D1527918

THE REGENCY COMPANION

GARLAND REFERENCE LIBRARY
OF THE HUMANITIES
(VOL. 841)

George IV   *Gill Ray*

New York Public Library
Picture Collection

THE REGENCY COMPANION

Sharon H. Laudermilk
Teresa L. Hamlin

GARLAND PUBLISHING, INC. • NEW YORK & LONDON
1989

823.08
L

Library of Congress Cataloging-in-Publication Data

Laudermilk, Sharon, 1949–
    The Regency companion / Sharon Laudermilk, Teresa L. Hamlin.
        p. cm. — (Garland reference library of the humanities ; vol.
841)
    Bibliography: p.
    ISBN 0-8240-2249-1 (alk. paper)
    1. Love stories, English—handbooks, manuals, etc.   2. Love
stories, American—Handbooks, manuals, etc.   3. Historical fiction,
English—Handbooks, manuals, etc.   4. Historical fiction, American—Handbooks,
manuals, etc.   5. Manners and customs in literature.
6. Great Britain—History—1789–1820.   7. England—Social life and
customs—19th century.   8. Regency—Great Britain.   I. Hamlin,
Teresa L., 1950– . II. Title. III. Series.
PR830.L69L38   1989
[GV1595]
823'.085'09—dc19   88-28203
                                                          CIP

Printed on acid-free, 250-year-life paper
Manufactured in the United States of America

Dedicated to all those who helped make *The Regency Companion* the best it can be.

Also acknowledged are the invaluable contributions of indexer Sally Raye and editor Phyllis Korper.

CONTENTS

INTRODUCTION

The capricious, frivolous *haut ton* of beaus, bucks, bedizened dames, demi-reps, and green girls ruled over by George, Prince Regent (1811–1820) continues to titillate and fascinate. Though Regent for less than ten years, throughout his father George III's final bout of madness, his opulent reign and heady influence on raffish high society overshadow the whole of the late Georgian Age. This continuing appeal is many sided.

First, it is a very exciting and understandable slice of history. It is not so far back in time so as to make the people seem alien to our modern eyes. And the era has everything—a large and dissolute royal family, a tyrant, Napoleon, and many heroes of the glorious and savage wars to depose him (from Nelson at Trafalgar to Wellington at Waterloo). It is a period of transition from eighteenth-century decadence to nineteenth-century prudishness. England of the time was under tremendous social and economic pressures.

Second, it is an era bursting with romantic ideals. The infinite appeal of the aristocracy adds a fairy-tale quality to the whole. Lords and ladies and dukes populate the landscape. The lovely female garments of the period—high-waisted, flowing, classical in inspiration—are tremendously entrancing.

Third, there are rules in this clearly delineated world. Men and women flaunt these rules at their peril. Though the female is expected to be much more circumspect than her male counterpart, each sex has to live within a framework that the Polite World recognizes as fit and proper.

This Regency companion has grown out of a deep appreciation for the period and contains a wealth of detail and insight into the *beau monde* in the first quarter of the nineteenth century.

THE REGENCY COMPANION

Chapter I

THE LONDON SEASON

Regency London! Raffish, exciting, dazzling. It gleamed like a multifaceted jewel for the upper reaches of society. A true diamond of the first water.

Like all great cities, there was staggering abundance for those in the first style of elegance and mind-boggling poverty for the Great Unwashed at the other end of the social scale. The word "slum" entered the English language about the time the Prince Regent began demolishing the wretched clutter of small streets and buildings to make a broad and beautiful thoroughfare from Carlton House to the grand Regent's Park planned by Nash.

For all the British Isles, London was surely the center of the universe. Here were housed the great banking houses, the Royal Exchange, and the magnificent new docks built during the long war with France by the East and West Indies merchants. The national government and bureaucracy that ran an empire and the headquarters of a military organization that was at war with the French for twenty years were also centered here. Culture in the form of literature, art, and theater made it a city of infinite variety and wonder. But the magnet that drew the bucks, dandies, grand dames, fops, eccentrics, the fashionable impure, and green girls of raffish Regency society was the fascinating frivolous world of fun and frolic called the London Season.

There was shopping in the Great Wen unrivaled anywhere. Fripperies, falderals, the latest mode in bonnets or books were all waiting for the shopper in Bond Street. Great shopping bazaars offered goods in epic profusion. The fashionable parks, Hyde Park and Green Park to name two, gave town beaus and young chits just out the school room a chance to see and be seen. Galleries, museums,

3

pleasure gardens like Vauxhall, concerts, and theaters of
every description offered a glorious abundance of unlimited
frivolity. Wouldn't you have to be henwitted or addlepated
to *not* come for the Season?

And come they did. All the nobs! Every spring the
high-born members of the upper ten thousand accompanied
by the ever-present hangers-on who followed where fashion
and wealth journeyed made for glittering and gay London!
The greatly improved travelling conditions at the end of
the eighteenth century made journeys to Town quicker and
easier.

In the spring everyone who mattered was in Town for
the Season which generally began in March or April and
lasted until sometime in June. The aristocracy and gentry
would then retire to the country to hunt, flock to a
fashionable seaside resort like Brighton, or take the waters
at an equally elegant spa. September saw the return of a
portion of the Polite World to Town for the Little Season,
which was noticeably thinner of company than the Season.
Other members of the *haut ton* might return to their
estates to host house parties or join house parties elsewhere.

Town emptied of the upper circles in November.
Parliament convened in January, and many fashionable
people especially those involved in government circles
returned to London. And then in the spring the whirl
began again.

Gaming was the great curse of the age. Captain
Gronow's memoirs included this story:

> George Harley Drummond, of the famous bank-
> ing-house, Charing Cross, only played once in his
> whole life at White's Club at whist, on which
> occasion he lost £20,000 to Brummell. This
> event caused him to retire from the banking-
> house of which he was a partner.[1]

Gronow goes on to talk of the losers who found
themselves "at the Israelitish establishment of Howard and

Gibbs, then the fashionable and patronized money-lenders."

Women, too, were addicted to the card table. And more than one story is told about a great lady deep in gambling debts settling her vowels by granting the holder of the notes her favors.

The fashionable who congregated to entertain and be entertained were of the first consideration. They were the *haut ton*, that is those members of the great landed families, which numbered over three hundred. They had to be plump in the pocket to sport the blunt it took to run both a mansion or great house in the country and a townhouse or another mansion in Town.

Their annual incomes ranged from a few thousand to well over eighty thousand pounds which the Duke of Bedford reaped from his estates in 1816. And money was essential. The Season could cost enormous sums of money. Literally thousands of pounds could be spent on stabling horses, housekeeping, entertaining, and keeping one's wardrobe apace with changing fashion. It was vital to be all the crack. More than one sprig of fashion could find himself in dun territory before the Season's end. And to add to these huge outlays of moneys, if the gentleman or lady of the house was addicted to gaming it could lead to disaster.

One example of many such financial disasters appears in an April issue of the *Morning Post* in 1805:

> The sum lately lost at play by a lady of high rank is variously stated. Some say it does not amount to more than £200,000, while others assert that it is little short of £700,000. Her Lord is very unhappy on the occasion, and is still undecided with respect to the best mode to be adopted in the unfortunate predicament.[2]

Scrope Davies of the dandy set lived for the gambling tables. For a number of years he managed quite well on his luck—but Dame Fortune eventually deserted him. Even the youth who had lost his entire fortune to Davies at the tables upon reaching his majority (and then had been granted the whole of his fortune back at the dandy's whim and a promise not to play again) turned his back on the debt-ridden Davies. His fortunes wrecked beyond repair, he sought repose and obscurity in Paris in 1820.

Even with all the monstrous expense, the London Season was essential if you were one of the upper classes. The *haut ton* gathered in London in the spring and its members had to be there or suffer a loss of prestige. It was a great occasion of the year. If you mattered, you were there.

This upper ten thousand or the Polite World was made up of the nobility and the gentry. Until the Reform Bill in 1832, the nobility reigned supreme in Great Britain. In 1801, there were 287 temporal peers and peeresses. The peerage of the United Kingdom excluding princes of the blood had five grades: duke, marquess, earl, viscount, and baron.

An Essential Guide to Addressing the Highborn

A peer could have several titles, but was known by his highest rank. If he had two titles of the same grade, he chose the style by which he wished to be known.

The highest non-royal rank was that of duke; a duke was formally addressed as "Your Grace" and "Duke" on social occasions. The Duke of Slyboots would sign himself as "Slyboots"—that is, simply by his title.

His duchess was also addressed as "Your Grace" formally and socially as "Duchess," and she signed herself with her Christian name and title, "June Slyboots."

The four lesser grades of the peerage were referred to as "Lord Featherbrained" in social situations. Usage of the exact rank was devilish queer. It was the first style of elegance to use the exact rank at a formal occasion except for a baron who should be referred to by that title only on formal documents.

The peeress in her own right took the style of her

male counterpart's wife. If they married, their husbands did not receive a title.

Wives of the lesser peerage were called: marquess — marchioness, earl — countess, viscount — viscountess, and baron — baroness. Whatever her rank (except that of a duchess), the wife of a peer is referred to as "Lady Cheese-paring" in conversation. As with her husband, specific rank was only referred to on formal occasions and not even then for Baroness Tittle-Tattle as with her Baron, her rank appeared only on formal documents.

Lady Cheese-paring was addressed as "Madam" in a formal situation. Socially, she could be called "Lady Cheese-paring." Menials would have addressed her as "My Lady" or "Your Ladyship." She signed herself by Christian name and title, "Clarrisa Cheese-paring."

The eldest son was always the heir to his father's titles. Primogeniture was and still is supreme in the United Kingdom. The oldest son of a duke, marquess, or earl could use a title that was one of his father's lesser titles. The Duke of Fustian's heir would be known as the Earl of Nipcheese if that was his father's title next in rank.

In the same fashion the Earl of Nipcheese's eldest son could use one of his grandfather's titles that was of a lower grade than the one his father had chosen. The grandson of the Duke of Fustian would possibly by courtesy be called Viscount Dryboots.

The younger children of peers were given courtesy titles also. The younger sons of a duke or marquess had "Lord" before their first name and last name. An earl's younger sons and all the sons of a viscount and baron had "The Hon." before their first and last names as did their daughters. Daughters of a duke, marquess, or earl had the courtesy style of "Lady" before both their Christian name and surname.

Widows of peers were known as Dowager Duchess of Fridayface or Dowager Countess of Buffleheaded. If there were already a dowager, the new widow would be known as Mary, Countess of Buffleheaded, until such time as she became the senior widowed peeress of the line.

The wealth of the peerage and the gentry was based on land. Fortunes made from other sources were suspect and generally unacceptable in the highest reaches of society.

Beneath the lofty heights of the upper reaches of the aristocracy there were 540 baronets and their wives who had Sir or Lady added to their Christian names. They could pass their title on to their heirs. Next in line were 350 knights and their wives. They were called "Sir" and "Lady" but could not transmit their titles to the next generation.

Beneath the titled Lords and Ladies, there was a huge circle of landowners (the Gentry) who were of old accepted families and authorized to bear a coat of arms. All the men below "Lords" constituted the lesser nobility but were very much part of the aristocracy that ruled England and made up the fashionable world.

Regency society teemed with men and women of rank and distinction, but behind their titles there stood a motley collection of rattles, rakes, jades, dandies, and highborn ladies with adjustable moral codes. And though titles and wealth were considered essential, the greatest fashion arbiter of the age was neither wealthy nor particularly well-connected. The audacious Beau Brummell, a man of infinite style, panache, and wit, ruled fashionable London until his escape from his creditors in 1816 to Continental exile. Urbane wit, address, and a fashion sense could carry anyone to the upper reaches of Regency society.

But a society that tolerated ladies of rank whose children each had a different father, none of which was milady's husband, could *not* tolerate other more innocuous and not-so-innocuous things.

Most unacceptable — the fellow one would certainly give the go-by or the lady one would assuredly give the cut direct — were those members of the fashionable world who had publicly disgraced themselves. The young buck caught cheating at cards, the woman divorced by her husband, a cow-hearted scapegrace who refused to meet an opponent in an affair of honor, or a baconbrained hoyden who made an unacceptable match in a runaway marriage. All these very public actions put them in a dreadful fix. Appearance was everything. This was an age of loose morals, but this lax morality was practiced behind closed doors. To defy the rule of discretion at all costs was to die a terrible social death. Lady Caroline Lamb, well-connected and wealthy, could not survive her very public disgrace with Lord Byron and the publication of her malicious novel *Glenarvon*. As far as the Polite World was concerned she was an anathema.

To those, however, who were acceptable, there was a wonderland of *soirées, levées,* balls, and entertainments awaiting them in the small world of fashionable Regency society. When high society came to Town, they spent their time in a very small area of London between Grosvenor Square and St. James's. The *beau monde* shopped on Bond Street and the gentlemen went to their clubs on St. James's and of course right off St. James's was King Street where the fashionable flocked to the very exclusive Almack's.

The *ton* walked in Green Park and rode or were driven in Hyde Park where the famed Rotten Row drew the fashionable and the not-so-fashionable residents of London (it was a public park) each afternoon. The great private palaces like Northumberland House, Grosvenor House, and Devonshire House were dotted through this stylish landscape of the West End.

Pall Mall was a highly modish street with many dwellings of stately aristocratic mein. Prinny's Carlton House and Marlborough House were two of many, but to go too far eastward would land one among poor abandoned wretches housed in filthy slums. Hovering at the edge of elegant London was always the specter of the impoverished and miserable lower classes.

Tottering at the head of the *haut ton* stood the magnificent Prince of Wales. Extravagant, spoiled, and always debt-ridden, he was like a great child of much charm and little sense. Foolish as far as money was

concerned, he was for much of his life considered a
parasite by the great majority of his subjects. Known as
Prinny, he set up his own court at Carlton House as soon
as he left his father's (George III) control. From that
time on he devoted himself to pleasure. His principal
interests were gambling, dress, building, decorating, and
spending large sums of money—which, of course, were not
so very different than the chief aims of elegant Regency
society. The "first gentleman of Europe" was a worthy
head of the fashionable world. He had great flair and
taste and, as a lover of architecture, had a strong visual
sense. Much as the elegant ones might mock and despise
him, where Prinny led they followed. When the Prince
removed to Brighton, so did society. Prinny gave trousers
his unofficial sanction in 1816, and the Polite World
followed like sheep. Considered by many as a fat, aging
libertine (he was forty-nine when he became Regent in
1811), he was an affable prince of great charm who
symbolized all the best and worst of his age.

    Another significant segment of Regency society were
the great political hostesses. Though not frivolous enough
to be truly ultrafashionable, these hostesses were noted for
having the most varied guest lists and best table talk in
London. Lady Melbourne, a tall Junoesque woman, reigned
as a Whig hostess. Byron called her "the best friend I
ever had in my life, and the cleverest of women." She
followed the prime rule of discretion all her life and was
noted for her many lovers. Her famous advice to her
daughter Emily Cowper on her death bed was to urge her
to be true to her lover rather than to her husband. At
the parties of these political hostesses the great issues of
the day were discussed and argued, something not
generally done in other fashionable drawing rooms.

    More intelligent conversation could be found at the
fashionable salon of Lady Holland at Holland House where
actors, writers, painters, and the high born met and
mingled. Lady Holland was (oh, horrors!) a divorced
woman and not accepted in the best circles by high
sticklers, but the quality of the company at her dinner

table drew the best of London to her doorstep.

But no matter who a dandy associated with or where a celebrated beauty was invited, there was really only one test that proved just how fashionable one was. If London was the Mecca that the Polite World journeyed to each year, then Almack's was the shrine where they worshipped. Captain Gronow writing of 1814 said:

> At the present time one can hardly conceive the importance which was attached to getting admission to Almack's, the seventh heaven of the fashionable world. Of the three hundred officers of the Foot Guards, not more than half-a-dozen were honoured with vouchers of admission to this exclusive temple of the *beau monde;* the gates were guarded by lady patronesses whose smiles or frowns consigned men and women to happiness or despair.[3]

These Lady Patronesses were the Ladies Castlereagh, Jersey, Cowper, Sefton, Princess Esterhazy, Countess Lieven, and Mrs. Drummond Burrell.

Almack's supplanted Carlton House as the top of the trees entertainment as Prinny became older and more tarnished. These assembly rooms were on King Street, St. James's, and arrogance and exclusivity in the form of the Lady Patronesses presided over a mesmerized social circle. The name Almack's was an anagram of a Mr. McCall who founded the club in 1765. The purpose of the anagram was said to be because he was a Scots, and the Scots were not popular at the time.

Exclusivity was Almack's trademark. The Ladies Committee ruled with arrogant thoroughness. Every name scrutinized for membership was put to a gruelling test of social suitability. Only the socially perfect need apply. Many peers of the realm were excluded, and though members had the privilege of taking a guest to the balls, their invited visitor had to pass rigid social tests too. These Patronesses issued a voucher to the chosen that entitled one to purchase a ticket.

Patronesses of Almack's (1814)

1. Lady Jersey (Sarah Sophia) was variously known as "Queen Sarah," "Silence," or "Sally" to her intimates. Head of the Committee in 1814, she was not noted for her kind heart. She was the eldest daughter of the 10th Earl of Westmorland and Anne, sole heiress of Robert Child, the enormously wealthy banker. She married the 5th Earl of Jersey in 1804 at Gretna Green.

2. Lady Castlereagh before her marriage in 1794 was Lady Emily Anne Hobart, the youngest daughter and co-heiress of the 2nd Earl of Buckinghamshire. Her husband, Robert Stewart, Viscount Castlereagh, and later 2nd Marquis of Londonderry, was a preeminent statesman throughout the period. At various times he was Secretary of State for War, Secretary of State for Foreign Affairs, and leader of the House of Commons. Lady Castlereagh as a society leader was noted for an aristocratic arrogance that rivaled that of Mrs. Drummond Burrell. She was also known for the oddity of her dress and appearance.

3. Princess Esterhazy was plump, pretty, and good natured except when persons of lower birth tried to step out of their caste. She had a true continental disdain for those less noble than she. She was the grand niece of Queen Charlotte and happily took precedence over the other ladies at public functions. Thérèse was the daughter of Charles, Prince of Thurn and Taxis by a daughter of the Grand Duke of Mecklenburg-Strelitz. Her husband Prince Paul Esterhazy served as Austrian ambassador in England 1815-42, and the Princess ruled over English drawing rooms during those years.

4. Countess Lieven rivaled Princess Esterhazy for Continental sophistication and arrogance. Count Christopher Andreievitch Lieven and his wife Dorothea arrived in England in 1812. He was the Russian ambassador to England for twenty-two years. Dorothea's extreme thinness, exotic beauty, and elegant carriage were her trademarks. Her arrival in London society created a

sensation.

5. Lady Cowper was as lovely, warmhearted, and gay as her husband was dull and stupid. The magnificient Lady Melbourne was her mother, and her father could have been any of her mother's numerous lovers. A leader in society all through the Regency (The Prince of Wales stood as godfather to her first-born son in 1806), she wisely followed her mother's advice and remained true to her lover, Lord Palmerston, and married this future Prime Minister after her husband's death. Emily was considered one of the kindest of the members of the Ladies Committee except for her attitude towards her crazed sister-in-law, Lady Caroline Lamb.

6. Mrs. Drummond Burrell was the most arrogant, disdainful, toplofty society dame who ever tread the assembly rooms in King Street. Later Lady Willoughby de Eresby, this heiress to the great Drummond fortune married Peter Burrell in 1807 uniting the Burrell estates (which in 1809 would be substantially increased by Peter's mother's inheritance from her brother, the childless 4th Duke of Ancaster) with her own inheritance. She terrified hopeful young misses on the town who were always warned to beware of the haughty Mrs. Drummond Burrell.

7. The dearest, kindest, and nicest of the group was Lady Sefton. Maria could always be depended on to help a friend in launching a girl in the marriage mart. Her husband the Earl was part of the inner circle at White's and a member of the Four-in-Hand Club.

All manner of sly and havy-cavy methods were used in attempts to influence the Patronesses. Rumor suggested that these haughty women used their position to revenge themselves on rivals and enemies by refusing them admittance. The husband of Lady Jersey was challenged to a duel by a captain of the Guards who discovered that the Countess had used her power to refuse him admittance. The Earl replied that if he had to duel with every person blackballed by his wife he would be a constant target. They did not meet at dawn in a royal park.

One point not to be overlooked was that the general

run of the *crème de la crème* at Almack's was entirely composed of high-born, blue-blooded nobodies with little historical or cultural relevance. In their own time they were relatively unknown outside their circle of friends.

Almack's Assembly Rooms served supper at each ball. Refreshments were not of the best. One visitor pronounced them to be perfectly wretched. One did not come there to eat. Low stakes card play was available though it was dull work for the high-flying Regency gamester. There were rigid rules that could be broken by no one. The doors always closed precisely at eleven. No one could enter after that hour. The proper mode for a tulip of fashion entering Almack's was decreed by the Ladies Committee. Knee breeches and a white neckcloth were *de rigueur*. The outfit would be topped by a dress coat with long tails.

Guarding the sacred portals was Mr. Willis. He was ever-vigilant so that no one ascended the staircase to the ballroom who wasn't properly attired. Even the Duke of Wellington, the darling of London society in 1814, was politely and firmly turned back by Willis, because his dress did not conform to the rigid rules of the social club. He dared to arrive in trousers! When Mr. Willis, with calm courtesy, told the great man he could not be admitted, the Duke goodnaturedly walked away.

Almack's lease was held by the Willis family during the Regency, and it also was referred to as Willis's Rooms. The building's exterior was judged very plain with its simple and undistinguished brickwork, staid pedimented Ionic doorcase marking the entrance, and dull design. The second story sported six windows with round arches which graced the ballroom. The Rooms had been designed by Robert Mylne in the 1760s. The ballroom in which the weekly assemblies were held was criticized as a huge, spare room with a terrible floor.

Before the introduction of the quadrille in 1816 and the waltz by 1812, the English country dance, the minuet, contredanse, Scotch reels, and the Ecossaise were favored by dancers in Almack's Assembly Rooms. Though the minuet had effectively been killed in France along with much of the aristocracy, refugees from the Terror kept the mincing artificial dance alive in London. The Prince Regent gave a large ball in 1813 that opened and closed with a minuet.

Predictably each ball at Almack's opened with a minuet and continued with country dances, contredanses and cotillions. Leading the orchestra was the Scotch violinist Neil Gow.

The introduction of the waltz brought open scandal to the ballroom floor. Born in Vienna, outrage and protest against this intimate dance stormed across Europe to England where ferocious moral affront greeted the new dance. A form of the waltz that had no scandalous close hold and featured an "Allemande" and intertwining arm movements had been seen in English ballrooms since 1800. The very shocking and risque "closed couple" waltz was a gliding dance very suitable to elegant footwear and highly polished ballroom floors. This indelicate dance quickly caught hold, and soon couples were waltzing in ballrooms all over England.

The waltz received formal acceptance when it gained the Prince Regent's blessing in 1816. This, however, didn't stop *The Times* from condemning the unseemliness of the dance. Dire warnings were uttered and parents were urged to protect their daughters from this vile contagion. Despite the denunciations in press and pulpit, the waltz had come to London to stay. And it wasn't so very licentious. There was plenty of space between partners.

The quadrille evolved from the English country dances that had been imported to France by the visiting English. It was a square dance with music in five movements in different tempos. In 1816 Lady Jersey saw the figures on a visit to Paris and brought the new dance back home to England. The first demonstration was given at Almack's by Lady Jersey, Lady Harriett Butler, Lady Susan Ryder, and Miss Montgomery with Count St. Aldegonde, Mr. Montgomery, Mr. Montague, and Charles Standish.

Of the two new dances, quadrilles were the most pop-

ular. Some people still violently disapproved of waltzing.
After each dance a partner brought his young lady back to
her mother or chaperon and made his bow. It was wise to
be as circumspect as possible. Under no circumstances
were bodies actually to touch while waltzing. Scandal
would follow any lack of decorum.

Almack's served several important functions in
Regency high society. It gave a certain cachet of exclusivity to those who gained admittance. Entry to "the
seventh heaven" conveyed a greater distinction than a
court presentation. Also the social power of the Lady
Patronesses as society leaders was reinforced each time
they gave or refused a voucher to a fashionable hopeful.
There was no second application for admittance. Almack's
remained the place to see and be seen for the socially
superior throughout the first quarter of the nineteenth
century.

Almack's primary function was as a marriage mart.
Here young ladies of good birth and little fortune could
make an eligible connection. A tulip of fashion with
pockets to let might repair the family fortunes by con-
tracting a brilliant match. Many grand and not-so-grand
alliances were cemented between the great families on
Almack's ballroom floor. The resulting dowries and
settlements could help to compensate parents who in
launching daughters in society and making generous
allowances to spendthrift sons on the Town had expended
enormous sums on a London Season.

An Essential Regency Guide
to the Language of Élegance

Elegance demands a language to set the fashionable
apart from the unfashionable. The language the English
drew colorful and stylish phrases from was French. Never
mind that Napoleon was called "The Monster" and war with
France was a way of life, modish gentlewomen and
gentlemen of the first stare sprinkled the following French
phrases and words throughout their speech.

À la cheribum—man's hairstyle.
Au coup de vent—man's hair style, tousled.
Bon mot—repartee.
Brioche—a kind of sponge cake or a blunder.
Carte de visite—visiting card.
Chère amie—dear friend or lover.
Concierge—doorkeeper.
Du vieux temps—out of fashion.
Faux pas—false step, social indiscretion.
Fête—an elaborate entertainment.
Habitué—frequenter, constant visitor.
Haut ton—high tone, the height of fashion.
Je ne sais quoi—I don't know what, beyond
    understanding.
Laisser aller—let go.
Le beau monde—the fashionable world, high society.
Levée—an afternoon reception attended by males only
    hosted by the British king or by his representative.
Mal à propos—out of place, unsuitable.
Mauvais sujet—black sheep.
Mauvais ton—bad style, unacceptable social behavior.
Mésalliance—undesirable marriage with one of lower social
    standing.
Modiste—desssmaker or milliner.
N'est-ce pas?—Isn't that so?
Nouveau riche—newly rich, a social climber.
On-dit—they say, it is said, people say.
Ouï-dire—hearsay.
Outré—overstated, eccentric.
Parti—matrimonial catch, a good match.
Parure—a set of jewelry.
Parvenu—one who pushes himself socially.
Pâté de foie gras—a pie made of gooseliver.
Pour faire ses adieux—to depart.
Protégé—to be under the patronage of another.
Que c'est?—What is this? What is that?
Raffiné—a fashionable rake.
Recherché—chosen with care.

Retroussé — turned up, most often said of the nose.
Roué — debauchee, rake.
Salon — drawing room. A gathering of distinguished guests
    at the home of a lady of fashion.
Savoir-vivre — knowing how to go on within society.
S'il vous plaît — if you please.
Soirée — an evening party or reception.
Tabac à priser — snuff.
Tabatière — snuffbox.
Tendre — a tender affection.
Tête-à-tête — head to head, a confidential matter.
Tiens — Indeed! You don't say so!
Ton — society's fashion, tone.
Tout le monde — all the world.
Trône d'amour — throne of love, a cravat style.
Un argent fou — endless money.
Vis-à-vis — face to face, sitting or standing opposite
    another.
Vivre le jour — to live for the moment.
Voilà tout — that is all.

NOTES TO CHAPTER I

1. Rees Howell Gronow, *The Reminiscences and Recollections of Captain Gronow,* 1:56.

2. John Ashton, *The History of Gambling in England,* p. 92.

3. Gronow, *Reminiscences and Recollections,* 1:31.

Chapter II

THE FASHIONABLE LADY

A fashionable young miss of the Regency came to Town for the Season to meet her destiny. The frantic, expensive shopping and whirl of dressmaking were all aimed at making her tempting fare. The unfledged female was being groomed to contract an eligible alliance.

Her options as a woman were severely limited, and she needed to secure an offer from a desirable *parti*. Young women of fashion had few other opportunities to make their way in the world. If they had money of their own, they could afford to spend years on the marriage mart, but if the fashionable chit was of a family in reduced circumstances or had no family and was without friends, a match with a gentleman of means was essential.

Every authority considered women to be inferior to men in intelligence. The popular conception at the time was that marriage was woman's natural condition. And the Season was centered around opportunities for courtship and dalliance.

Georgian England was a man's world, though women were very much the center of the London social whirl. Whether they were refusing hopeful applicant's vouchers to Almack's, accepting a *carte blanche* from a pink of the ton, or spreading the latest *on-dit* over a high-stakes hazard game, a host of women of many types amused themselves heartily.

A Guide To The Fair Sex

Abigail—a lady's maid.
Ace of spades—a widow.
Ape leader—an old maid: their punishment for not

multiplying is to lead apes in hell. The source is *Shakespeare's Much Ado About Nothing*, Act II, Scene I.

Article — a wench. A pretty girl. "She's a prime article."

Baggage — a familiar term for women and children. "She's a cunning baggage."

Bluestocking — a learned female who neglects the social graces.

Chit — a young girl.

Crone — an old toothless beldam.

Dandyess or dandizette — a female dandy of the Regency.

Devil's daughter — one who has married a termagant has wed the Devil's daughter.

Diamond of the first water — an especially fine diamond, one of great value judged by its size. The color is its "water." Used to describe an exceptionally lovely girl.

Dowdy — a coarse woman.

Green girl — a fresh young girl who is very inexperienced.

Harridan — a slatternly old woman.

Hell cat — a termagant.

Hoity-toity — a silly, thoughtless girl.

Hoyden — a romping, boisterous girl.

Hussy — an abbreviation of housewife, used as a term of reproach.

Jade — a term of reproach to women meaning worthless.

Jilt — a deceiving woman, who encourages the address of a man whom she means to abandon.

Long Meg — an insulting name for a very tall woman.

Milk-and-water miss — an insipid girl devoid of interesting conversation.

Mort — a woman or wench.

Romp — a forward girl.

Tabby — an old maid. Old maids being often compared to cats.

Toad Eater — a poor female relation in a great family subjected to all whims. Swallowing toads is likened to swallowing or putting up with insults, as disagreeable to a sensitive person as digesting toads.

Toast — an idolized woman whose health is often drunk by men.

Vixen—a woman of scolding and fiery disposition.
Wet Goose—a very stupid girl.

Education

The girl born in a well-connected family of means
was brought up at a distance from her parents. Wet
nurses breastfed her; nursery maids cared for her; and
governesses oversaw her education should she not be sent
off to boarding school.

The education of young girls was not the best.
Mothers and governesses were much more concerned with a
young lady's social graces than her ability to decline a
Latin verb. Upper-class housewifery skills were valued.
Sewing a delicate seam, painting a pastel watercolor, or
learning to dribble French phrases through her speech was
the extent of many a girl's accomplishments. Common
subjects taught by a governess were watercolors, French,
music, drawing, geography, and history as well as general
deportment.

Visiting masters were employed to help educate the
young girl at home, too. These would be music teachers or
drawing masters. Caper-merchants (dancing masters) taught
the minuet, cotillion, quadrille, and the waltz.

Walking and horseback riding were her chief recre-
ations. It was not unknown for a child of two to be
mounted on a horse and taught to ride.

Girls were sent to private boarding schools, too. The
schools aimed to "cultivate becoming postures for the
ballroom." These schools were private ventures for profit,
and the teachers were either impoverished gentlewomen,
poor relatives of the clergy, or retired servants of the
upper classes. Frequently a clever but poor pupil would
help to teach in return for reduced fees.

Deportment might be taught by the aid of Mrs.
Chapone's collection of polite letters called *Improvement of
the Mind.* It contained letters on the Regulation of the
Heart and Affections, The Government of the Temper, and

Politeness and Accomplishments.

Lesson books included *The Class Book* (1817) which contained lessons for every day of the year plus information on every subject with emphasis upon science, morality, or other basic knowledge, and was designed for young children. One very popular method of teaching pupils was by the question and answer method. *Mangnall's Questions* was a standard text book of the type.

A "finished" young lady could waltz, play a piano selection, or sing a song or two.

Clever girls were looked at with suspicion. They earned the title "bluestockings," and it was not a term of admiration. Early in the previous century "bluestocking" had meant a person renowned for learning, charm, and wit. The term was styled from a learned gentleman named Benjamin Stillingfleet who wore plain clothes with blue stockings to the parties at the fashionable salons. Boswell wrote that when Stillingfleet was absent from the company that, "We can do nothing without the bluestockings" was a comment frequently heard. The term stuck to the whole set of intelligent literate people who frequented Montagu House and other salons.

In the Regency, the term referred only to women of much education, little social graces, and poorly dressed figures. Women were thought to be fatally silly with a mind only fit for gossip and fashion. A young miss who thirsted for knowledge, however, could find a way to pursue advanced learning. She might cajole a doting father into letting her have lessons with her brothers at the local rector's or pursue a course of study of her own by plundering the books in the well-stocked family library. A determined girl could get an education though her path to learning was not an easy one, and her accomplishment was likely to be ridiculed.

The Young Miss in Town

At sixteen or so, the Regency miss put the school

room behind her and was introduced to the world. London's routs, balls, and assemblies became the hunting ground for her ultimate quarry—a husband.

A young girl's entry into the polite world was officially marked by a Court Presentation. It was a gruelling social experience and for one young lady even more so than usual. Lady Sarah Lennox's name was sent in as a candidate to be privately presented at King George III's Court as was then customary for Peer's daughters,

> but a request came that if she had a *second* name it might be used, as it was feared the name of Lady Sarah Lennox, his first love, might have an exciting effect upon the poor King; Lady Sarah, however, had no other name, and the King was informed she was to be presented. He immediately inquired if she was pretty, and, on being answered in the affirmative, he further inquired if she was like her namesake and great-aunt, the Lady Sarah Lennox of his young days; and he was told that there was said to be a resemblance. When the evening came Lady Sarah was taken up to the King, and to her great surprise and consternation he begged her to allow a blind old man the privilege of passing his hand over her features!—this he did, making no remark. Lady Sarah afterwards said she could not refuse, knowing the reason for his request, but she found it a very embarrassing position.[1]

Obligatory dress was ostrich plumes as a head dress and an elaborate gown with hoops. The *Memoirs of the Comtesse de Boigne,* 1815-1819, contained a description of one such outfit. A mandatory plume composed of seven huge feathers supplied by the stylish plumier Carberry topped her headdress. Plumes had to have at least seven feathers, but ladies were free to have more. Some massive plumes had more than two dozen feathers. The Comtesse's head-gear beneath her plumes consisted of a garland of white roses upon a ringlet of pearls, a diamond comb, diamond buckles, and white silk tassels. All these ornate trappings were rather repugnant to her classical tastes but necessary for court.

The elaborate plumage was just the beginning, however, of the outlandish style—for all ladies wore outmoded hoops to be in the proper mode. After putting on her bodice as usual, the Comtesse's huge hoop skirt of waxed calico over whalebone was tied at her waist. The hoop was very narrow at the sides and protruded out very far in front and back. Three layers of skirts rested on top of the hoop. A satin skirt lavishly decorated with silver embroidery was topped by a tulle skirt featuring a silver lace furbelow. The shortest and top skirt was made of silver-spangled tulle decorated with a garland of flowers. This last skirt was turned up and tucked so that the garland draped crosswise all around the skirt. The tuck openings had a flower bouquet set in silver lace as ornamentation. To complete the proper style, the bottom of the white satin dress was turned up in loops and did not reach the base of the hoop skirt. Only the queen wore a train. Even the princesses' dresses, though not turned up, did not quite touch the ground.

Every piece of jewelry which could find a place in the ornate toilette was put on display. After the last curl was in place and the final bracelet and brooch found a home, the Comtesse didn't quite know what to think. Torn between the desire to laugh at the sight or frown in irritation at the time and effort it took to achieve this ridiculous style, the Comtesse could decide only that it became her very well indeed.

The Comtesse's comment about the absurdity of the dress was correct. The high waist and hoops were a ridiculous combination, but court protocol must be obeyed. These elaborate Court dresses cost enormous sums of money, and purse-pinched families might call on a well-heeled connection to foot the bill.

The young women journeyed to Court in carriages

accompanied by liveried footmen wearing huge bouquets in their lapels. A long procession of carriages made their way down Piccadilly to St. James's Palace.

As Richard Rush, Envoy Extraordinary and Minister Plenipotentiary from the United States found one of the drawing-rooms that he attended well worth recording. Held in celebration of Queen Charlotte's birthday and also the first such function since the death of Princess Charlotte, Prinny's only child, it was a pageant that could not be matched anywhere in Europe.

The procession of carriages featured numerous footmen attired in lavish livery. Some carriages boasted as many as three footmen! Proud horses in prime style under elegantly appointed harness added to the colorful sight. Splendid scarlet-clad cavalry (rumored to be Waterloo veterans) paraded atop jet black horses. Guns were fired off from both the park and the tower. Trumpets sounded!

The real show awaited inside when one saw the guests congregating. The gloriously attired ladies, each sporting a plume, were the true spectacle. The whole room became a vast field of undulating feathers. All the colors of the rainbow—blue, green, red, yellow, violet, even pure white—could be seen. The glitter of sunlight on all the diamonds displayed added to the dazzling sight. But by far the most wondrous sight was the proliferation of hoops. Richard Rush thought the hoops amazing and the wearers graceful, grand, and utterly unique.

Young ladies in the crush of matrons and their daughters encased in hoops and encrusted in diamonds had been known to faint with excitement while waiting to make their curtsy. It was a gruelling, glittering, thrilling start to a damsel's coming of age.

After her Court Presentation, a society miss would have a large ball in her honor at the family's London residence. Her scheming mama would invite as many eligible young bloods as could fill her ballroom.

With luck, impeccable birth, friends in the right places, and a well-filled purse she would be approved by a haughty Lady Patroness to receive a voucher to Almack's.

The Court Presentation was essential for any lady of good birth, but Almack's was the pinnacle of social success. No young lady of fashion was of the first stare if she did not grace the Wednesday night balls in those heavenly assembly rooms during the Season.

The delights of London and the *haut ton* were all waiting for this highborn damsel. Routs, balls, assemblies in private homes, military reviews and balloon ascensions in royal parks, evenings at Vauxhall and Drury Lane—these kept her social calendar bursting with engagements.

But there was some devilish queer things that could spoil the wonder and excitement of it all. Gossip and scandalmongers abounded in Regency society. Tea was called "scandal broth" for good reason. A lady could lose her reputation on not what really occurred, but what the Polite World thought had occurred. Appearance was all.

A lady did not walk or ride abroad alone. If unaccompanied by a man, she took a friend or a maid. There were all sorts of dangers—from footpads, rakes, Bond Street loungers, and the malicious *on-dit* that would be touted about because she had ventured out alone.

Curiosity in the small select Regency society was rampant. Letters relayed the juicy bits of scandal to the four corners of the Kingdom. And this tittle-tattle was serious. Reputation loss meant being cut off from all decent (elegant!) society. High sticklers never forgave or forgot. Possibly the woman who did lose her reputation gained a suitable monetary compensation from her protector to soothe the wounds done to her good name.

There are several rules of behavior a fashionable young lady had to follow:

1. Never be seen driving down St. James's Street where all the men's clubs were. To do so would make one the object of every Town saunterer's lascivious stare. Very fast behavior.

2. Never let anyone suspect that one's expectations were small. Nothing could be more fatal to one's chances.

3. Never express an urge to be wear a warm pelisse

or shawl. The very lightest of wraps should suffice in every type of weather.

    4. And most important to achieve social success, a girl had to gain the approval of Beau Brummell (before his disgrace and exile). If the "Beau" was so obliging to bring one into fashion, a career as a reigning toast was assured.

The Regency Damsel's Future

    This whirl of social life that fired damsels off into the *ton* was, of course, aimed at one end — the eligible connection. These high-born chits were supposed to do their best to either wed a fortune, forge an alliance between political families, or join great landed estates. Any combination of the above and the young girl was considered the perfect flower of British womanhood.

    Misalliances were considered base. A girl should marry to increase her social consequence and thereby her family's. And certainly she should never marry beneath her. Matches between men and women of unequal social standing were threats to the rigid structure of society.

    This was not true of matches between personages of unequal fortunes. In an era where women had few options outside marriage, husband hunting constituted an honorable trade. A portionless miss of good family and high rank had a duty to seek out an eligible *parti*. Men were also hopeful that their future spouse would bring a substantial sum to their union, and this, of course, made the possibility of an eligible offer for a beautiful girl of little fortune small. But hope reigned eternal in the breasts of determined matchmaking mamas, after all the Gunning sisters had done the impossible!

    The sheer unlikelihood involved in the romance of the Gunning girls inspired ambitious mothers for generations of London Seasons. The two young ladies arrived in England in 1751. They came from Ireland in the charge of their father Mr. John Gunning of Castle Coote. Georgian society was agog! Beautiful, charming, and penniless they married noblemen far above their touch. The younger girl Elizabeth captured the Duke of Hamilton, and after his death she married the Duke of Argyll in 1759. The elder daughter Maria became the wife of Lord Coventry but unfortunately didn't live to enjoy her triumph long. Her early death was rumored to be caused by her predilection for a lethal beauty aid, lead-based cosmetics.

Marriage was the most secure and satisfactory role for the Regency belle. After marriage and upon filling her lordship's nursery with a pledge or two of her affection to insure the family fortunes for another generation, the young matron could have a dashing and unrestrained social life if she chose. Discretion was essential, but as she was now free of dominating parents and the strictures that confined the activities of an unmarried girl, London was her oyster.

Her large staff took care of the mundane affairs of running the household. Mornings were spent on deciding what to wear. Afternoons were full of social calls, driving in Hyde Park, and shopping on Bond and Oxford Streets. The nights were for the elaborate rounds of entertainment at balls and assemblies where elegant dalliances began.

Of course, some marriages where based on true affection, but it was a practical age. One was expected to look for pleasure outside an unsatisfactory marriage. Highborn ladies could have a quiverful of children, and none would share the same father. Lady Oxford (the family name was Harley) had a large brood who went under the collective name "Harleian Miscellany." The variety and number of different fathers were astounding even to her contemporaries.

Not every woman had the opportunity to marry, but an unmarried woman's state was not a happy one after she passed her first blush of youth. Spinsterhood was considered an unnatural state, and a woman on the shelf was ridiculed. A spinster was called an "ape-leader" in disparaging tones, for that was to be her fate in hell—to lead apes.

If a spinster had a respectable income, the possibility

of her own household was not out of the question. A paid female companion or needy elderly relation would reside with her to lend countenance to the situation. This way of life offered a certain freedom that a woman living in a relative's domestic establishment would not have.

Those young women who had no income to call their own were in a difficult position. If they had family, they could dwindle into that ignominious state of being the "poor relation." Living with a relative of means, the spinster would be set to onerous tasks from morning until night. In the worst of situations they became unpaid servants who taught the children, tended the sick, and mended clothing while they were ill-fed and ill-housed. Of course, this was the worst scenario to be imagined. The "poor relation" might be treated with great consideration and be an important part of the household.

The professions open to gentlewomen were few. The major and most viable possible profession was teaching. Governesses were employed at all the great country houses. Their pay was poor and they were relatively untrained. Socially despised, they existed in a limbo world between their upper-class employers and the inferior servant class. It was a hard life with few rewards and no personal independence. Many times the poor governess was put in charge of pampered spoiled children she was not allowed to correct. Her employer made sure every moment of the governess's work day was spent in giving value. Oceans of needlework could descend on the poor girl to fill each idle moment with drudgery.

Gentlewomen might also choose to become the paid companions of crotchety old dowagers with smelly pug dogs and numerous unnamed ailments. This, too, had all the possibilities of being a perfectly wretched situation. When spinsters reached the point of becoming general dogsbodies and whipping boys for eccentric old ladies, there was little hope left for a brighter future.

For a woman with exceptional talents and persever-ance there was the slim chance that she could earn a living by writing. Starting with Fanny Burney's success with *Evelina* (1778), *Cecilia* (1782), and *Camilla* (1793), writing became a respectable profession for women. A host of women authors entertained Regency readers—Jane Austen, Maria Edgeworth, and Hannah More.

Other professions open to women were not considered respectable or acceptable for one of gentle birth, but unhappy circumstances might push an unmarried damsel to ruin. The stage was one recourse. Acting was a precarious trade, but it offered opportunities for wealth and success if a girl had good looks, intelligence, natural abilities, and phenomenal good luck. It was also a profession where women were not in direct competition with men. Many actresses could retire wealthy women through their performances, either on the stage or in their boudoir.

The boudoir was the scene of the least respectable course a penniless lady might take to make her way in the world. A woman with no relations, fortune, or friends could seek a protector who would offer her a *carte blanche* arrangement. If she were clever, ruthless, and ambitious she could become a wealthy woman. For gently reared females, the life of the *demi-monde* was not a reasonable choice though the temptation was always present. For a girl alone and friendless, selling her favors to the highest bidder could be her only means to survive.

All in all, a gentlewoman's best opportunity to succeed lay in securing a husband of rank and fortune. In marriage, she gained status and security. And in some alliances, she was accorded the freedom to dally where she pleased.

A Refined Guide to Female Fashion

A lady of fashion was obsessed with her wardrobe. A good deal of her time was spent in making sure she was turned out in the first style of elegance.

At the beginning of the nineteenth century, women of rank had thrust off the lush restrictive fashions of the eighteenth century. The new mode of dress was based on the classical inspiration of Rome and Greece. Dresses were simple one-piece garments divided into bodice and skirt by a ribbon tied directly under the bosom. The bodice was very low, and breasts were very much on display.

Only the lightest materials were used in making these classically inspired dresses—light muslin, batiste, and lawn. And the delicacy of the fabrics put a lady's body contours on display as never before in modern Europe. The most outrageous fashions came from Paris, and Englishwomen copied them eagerly though they were never quite as free with their bodies as the French ladies.

The Countess of Brownlow wrote as an eyewitness when she recalled one special French lady who came to England during the brief peace in 1802. Madame Recamier created quite a stir when she appeared in Kensington Gardens in a mode of dress which was much more immodest and sophisticated than what the typical tonnish Englishwoman wore. She had donned a thin, clinging muslin dress which hugged her body à l'antique, that is, like the revealing draperies on an ancient statue. Her coiffure consisted of rather greasy ringlets clustering around her face and a long plait hanging down her back. To finish the antique classical look, a large veil artistically concealed her head. Needless to say, more than one person turned to stare, and a few even turned to follow this odd sight.

The preferred color for these flimsy gowns was white. There were two reasons for this. Classical scholars who were eagerly studying the treasures gleaned from contemporary excavations in Greece believed the exquisite statuary was in its original state—snowy white marble. They were unaware that in classical times the statues had been painted in rich strong colors. The other reason stemmed from Napoleon's preference for white. War notwithstanding, the English eagerly sought to emulate the elegance of the French Imperial court. If Josephine and the other ladies of the court wore white, the London belles did too.

The military influence was evident in fashion throughout the late Georgian period. Frogging and epaulets were copied and incorporated in attire. A variety of outfits were given war-related names. There was a Wellington mantle, a Kutusoff hat, and a Trafalgar dress, to name a few.

Luxurious materials for evening wear returned to fashionable gowns after 1809. More elaborate decoration and the return of colorful hues were the trends from 1810 to 1820, though white was still considered the most elegant of colors. Fashion during these years moved from simple classic lines in delicate materials in 1803 to elaborate gowns heavily frilled and decorated by Regency's end. The one constant was the waistline. It never moved too far from the bosom.

The Fashion Magazines

During this period fashionable women were kept informed of the latest mode in a wide range of magazines and journals. These fashion journals were also used by *modistes* and mantua-makers to give their customers a better idea of how dresses would look upon creation.

The major magazines were:

La Belle Assemblée, or Bell's Court and Fashionable Magazine addressed particularly to the Ladies. (1806-1868) This magazine contained a wealth of information on a wide range of women's concerns. It was a true women's magazine with celebrity anecdotes, instructions on manners, cosmetic advice, and beauty aids. Dress and fashion were covered in delightfully colored fashion plates—the best of which were from 1809 to 1820. Fashion plates were presented with lengthy, written descriptions, and modish gentlewomen pounced on the latest monthly issue.

This magazine was started by John Bell, the enterprising publisher of the *Morning Post, The World,* and *Bell's Weekly Messenger.*

The magazine was filled with advertisements that touted the wonders of various rouges, depilatories, powders, and corsets.

The Lady's Magazine, or Entertaining Companion for the Fair Sex (1770-1837)
This was the first of the true fashion-plate magazines that was issued regularly. The plates were not decorated with color until 1790. Before 1790, dressmakers would color the plates themselves to enhance the dress designs and entice their lady customers to order garments.

Le Beau Monde, or Literary and Fashionable Magazine (1806-1810)
This monthly journal usually presented two hand-colored fashion plates in each issue. It was filled with articles about theater, the arts, literature, and music. It was a close rival of *La Belle Assemblée* in content.

The Repository of Arts, Literature, Commerce, Manufactures, Fashion and Politics (1809-1828)
Started by Rudolph Ackermann, the *Repository* was issued in monthly editions, and besides fashion plates, it contained plates showing pictures, furniture, and portraits. There were several fashion plates in every issue. Each was described in great written detail. Ackermann's journal maintained high standards of execution throughout its existence.

Other magazines included:

The Ladies Monthly Museum, or Polite Repository of Amusement and Instruction: being an Assemblage of what can Tend to please the Fancy, Instruct the Mind or Exalt the Character of the British Fair. Edited by a "Society of Ladies." (1798-1832)

Fashions of London and Paris (1798-1806)

La Miroir de la Mode (1803)

The New British Ladies' Magazine (1818-1819)

Record of Fashion and Court Elegance
(1807-1809)

Dresses

Male critics complained that their sisters and wives were all shoulders and skirts, but the high-waisted dress reigned supreme in late Georgian England.

Women's clothes were geared to reflect the time of day and the activity. There was little or no notice paid to the changing seasons.

A fashionable lady had:
Carriage dresses
Court dresses
Dinner dresses
Evening dresses
Full evening dresses
Garden dresses
Morning dresses
Opera dresses
Promenade dresses
Riding dresses
Theater dresses
Walking dresses

The most elaborate was the hooped Court dress. The morning dress was the most informal and was called "undress."

A lady's gowns were made up after she visited a fashionable *modiste* or mantua-maker and selected designs from the latest fashion plates. They consulted over trimmings and fabrics, and then the gown was constructed. Delivery was made after satisfactory fittings.

Muslin was the fashionable material for day and evening, though more elaborate materials began to reappear about 1809 for evening. *The Ladies Monthly Museum,* June 1802, declared that dreses were now so thin they could be sent by the two-penny post.

The necklines were deep and square-cut on these high-waisted dresses. They had short sleeves known as *bretelles* (shoulder straps). All the fullness on the dress was in the back and many had trains. Trains on day dresses were popular until 1806, and they remained modish for formal dress for several years after that. The short sleeves began to be puffed about 1805. A lining of coarser muslin was used to give the sleeve body.

The fullness of the trained dress at the back gathers was held out by a small bustle pad. It was pinned in place on the center back at the high waistline and had tapes attached to it that tied around the waist to keep it in place. Pockets had been eliminated on dresses to a large extent. The transparent figure hugging styles demanded a sleek line, and reticules or "ridicules" came into fashion to carry feminine paraphernalia.

White muslin with delicate sprig, check, and spotted patterns stayed in style through the whole period. The most luscious materials came back in style around 1809 though they did not supplant muslin.

The simplicity in cut began to diminish as women grew weary of plain fabrics and pure lines. By 1805, another garment was worn over the classic dress. It could be either as short as mid-thigh or as long as the dress and cut open in the front. Elegant romantic ruffs of Brabant lace emulating Elizabethan styles came into fashion. Skirts shortened to reveal ankles and trains became completely outmoded by 1810 except for ornate court dress. By 1812, dresses were being trimmed with frills that made them much more elaborate. Collars became higher, and short sleeves disappeared.

The year 1815 marked significant changes in many areas and women's fashion was no exception. Waists became even shorter, and skirts flared a great deal wider at the bottom. The bottoms became much more heavily flounced, ruffled, and decorated. The entire ensemble was becoming more heavily embellished. Transparent materials worn over opaque ones were in vogue—such as a slip of colored satin with a dress of "patent" net worn on top.

Also, in 1815, the increased use of colored silks paved the way for a return of a riot of color in fashionable ensembles. Velvets and satins in rainbow hues were once more the rage.

The pure, simple, unaffected costume of 1802 was by 1818 considerably changed. Luxurious decoration adorned the gown's bodice, sleeves and hemline. The fashionable mode demanded lace, bows, and elaborate embroidery to decorate the still high-waisted dress. It forecasted the profusion of ornate elegance to come.

A Regency Riot of Colors

Stylish colors for dresses abounded! They were sometimes dubbed with French names, because fashionable dressmakers followed the lead of their aristocratic customers and made their goods more elegant with French phrases. A color might even be named for a place or a person. Welcome to the brilliant hues of the Regency!

Amaranthus color—shade of purple with a pinkish tint (1802).
Bishop's blue—blue with a purplish tint.
Blush-colored—pale shade of pink.
Bottle-green—dark green with a bluish tint.
Capucine color—dark orange color.
Carmine—bright red shade.
Clarence blue—medium blue shade (1811).
Devonshire brown—rich brown with a reddish tint.
Forester's or American green—a bright green (1817).
Jonquille—fashionable yellow, 1811 and later.
Manilla brown—light color (1811) taken from Manilla hemp.

Nakara color—pearl color, 1812 and later.
Pea-green—fashionable color in 1809 and later.
Pistache or Pistachio color—light delicate shade of green modish in 1819.
Pomona green—apple green (1812).
Poussière de Paris—color of light brown (1819).
Skeffington brown—a very special brown devised by Sir Lumley himself.
Spanish blue—popular dark blue color for mens coats (1809).
Spanish fly—rich dark green color (1809).
Willow green—delicate green color (1811).

Wraps and Outerwear

Though it was very fashionable to stand shivering in one's thin muslin gown with only the lightest wrap, a lady of the first stare had a large diversity of coats and wraps in her wardrobe.

Pelisses were very stylish. They were close fitting, really an overdress. They buttoned down the front and sometimes were several inches shorter than the muslin dress they topped. Fur was a common trim.

A mantle was the most simple and popular garment. It was a large rectangular piece of fabric gathered at the neck. Superbly simple in construction, it had no sleeves. Hoods either round or pointed were sometimes attached.

Most unique to the period was the elegant spencer. It was a short jacket that reached just to the high waist of the gown.

Kashmir shawls also came into fashion. They were large, light, and warm, prime requirements for an elegant young lady in a flimsy lowcut dress. The shawls measured between six and nine feet long and twenty to forty-two inches wide. A whole array of colors from dark red to bright yellow were used. The rich texture and lavishly woven borders stood out brilliantly on the white background of the muslin dress.

Fur cloaks were introduced around 1808 to wear over

fashionable ensembles in cold weather. And fur trims were used on many garments. Marabou and swansdown decorated street cloaks. Sable and ermine were the costliest and most admired, but nearly all the furs available today were known and used. These furs became linings or trims for outerwear. Never to be seen, however, were wraps with the fur worn on the outside except as a trim. Often a muff of immense portions made of matching fur was added to an ensemble that boasted fur trimming.

Some fashionable wraps and coats included:

Capot — an evening hood.
Caroline Spencer — made of white kerseymere with a cape and trimmed in blue satin, 1818.
Cottage cloak — with either a cape or a hood, it fastened under the chin.
Douillette à la Russienne — warmly lined and usually padded.
Hungarian wrap — a loose cloak made of velvet and lined with silk, wrapped about the person.
Kutusoff mantle — matching the hat, and featuring a wrinkled collar, it fastened at the throat.
Poland mantle — made of silk and it fastened with a shoulder brooch.
Zephyr cloak — long cloak of lace or net falling in points at the feet and sashed at the waist.

Shoes and Hose

The favored shoes were light, flat, low cut pumps called slippers. They could be fastened by a lace twined around a slender ankle or even thin bands of ribbon over the instep. They were given names like the Grecian sandal or Roman sandal though they had little in common with a classical sandal. Slippers were so simple some ladies made their own, but generally they went to a fashionable shoemaker like R. Willis at 421 Fish Street Hill in London who boasted a Royal Patent.

These delicate pumps were usually made of kid and covered with beautiful fabrics. The flimsy slippers could also be made of jean (a twilled cotton fabric), Spanish satin, or Moroccan leather. A lady of admired elegant style must have a pair to match every outfit. Evening slippers were the most fragile styles. They were made of the finest fabrics — brocade, satin, and *gros de naples*. Exquisite bead, bugle work, and embroidered bow knots often decorated them.

Half boots were the preferred style for walks or phaeton drives. They were generally heeless, pointed, and sometimes laced in the back. They could also be worn for evening and were made in satin and brocade. Ornate embroidery decorated the sides and toe.

Very stout boots were made of nankeen or sturdy leathers. In cold weather furlined boots made of velvet were stylish. It also became common for women to protect their delicate slippers by wearing boots over them.

For the most part, all pairs of shoes were "straights" — exactly the same with no left or right.

Silk hose in white and tied at the knee were standard. As the hemline moved above the ankle after 1810, highly decorated stockings were common. Openwork insets and embroidery featuring flowers or bownots were some of the embellishments.

Underwear

The nineteenth century opened with English women following their French sisters in discarding petticoats and corsets. Young ladies were known to wear their thin muslin dresses with nothing under them but flesh colored tights.

As one social observer recounted in June, 1812, a fashionable young lady addressed her partner at the Lord Mayor's Ball with an admonition to be very careful and not tread on her dress, because underneath was nothing to save her modesty.

The extreme of this fashion was the bare female form under a "dampened" clinging muslin dress. In reality underwear usually consisted of a single petticoat, which might be colored under the white dress. *Zonas*, a Grecian brassiere consisting of bands covered with silk, could also be found under these thin garments. The damsel wrapped the bands around her upper trunk, and it offered some support for her lower breasts.

"Bust improvers" were a major innovation of the period. Bosoms were the main focus of the figure. It was necessary to improve on nature's inadequacies for some ladies. These "bosom friends" were made of stuffed cotton or wax.

The most important fashion news of the age was the introduction of drawers although they did not become widely worn until after the Regency. They were accepted in the royal circles by 1811 and had been mentioned in fashion journals since 1805. They were also called pantalettes. They were usually trimmed with expensive lace and hung slightly below one's dress till around 1820 when they disappeared under dresses forever.

Small bustles in the shape of rolls could also be found among most ladies' undergarments. They were tied as high as possible under these high-waisted dresses in order to improve the fall of the skirt.

Corsets never completely went out of style. There were always figures that needed help. The short corset was frequently used by young ladies. Problem figures that needed greater aid would use a long corset that reached down to the hips. Shaped breast cups made their appearance at this time, a distinct change from the past when corsets either pushed up or flattened the bosom.

Beau Brummell's dictates on cleanliness had its effect on women's underwear as fashionable ladies began to pay more attention to their personal hygiene. Cleanliness meant changing more frequently and possessing larger quantities of underwear.

Hair

Classical dress styles demanded a head of hair that followed the Greek and Roman mode too. The fantastic bizarre coiffures on the enormous heads of the eighteenth century were replaced with smaller, neater styles. From 1800 to 1810, short hair, *à la Titus*, was very popular. The cropped cut had many variations. The hair could be cut short just in front, or front and sides with the back length left longer.

Many women regretted cutting their hair so short, and they kept wigmakers flourishing as they bought long wigs *à la Sappho*.

Hair was simply worn for daytime, often just ornamented with a riband entwined through curls. Full dress required more elaborate decoration.

If a lady couldn't bear to cut her hair, she had the option of pulling her long locks to the back of her head and tying them into a bunch of curly tendrils or arranging a bun.

All sorts of false hair, braids, jeweled combs, flowers, plumes, and even ropes of pearls were used to decorate the hair.

Hair styles were given names that alluded to their classical inspiration like *à la Venus*, but as clothes became more elaborate so did hair styles. The simpler skimpy cuts went out of favor.

From 1810 to 1820, the wispy curls delicately arranged around the face gave way to longer more elaborate curls and fantastical ringlets all around the hairline. The rest of the hair was dressed on the crown in a top knot. The top knot could consist of braids, curls, or a large bun alone or in any combination. Mr. J.B.M.D. Lafoy, a hairdresser who wrote *The Complete Coiffeure* (1817), voiced emphatically that a lady's best hairstyle was what suited her best. London was full of well-established hairdressers, and they visited their wealthy clientele to prepare them for special events. The first chore of a young miss new to Town would probably be acquiring a fashionable new cut.

Headwear

New hairstyles meant new types of headwear. The towering edifices of hair of the eighteenth century were gone. A short cut or long hair dressed close to the head was a elegant lady's preference. A huge variety of trim bonnets, lacy caps, and sumptuous turbans came into fashion to complement the new modes.

Bonnets and hats followed the shape and size of hairstyles. At the beginning of the period they were smaller and had a lower line. As the fashion for more elaborate styles featuring fancy top knots and lavish curls grew, the crowns became higher and the brims wider to accommodate them.

The number of different fancy bonnets and hats was astonishing. Straw and velvet were the preferred material though satin and crepe were used too. Trimmings of ostrich plumes, ribbons, and puffed or pleated fabrics dressed up the different styles. Sometimes large veils of net or lace were artistically arranged over the bonnet.

Bonnets could have names that reflected the events of the day such as the name of a military leader or a battle. *La Belle Assemblée* cautioned the fashionable lady not to appear in public two days in a row in the same bonnet. To comply with this dictate she might choose from the sampling of bonnets and hats below:

Coburg bonnet—crowned bonnet, tied under the chin, 1816.
Conversation bonnet—fashioned of chip, with a brim; silk-
    lined with matching ribbon tied in a bow on top, 1807.
Cossack hat—a rounded crown, front edged with pearls and
    feathers at one side, 1812.
Gipsy hat—straw or chip and tied with a ribbon.
Jockey bonnet—with full crown and eye shade, 1806 and
    later.

Kutusoff hat—bears the name of the Russian General who
commanded the Allies against Napoleon in 1813, fashioned
of cloth, tied under the chin, and boasting a feather.
Poke bonnet—bonnet that projected or poked over the face.
Spanish hat—a felt hat, with a plume, fashionable until
1807.

Caps were undress bonnets. They were worn both
indoors and outdoors by women of all ages. Jane Austen
described one of hers in a letter.

My cap has come home and I like it very much.
Fanny has one also, hers is white sarsnet and
laces of a different shape from mine, more fit
for morning carriage wear, which is what it is
intended for, and is in the shape exceedingly
like our own satin and lace of last winter,
shaped round the face exactly like it, with pipes
and more fullness and a round crown inserted
behind. My cap has a peak in front. Large, full
bows of very narrow ribbon (old twopenny) are
the thing. One over the right temple perhaps,
with another at the right ear.[2]

The cap could be cut away in the front so delicate
tendrils of hair showed to advantage on the forehead.
They were also worn under a bonnet. Lace was a very
fashionable material to make one's cap and ribbon was the
preferred trim.

Some different modes were:

Coiffure à l' indisposition—cap fashioned of muslin and lace
(1812 and after).
Cornette or French cap—cap covering the hair and ears
made of lace and net. A ribbon bow tied under the chin.
Regency cap—white satin cap trimmed with ostrich
plumage.

Some kind of headwear for full dress was a fashion
necessity. Turbans were one of the most fashionable styles
for evening wear and were worn throughout the period.
The height of their popularity was in 1809. It was said
they drew their original inspiration from the Egyptian
campaign.
Turbans could be very elaborate creations of satin or
velvet. Their size and ornateness grew with the increasing
size of the hairstyles and fancier decorations on gowns.
Towards the end of the Regency period all the most
luxurious fabrics were used—sometimes as many as three in
one turban! Plumes, pearls, jeweled brooches, and gold
fringe adorned these fanciful creations by 1820.

Some styles favored by the *ton* were:

Armenian toque—small turban fashioned of satin and
    feather-trimmed tulle, 1817.
Demi-turban—length of gauze or muslin wrapped around the
    head and knotted on the side. (1800-1812).
Turkish turban—fashioned of entwined gauze and silk, (1808
    and later).

Veils of muslin or lace (like the one Madame Recamier
wore on her visit to England in 1802) or half-handkerchiefs
could be draped over one's hair too.

Fans

Every fashionable woman regardless of age had a fan.
Fan language was memorized just as manners were learned
by every stylish woman of polite society. The Princess
Charlotte was given her first fan by her Aunt Amelia when
she was but two years old. As the princess learned
carriage and curtsying, she also learned the intricacies of
fan language. She knew how to peep through her fan,
over it, or to the side for maximum effect. Different
social situations required different gestures.

With fan in hand a lady was well on her way to cutting a figure in society. She could give a lingering look that was long enough to invite but not embolden. Or she could discourage and refuse without being rude. The fan added romantic flair to the intricacies of courtship.

Different occasions required a particular fan and a lady must have one for each event she attended be it royal entertainments, church, card playing, the theater, shopping, phaeton driving, or walking in Hyde Park.

A variety of fabrics were used to make these multitudes of fans. Painted silk, gauze, and lace were three of the most popular materials. Ivory was used for the sticks, and many fans featured jewels on them. A lady might even write a favorite verse on her fan.

Jewelry

Many portraits with the simpler gowns of the first decade of the century depicted necks and arms bare of jewelry. As the dresses became more elaborate, the use of jewelry also increased. Necklaces, bracelets, and family tiaras placed in classically inspired hairdos were very much in vogue.

Other jewelry to be seen were crosses on neck chains. The large shawls and wraps of different sorts ushered in the use of wrought gold and jeweled clasps. Cameos, too, were very popular for a time, especially at the French Imperial court. Suspended by a gold chain from the neck, small watches adorned the bosoms of more adventuresome ladies.

Parasols

Parasols were used to complement milady's ensemble as well as to keep the dreaded touch of the sun away from her face. A freckle might appear!

Very elegant with long slender handles, they had

whalebone frames shaped like a pagoda with silk stretched over them. Fringe might decorate the edge. Some had hinges near the top of the handle to tilt the top at an angle. A miniature version little more than two feet across was very popular all through the period.

Reticules

Reticules were also called popularly "ridicules" or "indispensables." The sleek lines of the flimsy dresses had eliminated the pocket. This early pocketbook was either bag shaped or flat and round. It might match a woman's slippers or be made of the same fabric as her gown. Some were ornately decorated with embroidery and jewels.

Shopping

To purchase her fashion accessories, a London lady could shop at one of the fabulous bazaars like the Exeter Change and Burlington Arcade. A bazaar was a building of more than one story that was under one management with many different shops and stalls. Not too different in concept from a modern day mall.

The goods included all sorts of gimcracks, gewgaws, and fripperies. Silk stockings, children's clothes, books, toys, and *papier mache* pretties to sit on milady's table were just a few of the dazzling amount of goods for sale.

During the Regency most shopping was done at individual shops. Prime shopping for a lady was the wealth of stores and shops situated around Oxford Street and Mayfair or Leicester Square and Covent Garden. There were silk mercers, milliners, corsetiers, linen-drapers, and haberdashers to outfit her in the latest mode. Jane Austen bought fashionable muslins at Grafton House when she was in London.

These delightful, bountiful shopping areas filled a

fashionable woman's idle hours. She only shopped in daylight and was always accompanied by her maid, footman, or page. Her reputation, you know!

The Lady's Maid

The lady's maid was the essential ingredient in keeping milady's fashionable lifestyle afloat—from dressing and undressing her mistress for each different activity to preparing a bath, or removing a stain, she was kept busy from rising to retiring.

A lady's maid was known as an abigail, a reference to II Samuel verses 24-28 when Abigail calls herself David's handmaid four times.

She was responsible for many things. A task of great importance was accompanying her lady on shopping excursions or walks in Green Park. A pearl beyond price was a maid who had a talent for hairdressing. She was also expected to inspect every item of clothing after it was used and repair any damage. Another duty of the abigail was to keep a lady's cosmetic pots filled with either homemade or purchased cosmetics.

Cosmetics

All sorts of lotions and potions were used to remove unsightly hair, dye gray strands, vanish wrinkles, and generally keep the fashionable lady young and beautiful. She might buy such products as Bloom of Circassia, Oil of Jasmin, L'Eau de Ninon, or Milk of Roses.

La Belle Assemblée in 1806 stated "on the toilet of a lady the rouge box is become perhaps the most essential attendant." Ladies eagerly colored their cheeks. Rouge was made from red sandalwood or orchanet root, and if used often, it damaged the complexion. It was artfully applied with a soft hare's foot.

Some ladies applied rouge with an overgenerous hand.

Mrs. Fitzherbert was said to be rouged to the very eyes. Caroline of Brunswick was another devotee of the rouge pot who strode through life with cheeks fearfully reddened. The most dangerous of the beauty aids was white lead and mercury water. A lady used these ingredients to keep her complexion snowy white and unblemished. Prolonged use resulted in death by slow degrees.

One of the worst disfigurements was a freckle! This awful blemish was attacked with various remedies. One was a wash of diluted hydrochloric acid. Another remedy was roman balsam, a paste made of barley flour, bitter almonds, and honey to be worn overnight.

Pimples were also treated with roman balsam. For blackheads, it was Darwin's ointment, an odious mix of sulphur flour, hog's lard, and mercury.

Whatever her problem, there was assuredly some noxious paste or expensive lotion available to combat nature's mistakes.

NOTES TO CHAPTER II

1. Blanche A. Swinton, *A Sketch of the Life of Georgiana, Lady de Ros*, pp. 7-8.

2. *Jane Austen's Letters to Her Sister Cassandra and Others*, ed. R.W. Chapman, p. 326.

Chapter III

THE FASHIONABLE GENTLEMAN

From the top of his head covered in short carefully tousled locks to the bottom of his glossy black boots (rumored to be polished with a champagne-based concoction), the prototype Regency buck could make milady's heart throb with yearning. He should have broad enough shoulders to show his beautifully cut formfitting dress coat to the best advantage. If properly made, this cut-away jacket made by Meyer in Conduit Street (a favorite of Prinny's), Weston, or Schweitzer and Davidson, took the aid of a valet or two in donning. For a man who desired a conservative military cut, Stultz who numbered Wellington among his clients would be the tailor of choice.

His waist should be slim as befits an athlete. A muscular thigh and calf would not go amiss with a young lady of discerning taste either. Skintight yellow pantaloons defined every bulge and lack thereof. Young men with spidershanks were known to pad out slender limbs with sawdust.

But beyond physical perfection and fashion sense our Regency beau should posses wit, audacity, and utter coolness. Nothing should rattle him. He should be awake on every suit, a Corinthian of courageous spirit ready to do his best. Coolness was all. It was the age where gentlemen wagered vast sums without the flicker of an eyelid. Estates were won and lost on the turn of a card.

Gaming was only one of the great vices that plagued the men of the age. Drunkenness was the other. Our Regency buck could well be a three-bottle man, but his imperturbable manner did not make him dangerous until he broached his fifth bottle.

There was a whole vocabulary built around the bottle and its consequences in the Prince Regent's London. Any

Regency buck would be well acquainted with the following terms:

A Glossary of Being Foxed

Accounts — casting up one's accounts: retching.
Altitudes — to be in one's altitudes: to be drunk.
Blue ruin — gin.
Chirping merry — happily stimulated from imbibing liquor.
Cup-Shot — feeling liquor's effects.
Disguised — intoxicated.
Flustered — intoxicated.
Foxed — inebriated.
Fuddle — drunk.
To cascade — to throw up.
Top heavy — intoxicated.
To shoot the cat — to retch from drunken excesses.

A Guide to Regency Males

While the beau ideal made the heart of many a green girl flutter, a host of other male characters populated the Regency scene.

Beau-nasty — fashionably dressed but none too clean fop.
Bow window set — Brummell, Alvanley, Mildmay, and Pierrepoint sat in the bow window at White's Club. They could be seen dressed in the first style of elegance by everyone who passed by.
Brother of the blade — a military man.
Brother of the quill — a writer.
Buck — a spirited young blood.
Buck of the first head — a debauchee in prime style.
Captain Queernabs — a poorly dressed man.
Captain Sharp — a roguish gambler who is well-schooled in cheating.
Chicken Nabob — an unimportant nabob who returned from

the East Indies with only an inconsequential fortune.

Corinthian — a relentless sportsman devoted to manly sports. The term comes from Shakespeare's Henry IV, Part I. — "... a Corinthian, a lad of mettle...."

Court card — a foppish fool.

Coxcomb — a foolish person full of conceit. The term comes from the strip of red on top of a jester's cap worn by court fools.

Crusty beau — a fellow encrusted with paint and cosmetics.

Dandy — a foppish man unusually attentive to dress.

Fop — a man dedicated to his appearance.

Fribble — an unmanly fop.

Gentleman of the green baize road — a gamester.

Greenhead — an immature youth.

Hell-born babe — a lascivious, wicked youth.

Man of the town — a profligate blood.

Man of the world — one who knows the ways of the world.

Nob — a man of consequence.

Out and outer — a man up to any challenge.

Pink of the *ton* — a flower of fashionable English manhood. The best of these was known as the pink of the pinks.

Quiz — an odd-looking man.

Rake, rakehell, or rakeshame — a libertine.

Scapegrace — a wild, morally loose fellow.

Scoundrel — a man who has not one shred of honor.

Scourers — wild bloods who sought entertainment by smashing windows, assaulting the watch, and harrassing every passerby.

Swell — a sartorially splendid gentleman.

Turk — a hard, cruel man who offered Turkish treatment to all.

Unique four — the complete dandies: Brummell, Alvanley, Mildmay, and Pierrepoint.

Unlicked cub — an immature lad.

Upbringing

As diverse as the male types in the upper reaches of society were, young men of good family had many elements of their upbringing in common. Such a young man was born at home with usually a midwife in attendance or perhaps a doctor. His mother was given laudanum or its stronger form, opium, for pain. Her chances of surviving the actual childbirth were good. However, surviving the doctor's or midwife's unwashed, germ-ridden hands were not. Childbed fever claimed the lives of many women before modern methods of sterilization became common later in the century.

The services of a wet nurse were engaged at the moment of birth or just before the bouncing babe was out in the world. No lady of the first rank would breastfeed her own child. The wet nurse was usually a woman of low birth, possibly a maid or perhaps the relative of a servant. Babies were sometimes dosed with gin to keep them quiet and docile. This was only one of many pitfalls our young male had to face in order to reach maturity.

He was given unpurified water to drink whereas adults mixed wine with their water. Many children never lived past the age of five. In the nursery, the young cub was dressed in petticoats and a cap. The large, drafty rooms of a country house could be very cold, and the cap and long dress gave a little extra protection.

His principal care after he was weaned from his wet nurse was given over to a dependant relative or a nanny engaged specifically for the task. His life was governed for ill or good by his attendant. They almost had the power of life or death over their charges. Parents only saw the child at specified times and then a servant accompanied the child. Georgian parents of means kept a certain distance between themselves and their children.

After the end of his nursery days, he would be tutored by the local clergyman who probably owed his living to the boy's father. Or perhaps a governess or tutor would be particularly employed to teach him his letters. When the little fellow could read and write, he was banished from the family circle to the revered institution known as the public school.

The public schools were open at a substantial fee to the sons of the nobility and gentry with a smattering of boys from the bourgeois. These hallowed halls of learning that trained the future members of the *haut ton* included Eton, Rugby, Harrow, Winchester, Westminster, and Charterhouse.

Georgian gentlemen wanted their sons trained for government and polite society. The course of learning was classical. The literature and language of Greece and Rome were the stuff of the daily study grind. French, too, was taught as some knowledge of this language was essential in the upper levels of society. Among the fashionable French was also a means of private conversation in front of the always-present servants. Drawing and fencing rounded out the curriculum. There were few science or mathematical courses.

Everyday life at these select schools could be filled with brutal unhappiness for the poor young fellow enrolled there. He was bullied by the elder boys, given minute portions of poorly cooked food, and put to bed under scanty bed coverings in a dank, chilly, crowded room.

The life was hard and brutish. Older boys were in charge of the younger ones and ordered them about unmercifully. This was called fagging — a system whereby an older boy used the younger as a servant to fetch and carry for him — and worse. Such prolonged ill-treatment could result in a suffering schoolboy exacting revenge on his headmaster. One such incident is said to have occurred at Harrow when the headmaster's carriage was blown to bits with gunpowder.

Brutality was not confined to fagging. Boys were severely punished with canes and rods on bare buttocks to such an extent that it was not unknown for a boy to bleed from his beating.

The true test at these schools was whether the young cub could survive. Flogging and fagging were supposed to

toughen the spirit and strengthen his backbone—essential
elements in acquiring a stiff upper lip. Educators and
parents subscribed to the principle that one was fit to
command only after one had learned to obey. And those
young boys of the gentry and nobility were there to learn
their place and destiny in England's highly structured
society.

The young Georgian gentlemen who survived public
school were now eighteen years old and could go on to
"Tory" Oxford or "Whig" Cambridge. During this period
both schools had somewhat declined in quality. Dons
teaching by tutoring and lectures gave all the instruction.
Here as in public school, the study of the classics prevailed. At the university he had the option of frittering away
his time or studying hard if his abilities turned in a
scholarly direction. Some undergraduates spent all their
time eating, drinking, and wenching. Most young bloods
did a bit of studying and a bit of carousing.

The Young Blood in Town

Traditionally a young man went on the Grand Tour
with a bear-leader or tutor, called so because he led an
unlicked cub. The two of them would travel the length
and breadth of Europe sampling all delights available. The
French Revolution, then Napoleon and the long war with
France took this option away from the young man of the
early nineteenth century. If the Regency buck saw the
wonders of the Continent, it would probably be from the
back of a cavalry mount.

A young gentleman was expected to be an all-around
sportsman, handy with his fists, his guns, on a horse, and
with a sword in his hand. The age was one of bare-fisted
fighting, and the spectacle of the boxing match was the
greatest draw of the time as a sporting event. Gentlemen
were expected to participate in the sport and to be adept
with their fists. A true fashionable male would be found
at Gentleman Jackson's Rooms, a boxing salon in Bond

Street, stripped and ready to go a round or two with the former champion once or twice a week.

For swordplay he would frequent Angelo's for tuition and practice. Angelo's Haymarket Room was *the* premiere fencing school. The great instructor Domenico Angelo turned fencing into a gentleman's sport in the Georgian age with scientific instruction at his London school. His manual, *The School of Fencing*, helped promote it as a sport of skill that enhanced a Regency buck's poise, grace, and general athleticism. Swordplay survived as a sport even as pistols were replacing them as the duelists' weapon of choice because of the spirit behind Angelo's artful instruction of such things as the thrust, the salute, the feint, and the execution of the *demi-volte*.

And these masculine martial skills could prove useful in preserving a young man of refinement's life and honor. The Regency has been called "the age of politeness" for good reason. There was a veneer of elaborate social behavior to avoid arguments. Quarrels could lead to duels among these touchy aristocrats who valued honor above all else. A meeting at dawn in a royal park to settle a matter of honor with pistols or swords was not an unusual occurrence. Courage or "bottom" was the most admired of gentlemanly virtues. "Neck or nothing" insouciance on horseback and elsewhere was the true mark of the nonpareil.

At large in Town and educated in the classics and the manly arts, the young man of style had several ambitions. The first of these was success at gaming. As he proved his courage on the hunting field so must he prove himself at faro, hazard, and whist. The coolness and courage that served so well in the boxing ring now had to surface to serve him in wagering huge sums on the possibilities of absurd happenings. One famous wager took place between Charles James Fox and the Prince of Wales during a promenade on Bond Street. Fox wagered with Prinny the number of cats that would walk on either side of the street. Fox chose the sunny side of the street, and since cats prefer sun to shade he won the wager with a count

of thirteen to zero. Fox stayed ever alert for wagers
likely to divert funds into his constantly empty pockets.
Our beau's second ambition was to receive society's
approval in his world with all the invitations and trappings
that made him a gentleman of the first stare. These
included memberships in the right clubs, invitations to balls
and assemblies of the first elegance, and society's general
acceptance of his superiority and modishness. And for
men, too, a voucher for Almack's was important. Men, as
well as women, thirsted for the fashionable world's
approval. They ruined numerous cravats to tie the perfect
"orientale" to impress their peers. Men of fashion were
captives of society's approval.

Another ambition of the young buck was to pursue
Town pleasures with unrivaled glee, and what could be
more agreeable than making a stir in the world at the
same time! Gentlemen who were newly arrived in Town
and desirous of worldly attention were advised to proceed
directly to Bond Street to begin the dreaded lounge!
Odious bucks established their credentials as Bond Street
loungers from the hours of noon until four. It was
essential to carry a walking-stick (a wonderful way to trip
passersby) and wear spurs (a handy hook to catch a pretty
girl's petticoat). Often fellows of like mind paraded up
and down the street together. Three Bond Street loungers
abreast could then amuse themselves by accidentally
running innocent bystanders off the pavement and into the
gutter. To have just the proper air, it was also recommended that these strollers have a quizzing glass ever on
the ready—so few fashionable fellows should be able to see
beyond the end of their noses. At all times the Bond
Street lounger is advised to make himself conspicuous by
employing his contemptuous superiority and haughty
sophistication on all and sundry.

Young men on the Town as a rule made themselves
obnoxious. In the park at night, gangs of young aristocratic fellows plagued night watchmen who called out the
hour and watched for troublemakers as they patrolled the
streets. These young bloods about town amused themselves

by knocking down the watchmen and passersby. The unwary were tossed in horsetroughs for a belly laugh. Sometimes one of their number would pretend to be a woman in trouble screeching for help, and then howling with amusement as helpful bystanders rushed to rescue the "damsel" in distress.

Perhaps his greatest interest, amusement, and even ambition were the women in his life. Of supreme importance was the continuance of his name and the debt he owed his family. If his family was facing financial ruin or hardship, it was his duty to marry money no matter how unattractive the package in which it came wrapped. A squint or a moustache were to be overlooked if a young lady's portion was large enough. Should the young beau be the heir to a great name he was expected to dedicate himself to the future of his family. It was his duty to get an heir of his body to preserve the line. Younger sons could go wild on the town and dissipate their time, wealth, and health. The heir must marry and reproduce.

Many men felt after they had bestowed their name and fortune on a woman that they had done their part. Marriage was an institution and not the proper place for passion. In marriage, a man made sure his heir was *his*. It was not unusual in fashionable marriages for husbands and wives to go their separate ways after a male child was born. Where a Regency buck looked for passions and pleasures was among the women of the town. Opera dancers, the fashionable impure, or just plain prostitutes were the receptacles of his animal lusts.

There was a complete parallel world of elegant courtesans who serviced the men of the *ton*. The most renowned of these were Harriette Wilson and her sisters. Harriette Wilson and her three sisters, Amy, Fanny, and Sophia, were four of the best known Cyprians of their time. Rumored to have been set about their trade by a mother who had been "in the business," these women of the town plied their trade for a good many years and reigned supreme in the world of the *demi-monde*.

They were all rather plain girls with a vivacity and

charm that took them to the top of their chosen trade. Only Sophia landed (through little effort) an aristocratic husband. Amy was the intelligent one, Harriette the witty one. The nicest of qualities belonged to Fanny, and dim-witted Sophia was the one with a childish, naive charm.

Amy's house was where their admirers gathered to bid for their favors. Harriette charged a hundred guineas for a few hours of dalliance, though their company was sought many times just for witty conversation and a congenial evening of a buffet supper, a party, or a reception. Harriette lived under the protection of many men and named names in her infamous *Memoirs* published in 1825. There was to have been a second volume about her exploits, but certain nervous gentlemen who provided large monetary payments stopped a sequel.

Brummell, Alvanley, Palmerston, and Luttrell could be seen among the elite in Amy's drawing room. To be seen at the Wilson's was just as important as being seen at White's or the Argyle Rooms. They were all the crack and men of fashion lined up for them. If a man about town wished to be discreet about keeping a mistress, he would establish his bit of muslin in an out of the way district. But such subterfuge was rarely used. What would be the distinction of winning a prime article and not having the gratification of being envied and admired by the fellows who lost out?

A kept woman milked her protector for every bit of blunt she could and was shared by other lovers in his absence to save money against the day that her protector grew tired of her and moved on to the next ladybird. For many women being in some man's keeping was the only road to survival in a society that had few opportunities for women beyond marriage and domestic servitude.

The "Bits of Muslin" Glossary

Abbess — the mistress of a bawdy house.
Bit of muslin — a wench.

Carte-blanche — blank paper denoting unlimited authority. Gentlemen offered "ladies" a blank check to lure them into their protection.
Covent Garden Abbess or nun — a prostitute. Covent Garden was frequented by women of easy virtue.
Cyprians — loose women. Cyprus was renowned for its love of Venus.
Demi-rep — from demi-reputation. An unchaste woman.
Doxy — a wanton woman.
Easy virture — a woman of easy virtue: a prostitute.
Fille de joie — a courtesan.
Impure — a loose woman.
Ladybird — a kept woman.
Nunnery — a house of ill repute.
Phrynes — impures. Phryne was an Athenian courtesan in ancient Greece.
School of Venus — a house of ill fame.

The everyday preoccupation of the fashionable Regency gentleman was, of course, clothes and appearance. The man who ruled society in the late Georgian age was a person whose philosophy and fashion dictates lived long past his life span. He was the supreme dandy and Regency beau — George Brummell. Brummell's grandfather was rumored to be a personal servant, but his father was secretary to Lord North. Though he had neither birth nor wealth, he was sent to Eton at the age of twelve in 1790 where he became very popular. He was dubbed "Buck" by his intimates because of his close attention to personal cleanliness and his dress. It was not long before the Prince became enthralled by him and gave him a cornetcy in his own regiment, the 10th Hussars, in 1794.

Brummell soon became the Prince's intimate and spent much of his time on military leave. An inheritance of £30,000 and the threat of being posted to Manchester, which he insisted was "foreign service," led him to resign his commission and set up his own bachelor establishment in 1798 at No. 4 Chesterfield Street. He soon became the *arbiter elegantiarum.* His lengthy morning toilets were legendary. He informed his intent admirers that not one but three hairdressers attended his locks – one for the back, one for the temples, and one for the front. And he had been known to discard numerous cravats as failures before tieing neckcloth perfection.

Extravagance, gambling, and his impudent tongue caused his ruin in 1816. He fled to Calais and lived the remainder of his life in straitened circumstances. But while he reigned supreme in Regency London he was the absolute arbiter of fashionable taste. As Thomas Raikes described him:

> he was in his time the very glass of fashion; every one from the highest to the lowest conspired to spoil him; and who that knew him well could deny that with all his faults he was still the most gentlemanlike, the most agreeable of companions? Never was there a man who during his career had such unbounded influence, and what is seldom the case, such general popularity in society.[1]

Beau Brummell's dictates on fashion were important for any young man on the town to follow if he wished to succeed in the fashionable world. Beau decreed that a gentleman's clothes should be indiscernible in material and exquisite in cut and fit. The emphasis on cut and fit saw the demise of silks, satins, and brocades for men's wear. Brummell's new male creation was dubbed "a dandy," a silly, effeminate fellow who put his main emphasis on clothing.

Beau's all-pervasive influence pulled smelly English squires out of their stables, gave them a long, thorough wash, shaved them well, and dressed them in spotlessly clean clothes that were cut to fit perfectly. His belief in good country washing and lots of clean linen brought about a revolution in male grooming. When Brummell was through with a man of fashion, he was immaculately clean with a smoothly shaven face and sported snowy white neckcloths plus gleaming Hessian boots.

Beau Brummell's dandies believed to show emotion was bad form and that life was a bad joke. The cool, clever Regency buck full of audacious wit and supreme self-confidence personified Brummell's manner. Raikes remembered him as

> liberal, friendly, *serviable,* without any shuffling, or tortuous policy, or meanness, or manoeuvring for underhand objects; himself of no rank or family, but living always with the highest and noblest in the country, on terms of intimacy and familiarity, but without *bassesse* or truckling; on the contrary, courted, applauded, and imitated, protecting rather than protected, and exercising an influence, a fascination in society which no one even felt a wish to resist.[2]

A Guide to Men's Fashion

From 1800 to 1810 men's fashion saw the fineness of English tailoring supersede the French influence. The French would retain their stranglehold on women's fashion, but English tailors with their superb cut and fit (Brummell's influence) were to be the dominant force in men's clothes.

Despite much opposition even from church pulpits, long trousers firmly replaced knee breeches. Prinny gave unofficial sanction to the new style in 1816 when he appeared clad in trousers.

Trousers began their triumphant march toward supremacy in the years 1805 to 1810 in fashionable society. After Waterloo only elderly men wore knee breeches. "Small clothes" were reserved only for very formal or ceremonial occasions. In general, day wear became plainer, neckcloths smaller, and hair shorter.

Coats were cutaway and waistcoats were cut deep with a frilled shirt protruding from a deep vee. The coats and waistcoats were of different materials and colors. The coats were usually in darker colors — claret, green, black, blue, or brown. Such fine woolen cloths as superfine, and kerseymere, which had a smooth dress surface, were used for coats. White waistcoats were *de rigueur* for evening wear and were made in a variety of colors (including even patterns) for day wear. Stylish bucks often let their creative impulses run riot when choosing the fabric texture and color used to construct waistcoats.

Throughout the period fashionable male attire was somewhat confining with its high, intricately tied, starched cravats and superbly fitted, tightly clinging coats and pantaloons. But the dandies, fops, and exquisites who wore these clothes, after all, were gentlemen of leisure. These Town beaus were obsessed with their clothes and the dress of others. No one found it unusual for a stylish buck to criticize a woman's taste in dress. The dandy spent much of his time and effort on his own clothes and was perfectly willing to use this expertise to needle a young and lovely green girl.

> Brummell was as great an oracle among the women of the highest rank in London, and his society as much courted and followed, as amongst his male associates. His opinion on all matters of taste and dress was implicitly adopted.[3]

Coats

The dress coat was a tail coat and used on almost all formal occasions. It was constructed from materials of suppleness and flexibility that was unlike the stiffer cloths and fabrics used in the eighteenth century. The coat was cut away in front in a straight line slightly above the gentleman's waistline. Either single- or double-breasted styles were acceptable.

The morning or riding coat had a tail and sloping

front edges. The horse-mad Regency buck rode frequently, and the riding coat did double duty as a morning coat. He also donned this style on more formal occasions.

The new fangled frock coat was first seen in the years following Waterloo. Military in design, it took its form from the great coat though it was more fitted. In the Regency it was only worn on informal occasions.

The great coat was worn year round. There were two basic styles, the surtout and the less-fitted box coat. The surtout was double-breasted, collared, and often had a cape attached, and could be worn very long (some were even ankle-length). Layers upon layers of shoulder capes of varying lengths distinguished the box coat which fastened down the front with a long row of buttons.

Waistcoats could be single- or double-breasted with or without lapels or collars. Dandies often gave their florid tastes full reign by selecting waistcoats in bold colors and gaudy prints.

Pantaloons and Trousers

Pantaloons and trousers were always in light hues, such as buff and yellow. They were made from light-weight materials that differed from the coat's fabric. Merinos, doeskins, and kerseymeres were among the fabrics used. Legwear was constructed of nankeen, a heavy twilled cotton or drill for warmer weather. By the beginning of the Regency, trousers and pantaloons were the ultimate in daywear.

Pantaloons clung snugly to a gentleman's limbs. Calf length until 1817, they then continued down to the ankles. A side slit that buttoned kept them skintight, while straps under the instep kept them firmly in place. For evening wear, the elegant silk stockings, either plain or patterned, were worn.

Trousers of mid-calf length were acceptable for daywear and were often so body-hugging that they were barely discernable from pantaloons. They, too, were worn with straps tied under the instep, and by the end of the Regency reached the shoe top. "Cossacks," donnned during the Tsar's visit to London in 1814, were wider cut trousers which were gathered at the ankles and waist.

Neckwear

Magnificient neckwear was the principal vanity of the Regency dandy. He wore a collar that was attached to his shirt. It was long enough to be turned up so a bit of it appeared over the magnificient cravat. Collars could reach absurd heights.

The cravat consisted of a sizeable triangular or square-shaped piece of starched silk, lawn, or muslin. Black or colored cravats were thought very informal. Cravats always had to be snowy white for formal wear. Much patience, expertise, and artistic talent were needed to form a masterly tied neckcloth. An 1818 tome on the intricate art of cravats was published in London entitled *Neckclothitania, or Titania: Being an Essay on Starchers, By One of the Cloth.*

Some of the many modish styles were the American, the Napoleon, *en cascade*, mailcoach, Osbaldestan, and Irish. The mathematical style was triangular in shape and considered just slightly less austere than the famed orientale, which was so high fashionable fellows could not see where they were going and starched so stiffly that they could not turn their heads.

Footwear

The boot in black was for all walks of life, the most popular footwear. The English bootmakers, Hoby at the corner of St. James's and Piccadilly in particular, made the most elegant ones. They came in every style and weight. Generally all sported low heels. Military men and events influenced greatly the boot's style and name. Wellington and Blücher boots were named after the famous generals. The top boot was an eighteenth century style that survived into the Regency. Such boots were known as "tops." They were very fashionable for foxhunting. The boot was snugly fitted to the gentleman's leg and foot and finished at the knee with a buff or white leather turned down top—the origin of the name.

Blüchers were a popular style of riding boot named for the famous Prussian general and England's darling during the Peace Celebrations of 1814. It weighed more than the Wellington boot. Gentlemen especially thought it a much better boot in bad weather and for riding than the Wellington.

The Hessian boot was introduced around the beginning of the nineteenth century. This subtle leather boot was worn outside the trousers. It curved just under the knee. At the top of the curve or peak in the center front, a decorative tassle dangled down. It was firmly ousted from fashion by the Wellington boot in the last years of the Regency.

The Wellington boot remained in fashion until the mid-nineteenth century. It was a closely fitted boot of black calf skin. They were worn under breeches which fitted snugly and tied under the foot. The breeches were known as Wellington's, too, and were said to have been introduced during the Peninsular War by the Duke. Half Wellingtons were a shorter boot of similar style that were worn under trousers.

Fashionable bucks wore spurs at every hour of the day, whether on horseback or not. Special boot loops aided a fellow in pulling on his tight boots. A potion called *vin de champagne* was used to achieve the glossy shine mandatory for beaus of the first stare.

Black pumps were worn with evening dress. These evening shoes were either without heels or very low-heeled. Black kid and the new patent leather were the materials used. Dandies ornamented them with delicately tied bows or a jeweled buckle. Silk stockings set off a nicely turned male leg.

A new material for shoes was glossy patent leather hailed as waterproof. The shiny surface was achieved by several coats of varnish. It was also called japanned leather but was most popularly known as "patent" because a royal patent was sought upon invention of this marvelous new leather.

Hats

The top hat in all its sizes and styles remained popular throughout the Regency. Hats were often made of beaver, and when they became worn, the gentleman of limited means could have them repaired. Hats were made even more expensive by being the only article of personal clothing on which there was a tax.

Lock's was where a tulip of fashion might choose his latest hat. The shop was located at No. 6 St. James's Street. Before the Battle of Trafalgar in 1805, Lock supplied Nelson with a cocked hat complete with special eye covering.

Gloves

If the fashionable male followed Brummell's strictures, his gloves would have the fingers cut out and sewn at one glovers and the thumb at another establishment to ensure a perfect fit. Gloves were usually constructed of either cotton or leather.

Hair

By 1800 wigs were no longer fashionable and long hair had become out of date. In 1804 the pigtails worn by soldiers in the British army were shortened. In 1808 they were shorn of them completely.

Older men though they might have put off their wigs

often still wore their hair long in eighteenth century styles. A fashionable young man wore his hair cut extremely short or a little longer and brushed forward to fall artistically in graceful curls on his forehead. Many hair styles found inspiration from Greek and Roman classical styles as exhibited in ancient statuary and on vases. Straight hair became a curly profusion with the aid of a crimping iron. Side whiskers were ordinary by 1810.

Snuff

Snuff taking was common to both sexes though more prevalent among men than the fair sex. Brummell made snuff taking an art form. His precise technique was copied just as the cut of his coat was by the fashionable world. He used only his left hand to hold and open his beautifully decorated snuff box. Elegant hand movements were the hallmark of his style. It was essential that the delicate fluttering of the lace draped over his wrist highlighted elegant, much pampered hands as his right hand raised a pinch of the pungent sort to his quivering nostrils and was daintily inhaled.

The Prince Regent as the "first gentleman of Europe" was *bon gré mal gré* — whether one will or not — a connoisseur of snuff. Though Prinny disliked snuff, he was above all else fashionable. He practiced the elaborate snuff-taking ritual with credible zeal. His snuff cellar contained varieties from all over the world. And as required for a dandy, different sorts were carried by him at different times of the day. Prinny's favorite blend was The King's Carotte, mixed exclusively for him by Fribourg & Treyer, the supreme tobacconists of the day. Other sorts he chose from were Bureau, Martinique, Old Paris, Bordeaux, Cologne, and Queen Charlotte's mixture. Queen Charlotte, the Prince's mother, used snuff from the age of seventeen until her death. Her preferred mixture contained ambergris, attargul, and powdered bitter almonds.

Prinny himself held his snuff box in his left hand and

opened it using his right thumb and forefinger. He would take a pinch with the same right thumb and forefinger deliberately losing it before it reached his nose. His snuff boxes were beautiful works of art. Each box contained a different variety of snuff and he had a superb collection of these art objects. Classical scenes were popular decorations for the little boxes which were upon occasion used to store precious momentoes, such as locks of hair and special trinkets.

Lord Petersham was famous for being the owner of a different snuff box for every day of the year. A Bond Street beau might purchase a snuffbox of ornate elegance at the jewelers Rundell and Bridges or at Jefferys.

Also purchased with the snuff box was a small silver shovel. This implement was designed to ladle the proper amount into the waiting nostrils of a heavy snuff user.

Smoking was something out of the ordinary. Tobacco was usually enjoyed in clay pipes outside. It was not very elegant for a Town beau to be seen smoking. Snuff was the fashionable vice of the day.

The prime rule in snuff etiquette was to never request a pinch of snuff. To be offered a pinch and accept was unobjectionable but to ask was terribly rude. This iron rule led to the quarrel between Prinny and the Beau. At Brighton Pavilion the Bishop of Winchester asked Brummell for a pinch of his snuff. Rather than overlook such a discourteous request, the Beau so forgot himself in his rage at this rudeness that he instructed his servant to toss the rest on the floor or in the fire. The Prince always mindful of his royal duties to guests was enraged that the Beau who considered himself to be a fashion leader would exhibit conduct unbecoming to a gentleman. He strongly expressed his displeasure to Brummell the next day. And so snuff began a quarrel that helped lead to Brummell's ultimate downfall. The audacious Beau forgot too often which one of the two of them was the royal personage.

Jewelry

Brummell wore no ornate jewelry. Snuff-boxes and elegant walking-sticks made up the bulk of his jewelry accessories. Well-dressed gentlemen might also wear cravat pins, rings, and fobs. The fob was the short chain or ribbon with a watch at the end of it that was carried in a fob pocket with a decorative ornament attached to it. Fobs dangled at the top of skin tight "inexpressibles."

One type of fob was a chatelaine, a series of ornate plaques that attached to the waist and from which a watch was hung. The watch was decorated to match the series of small plaques and its back was turned to show the design. Sometimes the watch was even eliminated. These chatelaines could be equipped with small chains or hooks, and a diversity of tiny objects were suspended from them. The enamel plaques might depict scenes from classical mythology. They were made from all types of metals and stones. Cameos were a popular decoration, too.

Quizzing Glasses

For the Regency dandy it was essential to have a quizzing glass dangling from his buttonhole. Odious fops quizzed everything as they strolled through the streets of London and ambled through fashionable salons. The pleasure-loving buck applied his glass to his eye with the same steadfast diligence to view the abundant charms of a modish damsel in a low-cut gown as he did to the elegant and lavish variety of food that made up his dinner.

Scent

Despite Brummell's dictate that blueblooded men should merely smell delightfully of the good washing and fresh clean air, Town beaus used a variety of fragrances.

Favorites included a variety of sweetwaters such as Imperial water (made of among other things, frankincense, cloves, and benzoin), and it was sometimes used as a mouthwash. Also popular was Hungary water, honey water, and rose water.

Eau de cologne was a fairly recent fashion. The Farina Brothers, Italian silk merchants in (where else!) Cologne, invented the product in the eighteenth century. It rapidly became popular, and its use swept across Europe.

The Valet

Overseeing the dressing and ornamenting of our finely turned out dandy was the devoted manservant called the valet. He provided the hugh stack of snowy white cravats that an artistically inclined gentleman might go through to achieve the ultimate in neckcloth art. Robinson, Brummell's valet, experimented some months to discover just the precise stiffening needed to achieve the best results. He kept his master's clothes in good order and repair, and might even make suggestions about a garment's suitability.

The valet was an essential actor in the play of life in the fashionable world. He kept his master immaculate, shaved, and in prime style, separating him conclusively from the Great Unwashed.

He was definitely one of the upper servants; a gentleman's gentleman. But a tulip of fashion had of necessity to be careful that his invaluable manservant's taste did not supersede his own. It should never be said that a dandy was made by either his tailor or his valet. The elegant man about town should have his own individual style. Brummell was never a slave to fashion.

NOTES TO CHAPTER III

1. Richard Henry Stoddard, ed., *Personal Reminiscences of Cornelia Knight and Thomas Raikes,* p. 268.

2. Ibid., p. 278.

3. Ibid., p. 269.

WEDDING NIGHT or the FASHIONABLE FROLIC.

Prince marries Mrs. Fitzburgh while friend fiddles.   *Unknown*

New York Public Library
Picture Collection

Chapter IV

ROMANCE, COURTSHIP AND MARRIAGE

Whether a young man on the Town was the biggest prize on the marriage mart or a younger son with limited prospects and highly ineligible, there was a prescribed procedure for a proper courtship.

On the surface at least, a demure damsel was pursued by the male. It was he who must arrange an introduction through a third party. This was not to say a matchmaking mama or relative might not throw a desirable potential mate in the way of a likely bachelor.

The introduction could take place on a ballroom floor as the young gentleman scanned the assembly and spied a lively chit making her debut in the *haut monde*. Soliciting an introduction from her chaperon or perhaps his hostess, he would then ask her the favor of performing a dance with him. The *Lady's Magazine* in 1818 cautioned young ladies to beware the dangers of waltzing. Human nature was so depraved that even the men of great purity could not be trusted. After all one must remember what lustful beasts were the best of the male sex!

Introductions could also take place at a house party, at the theater, or in a variety of ways. The proper way, of course, was the formal introduction.

After the introduction, a gentleman would pay calls on the lady who had captured his affection. The visits would be chaperoned and could take place in the morning or afternoon. The correct time for a call was ten to twenty minutes because any longer was considered a serious breach of etiquette.

He might ask the young lady to accompany him for a drive in Hyde Park during the fashionable hour. However, cow-handed young men with little skill had best leave tooling a dazzling damsel around Town to others more skillful.

One of the other fashionable ways to proceed with a courtship in the best circles was to send a posey to the young lady before an important ball or even an elegant trifle like a delicate hand-painted fan. An ardent swain might also seek to tempt the young lady that he fancied with delicious out-of-season treats such as strawberries in January.

The couple were in the same stylish circles and therefore were very likely to meet in many different situations. The fashionable flocked to the same balls, plays, concerts, assemblies, and other entertainments. How each hot-blooded young buck and his older elegant counterpart made use of these opportunities was left up to his own skill and imagination.

Of course, while these bewitched bachelors pursued their quarry through London's elegant drawing rooms, they, too, became fair game. Young girls shot off into the ton each year were encouraged by their parents to believe that they had all the qualifications to fill a great position. These ambitious young ladies invariably set their caps at unwary men of means.

Courtships might also continue over long distances. Correspondence could further the romance along, but a suitor must follow a restrictive set of rules. No young woman could be written to or reply to a letter without her father's or guardian's permission. For content in his letter, the eager young buck might rely on *The New London Letter Writer* by Samuel Johnson, M.A., which was published in the 1790s. Numerous examples abound for the young lady and her suitor to follow as they correspond with each other and fan the flames of their mutual desire.

Though some young men and women chose ambition as the ruling factor in choosing a life mate in Regency London, many more were felled by Cupid's bow. The elegant miss who hid her schemes behind a fluttering fan was most likely motivated by romantic love.

However the match came about, there were procedures to be followed. The modern way was to propose to the young lady first and then seek approval from her family.

This new way was deplored by the old guard. The virtuous and outmoded course was to seek the approval of the young lady's father first, and if it was denied, to gracefully bow to parental dictates and withdraw one's suit.

After the couple was betrothed, the engagement was puffed off in the *Morning Post*, the *Gazette*, or *The Times* or all three. After this formal announcement, the gentleman who made the offer had no honorable way to withdraw. The bride though might balk before the pair came to the altar, if she was strong enough to withstand the gossip and the label of "jilt."

An offer need not be voiced but only accepted generally as made unsaid. The Iron Duke himself fell into such a trap that honor made. Wellington at the age of twenty-four loved Miss Kitty Pakenham. They parted, and he served most of these years of their separation overseas. During the entire time — twelve years — he never wrote to her and she never communicated with him. When informed that his friends considered him obligated to her and her feelings were still loverlike and constant, he did the only honorable thing. Wellington entered into a passionless marriage to satisfy duty and honor in 1806. Youthful infatuation died an ugly death.

Prinny's courtship of the woman he would marry first — Mrs. Fitzherbert — was in stark contrast to Wellington's. Hysterically, the Prince pursued the older widow — tearing his hair, beating his brow, threatening all manner of self destruction until the crowning touch — a supposed stab wound or at least the sight of blood oozing from the side of his body. Mrs. Fitzherbert eventually went through a marriage ceremony that had no validity under English law. It was a painful, exhausting episode in royal courtship.

One of the longest courtships of the period was the love affair of Emily Cowper and Lord Palmerston. They remained adulterously faithful to each other until the lovely Emily's husband obligingly died of natural causes, and they married after many years of waiting.

Beau Brummell, too, had his moment in the sun. He

loved a lady, but, alas, it came to naught. The reason?
Beau explained it all with one deadly sentence. The lady
had an unfortunate predilection for cabbage!

The oddest love story no doubt concerned a noble
lord who married for convenience when he was a boy and
never lived with his bride. Several years later on meeting
an exquisite beauty at the theater, his somewhat improper
advances to her turned out not to be so improper. She
was his wife!

The Regency Match

Jane Austen wrote to her niece about sentiments that
reflected the heart's desire of every female from green
girls just launched into the *ton* to every ape-leader ever
placed firmly on the shelf—"... Anything is to be preferred
or endured rather than marrying without Affection...."[1]

The thrilling romances that entertained a young lady
in her idle hours mirrored society's new attitudes towards
love and marriage. Courting in the decadent eighteenth
century had been a seducer's art, but at the dawn of the
new century it was a young man's road to the wedding
altar.

Romantic love irrevocably linked to marriage was an
idea whose time had come. The cynical matches of
marriage between fortunes and great estates still existed in
the upper ten thousand, but love matches were common and
in most cases considered all the crack.

The arranged marriages of grand and noble families
where the potential bride and groom neither knew or
approved each other before the ceremony had often proven
devilish queer. Ladybirds, Cyprians, and cicisbeos enlivened
these boring loveless alliances. A young lady who married
a chap with twenty thousand a year usually had substantial
"pin money" to indulge her passions—for cards or other
things. And the fashionable buck on the Town had ample
opportunity to do the same. Loveless marriages bred
bored, restless spouses. It made sense that love matches

would avoid many of these marital pitfalls for the *haut ton*.

The changing attitudes towards romantic courtship and marriage had evolved over a century and a half. Parents until around the mid-seventeenth century chose their children's lifemate with no consideration or consultation with their offspring, though family friends might have a say in the final decision and sometimes even made the original suggestion. Children were only allowed to exercise the right to veto a parental choice after meeting a potential spouse at the beginning of the Georgian Age. And this right was in the beginning much more likely to be granted to a male child.

An alliance arranged by Regency parents with or without the child's consent was not uncommon among the great families in the upper ten thousand. The well-endowed heirs and heiresses were the least free to choose where to bestow their hearts and hands. Their only freedom might lie in the fact that their parents were dead or they had plenty of blunt at their command. Even with the freedom to make their own choice, many a beau and miss were tempted to look as high as they could for a match.

With the fashionable who were not confined and restricted by a great estate, the desire to make a match with affection at its base was considered essential to marital felicity. This compatible affection need not be a deathless passion but merely a comfortable tolerance to make a marriage of convenience an agreeable enterprise.

Marriages of convenience could be based on many different reasons. A young lady might feel it necessary to sacrifice herself on the altar of family duty by marrying a gentleman of means who could settle an improvident sire's gambling debts. It might also be convenient for a titled young blood to marry the heiress of the great estate that bordered his own country estate.

It should also be kept firmly in mind that it was very inconvenient for a young woman to remain unmarried who had no independent means. An impoverished chit had best set her cap at a man of means for the alternative was not pretty.

The first-born male child's marriage was crucial to the family's future. Sometimes pluck to the backbone was needed as the aristocratic heir screwed up his courage to ask a wealthy mill owner's daughter to bestow her hand in marriage. As one aristocratic French mother told her son — "to marry advantageously beneath oneself is merely taking dung to manure one's acres." This approach to the wedded state brought a certain cynicism to the nuptials.

Younger siblings had their duty, too. Younger sisters and brothers were looked on by the head of the family as elements to be guided by him to insure the family's power and wealth. Younger sons sought careers in politics, the church, the branches of military service, or the East India Company to advance themselves. A marriage of convenience was made to supplement the rewards of these careers. A lady of good birth was essential and a rich dowry icing on the cake. Young women, too, knew their duty to family and themselves.

Though the lure of wealth, position, or security, or all three might propel some to the altar, the multitude desired to make a love match. The love match meant that young people must meet and mingle with their peers in order to evaluate each other's qualities and a whole set of institutions developed to enchance this courting process.

Balls and card parties in the assembly rooms in country towns were ways young people might begin the courtship dance. The London Season itself and watering places, such as Bath, were ways that society provided the ways for elite offspring to meet their contemporaries across county lines. After clandestine marriages were made illegal in 1754, aristocratic children were allowed even more freedom to mix in society and choose where to bestow their hearts and hand.

The marriage of choice varied from individual to individual and family to family. The pressures that could come into play were many. The legal age for women to marry was twelve, for men fourteen, but parents had to consent to any union of an individual under twenty-one.

Often young men and women were emotionally or physically blackmailed into a match. The promise of money to clear his debts propelled Prinny into marriage to the obnoxious Caroline. More than one young aristocrat similarily followed his head rather than his heart.

Young women, also, had worldly ambitions. A splendid offer that led to a brilliant match often was much more appealing than a love match with an impoverished younger son. And girls, too, would sometimes sacrifice married love to help their families.

The Laws and Customs of Marriage

Lord Hardwicke's Marriage Act

The most profound effect on the wedding ceremony and the act of marriage was Lord Hardwicke's Act of 1753. In his bill any person solemnizing matrimony in any other than a church or public chapel without banns or license, should on conviction, be abjudged guilty of felony and be transported for fourteen years, and all such marriages should be void.

Zealous opposition to the bill was led by Mr. Henry Fox but to no avail. Clandestine marriage had long been abhorrent to the Church of England. This attitude plus the desire of the upper classes to protect their children, who were the future of the family, from easily contracted marriages with unsuitable partners allowed sure passage of the bill. Too many heiresses had been lured away from their families by scoundrels.

These clandestine marriages (especially of minors) were performed in rooms and taverns near the Fleet, a notorious debtor's prison on Farringdon Street. Defrocked and disreputable ministers, imprisoned for debt in the Fleet, earned the ready by performing surreptitous marriages. And until Lord Hardwicke's Act went into effect as law in 1754, such marriages were perfectly legal.

The common people were outraged that this cheap and

easy wedding ceremony was to be outlawed, but the quality had their way. If young men and women of the Polite World were allowed to easily meet and mingle, marriage had to be elaborately managed by church and state. The new law took effect on Lady Day (March 25), 1754.

A provision of the law was that a couple were directed to have banns published in the church on three successive Sundays preceding the solemnization of marriage. This was done immediately after the second lesson.

If the couple lived in different parishes, the banns had to be proclaimed in each parish, and proof in the form of a certificate had to be supplied to the curate performing the marriage service. Of course, parental permission was required to post banns for minors under the age of twenty-one.

Quicker marriages were available for those plump enough in the pocket to afford it. A special license could be obtained from the archbishop or his representative. These licenses did away with the need to have the banns called, and therefore meant the ceremony could take place immediately. The couple could also choose the location and time of day to suit themselves rather than be confined to a church between the hours of eight and twelve in the morning.

The Act also made destroying, forging, or falsifying with evil intent an entry in a marriage register a capital offense. Binding pre-contracts (betrothals being as serious as marriage) were done away with completely.

Members of the royal family, Quakers, and Jews were exempt under the Act, but Catholics were not. The only legal marriage a Roman Catholic could contract under English law had to be performed by an Anglican.

Mr. Henry Fox did manage to provide one big loophole for runaway lovers. Scotland was declared exempt from the new law. And so the romantic legend of Gretna Green was born!

Impediments to Marriage

The Anglican Church had three impediments to marriage. They were:

1. A preceding marriage, contract, or any controversy or suit concerning them.
2. Consanguinity or affinity.
3. Need of the consent of parents or guardians.

Perhaps the only one that needs clarification is the curious relationship called affinity, that is, a man marrying his deceased wife's sister.

This prohibition seems to have arisen in the time of Henry VIII who dissolved his first marriage on the grounds that his wife had previously been wedded to his brother. During the Regency these marriages were not void but voidable, that is, they could only be set aside by a decision in an Ecclesiastical Court. Eminent personages who had contracted these marriages and who feared they might later be declared void, and in consequence their children declared illegitimate, fought to have their position stabilized. A bill was introduced by Lord Lyndhurst to regularize marriages of affinity or which had forbidden degrees of consanguinity. The bill was amended by the Church to legitimize all such marriages in the past but it declared them in the future to be *ipso facto* void. These marriages still took place. Often the couple resided in another country to have their union legally solemnized. In 1857, the Court of Chancery decided that all such marriages, no matter where performed, were illegal.

Weddings

The wedding itself according to custom could take place at any time of the year though Lent was considered a little too oppressive. Marriage was not to be entered into lightly, true, but the somberness of this season was to be avoided.

Church weddings had to take place between the hours of eight and noon. Ecclesiastical authorities decreed that this solemn ceremony had to be celebrated in the daylight hours for honorable people had no fear of the light, and it was supposed that couples would be more serious in the morning.

The twelve noon deadline for the performance of the wedding ceremony meant the celebration or party that followed the service was very early in the day. As a consequence wedding breakfasts or *déjeuners* were very popular. Even if the wedding took place just before noon, the midday meal that followed was called a breakfast.

The church or a chapel in one of the bigger country houses was considered to be the best place to exchange sacred marriage vows. Marriage was performed with proper reverence to its condition as a holy vow. Marriage was not a civil contract to enter into lightly.

The wedding group in the church was very small at the beginning of the nineteenth century. It gradually increased in size until it reached gigantic proportions in the weddings of the fashionable in the 1860s and 70s. Usually a wider circle of relatives and friends were asked to the Regency wedding breakfast. The breakfast could be a full-course meal and there was a brides-cake to celebrate the nuptials. It was not called a wedding cake until Victorian times.

The supporter of the groom was called a groomsman. He need only have two qualifications—to be a friend of the groom and to be a bachelor. There was no male equivalent of the matron of honor. The term "best man" to describe the groomsman is firmly rooted in Victorian times and was unknown in the Regency.

The bride's mainstay was a brides-maid whose responsibilities did not end at the wedding ceremony. After the happy couple returned to Town, the chief brides-maid might help in directing envelopes if the bride had "cards." Cards were a printed notification that the wedding had taken place. A bride's nuptial card provided her new name and address, the date of her return from "going away," plus those days she would receive callers and delight them with wine and cake.

During the ceremony itself, the brides-maid might hold the bride's posey or have a hartshorn or vinaigrette on the ready. A socially correct bride should be overwhelmed with delicate virginal sensibilities.

The bride-clothes should be white and silver in the fashionable high waisted gowns of the period. Brides in these delicate draperies were all skirt and shoulder. A bridal veil of sorts was used. It was a trailing scarf of lace or gauze pinned in the center of the hair with long ends draped loosely around bare arms. The veils were for decoration only and fell down behind the bride to near the hem of her gown. They were *not*, however, worn over the face. This fashion was not generally seen until the mid Victorian times. It was extremely rare and unusual in the Regency.

Very common was a floral headdress for the bride. Princess Charlotte of Wales wore a wreath of roses on her head. Her royal aunts favored diamonds and fancy plumage as headdresses for their weddings.

Widows on remarriage could not wear white. A sober hue should always be chosen.

Men were in regular fancy dress in fashionable colors. Black was not fashionable for weddings until Victorian times.

On the great estates, servants, and tenants had their own festivities to celebrate an heir's nuptials. Servants might be given new livery. The poor of the parish could benefit, too, as the groom's or bride's family gave donations to the poor to mark the grand occasion.

A newly wed couple whose marriage cercmony occurred so early in the day had plenty of time to get started on their honeymoon or "going away." Sometimes they would leave their bridal party to celebrate without them.

Society couples came back to town to receive and return the calls of well wishers, and any girl who had the *entrée* at Court was expected to be presented anew, as a married woman. Most brides wore white and silver to Court as they had also worn to their weddings.

Gretna Green

The stringent inflexible terms of Lord Hardwicke's Act left one glaring loophole. Runaway couples where one or both of the parties were minors could legalize their union only in Scotland.

Infatuated couples — or perhaps a penniless groom who had captivated a heiress yet to reach her majority — made mad flights north to Gretna Green. Here a lucrative and sometimes disreputable traffic in irregular marriages flourished for almost one hundred years.

Gretna Green was the little village that was the first stopping place for runaway couples from England. It was in Dumfriesshire near the river Esk and located almost ten miles from Carlisle, nine from Annan. The last English posting stage and fresh horses were in Carlisle.

Here couples had an easy way round any impediments they might find from relatives. Scotland did not require the consent of parents or guardians, the publication of banns, and, therefore, delays. Scotland only required a mutual declaration exchanged before witnesses. This ceremony was quick and the participants need not have reached their majority. The couple could return to England as soon as they declared themselves married and their marriage was valid under English law.

Popular legend had it that a blacksmith performed these marriages, which were called "over the anvil." In actuality, professional witnesses were engaged to perform this task.

Pennant, in his *Tour in Scotland,* described Gretna as a little village characterized by a small grove of firs, and just a brief way from the bridge. Loving couples fleeing the disapproval of their more prudent relatives could be immediately joined in matrimony by an obliging fisherman, blacksmith, or joiner for a guinea or two or just the offer of a glass of whiskey. Postilions who drove the cooing couple from Carlisle were often in the pay of professional witnesses, and Pennant assured his readers that they would also share in the fee charged by their witness. He also reported that the couplers of these fleeing lovers were despised by the Church of Scotland who could do little with the enterprising witnesses at Gretna.

Two of major witnesses or "blacksmiths" were Joseph Paisley and, after his death, his son-in-law Robert Elliott. The word "blacksmith" referred to Vulcan's occupation as the celestial priest of marriage.

Robert Elliott who published *The Gretna Green Memoirs*, recorded that between the years 1811 to 1839 he united no fewer than 7,744 couples. He informed *The Times* that he had numerous records from the beginning of his career which would be open for inspection by anyone in order to prove his claims.

Rivaling Elliott for prominence was an old soldier named David Laing. Competition between these professional witnesses was fierce. All sorts of methods were used to get the greatest number of runaway couples. The most helpful cohorts were the postboys who drove where they pleased. Each "blacksmith" had his own place to witness marriages and postboys were sometimes given half the fee as a commission. Gretna Green "blacksmiths" always charged a fee for their services. It was not unheard of for a particularly rich groom to pay the witness a hundred guineas.

The marriage ceremony performed by Elliott was very simple and followed the pattern of traditional nuptials. He first asked the couples their names and addresses, then told them to stand up, and asked if they were single. On an affirmative answer, he then asked if they were both there of their own free will (this could be important later if the validity of the marriage was contested). On their "yes" answers, he filled out the certificate and proceeded to the heart of the ceremony which included the groom placing a ring on his bride's left hand, and an admonition,

"What God joins together let no man put asunder." Elliott
then declared the couple man and wife.

The runaway match of the Earl of Westmorland with
Miss Child, the heiress of the great banker, was one
famous clandestine match long talked about in Regency
society. The pair was closely pursued by her father and
nearly overtaken at the border. The Earl to gain a few
minutes drew his pistol and shot the leading horse of Mr.
Child's carriage. Needless to say, the couple made it to
the border. The elder daughter of their marriage inherited
the great fortune of her grandfather, married Lord Jersey,
and reigned over Almack's in the Regency.

Two famous Gretna Green marriages of the Regency
were:

> 1812 — C. Ewen Law, son of Lord Ellenborough and
> Miss Nightingale.
> 1816 — Lord Chief Justice Erskine, who gave Elliott
> twenty pounds. Within a year he sought a divorce
> under Scottish law but could not because the
> marriage was declared legal and valid.

A young heiress spirited away from her family and
carried off to Gretna against her will was encouraged by
her abductor to pay the "parson" — and often to hire horses
for the last stage from Carlisle to prove her willingness.
This kind of evidence would stand up in court if her family
or she herself attempted to overturn the marriage.

After the ceremony, the couple might adjourn to a
special "wedding chamber." This chamber was provided for
a fee so that newly married couples could savor the first
pleasures of love.

Wives and Real Property

The Regency miss on her marriage to a fashionable
buck became one with her new husband under English
Common Law and as Blackstone put it, the husband is that

one. When a newly leg-shackled pair walked back down the aisle, all the bride's property and all the property she was entitled to at the time of her wedding was now firmly under the control of her husband. Even after the acceptance of a proposal, the betrothed miss could not dispose of any property without her fiance's approval and consent.

The bride's property that her groom would have jurisdiction over was made up of two types—real property (land, animals) and personal property (household goods, clothing, jewelry). Real property was protected for her heirs, but her personal property was not protected at all. Property laws had derived from precedents in the Middle Ages when real property was where wealth resided and female fripperies were considered less than nothing.

During their marriages wives had no property at their disposal. Even blinded with love, it behooved a bride to realize just exactly what she was losing with marriage. Single women and widows had the same property rights as men, except to vote. Upon marriage a Regency husband assumed ownership or at least all control of his wife's property.

If a wife survived her husband, her real property remained hers legally and it reverted back to her complete control. Probably more than one unhappy wife heaved a huge sigh of relief when a spendthrift husband broke his neck on the hunting field or fell and cracked his skull after broaching his fifth bottle.

Also, by ancient rights of dower and free-bench, the widow enjoyed a life interest in her husband's lands. The Statute of Uses of 1535 provided that with prenuptial agreements with her future groom, she could give up her dower rights in exchange for a jointure, a settlement of land upon her at least during her own lifetime. Jointures were used to support a widow until her death, and they were rarely on the same level as the dowry a woman brought to the marriage.

Without the settlement of a jointure in a premarital contract, the bereaved (or elated) widow had a right to a life interest in one third of the freehold lands in her husband's hands at the time of her marriage. The only way the widow could lose these rights was if her husband or herself was found guilty of treason, felony, or adultery.

If the Regency wife died before her husband, her real property went on to the children or grandchildren. Should she not be blessed with any little darlings, the property went to her father, mother, or siblings. At the same time a widower had a life interest in all his dead spouse's land, not just one third.

Marriage and Personal Property

A fashionable married lady's personal property was her husband's completely. The Regency husband could do anything he chose with it. The wife had no protection under common law if he chose to sell it or will it away. Her children and relatives had absolutely no claim on it. In fact, the woman who had entered into the married state could only will away personal property with her husband's consent — consent that he could withdraw at any time and for any reason.

The only possessions that a wife had some control over after her husband's death were what was called "paraphernalia." This was the clothing and personal ornaments that she possessed at the time of her marriage or that her husband had given her during the marriage. Though these items could be disposed of by the Regency husband at any time during his liftime, after his death they reverted completely to his widow. Unless, of course, she needed the ready to cover his debts! Even her "paraphernalia" could be sold to meet his monetary obligations.

A Georgian gentleman's personal property could be settled in any way he saw fit. His wife had no say in its disposal. He had no legal obligation to leave his children or wife any part of his personal property.

If he died with no will, his wife received one third of his personal property and his progeny a two-thirds share. A childless wife got a half share if there was no will. The other half went to her husband's nearest relations.

Other Marital Legalities

One happy result of marriage for the woman was that her groom assumed all legal responsibility in actions involving her before the change in their estate. He became totally responsible for any debts his wife had and any contracts she had entered before their nuptials. This liability remained his no matter whether or not he received property from marriage.

As far as disciplining a wife, a husband could beat his spouse although the stick should be no thicker than his thumb. Cruel unjust punishment inflicted on a woman by her husband was prosecutable. A wife could charge her husband with assault and battery or could "swear the peace" by which a court could order her husband to keep the peace if he had inflicted bodily injury, imprisonment, or other cruelties on her.

Her wages for work were considered personal property and as such were a husband's property absolutely. It was even difficult for a woman to carry on her own business because of her virtual incapacity under law to make a contract. A husband often hesitated to agree to a wife conducting business separately when he could not profit from the trade but was in every way legally responsible for the business.

Even under cases of separation and desertion, the Georgian husband still had common-law rights to his wife's property. He still controlled and received income from her lands and completely owned her personal property. Only under mutual agreement was a maintenance allowance given to a separated wife, and this contract was not legally enforceable.

The children's custody was the father's absolute right. Under common law, the mother had no rights at all. Fathers could take offspring against the mother's will and deny her all access to them. The common law made no

judgement between characters of the parents. No matter
how reprehensible the father's personality and lifestyle and
how unsullied his wife's, the man always prevailed. The
children were his to dispose of as he pleased.

Equity

The harsh blindness of common law was tempered by
the development of equity. To protect the heiresses of the
propertied class a system of trust settlements of property
developed.

The jointure, the settlement on a bride by her future
husband of a freehold estate secured for her widowhood,
came into practice with the Statute of Uses (1535). To
receive this settlement the prospective wife had to
surrender her dower rights.

Equity developed over a long period of time and came
to mean much more to the Regency wife. The system
created a special category of property—the separate estate
of a married woman. Under this system, property could be
settled on the married woman for her exclusive use under
the management of a trustee who answered to the court in
carrying out the terms of the trust. Trust property could
be protected by the Court of Chancery against a husband
or any one else, according to the desires of the donor.

Separate property in equity could be anything—a
shipping fleet, mills, a great estate, a handful of unset
gems. A trust could also be created at anytime by anyone.
The usual way to set up the terms was in a written
document, either a will or deed disposing of the property
or in a marriage settlement, a contract negotiation between
the bride and groom or their families. Usually a trustee
was named or the Court of Chancery recognized the
husband as trustee, who was still bound by the terms
specified in the trust and could not treat the property as
his own.

The premarital contract many times had a clause
inserted that dealt with "pin money." This guaranteed the

Georgian wife a fixed income that was at her exclusive disposal during her marriage. Her clothing bills and gambling debts would be paid from the allowance that would be doled out—perhaps quarterly. Under common law, however, all her debts were her husband's legal responsibility, so no matter how much she spent, he had to pay if she dared his wrath and presented her bills for his settlement. Many wives preferred to live in dun territory or under obligation to another gentleman rather than risk a confrontation with an irate spouse.

The Court of Chancery also recognized as separate property one unique category—wedding presents and "paraphernalia" (clothing and jewelry given by a third person). Though a Regency wife might have no legal rights during her husband's life span to articles of a personal nature that he had given her, equity could ensure that she would possess the gifts of friends.

The separateness of the property also protected her from her husband's creditors. Neither she nor her trustee could sell her separate property if the terms of the trust stipulated otherwise. As much as a fond and doting wife might want to help her husband financially, it was beyond her control.

Equity offered much relief to the fashionable lady married under brutal common law, but the protection was only affordable for the upper class. Drawing up a marriage settlement cost around £100 and only one tenth of English marriages were covered under equity.

Divorce

Incompatible couples who chose not to live separate lives in the same household or did not wish to maintain separate residences could take the irrevocable step of petitioning for divorce.

Divorce was in no respects an easy decision or one in which either partner even considered taking except in the most extreme of situations. A divorce put both parties, whether innocent or guilty, beyond the pale. Divorces were lengthy and costly. Only Parliament was invested with the right to grant divorces. Before a divorce case was presented the offended party had to have brought forth successful suits in the Ecclesiastical Court for separation from bed and board and in the civil court for financial damages. Few could afford the astronomical costs that the private Act of Parliament required.

The notoriety was also a deterrent. Few men of honor wanted their names bandied about in the press and among the Great Unwashed. Both the guilty and innocent were shunned by the highest levels of society, and they were forever banned from Court. A few, like Lady Holland, rose above this social stigma. She gathered around her the best conversation in London at Holland House, but for all her wealth, power, and personality she was never allowed to set foot in Almack's or be presented at a drawing room.

It should also be remembered that only after 1801 could women obtain a divorce, before then only the males had that privilege. And most telling statistic of all, only 317 divorces were granted before the law was liberalized in 1859.

Annulments

The lengthy, expensive divorce procedure might be avoided if the couple could get an annulment. Only for the reasons listed below could an annulment be granted that would allow either party to legally remarry.

1. The husband had been impotent for three years.
2. The parties involved had a close family relationship.
3. One party had a prior contract with another person who was still living.

In the case of a spouse missing for more than seven years, the husband or wife could also remarry. Annulment had neither the bad odor of divorce nor its permanent social stigma.

Royal Weddings

Royal marriages were governed by the Royal Marriage Act. The Act stated that every marriage or marriage contract entered into by the descendants of the body of the late King George II (excluding the issue of princesses who marry into foreign families) should first obtain royal consent. If the petitioner was over the age of twenty-five and the sovereign refused consent, he or she could petition Parliament to overrule and consent to the marriage. No marriage contracted without receiving Parliament's or the sovereign's approval and consent was legal or binding.

Under the Act no member of the royal family could follow their heart even if they were willing to risk the censure of the world. No union without consent was binding.

Prinny's legal marriage to the ghastly Caroline of Brunswick in 1795 was not the first wedding ceremony at which he had been the groom. In December 1785, the infatuated, obsessed Prince of Wales secretly married a twice-widowed Catholic named Mrs. Fitzherbert. The marriage was illegal and non-binding. Their relationship continued off and on for many years even after his wedding to Caroline.

Prinny forced by his debts to do his duty emanated grave disappointment as the Archbishop of Canterbury presided over his nuptials with a smiling Caroline. As the Archbishop asked if there were any impediments, the Prince openly wept. The Duke of Bedford helped to prop up Prinny who had drunk several glasses of brandy to enable him to go through the ceremony.

He managed to do his duty and Caroline presented him with a daughter, Charlotte. There would be no other children — the couple spent the rest of their lives despising each other and living separate lives.

In Princess Charlotte rested the future. Her marriage to Leopold of Saxe-Coburg-Saalfeld in May 1816 and pregnancy announced later that year ensured the line of succession. The whole nation mourned when she died in childbed in 1817 and wondered where the legitimate heirs of the next generation were?

The three unmarried though not uncommitted Royal Dukes — Cambridge, Kent, and Clarence — did their duty (and received monetary reward for it from Parliament). All married suitable brides in 1818. The winner of the royal stakes? The Duke of Kent! His first and only legitimate child was a daughter. They called her Victoria.

The Language of Love and Marriage

April gentleman — a newly wed man.

Buckled — To get buckled; to get married.

Cap — To set one's cap at a bachelor — a lady's pursuit of a favored gentleman.

Cast sheep eyes upon — express an interest in a member of the opposite sex.

Cat's foot or paw — Living under the cat's foot, being under the control of one's wife.

Cicisbeo — A male escort of a married woman. The term comes from Italy where fashionable men did not associate with wives in public.

Comfortable importance — a man's wife.

Cream-pot love — The pretended love which young fellows offer to dairy maids, to wheedle cream and other things from them.

Cry off — To jilt one's future spouse. An announcement inserted in the proper papers informed the world.

Last Prayer — An unmarried girl past her first blush of youth is said to be at her last prayer.

Mariage de convenance — a marriage arranged to suit the practical demands of the bridal couple.

Marriage mart or market — Assemblies or places associated with matchmaking — such as Almack's.

Mousetrap—The parson's mousetrap, the state of matrimony.

Pay one's court to—offer tender attentions.

Petticoat government—A woman controlled household has a petticoat government.

Puff it off to the papers—To send the marriage announcement to the *Morning Post* or other appropriate papers.

Settlements—prenuptial agreements.

Shelf—A spinster who has no more hopes of marriage is on the shelf.

Smelling of April and May—said of a couple in love and possibly planning marriage.

Tie the nuptial knot—to marry.

NOTES TO CHAPTER IV

1. *Jane Austen's Letters to Her Sister Cassandra and Others*, ed. R.W. Chapman, p. 410.

The Four-in-Hand Club, St. James Street   *Unknown*

New York Public Library
Picture Collection

Chapter V

HOW THEY PLAYED

The rush to Town in the spring of each year by the members of the *haut ton* was as predictable and unchanging as the seasons themselves. London was a great bustling center of excitement. The Polite World came to entertain, to be entertained, and to wallow in the unrestrained pursuit of pleasure. Whether the visitor be a dazzling young chit being fired off into the *ton*, a dissipated rakehell acquainted with every vice, or a young swell flirting with dandyism, Town life had something for everyone.

Men amused themselves in their clubs or at the latest grisly spectacle of Regency sport. They also dutifully escorted the females in their life to public and private entertainments.

The fashionable entertained each other at dinners, card parties, suppers, routs, breakfasts, balls, *soirées,* musicales, and *levées.* Many were excluded from the upper echelon that gathered at Almack's.

They went to Covent Garden and Drury Lane. They listened to Catalani at King's Theatre and strolled through the Chinese lanterns at Vauxhall Gardens. They traipsed through London's hoary old monuments and drove, rode, or strolled through her parks.

Dazzling London was at their feet. Even though they had to step around the ragged urchins in the street to make their way to the fashionable *modiste* or tailor who would work that special magic to set them apart from their fellows, they exalted in their toplofty exclusiveness.

To the fashionable world London was a vast playground. This playground had a special rule though: an elegant lady was barred from the men's world of entertainment. A male of rank and fashion had freedom to do what he chose, whenever he pleased. A lady had no such

choice; she was restrained by her sex and position. She
dared not venture out alone in Town. Her reputation, you
know!   Much of the amusement that entertained the
fashionable was strictly male — the world of clubs and sport.

A Gentleman's Pleasures in Town

Society in the late Georgian Age were most definitely
a man's world, and there were a multitude of amusing
pursuits to entertain a beau on the Town.   The most
elegant of these could be found in the men's club.
The clubs were noted for their deep play, heavy
drinking, and exclusivity.   New members were refused by
the single blackballing of one member.   The upper reaches
of society were a small enclosed world and entry was
gained through either birth, wealth, or wit — each alone or
in any combination.
Deep play was the bane of the gentlemen's clubs.
Fortunes and great estates were won and lost on the green
baize tables of the London clubs.

The Men's Clubs

White's

Foremost among the clubs, White's was the oldest
and most splendid of the gentlemen's clubs on St. James's
Street.   Brummell reigned supreme here until his downfall
in 1816.   The bow window that became his exclusive
preserve was added in 1812.   Here he gathered his inner
circle — the Duke of Argyll, Lords Alvanley, Sefton, Worcester, and Foley, "Poodle" Byng, "Ball" Hughes, and Sir
Lumley Skeffington.   No one dared sit there who had not
been favored by the Beau.   Everyone in the "bow window"
could be seen by those who passed by the club, but
Brummell's   stringent   ruling   made   the   recognition   or

greeting to any passerby a dreadful breach of etiquette. Gambling and betting were the chief forms of entertainment. White's Betting Book was famous for the vast array of subjects listed within it. Fashionable gentlemen could and did have differences of opinion on an infinite variety of topics. Through the years of Napoleon's ascent, bets on his downfall or victory were commonplace. Life and death matters were also sometimes argued—who would bear a child first, who would die first, when would they die or marry. Nothing was too sacred or absurd to make a wager on.

Regular gambling went on in the card rooms. Dedicated players might wear a special costume to protect their elegant rigs. Frieze coats were worn over their clothes, and a type of leather mitten was pulled up over the white cuffs. Glaring lights were combated with broad-brimmed straw hats, which had the added benefit of shielding one's expression. Every advantage helped. Stakes sometimes leapt to incredible heights. Fifty thousand pounds could change hands in one sitting at the card table.

Raggett, the owner of White's, had begun life as a poor man. His rise to riches was recounted by Captain Rees Howell Gronow:

> Raggett, the well known club proprietor of White's, and the Roxburgh club in St. James's Square, was a notable character in his way. He began life as a poor man, and died extremely rich. It was his custom to wait upon the members of these clubs whenever play was going on. Upon one occasion, at the Roxburgh, the following gentlemen, Hervey Combe, Tippoo Smith, Ward (the Member for London), and Sir John Malcolm, played for high stakes at whist; they sat during that night, viz., Monday, the following day and night, and only separated on Wednesday morning at eleven o'clock; indeed, the party only broke up then, owing to Hervey

Combe being obliged to attend the funeral of one
of his partners who was buried on that day.
Hervey Combe, on looking over his card, found
that he was a winner of thirty thousand pounds
from Sir John Malcolm, and he jocularly said,
"Well, Sir John, you shall have your revenge
whenever you like." Sir John replied, "Thank
you; another sitting of the kind will oblige me
to return again to India." Hervey Combe, on
settling with Raggett, pulled out of his pocket a
handful of counters, which amounted to several
hundred pounds, over and above the thirty
thousand he had won of the baronet, and he
gave them to Raggett, saying, "I give them to
you for sitting so long with us, and providing us
with all required." Raggett was overjoyed, and,
in mentioning what had occurred to one of his
friends, a few days afterwards, he added, "I
make it a rule never to allow any of my servants to be present when gentlemen play at my
clubs, for it is my invariable custom to sweep
the carpet after the gambling is over, and I
generally find on the floor a few counters,
which pays me for the trouble of sitting up. By
this means I have made a decent fortune."[1]

Whist was the game that most dominated the gamblers
at White's. As Captain Gronow remembered:

It was here that play was carried on to an
extent which made many ravages in large
fortunes, the traces of which have not disappeared at the present day. General Scott, the
father-in-law of George Canning and the Duke of
Portland, was known to have won at White's,
£200,000; thanks to his notorious sobriety and
knowledge of the game of whist. The general
possessed a great advantage over his companions
by avoiding those indulgences at the table, which

used to muddle other men's brains. He confined himself to dining off something like a boiled chicken, with toast-and-water; by such a regimen he came to the whist-table with a clear head, and possessing as he did a remarkable memory, with great coolness and judgment, he was able honestly to win the enormous sum of £200,000.[2]

Watier's

On the east corner of Bolton Street at No. 81, Piccadilly stood the greatest gambling club in all Regency London — notorious Watier's. Ominously, it stood on the site of what had been a particularly bad hell. The club had a brief, brilliant life span before its demise in 1819.

The beginnings of the club were at Prinny's dinner table. The Prince asked his guests who were members of White's and Brooks's and what the food was like at their clubs. Sir Thomas Stepney replied that the food was all the same — "the eternal joints, or beef-steaks, the boiled fowl with oyster sauce, and an apple-tart — this is what we have, sir, at our clubs, and very monotonous fare it is."[3] Impetuously, the Prince rang Watier, one the royal cooks, and asked him if he would care to take a house and start a club. Watier agreed and with Madison, the Prince's former page acting as the manager, and Labourie who also came from the royal kitchens acting as the chief cook, the club Watier's was born in 1805.

Byron called it the Dandy Club with good reason. Brummell reigned supreme here. His position as the arbiter of fashion allowed his dictates in dress, social behavior, and even snuff boxes to be strictly followed.

Macao, a simple game very adaptable to varying stakes, was the primary road to ruin at Watier's. Brummell was particularly susceptible to the lure of macao. After losing a phenomenal sum at the club one night, Brummell in comic despair called out to a waiter to bring him a flat candlestick and a pistol. Bligh, a member and an extremely odd fellow, calmly pulled out of concealment two fully loaded pistols and said he would be happy to oblige Brummell's wish to stick his spoon in the wall. Those about them remained silent as expected given the armed bedlamite's presence.

Brooks's

While White's had a Tory bent, Brooks's at No. 60 St. James's Street had a Whiggish character. The club was founded by William Almack and named for the first manager William Brooks. As Captain Gronow remembered the fashionable club:

> Faro and macao were indulged in to an extent which enabled a man to win or to lose a considerable fortune in one night. It was here that Charles James Fox, Selwyn, Lord Carlisle, Lord Robert Spencer, General Fitzpatrick, and other great Whigs, won and lost, hundreds of thousands; frequently remaining at the table for many hours without rising.
>
> On one occasion, Lord Robert Spencer contrived to lose the last shilling of his considerable fortune, given to him by his brother, the Duke of Marlborough; General Fitzpatrick being much in the same condition, they agreed to raise a sum of money in order that they might keep a faro bank. The members of the club made no objection, and ere long they carried out their design. As is generally the case, the bank was a winner, and Lord Robert bagged, as his share of the proceeds, £100,000. He retired, strange to say, from the foetid atmosphere of play, with the money in his pocket, and never again gambled....
>
> Lord Carlisle was one of the most remarkable victims amongst the players at Brookes's and Charles Fox, his friend, was not more fortunate, being, subsequently always in pecuniary diffi-

culties. Many a time, after a long night of hard play, the loser found himself at the Israelitish establishment of Howard and Gibbs, then the fashionable and patronized money-lenders. These gentlemen never failed to make hard terms with the borrower, although ample security was invariably demanded.[4]

Boodle's

Boodle's, named for its first manager and founded by William Almack in 1762, was located at No. 28 St. James's Street. Though such illustrious gentlemen as the Beau, Wellington, and Wilberforce held membership here, the majority of the members were country gentlemen who came to gamble and partake of the especially good food. Like White's, it, too, had a famous front bow window.

The Guards'

The Guards' Club was a project of Prinny and the Iron Duke who were concerned that the officers returning from the Peninsular Wars in 1810 should have somewhere to meet. The club was placed directly opposite White's on St. James's Street.

As Gronow recalled:

> The Guards' Club was established for the three regiments of Foot Guards, and was conducted upon a military system. Billiards and low whist were the only games indulged in. The dinner was, perhaps, better than at most clubs, and considerably cheaper.[5]

The proximity to White's gave Colonel Sebright "one of the most eccentric men of the age" and a daily visitor to the Guards' a surfeit of ammunition. His entertainment

was
finding fault with everything and everybody
connected with the changes taking place in the
dress, &c, of the army, and of the English
gentlemen. From the windows of the Club he
used to gaze at White's, which was opposite, and
abuse the dandies, especially Brummell and
Alvanley, who were his especial aversions,
ejaculating "Damn those fellows, they are
upstarts, and fit only for the society of tailors![6]

Other clubs in St. James's Street that a pleasure-
seeking buck on the Town might frequent were Arthur's
and Graham's. Gronow described them both as less
aristocratic than the others. Graham's at No. 87 St.
James's Street was where Sir Henry Bentinck invented
"Blue Peter," a call for trumps. Also at Graham's in a
regrettable incident a nobleman of the highest position and
influence was accused of cheating at cards. After a trial
that went against him, he died of a broken heart.

Arthur's, a descendent of an earlier chocolate house,
was established in 1811. A very expensive club, the
membership roster included a good many country gentleman.
In the hall hung a portrait of Kitty Fischer, who was a
celebrated lady of pleasure.

The Hells

While the fashionable clubs were run in an above-
board manner, the semi-public hells were lying in wait for
greenhorns.

If a pigeon be refused admittance on the
score of not being known, and received the *stale
answer* — 'Sir, this house is only open to the
gentlemen of the Club,' he has only to *go down*
St. James's Street into the Square or to Pall
Mall, and he will find accommodation all the
way: the descent is easy even to the most

intoxicated dandy or guardsman, who will experience the truth of the *"facilis descensus Averni."* [the descent to Hell is easy—Vergil][7]

Those infernal places called gaming "hells" awaiting the pleasure of London's fashionable males included in 1817:

The Pigeon Hole, No. 10 St. James's Square—A decidedly low house. It netted thirty thousand pounds within a year's time. One of the owners was reputed to be the "Abbot" of a "nunnery" and worth a hundred thousand pounds.

No. 77 Jermyn Street—This house was noted for the notoriously unfair hazard table.

The Two Sevens, No. 77 St. James's Street—Stakes were set at levels of only fifty pounds, giving the bank a decided advantage. Players were known to grumble about the scurvy refreshment and the surly attitude of the house toward winners.

A Club House, Bennet Street, St. James's—A red baize door on this corner house set it apart from its neighbors. It was known as a "topping house" where high rank and title abounded.

Also worthy of notice was a gambling haunt in Pickering Place, the short narrow way next to Berry Brothers and Rudd in St. James's Street.

The Lisle Street, Panton Street, and Covent Garden hells were considered beneath notice for the better sort of gentleman.

The Gamesters

Gambling was a mania and many succumbed to the lure of the board of green cloth. Fortunes were lost and lives ruined. Some gamblers careened from one sort of bad luck to another.

The late Lord Clinton, then quite a young man, became a member of Watier's Club, and unfortunately lost a considerable sum at whist; wishing to raise some money for this purpose on mortgage, he sent the title-deeds of his family estate to be investigated by a lawyer; this man, on looking over the deeds, found that an old claim existed on the whole property in favor of the Cholmondeley family, and forthwith informed his lordship of the circumstance, who lost no time in commecing his action for the recovery. It made a great noise at the time; and as appearances at first were very much in favor of the suit, it was considered not only a very hard case upon Lord Clinton, who would thus be totally ruined, but an act of rapacity on the part of the other, who was in such very affluent circumstances.[8]

While a fashionable fellow might let his tailor's bill go unpaid for several years, his gambling debts had to be settled! It was a debt of honor, and, as such, all losses at cards must be paid at once if one had any pretension to being a gentleman.

To help settle these enormous debts, men of fashion sought the aid of the bankers, Coutts or Drummond. They might also consult with an Israelitish money lender, such as Howard and Gibbs, the "cents per cent" people. One club was said to have a very special room set aside downstairs known as the "Jerusalem Chamber," in which the obliging moneylenders would interview the members who needed immediate assistance.

An easily gulled pigeon under the hatches might also repair to the jewelers Rundell and Bridges or Hamlet's to raise some of the ready by pawning the family jewels.

Whatever the course a gentleman took to honor his vowels, they had to be paid!

The latest disaster at gaming kept London society entertained at the breakfast tables. Besides the titillating on-dit circulating in drawing rooms, newspapers printed intriguing tidbits such as:

March 28, 1811:
The brother of a Noble Marquis is said lately to have won at *hazard* upwards of £30,000 all in one night![9]

or

April 3, 1811:
A young gentleman of family and fortune lost £7,000 on Sunday Morning at a gaming house in the neighborhood of Pall Mall.[10]

Disaster never remained a secret for long.

The fabulously wealthy "Ball" Hughes, the dandy dubbed "the golden Ball," dwindled his immense fortune down to one fourth of its original amount. Captain Gronow considered him the greatest gambler of his day.

His love of play was such, that at one period of his life he would rather play at pitch and toss than be without his favourite excitement. He told me that at one time he had lost considerable sums at battledore and shuttlecock. On one occasion, immediately after dinner, he and the eccentric Lord Petersham commenced playing with these toys, and continued hard at work during the whole of the night; next morning he was found by his valet lying on the ground, fast asleep, but ready for any other species of speculation.[11]

Though the clubs and hells were exclusively male — or as in the case of the hells — a place where no "lady" would be found, there were reckless, zealous gamblers among the fair and frail, too. The notorious gambling house hostesses such as Lady Buckinghamshire and Lady Archer were no longer in business, but a determined lady with a bad dose of gaming fever could find a game of chance to suit her fancy.

Georgina, Duchess of Devonshire, lived a life consumed with her passion for cards. She borrowed the ready from friends and lovers till she could borrow no more. She even granted her favors in lieu of money owed as she continued to lose incredible sums in her mania for deep play.

The most famous victim of the gaming mania was the epitome of Regency society himself — the elegant, whimsical Beau Brummell. His ultimate downfall was most surely connected to his bad luck in gambling rather than the break with Prinny or his waning popularity. His exile to the continent began in the elegant card rooms of Brooks's, Watier's, and White's.

The Games

The dice, wheel, and card games that whiled away a gentleman's leisure hours were many and varied. Some of the most popular were hazard, faro, whist, *rouge et noir,* and E.O.

Hazard

This dice game and a particular favorite of Scrope Davies was the forerunner of craps. It was an excellent game for an intelligent player who could master the odds.

The rules? Throwing two dice together, the player (caster) continued until he scored five, six, seven, eight, or nine. The one he threw was called the "main." Then the caster threw again. If the second score (the "chance") equaled the "main," he was said to have "knicked it" and won all the stakes. If he threw "crabs" (two, three, eleven, twelve), he "threw out" and lost. If he neither "nicked it" or "threw out" he had to continue casting the dice until he either equaled the "main," thus losing, or cast his second score the "chance" netting him a win.

E.O.

A favorite wheel game was the amusement of E.O. (Even-Odd), known as the E.O. Table. Resulting from an Act of Parliament passed in 1739, this rotating entertainment, resembling roulette, was contrived to circumvent a blanket banning of those games of chance bearing "numbers thereon," for these were subject to fines. Another Act in 1745 made E.O. illegal thus making its popularity permanent.

Faro

Originally called Pharaoh, this game originated in sixteenth century France and arrived in England as early as 1700. It was played on a special faro table of green felt or baize with representations of the thirteen cards painted or enameled on the top. The dealer drew cards from a box face up. The player placed bets against the house on the card representation, speculating on what the dealer turned up and winning if his guess was right.

Whist

A particular favorite in the card rooms of White's, this four handed card game was the forerunner of modern bridge. The dealer dealt out thirteen cards to each player and turned up the last card whose suit was named trumps for that deal. The purpose was to win as many tricks as possible. The players opposite each other at the card table were partners. Points were accumulated at the rate of one each for each trick over six.

Rouge et noir

The first establishment dedicated to the French import, *rouge et noir*, also known as *trente et quarante*, was opened up in Pall Mall by a man named Roubel in 1815. Afternoon play began at two o'clock and continued until three o'clock in the morning. The profits were tremendous and other establishments soon followed including Fielden's located at the corner of Bennett Street and St. James's Street and Taylor's at No. 57 Pall Mall.

The game was played on a table which had red and black diamond shaped compartments whence came its name. The gambler placed his wager on either the red or the black.

Two rows of cards were laid out. The first was *noir*, the second *rouge*. The length of the *noir* row was determined by the combined amount of the cards. The dealer stopped when the cards totaled thirty-one or more. The second row was done exactly the same way. The bets on *noir* were victorious if that row was nearer thirty-one, *rouge* if that row was closer the magic number of thirty-one.

Wagers were also placed on *couleur* or *inverse*. The *couleur* bettor won if the first card dealt was of the same color that the row was designated. The opposite color gave the wagerer on *inverse* the victory.

Numerous other games of chance enlivened the nights of Regency gamester they included:

> *Vingte et un*
> Macao
> Lanterloo or Loo
> Basset
> *Jeu d'enfer*
> Blind-hookey
> Picquet

Hoyle's Games, the 1814 edition of the famous reference revised and corrected by Jones, was the indispensable aid to the intricacies of these fashionable games of chance.

The Gaming Glossary

Children in the wood—dice.
Cleaned out—having lost all your money, beaten, ruined. The fate of gamblers who visit hells where money is spent like dirt.

Dispatchers — false dice.

Done up — ruined by gambling.

Elbow shaker — a gamester casting dice.

Flats and sharps — persons easily taken in by thoses ready to take them in on all occasions. Without flats, sharps would become extinct.

Fulhams — loaded dice.

Gulled — deceived or cheated.

Gullgropers — money lenders.

Hatches — under the hatches — in debt.

Hells — gambling houses where infernal practices occurred located mostly near St. James's Street.

High-flyers — gamblers for highstakes.

History of the four kings or child's best guide to the gallows — a pack of cards.

Legs — bookmaker or blacklegs.

Nick — to win at dice or to hit the mark just in the nick of time.

Ready — the money.

Speeling — gambling.

Tapis vert — gaming table.

Uphills — false dice that have mostly high numbers.

Vowel — "to vowel a debt." Where the acknowledgement of the debt is expressed by the vowels I.O.U.

Sports

Boxing

A variety of grisly, manly sports amused our Regency buck, but the contest between two prime milling coves was by far the most popular sport in the country. Such amazing practitioners of the sport as Tom Hickman the Gaslight Man, Mendoza the Jew, Henry Pearce known as "the Game Chicken," Jem Belcher, and Tom Cribb who was for a number of years the unchallenged champion enthralled men at all levels of society and education.

Boxing was firmly entrenched as a true test of manliness. To be a proper man with his fists and to clear a lane of men with his "morleys" was the height of a young man's ambition. Englishmen learned courage, honor and sportmanship from pugilistic contests. What man would not appreciate the fortitude and nobleness of spirit that kept these bruisers on their feet for double digit rounds of punishing bare-fisted fighting? These stalwart gladiators were stripped to the waist and fought many times with naked fists, though by 1814 boxing with gloves was becoming more fashionable.

In spite of the many regulations and laws against boxing, little interference from the authorities was made against prize-fights. Matches like those between Cribb and Molineaux or Gentleman Jackson and Mendoza the Jew were arranged in places and at times to avoid the law, though few officials of the Crown were likely to risk the riot that an angry mob of avid boxing fans could start.

Fights were usually held outside cities and towns but were always close enough to be easily reached by boxing fans. When the date and place had been announced hordes of spectators set out on foot, or horseback, or driving fancy carriages. The great improvements in roads and communication made sporting matches of interest to everyone, and most particularly the aristocracy who ruled over these events.

For a fight between Randall and Martin at Crawley which was only thirty miles from London, the Fancy began scurrying out to the site early the day before when they caught the first hint that a pugilistic contest was scheduled. By eight o'clock that evening, every public house and inn in the surrounding countryside was filled two and three times over with avid sporting men. Many could not obtain beds and settled for whatever they could get or stayed up all night. Those fellows lucky enough to get a bed often found sleeping impossible as the carriages, full of eager boxing fans, rattled past all night. And the flood of traffic continued through the morning when the rich fellows of the highest distinction poured in from Town and Brighton in their elegant barouches. The roads stayed jammed with traffic. When the contest began at noon, thousands of spectators huddled around the chosen match site at Crawley Down.

John Broughton laid down the rules of prize-fighting. A round, a set-to, and a bout were designated as well as the time limits between them. A fighter on his knees was to be considered down. He also instituted roped or railed boundaries. Before the use of rails, the fighting area was only a scratched square measuring a few yards in both directions. The mill continued until his seconds could no longer "bring him up to scratch" or place his feet on the mark.

Champions of England

Mendoza — 1792
John Jackson (retired) — 1795
Jem Belcher — 1803
Pearce (the Game Chicken) — 1805
John Gully (declined the office) — 1808
Tom Cribb — 1809
Tom Spring — 1824

The London centers of pugilistic endeavors and fellowship were many and included among them:

Daffy Club — Tom Belcher, the landlord of the Castle Tavern, Holborn, hosted the start of the Daffy Club begun by Mr. James Soares. This sporting society could well be called the "Gin Club" for all its members were always in "spirits." Blue ruin was the sporting man's drink of choice in Cribb's Parlour as the most informal of clubs met here.

Jackson's Rooms, Bond Street — Gentleman Jackson, a former champion of the ring was the proprietor of this famous boxing saloon. A long-time connection between the patrons of the ring and Regency bruisers, his honorable reputation allowed him to realize a handsome living and enormous respect among all English gentlemen.

Limmer's Hotel—the site of much socializing of the Fancy. Gregson, Gully, Broughton, and Slack were some of the pets of the Fancy to gather there with their pupils and patrons.

Offley's—A sporting hotel in Henrietta Street, Covent Garden. It was known among the Fancy for its unrivaled beefsteak. The excellence of the ale was also notable.

Pugilistic Society—Its first meeting was at the Thatched House Tavern on May 22, 1814. It had been established to add the same respectability to the sport that the Jockey Club had done for horseracing.

The Animal Sports

Bull baiting and bear baiting were two of the violent crowd-pleasing sports that enjoyed popularity in the Regency, but the animal sport that claimed the bulk of gentlemanly attention was the exciting but cruel cock fight.

In specially-built indoor arenas such as the Royal Cockpit, Birdcage Walk, the sport was avidly followed and great sums wagered on the outcome.

The birds had sharpened spurs, and rich cock owners might equip their fighters with metal spurs. The fight between battling cocks could be long or short, but the extraordinary violence and cruelty was always present. The excited spectators were known to wager enormous sums of money. Needless to say, no ladies were ever present.

The Earl of Derby, for which the famous horse race was named, was reported to have had some three thousand birds at one time. His birds were carefully cared for until the fight. Diet was controlled so that the bird might begin in "fighting form." The phrase "fed like a fighting cock" came from the birds being fed a special diet of hot wine, eggs, and butter. John Gilliver was a well-known game-cock feeder. Exercise for the precious fighters was the fight itself.

The Public Amusements

A Night at the Theater

A night in a Regency theater was a boisterous, exciting evening where anything might happen. The troublesome, petulant audience demanded that the actors and managers deliver a pleasurable performance. No one suffered in silence with bad acting, bad staging, or bad plays.

The performance generally began around six o'clock when the music started and the curtain rose for the only time that evening. There was no lowered curtain between acts.

Actors were applauded as they entered through the stage door. Customers who chose to leave at the end of the first act had their money collected by the management, and at the same time other customers took advantage of the half price or lowered rates that came into force.

The fearsome, critical audiences could terrorize the actors and managers. They wanted to see the best and at the least price. Badness was ferociously punished with hisses and boos as well as physical abuse from highflying missiles directed at the offending actor.

The orange girls who circulated through the house passing messages and selling fruit helped to supply some of an angry audience's ammunition. Orange peelings, apples, and sticks were hurled at the stage and frequently missed their targets. Sometimes unlucky members of the audience in the pit were struck instead!

Howling, maddened audiences could sometimes be quieted by profuse and humble apologies from the actors and managers. Macready had to apologize for performing in a part that did not suit him.

But occasionally even apologies couldn't soothe the

savage audience beast. Junius Booth was on the stage for a good part of the evening and could not be even heard so he could apologize. Stage hands pulled banners across the stage "Pray Silence to Explain." The audience howled on. Next came, "Mr. Booth will apologize." And then, "Can Englishmen Condemn Unheard." It seemed they could, and the noisy outrage did not diminish. Even Kean at the height of his career was once at the mercy of an outraged, merciless audience.

The usual program of a London theater consisted of several elements which might include a one-act play, a Shakespearean tragedy, and a farce that featured a rendering by a popular vocalist and possibly even a few conjuring tricks. Covent Garden and Drury Lane were the only theaters licensed to perform legitimate drama, which dated from the royal patents granted by King Charles II. The other theaters were licensed only to perform farce, pantomine, and musical pieces. Opera could and was performed at all the theaters, but the versions used had been bowdlerized, botched, and in general, made nonsense of the Italian operas performed. Only at King's Theatre were the operas performed to meet the composer's requirements.

The fashionable occupied the boxes that were to the left and right of the stage in the semi-circular auditorium. Courtesans also used the boxes to display their wares. A recent innovation in the boxes much approved by the audience had been to replace the backless benches with more comfortable chairs. The less fashionable sat in the galleries and the hoi polloi made do with the cheap seats in the pit.

Whatever the station in life, the members of the audience never hesitated to give voice to rooster crows, lion roars, or dog howls, if the performance was boring or the acting badly done.

Management tried to prepare themselves by sometimes putting iron spikes over the orchestra to prevent an angry mob from storming the stage. But there was little they could do to stop the fights that broke out between different sections of the theater when they had a difference of opinion.

The performances generally ended by midnight, and in the next day's papers the theater goers might read Hazlitt's review in the *Morning Chronicle*.

The Theaters

Covent Garden (Royal Opera House) — Located in Bow Street, it was the most ornate theater in London when it opened in 1732. A fire devastated the theater in 1808. Not only was the theater destroyed but so was Handel's organ and many of his manuscripts as well as the entire stock of wine put up by the Beefsteak Club!

The Prince of Wales and others offered considerable financial aid and the new theater was opened in September 1809. The magnificent new building had been designed by Robert Smirke who had modeled it on the Temple of Minerva at Athens with a Greek Doric portico as a main feature of the Bow Street facade. An ornamental frieze of literary figures by English scupltor John Flayman also enhanced the building's elegant style.

Le Beau Monde reported on the fabulous new interior in detail and with vivid descriptions in September 1809.

> The interior is elegant, but is scarcely answerable to the magnificent idea with which the portico impresses any one about to enter the theatre. The vestibule is grand, and the staircase, ascending between two rows of Ionic columns, between each of which is suspended a beautiful Grecian lamp, has a splendid effect. At the head of the staircase is an anti-chamber surrounded with Ionic pilasters, in which the statue of Shakespear meets the eye, on a pedestal of yellow marble. The figure of Shakespear is by Rossi, and is in the costume of his age: he holds a roll of paper in his hand, but

his air is rather that of a barrister than a poet. We cannot account for this deficiency of expression, which we are sorry to observe in the works of Rossi. From the anti-chamber you come into the lobby of the lower tier of boxes: it is in the same style of Ionic architecture, and is divided with arched recesses, the semi-circular parts of which are filled with paintings from various scenes of Shakespear painted in *relief*. The fronts of the boxes are elegant and simple; a fretted gold flower of antique form, runs along each tier, upon a pale coloured ground: above and below the flowers are rows of stars. None of the boxes project beyond the others, in the manner of those usually termed stage boxes; and the fronts are perpendicular, without any of that rotundity which rather hurt than enriched the *coup d'oeil* in the former theatre. Slender pillars, richly gilt, separate the boxes; and from a golden bracket, above each pillar, is suspended a chandelier of cut glass, which are novel in their form. The seats are covered with light blue cloth, and are more in number than in the boxes of the old theatre. The pit is divided by two passages through the middle of it, and the seats are much elevated above each other. The two-shilling gallery is more ample than has been represented, and the slips are very wide and commodious. The most remarkable novelty consists in the construction of the shilling gallery: here the architect, to preserve the uniformity of his design, has rested the piers of a row of arches which support the roof, in such a manner that the gallery is divided into five parts, resembling separate boxes.

The stage is large, and well calculated, by its depth, for the exhibition of processions and extensive scenery. Two very elegant and lofty pilasters support a semi-elliptical arch, over which are the Royal Arms. Two figures are painted on each side of the arch *in relief*; they are females, holding wreaths of laurel, trumpets, &c. A crimson drapery in rich folds is painted within the arch, and covers the supporters of the curtain. The ceiling is painted to resemble a cupola, divided into square compartments, and surmounted with the figure of an ancient lyre. This, how ever, wants shadow to give it the appearance of concavity; it looks flat and deformed. The shape of the house before the curtain is that of a *horseshoe*, wide at the heel. This shape is continued from the bottom to the top of the house with unbroken uniformity, with the view that each sound as it enters may be regularly diffused, and the slightest whisper rendered audible.[12]

The enormous sum of three hundred thousand pounds was spent to rebuild the theater and its manager John Kemble increased the prices of tickets to offset the tremendous expense. The perverse, excitable mob called a London audience would have none of it. *Macbeth* and the farce *The Quaker* were not heard on that opening night. Neither was much else performed as riots continued for sixty one days. These O.P. (Old Price) riots featured a wild, rowdy audience screaming "O.P.", ringing bells, foot stomping, and blowing trumpets. Kemble and his actors did their best to continue performing. Bow Street Runners were hired to apprehend the ring leaders but to no avail.

Finally Kemble conceded defeat to his audience and bowed to their demands. An agreement was signed at the Crown and Anchor to retain the box price of seven shillings. As other managers had done in the past and would do again in the future, Kemble most humbly apologized from the stage and the victorious audience in the pits lifted up a sign reading "WE ARE SATISFIED."

One of the most notable theatrical phenomenons of the late Georgian theater that premiered at Covent Garden was the renowned Master Betty. The young man had played the provincial theaters and was touted as the amazing *enfant prodige*, an acting genius at the age of fourteen. His first London appearance took place at Covent Garden December 1, 1804, as the character Selim in *Barbarossa*. His anticipated performance created hysteria among the crowd that started gathering outside Covent Garden at ten o'clock that morning. In the afternoon a crowd of thousands had formed. When the doors finally opened at five, an immense rush of eager spectators rapidly filled up the two galleries, the pit, and all the boxes. The great pressure generated by the crowd shoved some hapless souls physically out of the boxes and into the pit. Fortunately, the crowd raised them up and passed the stricken ones to the lobby. Bruises and a few faints from the terrific heat were luckily the extent of injuries to the avid audience.

Master Betty was not seen until the second act when he was greeted by resounding applause. From that moment forward, he broke all previous box office records and continued to do so until he retired in September 1808 to attend Cambridge. He earned about £30,000 during his career and lived until the age of eighty-three.

Another notable event was Kemble's staging of *Bluebeard* which featured sixteen horses on stage in 1811, and the pantomine in 1812 that featured an elephant.

Kemble's sister the revered Sarah Siddons retired from the theater in 1812 at Covent Garden though she did continue to appear occasionally in benefits.

Between 1810 and 1824 the musical director Henry Bishop adapted Scott's novels for opera and was responsible for the first English performance of Mozart's *Don Giovanni* (1817), and Rossini's *Barber of Seville* (1818).

Theatre Royal Drury Lane — This theater on Catherine Street was built in 1663 and has a long and illustrious history. Like Covent Garden, it, too, had a Royal patent and like many other London buildings it burned down more than once and as a phoenix from the ashes rose again.

The theater design familiar to Regency audiences was

the one created by Benjamin Wyatt that opened in 1812 after the theater's earlier complete destruction by fire in 1809. The new building was modeled on the great theater at Bordeaux and cost over one hundred and fifty thousand pounds. One of its most impressive features was a domed Corinthian rotunda that was approached by a perfectly splendid double staircase from the vestibule.

Notable romances began in Drury Lane. Here Prinny first saw Mary Robinson (Perdita to his Florizel) and his brother, the future William IV, first saw his longtime paramour and mother of his numerous illegitimate children, Mrs. Jordan.

Acting triumphs included Mrs. Siddons debut in 1775 as Portia in *The Merchant of Venice* and John Kemble's debut as Hamlet in 1783. The newly reopened theater in 1812 couldn't compete with Kemble at Covent Garden until the appearance of the amazing and marvelous Edmund Kean in 1814.

Kean was a small man with an ugly countenance who became transformed by a glorious power when on stage. His style was modern, original, and ushered in a whole new age of acting. Kean's portrayals of Shylock, and Richard III galvanized critics. His fantastic success gained him entry everywhere, but his restless, morose personality betrayed him time and again. A predilection to drink finally dimmed his bright star.

Also from the Drury Lane stage the incomparable clown Grimaldi retired in 1818. Clowns owe their classic makeup and costume to the genius Grimaldi, who rung laughter or tears from admiring audiences at his whim.

King's Theatre (Royal Italian Opera House) — This Haymarket theater was destroyed by fire in 1789 and rebuilt as an opera house in 1791. Though the Drury Lane company acted there from 1791-1794 while awaiting the rebuilding of their theater after one of several fires, the house was otherwise used exclusively as an opera house. Michael Novosielski built the great horseshoe auditorium that was the largest theater in England to be used for opera productions. There were five tiers of boxes, a pit, and a gallery that sat an astounding 3,300 people.

Some of the fashionable world that came to hear opera (and pay as much as £2,500 for a box sold on a subscription basis) were Lady Melbourne, Lady Jersey, the Duchess of Richmond, Prinny, and the Royal Dukes Cumberland and Gloucester. Not only the fashionable came to be seen and to see, the women of the town had boxes to display themselves to potential clients.

The shining star of the King's Theatre was the dazzling, temperamental Catalani. London's highest-paid prima donna drew enormous crowds and equally enormous fees for her performances. Her rich, beautiful voice sang *Semiramide* and several Mozart operas to enraptured Regency audiences. Other stars to grace the Opera stage were Bianchi, Tramezzani, and Naldi.

Opera performances though got no more reverence from their audiences than did other types of entertainment. The elegant fops and dandies made such a commotion that the harried management built a special lounge to lure them out of the theater. Needless to say this maneuver was fruitless.

Sadler's Wells — Located in Rosebery Avenue. A typical evening's performance as advertised in *The Times* could include,

> an entirely new musical Ballet of Action, called VITTORIA; or, WELLINGTON'S Laurels. In which will be snug [*sic*], "The Marshal's Will," by Mr. Lund. Trio, "Ifs and Buts," Messrs. Mezzia, Daley, and Barclay; and the "Gazette of Glory," by Mr. Rees. To conclude with a fancy Scene, illuminated in honour of the great Captain, with a portrait of the Hero. After which a new Pantomine, with new Music, Scenery, Dresses, and Decorations, called THE BRACHMAN; or Oriental Harlequin. Clown, Mr. Grimaldi. The Entertainments to conclude with a new superb Aqua-Drama, called ROKEBY CASTLE. The last Scene exhibits the immense body of Real Water,

on which will be exhibited an engagement between two ships.[13]

The aquatic spectacles were synonymous with Sadler's Wells and very popular.

Surrey Theatre — Located in Blackfriars Road. Made a theater in 1809, its typical bill of fare in the Regency could include as advertised in *The Times*

> the new grand Welsh Historical melodramatic Burletta Spectacle, called LLEWELYN, PRINCE of WALES; or, Gellert, the faithful Dog. After the Melo-Drama, Mr. Pack will go through his wonderful Protean Transformations and Ground Posturings. With (never performed) an entirely, new Comic Pantomine, which has been some months in preparation, with new Music, Scenery, Dresses, and Decorations, called HARLEQUIN WATERMAN; or Above and Below Bridge.[14]

Coburg — Constructed out of the stones from John of Gaunt's palace, Savoy, and named for Princess Charlotte's husband of the House of Saxe-Coburg, it opened in the spring of 1818. A mixed program of melodramatic spectacle, ballet, and a pantomine made it immediately popular with London audiences.

The Pleasure Gardens

Vauxhall

Fascinating and delighting Londoners in every walk of life for many decades, Vauxhall, an amazing entertainment, flourished in Regency London. First opened in 1661 when it could only be reached by water, these lavish gardens survived because of the changing variety of their marvels and the unchanging lure of their slightly illicit walks.

The gardens were located just north of Kensington

Lane and the original entrance was to the west.

Admission to the Gardens was two shillings in 1792 and three shillings in 1809. Gala nights were used to pay tribute to heroes, military victories, and royal birthdays among other things and these events raised the admission price to as much as a guinea. The stupendous Vittoria Fête of July 20, 1813, which was attended by the Prince Regent and all the royal dukes cost a whopping two guineas and a half for an admission.

There were five graveled, tree-lined walkways that made up the main design of grounds. The entrance avenue, the Grand Walk, was nine hundred feet long and thirty feet wide with elm trees on either side.

The South Walk that ran parallel to the Grand Walk had three distinctive archways which featured a very realistic painting of the ruins of Palmyra. At a distance the unwary visitor to the grounds often thought they were real. Replacing the portrait of the ruins was a Gothic Temple with an artificial fountain in the center that only opened on Gala nights. This walk was about the same width and length as the Grand Walk.

The most scandalous of the walks was the Dark Walk or Lover's Walk. It, too, ran parallel to the walks mentioned above and was the furthermost promenade in the Gardens. Very narrow, it was dearly beloved by clandestine lovers and romance novelists.

At the left of the Grand Walk and parallel to it also was the smallest of the walks known as the Hermit's Walk, which took its name from the transparency of a seated hermit before a hut at the upper end. On the right of the walk was a wilderness and to the left a rectangular rural downs.

Traversing these four walks was the very widest of the avenues, the Grand Cross Walk. It ran through the center of the grounds and the approximately one hundred and twenty five feet between the Grand Walk and the South Walk bounded by the Cross Walk was known as the Grove.

The fashionable promenaded through these walkways,

and young bloods on the strut often lay in wait for an unprotected female on the darker byways. It was not unheard of for one of these bucks to drag a miss of tender years from the side of her mother into the wooded areas. They also engaged in ogling any and all women within the Gardens. Whomever caught their interest enjoyed fixed attention, and many a female was put out of countenance.

Advertisements were placed in the newspapers by bloods with a fancy for an unwary female observed in the gardens. The poet John Keats wrote *Sonnet to a Lady Seen for a Few Moments at Vauxhall* in the same spirit.

A dazzling draw to the crowds was the famed Cascade that could only be viewed at nine o'clock for fifteen minutes. The delightful extravaganza changed over the years to keep the enthusiasm of the patrons. The clang of a bell signaled it was time to witness Vauxhall magic and people gathered to see a miller's house with a rippling waterfall that had frothy foam at the bottom as it turned the miller's wheel. In later years the background was changed to a mountain scene.

Music, food, and fireworks were three of the mainstays throughout the Garden's history. The concert in the Grove began in early days with a small group of players and grew to a sizable orchestra with vocalists. By the Regency the musical entertainment had progressed to two acts with the music of Haydn, Handel, and Hook. Between the two acts, the bell rang to signal the Cascade's appearance.

There were three prominent musicians featured during the Regency. The organist and composer, Mr. James Hook performed from 1774 to 1820. Mrs. Bland was a popular ballad singer who first gained attention in 1802. Charles Dignum was also a well-liked vocalist.

Visitors to Vauxhall, tucked away in supper boxes, indulged in expensive suppers that included chicken, pastry, beef, ham, and a selection of wines.

Supper-boxes numbered over one hundred and were located next to the Grove. Inside each box were paintings by Francis Hayman that were retouched or redone as they were worn out by the curious fingers of the crowd. The paintings were of scenes such as the maypole dance and leap frog. Each box seated six to eight people.

Food prices at Vauxhall were costly. A dish of ham cost one shilling and was considered grossly overpriced. The extremely thin shavings that passed for slices were attributed to a carver rumored to be able to cover the surface of the Gardens with one lone ham.

In addition to these muslin-thin slices of ham, Regency palates were titilated by miniscule chickens reputed to be no larger than a sparrow. In 1817, a minute portion of notorious Vauxhall ham and two tiny chickens cost eleven shillings. An assortment of biscuits and cheese-cakes added another four shilling six pence to the bill. To wash down these dubious delights Vauxhall patrons could purchase a quart of arrack for seven shillings.

Though guests at the pleasure gardens complained continually about the tiny portions and the high cost, visitors consumed staggering amounts of food and drink. At a masquerade in 1812 the teeming crowds lapped up, among a large variety of viands, 400 quarts of ice cream, 200 ornamented hams and tongues, 150 chickens and other fowls, and enormous quantities of cherries, strawberries and other fruits. At the grand 1813 fête to honor Wellington and celebrate the Vittoria victory over 1300 people invaded the pleasure garden to dine on such things as 150 dishes of chicken, 250 enormous tureens of turtle, 30 pigeon pies, and 15 hams.

The wines served with these enormous repasts were of the best vintages. Vauxhall punch renowned for its strength and pungent alcohol content, was a particular favorite. Boisterous bucks promenading through the various walks often owed their good spirits to this potent brew.

Fireworks were first seen in the Gardens on June 5, 1798, but only became a permanent entertainment showpiece in 1813. Patrons demanded bigger, better, and more dazzling effects every year, and the proprietor was hard put to come up with new and more lavish creations. Noisy wheels of fireworks that hissed and blazed as rockets shot off across the sky were the main ingredients in the exciting display.

Vauxhall Gardens was always trying new enticing entertainments to lure in patrons. In the first part of the nineteenth century a host of death-defying feats and amazing spectacles were put on to amuse and delight London.

A major attraction in 1802 was an astonishing fire balloon ascent. Mr. Garnerin was seen by a large crowd to rise in the sky incredibly fast. And soon after his wife escorted by a Mr. Glassford ascended to the heavens. The same year the Rotunda was changed to the Pavilion of Concord exhibiting allegorical devices representing the marvelous four corners of the globe.

In 1814 at the end of the Grand Walk was the Naumachia or the Sea Battle Enactment. Cannons were heard accompanied by the fire and smoke of a burning ship. Other ships performed basic maneuvers. But these wonders were no match for the many free celebrations in the victory year of 1814 and Vauxhall lost money.

A permanent colonnade was erected in 1810 when part of the Grove and Grand Walk were razed to accommodate this new addition. Awnings had covered parts of the walkways since 1769. The colonnade was brightly lit with lamps and was of particular pleasure in inclement weather. The Grand Walk's gravel was replaced with imported Flanders brick at one time.

In 1815 the Gardens opened on June 8 under the patronage of his Royal Highness the Prince Regent featuring one Signor Rivolta who performed on six or eight instruments at the same time.

The most remarkable attraction was the famed Madame Saqui who amid Chinese fire scaled a mast and walked a tightrope. Her appearance was masculine, and her legs were said to have been worthy of a strong man as she amazed the crowd with her rope dancing. Dressed in tinsel and spangles and sporting a plume in her hair, she created an almost supernatural spectacle that was long remembered by all who saw her. She was sometimes joined

by her husband and child.   For her performances she
earned one hundred guineas weekly.
Visitors in 1817 left the premises about one o'clock
though many pleasure seekers lingered until four.

Ranelagh Gardens

Vauxhall's chief competition in the eighteenth century
barely survived into the nineteenth.   The Rotunda and
Pleasure Gardens of Ranelagh opened April 5, 1742,
deriving its name from the private residence built in 1690
by Richard, Viscount Ranelagh who also constructed a
formal garden.   The Rotunda was commonly known as the
Amphitheatre and measured five hundred and fifty five feet
in circumference with the interior being one hundred and
fifty feet.   This resort became a fashionable entertainment.
The entrance was through four Doric columns into a
structure composed primarily of wood.
The royal dukes were often here, thus drawing crowds
resulting in a direct competition with Vauxhall Gardens.
Writers of the day compared Ranelagh to the Pantheon in
Rome.   Admission in the early years was twelvepence.   In
later years it was about three shillings with the exception
of special events, which cost more.
Within the Amphitheatre were fifty-two supper boxes
each containing a painting, bell-shaped lamps, and room for
six to eight guests.   The main amusement was the promenade termed by participants as "the circular labor."
Ranelagh was open on Monday, Wednesday, and Friday
having masquerades, concerts, fireworks, and transparent
pictures as permanent fixtures.   Sometimes the masquerades
lasted until six or eight o'clock in the morning.
The gardens were formally laid out in gravel walkways
with elms and yews on each side.   There were flower
gardens and a grass pattern of an octagon shape.   The
main avenue extended from the south of Ranelagh House to
the base of the gardens, where sat a circular Temple of
Pan.   Lamps were attached to the trees and a canal with a

building described as both a Chinese House and a Venetian Temple.

A chief diversion was created May 7, 1772 — a fake Mount Etna housed in a special facility. An advertisement described it as "the Cavern of Vulcan with the Cyclops forging the armour of Mars." Visitors saw smoke, flames from the crater, and a lava eruption flowing down the mountain ending with an explosion. This quite naturally became a prized attraction.

The year 1802 was a good one for both guests and management. On June 2, Boodle's Club gave a ladies dance at which dresses were silver and white accented with diamonds. A lottery booth was erected so that the ladies could draw for trinket prizes. June 28 was the date chosen by the Picnic Society for an afternoon breakfast with the renowned French aeronaut Mr. Garnerin, who ascended in a balloon at five o'clock.

On September 23, 1802 the assembled crowd laughed uproarishly at the spectacle of one Thomas Todd. Dressed in leather and metal he was to stay underwater in a large drawing tub. His demonstration lasted less than five minutes due to his suit being "misfitted by his copper-smith."

The· last entertainment of interest to guests occurred June 1, 1803, as a ball held for the installation of the Knights of Bath. Though Ranelagh had amused patrons for over one hundred and sixty years, the promenade no longer held their attention. July 8, 1803 was the last time the Rotunda opened. On September 30, 1805, Ranelagh House was demolished. The remains of the foundation could still be seen in 1813.

Bagnigge Wells

Less prestigious than Ranelagh or Vauxhall, the pleasure gardens of Bagnigge Wells began about 1760 when a doctor named John Bevis published a pamphlet extolling the benefits of the wells found in a hollow called Bagnigge

Vale. A Mr. Hughes, the property's owner, discovered the iron salts within the water and had Dr. Bevis test it. The two wells were about twenty feet deep, and water was drawn from a double pump under a dome supported by columns known commonly as the Temple.

The average dosage at the pump was three half pints priced at threepence a drink. A half guinea purchased a season's ticket. In later years the price was raised to sixpence.

The center of activities at this pleasure garden was a banqueting hall known as the Long Room measuring about seventy-eight by twenty-eight feet. A bust of a woman in Roman dress said to be Nell Gwynne was placed in a wall niche because Bagnigge Wells was rumored to be her summer home in earlier times.

Within the Long Room was a distorting mirror at one end and an organ at the other end. Both were sources of much amusement. As with the other gardens, often the main entertainment was seeing and being seen. People from all classes visited here as they did Vauxhall Gardens though from 1780 Bagnigge Wells was considered to be a place mainly frequented by the lower ranks. Soldiers continued to find amusement here throughout the years.

Sunday was a busy day. Hundreds came to drink tea and perhaps to indulge in a bowl of negus between the hours of five and eight o'clock.

The grounds were laid out in formal walks between hedges of boxwood and holly. There were many ponds containing gold and silver fish with the center pond featuring a fountain of cupid astride a swan. The Fleet River ran through the gardens and seats dotted its banks. Three rustic bridges crossed the river, and nearby arbors entwined with honeysuckle were available for trysts. Also on the grounds was a rustic cottage divided into two apartments and a grotto. A bowling green was another feature.

The water organ played on weekday afternoons as it had since the 1770s. Around 1810 Bagnigge Wells was most definitely thought of as a gathering place for the lower and middle classes and went steadily downhill in attendance. In 1813 the gardens went bankrupt, and in December of that year the establishment was placed on the auction block. The next few years saw a frequent change of ownership with a Mr. Thorogood leasing the property in 1818.

Other Amusements

Astley's Royal Amphitheatre

The Regency entertainments at Astley's were based on the marvelous equestrian exploits of John and Hannah Astley, son and daughter-in-law of the founder, Philip Astley. It was begun in 1768 as a riding school and served as the first circus. Like other London buildings it, too, burnt to the ground and the building familiar to Regency audiences had been erected in 1803 as "the handsomest pleasure haunt in London."

Though unimposing on the outside, the interior was perfectly splendid. There was a huge chandelier that held fifty patent lamps! Directly below this dazzling sight was a sawdust ring, which was at some distance from the lively orchestra and London's biggest stage. The stage was in front of an arch as high as the gallery. The best seats in the house were in the three tiers of boxes.

The performances were an exciting rough-and-tumble hodge-podge of acrobats, pony races, clowns, magicians, and sword-fights. A typical bill of fare as advertised in *The Times* in 1813 was:

Royal Amphitheatre (Astley's)

This and every EVENING will be presented (by the permission of the Proprietors of the Theatre Royal, Covent garden), a new grand Equestrian Burletta Spectacle, founded on the Melo-Drama, called The SECRET MINE; introducing the Unit-

ed Stud of Horses.   In the course of the
evening, various Feats of HORSEMANSHIP; a
new Song, called "The Bourbon Cockade."   To
conclude with an entire new Comic Pantomine
called MERLIN'S CAVE; or, Harlequin's Masquerade.   First time, a DIVERSTISEMENT, in
which the Misses Adams and Monsieur Bustann
will   appear.   Doors   open   at   half-past   five.
Second price, at half-past eight.[15]

Argyle Rooms

These rooms were on the east side of Regent Street
at the corner of Little Argyle Street and opened in 1806.
All sorts of balls, masquerades, and plays were put on
here.   A vivid description of the rooms appeared in *Le
Beau Monde* whose critic was most impressed.

The entrance hall is extremely beautiful, the
sides being painted in fresco, representing Corinthian pilasters and compartments, with a verd
antique marble basement, and lighted up with an
elegant Grecian lamp.   From this the company
proceed through elegant folding doors covered
with crimson, into the vestibule, and from thence
up a grand staircase, lined with green cloth,
over which   is   a   beautiful   morode   carpet,
bordered with *a-la-grec*.   The staircase is lighted
up with four Grecian lamps and patent burners;
at   the   head   of   the   staircase   is   an   elegant
lounge, designed and painted after the cell of an
Athenian Temple, supported by Ionic columns.
On   the   right   of   this   lounge   are   intersected
staircases   (which   lead   to   the   boxes),   covered
with   crimson   cloth,   and   elegantly   illuminated
with   chandeliers,   &c.   The   first   room   the
company enter is the Turkish room; the floor of
which   is   covered with elegant blue carpets; the

sides are hung with blue drapery, and round the
room are placed Ottoman sofas. The ceiling is
beautifully painted, with an eagle grasping a
thunderbolt, from which is suspended a large
chandelier. On the left of this room is the
Saloon Theatre, one hundred feet long, which is,
without exception the most beautiful of the kind
in Europe. The walls are decorated with a grand
screen of Corinthian columns in entablature,
which supports the cove of the ceiling, representing an open sky. Between each screen of
columns is a *basso relievo* ornament, under each
of which is a picture of Telemachus's search
after his father, Ulysses, attended by his
instructor, Mentor. The basement is decorated
with curious African marble, and the caps of the
columns ornamented and heightened with
gold.—From the archtare are suspended six
beautiful balloon cut glass chandeliers, each
containing twelve wax lights. At the upper end
is constructed twenty boxes (for the accommodation of the patronesses and their friends),
decorated with bronze musical figures, on white
ground with gold mouldings; each tier is
supported by antique bronze and gold fasces;
round the front of the boxes are suspended from
bronze brackets, representing entwined serpents,
eighteen beautiful antique chandeliers, the only
of the kind in England. The boxes are trimmed
and lined with scarlet. At the lower end is constructed an elegant, though small stage, the
frontispiece of a circular plan, decorated similar
in architecture to the Saloon. The scenery is of
the most costly kind, and entirely new.

The Orchestra is fitted up on a new construction, opened in the centre by tracery
wirework, to admit the sound into the body of
the room; on the right of the Turkish room is
the grand dining room, the furniture of crim-

son, and crimson curtains; the ceiling of which is most superbly painted, representing Apollo and the Nine Muses, from which are suspended several elegant cut glass chandeliers and Grecian lamps with patent burners; on the right of this room are several refreshment rooms, all decorated and lighted up in a superior manner; on the ground floor are several beautiful supper rooms, which were superbly lighted up.

The greatest praise is due to the proprietors for the elegance of their designs, as neither expence or labour has been spared in the decorations and embellishments of this noble mansion, as well as for their attention to the comforts of the subscribers. Mr. Cundle, of Lower Brook-street, has completely established his fame as an architect, in the building and decorations of the above place.[16]

The fashionable rooms hosted the annual Cyprians Ball during the Regency. The elegant gentlemen who had graced Almack's the night before indulged their fancy in the company of charming demi-reps. These fashionable doxies in provocative gowns that conveniently slipped down well-endowed bosoms cavorted with their wealthy protectors all through the night.

More respectable entertainment in the Rooms were the concerts of the Philharmonic Society, which were held there from 1813 until the building burned down in 1830.

The most earthshaking event took place in 1813. Alvanley, Pierrepoint, Mildmay, and Brummell held a ball at the Argyle Rooms to celebrate their gambling successes and invited Prinny despite his quarrel with Brummell. All Regency society gasped as Brummell insulted the Prince Regent beyond repair. Given the cut direct by the Prince Regent, Brummell inquired, "Alvanley, who's your fat friend?"

Books

Every gentlemen who had some pretence to culture kept a well-stocked library and every young lady who longed for love sought out "gothick" romances to while away her leisure hours. Books in London meant Hatchard's to the fashionable *ton*. The shop was located in No. 187 Piccadilly after 1801. More than a book store it was a meeting place for opulent London. The book shop had a club-like atmosphere with the daily papers laid out on the table by the fireplace. Benches stood outside the store for the servants of the customers. Queen Charlotte chose them as her bookseller, and the firm has held a Royal Warrant since then.

Jane Austen's works, Byron's latest epic poem, or Sir Walter Scott's adventurous, romantic tales might be among the books chosen by Regency patrons. No doubt one publication in particular galvanized the upper ten thousand more than any other. Lady Caroline Lamb's thinly disguised tell-all—*Glenarvon* (1816). If there was ever any hope that she may resurrect her dead social life, this book put the last nail in her social coffin.

Glenarvon was a wild fantasy with Gothic overtones. The hero-villian Glenarvon was obviously Byron. Pilloried in these pages were the high society circles of Lady Holland and Caroline's mother-in-law, Lady Melbourne. These three slender volumes bound in leather and trimmed in gilt were an immediate sell out!

To cater to the appetites of young ladies and older dames that Coleridge called "a kind of beggarly daydreaming," was Mr. Lane's Minerva Press. A publisher of this titillating product, he founded a book shop beside his press and made his fortune.

Lane's novels generally came out in three volumes with mottled covers. Horror tales included *The Discarded Son, Midnight Bell*, and many others in the grand tradition of Mrs. Radcliffe's famous *Mysteries of Udolpho*. Other romantic titles included *The Mutual Attachment, Frederick and Caroline*, and *The Mysterious Freebooter*. And all this ravishing excitement could be bought for a few shillings!

The establishment was also one of the circulating libraries that had become so profitable and popular. Yearly subscribers were entitled for four pounds, four shillings to borrow up to eighteen books in Town, or twenty-four in the country. The lowest subscription rate was one pound eleven shillings and entitled the borrower to four books a year in Town or eight in the country. Other popular circulating libraries in London were Hookam's and Colburn's.

Art

For the art lover, viewing private collections was the best means of enjoying the various disciplines. The National Gallery was still many years in the future. The nucleus of what would become the National Gallery was the fabulous gallery of John Julius Angerstein, Esquire, in his Pall Mall house.

Another glorious collection not to be missed was that of the antique busts and statues of Mr. Charles Towneley. Art lovers would also be advised to make appointments to view the private collections of Lord Radstock, the Duke of Northumberland, the Duke of Devonshire, the Duke of Bridgewater, and the Marquis of Lansdowne.

The Royal Academy of Art, Somerset House, was the place for taking life classes and instructions. The famous annual exhibition established the Academy at the forefront of the art world. It was extremely difficult to be accepted as a viable artist without the support of the Academy. Notable contributors to the exhibition included J.M.W. Turner.

Art to the fashionable also meant portraits and the wealthy inhabitants of London during the Season might well make plans to have their own or a family member's features immortalized.

Sir Thomas Lawrence was the most fashionable of the portrait painters. His elevation to prominence can be traced through the steep rise in his fees from 1800 to 1810. In 1802, Lawrence charged thirty guineas for a three-quarter-size portrait. In 1806, he charged fifty guineas for a three-quarter-size and two hundred guineas for a full length portrait. By 1810, he charged one hundred guineas for a head and four hundred guineas for a full-length portrait!

Other fashionable portrait painters were Sir William Beechey, portrait painter to Her Majesty Queen Charlotte, Sir Martin Archer Shee, and John Hoppner.

London Sightseeing

London offered the Regency visitor many curiosities, much history, and numerous sights to see. Such visitors were curious creatures, and some of the marvels and monuments they viewed and exclaimed over as they made their progress through the city included:

British Museum
This museum was located on Great Russell Street. Significant acquisitions and dates were:

1801 — Rosetta Stone taken in looting at Alexandria after Bonaparte's defeat.
1805 — Charles Towneley's classical sculpture collection.
1816 — Lord Elgin's marbles taken from the Erechtheum and Parthenon.
1823 — George III's library of 120,800 books.

Cadiz Memorial
Located in the Horse Guards Parade, it was a cannon captured from the French and rested on a Chinese dragon made of cast iron. The cannon commemorates the victorious siege of Cadiz by Wellington and victory over the French at Salamanca in 1812. The cannon was given as a token of respect to the Prince Regent by Spain. Critics called it the Regent's Bomb, and it was depicted in several caricatures.

Duchess Street

This was on the Portland estate. A house located here, originally designed by Adam and owned by Thomas Hope, admitted people by means of a written request beginning in 1804 to view the owner's treasures. Upon entering they saw a vase collection, sculptures in a Grecian temple, an Egyptian Room, Indian Room, Dining Room, three Vase Rooms, and a Lararium with an idol collection. In 1819 there was an art gallery addition.

Madame Tussaud's

Until 1835, this wax figure museum had no permanent address, but travelled from place to place. Coming to England in 1802 from France Madame Tussaud had with her 35 figures done in wax that had been bequeathed to her by an uncle. Authenticity and attention to detail won her acclaim. The figures were clothed in either exact duplicates or if possible the original apparel. The Duke of Wellington was very pleased with the Napoleon waxwork.

Newgate Prison

Located in Newgate Street this prison was in existence since the 1100s. Hangings were an attraction here. Usually a short biography of the most famous criminals was written and distributed on the day of the hanging. The Cato Street conspirators were the last to be beheaded at Newgate in 1820.

Pantheon

Located in Oxford Street, this structure was said to be the most magnificent in all of England by Horace Walpole and others. Assemblies, exhibitions, concerts, and fêtes were held there before it became the King's Theatre, Pantheon in 1791. Fire gutted the building in 1792, and it was rebuilt and reopened in 1795 with a masquerade. Various owners and enterprises met with failure on the premises. In 1813 it was closed completely. It did not reopen in its new life as a bazaar until 1834.

Tower of London

Located on Tower Hill, the Tower began as a means of defense in medieval times. In the 1200s the first wild animals arrived to form what came to be called the Menagerie. Henry VIII brought severe treatment of prisoners and the beheading of his wives to Tower Green. The last king to have his palace in the Tower was King James I. In 1822 the royal menagerie consisted of one elephant, one grizzly bear, and one or two birds.

Week's Mechanical Museum

Located in Haymarket, it opened in 1803 and the most talked about attraction on exhibit was the mechanical tarantula whose movements startled the fair sex especially. Musical clocks as well as mechanical birds, mice, and other animals made up the collection.

Westminster Abbey

Near King street and the Houses of Parliament. William I was crowned here. Gothic architecture with flying buttresses and a basic French design distinguish the Abbey. Several tombs and monuments as well as chapels and naves make up the interior.

To be seen in the Abbey:

The Coronation Chair—made for King Edward I and brought into the Abbey in 1277. It was used in every coronation in the Abbey.

Tombs—Edward the Confessor, Henry III, Edward I, Eleanor of Castile, Edward III, and Richard II. Also buried here are Henry VII, Anne of Cleves, Edward VI, Mary Queen of Scots, James I, Charles II, Mary II, Queen Anne, and George II.

NOTES TO CHAPTER V

1. Rees Howell Gronow, *The Reminiscences and Recollections of Captain Gronow*, 2:286.

2. Ibid., 1:55-56.

3. Ibid., 1:57-58.

4. Ibid., 1:56-57.

5. Ibid., 1:57.

6. Ibid., 2:293.

7. John Ashton, *The History of Gambling in England*, p. 111.

8. Richard Henry Stoddard, ed., *Personal Reminiscences of Cornelia Knight and Thomas Raikes,* p. 313.

9. Ashton, *Gambling,* p. 93.

10. Ibid.

11. Gronow, *Reminiscences and Recollections,* 2:92.

12. *Le Beau Monde*, September 1809, p. 324.

13. *The Times*, July 12, 1813.

14. Ibid.

15. Ibid., April 19, 1814.

16. *Le Beau Monde*, March 1808, pp. 176-77.

Chapter VI

HOW THEY LIVED

Whether one was as rich as a nabob, in dun territory, or just managed on an easy competence, the glittering allure of a London Season enticed the Polite World to Town in the spring.

Some families with numerous progeny only came to Town to make sure their children formed suitable alliances with eligible connections. Eligibility was always associated with the size of settlements. Others came to shop, go to theatrical entertainments, and to enliven *ennui* from dull winter months on country estates. Still others looked to the fashionable life in London as an end in itself. They dressed in styles bang up to the nines and gave entertainments that were all the crack. Elegant pursuits for pleasure's sake was their only occupation.

The gathering of the *haut ton* to meet, to mate, and generally amuse themselves during their annual spring migration demanded the first style of elegance in their Town residence as it did in their dress.

Families with deep pockets built enormous London palaces to impress all the world and his wife with their consequence. These Town houses built and decorated with magnificent luxury gobbled up enormous sums of money. The Londonderrys squandered £200,000 on Holdernesse House in Park Lane, which they purchased in 1821 for £43,000, before they found it worthy to entertain the *beau monde*. The Lambs spent over £100,000 on Melbourne House (later known as the Albany) in the 1770s.

Embellishing one's Town residence, adopting the latest fad in furniture and decoration, and assembling glorious art collections were considered occupations befitting a gentleman. They were mandatory tasks for all who wanted to make a stir in the world.

141

Even more modest Town houses proved expensive and one didn't always get what one desired. Lady Caroline Stuart Wortley wrote her mama in 1818 about the house her husband had purchased in Town after he became the member for Yorkshire, and his governmental career necessitated lengthy sojourns in London. They purchased a house in Curzon Street for £12,000 and a lease of 900 years. Lady Caroline thought it was in a rather dismal situation though she liked the house very much, but, oh, if only it could be in a square or near a park!

For families only in Town to propel their children into the marriage mart, the purchase and ruinous upkeep of a second dwelling was above their touch. Adequate abodes with decent addresses could be hired for the season at a price. Social necessity dictated that even the most modest of fortunes had to provide a residence of adequate size to entertain! A worthy house might let for a thousand pounds.

Owners of the luxurious Town palaces hosted large extravagant parties. Cards sent for receptions could number in the hundreds. Louis Simond, visiting London in 1810, described an "at home" of the first consequence. Invitations were issued a month or more before the grandly planned reception. Dutifully waiting in long lines of carriages that clogged the streets, the elegant guests often waited a half-hour or more to be received by their hostesses. None of the guests sat down. No conversation, no cards, and no music enlivened the scene. The *ton* just elbowed and twisted their way from room to room. At the end of their mandatory fifteen minute visit, the fashionable visitors dashed to the hall to wait impatiently for their carriage. Guests often spent more time with the footman who scurried to help them at the threshold than their host and hostess above stairs.

No "at homes" were top of the trees unless the guests declared it a dreadful squeeze! A hostess's reputation soared if at least one lady fainted amidst the well-dressed nobs in tightly packed rooms.

When guests departed after the required fifteen

minutes or so, they racketed off to the next "at home" and so on until the wee hours of morning.

Elegant London amused themselves at a variety of other fashionable entertainments in each other's residences. Hostesses not only gave "at homes," but kept the days and nights of the season crowded with dinner parties, drums, balls, routs, fancy balls, Venetian breakfasts, card parties, *soirées* and musicales.

There were many grand and glorious Town houses populating the London landscape. Some of the most noted residences were:

Apsley House

The British government bought Apsley House for Wellington from his brother Richard Wellesley in 1816. Situated at Hyde Park Corner, this Adam designed house was originally built in 1771-78 for Henry Bathurst, whose second title was Baron Apsley.

The Iron Duke spent over £40,000 transforming his acquisition. Notable among the numerous improvements was the magnificent Waterloo Gallery. Every year on June 18, Wellington held the Waterloo Banquet as a remembrance to all the men who had fought at Waterloo. Upon the lengthy dining table stood the Portuguese dinner service, an epic-sized centerpiece 26 feet long with over 1,000 silver and silver gilt items adorning it. The last commemorative dinner was in 1852.

Architect Benjamin Wyatt carried out the splendid improvements to the ducal establishment. Mrs. Harriet Arbuthnot dined at the Duke's table on the first day of the new dining room and declared it a magnificent room and a great improvement in the house. As his country's representative, the Prince of Wales, gave Wellington a most fitting gift to grace his home, Canova's statue of Napoleon.

Carlton House

Carlton House, residence of Prinny from 1782 to 1825, was the hub of his rakish social circle. The original house sheltered the Dowager Princess of Wales, mother of George III, until her death in 1772. George III granted it to the young Prince of Wales in 1783. He spent the next thirty years repairing, renovating, and decorating his home.

The spendthrift prince spared no expense in creating his fantasy palace. From the vivid bow-windowed bedchamber to the Chinese drawing room, only the best, most expensive, and elaborate furniture and decoration were up to snuff. His contemporaries concluded that it was either "overdone with finery" or a magnificent "English Versailles."

Gronow despised the princely residence. He wrote:

> One of the meanest and most ugly edifices that ever disfigured London, notwithstanding it was screened by a row of columns, was Carlton House, the residence of the Prince Regent. It was condemned by everybody who possessed taste; and Canova the sculptor, on being asked his opinion of it, said, "There are at Rome a thousand buildings more beautiful, and whose architecture is in comparison faultless, any one of which would be more suitable for a princely residence than that ugly barn." This building was constantly under repair, but never improved, for no material alterations were made in its appearance. The first step towards improvement should have been to give it a coat of "lime-wash," for it was blackened with dust and soot.[1]

One of the grandest of occasions to take place here was the magnificent fête held on June 19, 1811 to celebrate the establishment of the Prince of Wales as Regent. All the men were required to wear court dress or uniforms while the women out-blazed each other in the richness of their ensembles. Prinny himself wore a heavily embroidered field-marshal uniform.

Prinny utilized the whole of Carlton House, including the basement. Around 2,000 of the best people arrived from nine until after midnight. The house rang with noble chatter as the hall and state apartments overflowed with nobility.

The tables groaned with every delight which rank and wealth could obtain and every fancy the confectioner's art could conceive. Most notable of the numerous extraordinary decorations was the stream that flowed from the Prince Regent's seat down to the end of the table. Beginning with a round basin exhibiting a finely worked temple in its center placed in front of Prinny, water trickled between pictorial green banks. Several bridges crossed over the tiny stream as it journeyed down the table. Even fish of gold and silver swam in the mock stream.

Though reactions to the fête were mixed, London's interest was whetted. Crowds thronged the streets as the Prince flung open his doors until June 26th to show off his treasured mansion. The Horse Guards had to be called out to control the numerous visitors who were in a frenzy to gain admittance on the last day. The crowd in Carlton House had grown so much the gates had been closed at one o'clock. As a result of this, the waiting crowd outside the gates grew to an enormous size. Carriages filled up Pall Mall to the top of St. James's Street. Ladies, impatiently waiting in the long stream of carriages, left their elegant equipages and tramped on foot to Carlton House, each determined not to miss a viewing. The crowd swelled tremendously and wise onlookers retreated from the waiting horde. Those who did not exercise such shrewdness became crushed in a fevered mob. The back of the crowd surged forward and some women fell and were trampled. More than one bruised and battered soul had to be helped from the scene. Inside the gates, at last, several crowd-mauled females could be seen in various tattered clothing remnants. One lady even had her leg broken and others were almost completely undressed from the force of the frenzy. The Horse Guards attempting to control the crowd outside struggled with their unruly mounts among the restive throng. Several people got into the way of rearing hoofs and sustained injury. Men fainted, women screamed, and surgeons were called to the scene. Though Carlton House hosted many elaborate and memorable occasions, nothing ever equaled the amazing spectacle of this day.

Sadly, the Prince Regent decided after his ascension to the throne that Carlton House was not nearly grand enough for George IV and the building was demolished on his orders in 1826-27. His attentions now turned to Buckingham House and Windsor.

Chesterfield House

Located in Great Stanhope Street, this Palladian style house was designed by Isaac Ware for the 4th Earl of Chesterfield.

One of the house's outstanding features was the magnificent grand staircase of white marble. Lord Chesterfield wrote to a friend that the staircase would form such a scene unknown in England. He also lamented that the expense would ruin him, but his enjoyment in the sight was worth it. Also notable is that each room is in a different style. Work was completed on the building in 1749.

A legendary Georgian love story took place within the walls of Chesterfield House. It was here that the Duke of Hamilton wooed and won Elizabeth, one of the beautiful and penniless Gunning sisters who took London by storm.

During the Regency, the house was occupied by the 3rd Earl's adopted heir, a distant cousin named Philip Stanhope.

Devonshire House

Built for the 3rd Duke of Devonshire in 1734-1737,

Devonshire House occupied the site of Berkeley House which had been destroyed by fire. During the reign of the 5th Duke and his charming frivolous duchess, Georgiana, the house became a nucleus for Whig opposition to George III's Tory government. Charles James Fox, Prinny, and Sheridan were all habitual visitors.

The 6th Duke continued lavish entertaining during the Regency. A bachelor, he was hotly pursued by every title-hunting miss in Town. As Gronow remembered it....

> The Duke of Devonshire, then young, graceful, and distinguished, was hunted down by mothers and daughters with an activity, zeal, and perseverance — and, I am sorry to add, a vulgarity — which those only can conceive who have beheld the British huntress in full cry after a duke. It was amusing to see how the ambitious matrons watched every movement, and how furious they became if any other girl was more favoured than their own daughters by the attention of the monarch of the Peak. The young ladies, on their side, would not engage themselves with any one until all hope of the Duke asking them to dance was at an end. But as soon as he had selected a partner, the same young ladies would go in search of those whom they had rejected, and endeavour to get opposite or somewhere near him.[2]

The bachelor Duke began renovating the mansion in 1811. By 1820, the house was transformed. A lavish abundance of gilding put the house in prime style. The simple entrance hall was transformed into a grand new saloon and a new entrance opened up on the north side of the house. A new staircase ushered visitors up to the new doorway.

Alas, no lady ever shared the ducal residence. To the despair of many hopeful mamas, the Duke died in the single state.

Holland House

During the Regency, Holland House housed Henry Fox, the 3rd Baron Holland, and his wife the imperious Whig hostesses, Lady Holland. Married at sixteen to Lord Webster, she eloped with Henry Fox and married him after her divorce became final in 1797. The house itself was Jacobean in design and attributed to architect John Thorpe. Princess Liechtenstein described the dining room:

> Besides many likenesses speaking to us from its crimson damask walls, it has a sideboard rich and glittering with venerable family-plate, a great looking glass in which a merry party may have the satisfaction of finding itself repeated, and a gay china closet, filled mostly from the East.[3]

Among these many likenesses were Lady Fox by Kneller, Rogers by Hoppner, Moore by Shee, and Russell by Hayter.

The library at Holland House had bursting shelves loaded with the wisdom of the ages and measured 90 feet long and only 17 feet 4 inches wide.

Lady Holland was not accepted by the highest sticklers of the *ton*, but this was unimportant to this most political of hostesses. Holland House hosted the Whigs and a legion of prominent figures from every field of endeavor. George Canning, Melbourne, and Talleyrand were only three of the multitude who came to dine at her table. Her dinner table was always crowded.

Greville believed that Lady Holland delighted in an excessively crowded table and was never happier than when her dinner guests had their arms prettily pinioned together. Lady Grey deplored dining sixteen to a table for nine. Less important persons were known to be ousted for more important ones at the Holland table. Once she told the wit Luttrell to make room for another guest and he replied, "It must certainly be *made*, ... for it does not *exist*."4

The eccentric Lady Holland feared no one. She and her husband openly supported Napoleon. When the mighty emperor was incarcerated on Elba, they sent him plum jam and books to buck up his spirits!

Hotels

If one came to town to sample her pleasures for a few days, had no Town house and saw no necessity to let one, London boasted several hotels that catered to every taste.

During the Regency the Clarendon Hotel was run by a former cook of Louis XVIII, Jacquiers. Captain Rees Howell Gronow writing in his *Reminiscences* declared: "This was the only public hotel where you could get a genuine French dinner, and for which you seldom paid less than three or four pounds; your bottle of champagne or of claret, in the year 1814, costing you a guinea."

He also described other hotels of the era:

> Limmer's was an evening resort for the sporting world; in fact, it was a midnight Tattersall's, where you heard nothing but the language of the turf, and where men with not very clean hands used to make up their books. Limmer's was the most dirty hotel in London; but in the gloomy, comfortless coffeeroom might be seen many members of the rich squirearchy who visited London during the sporting season. This hotel was frequently so crowded, that a bed could not be obtained for any amount of money; but you could always get a very good plain English dinner, an excellent bottle of port, and some famous gin-punch.
>
> Ibbetson's hotel was chiefly patronized by the clergy and young men from the universities. The

charges there were more economical than at
similar establishments.   Fladong's, in Oxford
Street, was chiefly frequented by naval men; for
in those days there was no club for sailors.
Stephens's in Bond Street, was a fashionable
hotel, supported by officers of the army and men
about town.   If a stranger asked to dine there,
he was stared at by the servants, and very
solemnly assured that there was no table
vacant.   It was not an uncommon thing to see
thirty   or   forty   saddle-horses   and   tilburies
waiting outside this hotel.   I recollect two of my
old Welsh friends, who used each of them to
dispose of five bottles of wine daily, residing
here in 1815, when the familiar joints, boiled
fish, and fried soles, were the only eatables you
could order.[5]

The fashionable world also put up at Grillon's Hotel
at No. 7 Albemarle Street.   This hostelry had the
distinction of housing Louis XVIII in the days just before
he returned to France in 1814 to reclaim his throne.   The
ambience of the hotel was devilish flat and very
respectable.

The Pulteney was located in Piccadilly.   Tsar
Alexander I of Russia and his sister the obnoxious Grand
Duchess Catherine occupied quarters here during their visit
to London in 1814 for the victory celebrations.   She was
most pleased with Pulteney's modern convenience—water
closets.

The popular Tsar graciously acknowledged the
cheering throngs from Pulteney's balcony.   The hotel staff
were not, however, among Tsar Alexander's admirers.   They
were much too irritated by dreadfully low vails (gratuities)
emanating from the Russian visitors!

Lodgings

Gentlemen enjoying single blessedness and had no

family in Town from whom they might cadge hospitality or who had an independent income and much preferred to cut loose the apron strings set themselves up in lodgings or small apartments. Good addresses were preferable, but gentlemen forced to economize made do with unfashionable quarters. After all, a fellow had to have a sporting chance at well-dowered quarry.

London newspapers overflowed with "to let" advertisements of places for a gentleman to rest his head between social engagements. *The Times* of July 1, 1813 included these advertisements.

> Apartments, well furnished, in a superior, pleasant, and eligible situation, for a summer or winter residence, near Whitehall, with a cheerful view of St. James's Park, in a respectable family, where there will not be any children, or other inmate; suitable for a Gentleman and his servant, or Member of Parliament, who may have every family accommodation. Reference at Mr. Price's, Italian warehouse, No. 3, Haymarket.
>
> Apartments, Abingdon-Street. To be LET, furnished, a FIRST FLOOR, with servant's room, suitable for the residence of a Gentleman belonging to either House of Parliament. Cards of address at Riche's Italian warehouse, Little Charles-street, Parliament-street, Westminster.[6]

Several smaller listings appeared in the same paper. "To be LET, Apartments, genteelly Furnished, No. 2, New Bridge-street, Blackfriars."

The Fashionable Interior

Members of the Polite World who sought the accolade "of the first stare" forever chased the latest mode. Stylish townhouses had to shed their old-fashioned furnishings and outmoded decor. By Jove, how could a fellow hold up his head with a drawing room decorated during Queen Anne's reign?

Fashionable matrons shopped endlessly, consulted experts, hired skilled professionals to carry out detailed plans, and shopped some more for just the right touches for each room. Most sought after were the severe elegant lines of neo-classical Regency style. Robert Adam and Henry Holland fathered this English adaptation of ancient Graeco-Roman furniture and decoration. Holland's successor, Thomas Hope authored a very influential style book, *Household Furniture and Interior Decoration,* 1807.

Regency furniture featured severe neo-classic simplicity in outline. Bold curves, straight lines, both horizontal and vertical, in addition to the lesser role of ornamentation hallmarked the style.

Design books by innovative stylemakers included:

Etchings Representing the Best Examples of Ancient Ornamental Architecture (1799) by Charles Heathcote Tatham

A Collection of Designs for Household Furniture and Interior Decoration (1808) by George Smith

The Rudiments of Drawing Cabinet and Upholstery Furniture (1820) by Richard Brown

The Repository of Arts (1809-1828) Rudolph Ackermann's well-illustrated magazine.

The Cabinet-Maker's and Upholsterer's Guide (1828) by George Smith

Each book left no doubt that classically inspired design was all the crack! Whether the ruins and excavations were Roman, Etruscan, Greek, or Egyptian, England's upper classes sought out the ancient past to embellish their drawing rooms and bedrooms. Included among the many manufactories and warehouses where fashionable ladies and gentlemen made their selections were:

Buhl Manufactury
No. 19 Queen Street, Edgware Road. Owned by Louis Le Gaigneur, a French émigré, the workshop made Boulle furniture that captured Prinny's attention.

G. and R. Gillow & Co.
No. 176 Oxford Road. The fashionable quarters of their showroom were stuffed with solid mahogany furniture of all types.

Morgan and Sanders
Catherine Street, the Strand. They manufactured a large variety of furnishings. Tent bedsteads, Trafalgar sideboards and Imperial dining tables numbered among their inventory.

Oakley, Shackleton & Evans
No. 8 Old Bond Street. Very fashionable cabinetmaker with goods in the latest mode. Loo-tables, satinwood wardrobes, and mahogany library cases in the Greek style made up a small part of their wonderfully large warehouse.

Perry & Parker
No. 8 Fleet Street. An important glass manufacturer who offered a variety of chandeliers to its wealthy clients which included the Prince Regent. In 1817, the company moved to No. 78 New Bond street and changed its name to Perry & Co.

The Regency Styles

Chinese

Dragons, pagodas, and mandarins adorned the furniture, ornaments, and wallpaper. Bold Chinese red dominated the color scheme. Small chairs and tables made from beech were carved to resemble bamboo. Other features included Chinese lanterns, lacquered cabinets, trellis work, and use of the claw-and-ball foot.

Prinny delighted in fantastical Chinese style furniture and ornaments. His ardor for dragons spurred on a revival of this mid-eighteenth century fad. Notable use of oriental motifs can be seen in Carlton House's Chinese drawing room designed by Henry Holland and completed in 1790, the exquisite Chinese gallery at Brighton Pavilion completed in 1802, and the extensive remodeling and redecorating of the Royal Pavilion carried out between 1815 and 1823.

"Japanning," imitation Oriental lacquer, was the technique used to paint and varnish furniture. Black and green were the most popular colors used.

Egyptian Style

Baron Dominique Vivant Denon accompanied Napoleon's Egyptian campaign in the 1790s. The illustrations in his *Voyages dans la Basse et Haute Egypte*, coupled with Nelson's decisive defeat of the French fleet at the Battle of the Nile, propelled the exotic motifs of ancient Egypt into vogue. Thomas Hope made some use of Egyptian decorations.

The height of the craze was around 1810. Typical of Egyptian style furnishings were library tables supported by sphinxes, sideboards decorated with Egyptian lotus and water lily, and a cellaret or wine cooler in the shape of a sarcophagus. The use of sphinx heads, lions, crocodiles, and serpents as motifs helped make the style easy to exaggerate.

French Styles

French influences on furniture trickled through the barriers of war and blockades much as fashions in clothing did. Designs popular during the Consulate, Directoire, and

Empire made an impact on English taste and design. The Prince Regent's fondness for Boulle marquetry furniture assured its popularity. Marquetry ornament and brass inlay as decoration on standard furniture pieces were much sought after by the *haut ton*. The restoration of the French monarchy in 1814 sparked brief interest in a revival of Louis XIV style.

Gothic Revival

The Gothic or Old English fashion heralded a return to good solid English furniture. It had a strong emotional appeal for Britons tired of ancient severity and Oriental fantasy. Its popularity paralled the Romantic Revival in literature.

First featured in Sheraton's *Encyclopaedia*, 1804, this heavily carved, solid furniture was usually made of oak in either the Elizabethan or Tudor style. The skilled workmanship required made it more expensive than many other styles.

Greek Revival

The Grecian style was predominant among the many elements that made up Regency style Henry Holland first used extensively.

Indicative of the anciently inspired style were the lion paw foot, lion monopodium, and the distinctive lyre shapes used for chair backs and table supports. Artisans fashioned these bare, elegant shapes from mahogany, rosewood, and kingwood. Dark woods made exquisite backdrops for the brass lion mask mountings. Carved acanthus sprays and anthemion were used for detail. Heavy gilt often lavishly decorated the furniture.

A typical Grecian chair had boldly curved back and front legs. The forward curve of the front legs provided balance. Decoration included spiral reeding, lion feet and lyre-shaped splats. Winged paw feet were also popular.

Regency furniture makers applied the principles on ancient severity to all sorts of new fangled furniture! If a classical prototype existed, the style was slavishy followed by designers. The couch, round table with lion monopodium, and cross-framed stool were all examples of this. Sideboards and firescreens did not exist in classical times, but craftsmen applied the Grecian touch conforming them to the antique ideal.

The best examples of Regency interior decoration unified a room by basing its concept on a single fashionable theme. A workable theme could center around spare elegant Graeco-Roman style or the most fantastical Chinese motifs.

Prinny's Royal Pavilion at Brighton stands as a monument to dazzling rooms dedicated to a single theme. The Red Drawing-Room as designed by Nash was Oriental fantasy come to life! Columns became brightly colored palm trees with bamboo trunks. All the woodwork grains were teased into the illusive shapes of Chinese dragons. The hand painted wall covering design repeated the swirling dragons in white on a carmine red background. Dotted throughout the room were imported bamboo chairs. Every element enhanced the Oriental dream!

The worst Regency taste conjured up a nightmare of battling motifs. Miss Mitford described such a horror in *Our Village:*

> Every room is a masquerade: The saloon Chinese, full of jars and mandarins and pagodas; the library Egyptian, all covered with hieroglyphics, and swarming with furniture crocodiles and sphynxes. Only think a crocodile couch, and a sphynx sofa! They sleep in Turkish tents, and dine in a Gothic chapel ... the properties are apt to get shifted from one scene to another, and all manner of anomalies are the consequence. The mitred chairs and screens of the chapel, for instance, so very upright, and tall, and carved, and priestly, were mixed up

oddly enough with squat Chinese bonzes; whilst
by some strange transposition a pair of nodding
mandarins figured amongst the Egyptian
monsters....[7]

Servants

A formidable array of domestics in even the smallest
of fashionable dwellings served milord and his lady during
their sojourn in Town. The grandest residences had a
literal army of men and women to do the onerous chores
of early nineteenth century households.
Males dominated the top of the servant hierarchy in a
gentleman's establishment. Because landed noblemen had
many residences scattered throughout the country, each
house usually had its own house steward to oversee
everything. He was responsible for the entire staff,
household accounts, hiring new staff, and paying wages.
Serving as his master's personal secretary, the steward
kept abreast of his business and paid all the household
accounts. This position was particularly suitable for
educated young men who had their way to make in the
world such as sons of clerics and professional men. The
most superior of the house servant clan were addressed as
the *Major Domo* or *maître d'hôtel*.
Next in rank came the valet, the butler, and the
groom of the chambers. Only in gigantic households would
there be four male servants in the upper levels of domestic
service. More frequently the valet and butler combined the
duties entailed in their own jobs plus the responsibilities of
the house steward and groom of the chamber.
The valet was very important to the household and
among the servants because of his proximity to the master.
His interests should be inseparable from his employer's
needs and desires. This closeness bred a need for valets
to present to the world a picture of a true gentleman's
gentleman. The wise, fashionable valet cultivated an all-
knowing manner and dropped a French phrase here and

there. His duties included overseeing his master's stylish wardrobe of superfine coats and inexpressibles, barbering, and everything else related to grooming and personal needs. Compliments on his master's snowy white cravat folded in the most exquisite design reflected great credit upon his prowess as an artist in the dressing-room.

The butler oversaw everything that pertained to the serving of food and drink. Under his guardianship rested the sanctity of the wine cellar. He not only protected the delicate spirits from spoilage, but guarded against pilfering servants. The safety, cleaning, and inventory of all the dinnerware, glassware, and plate were also his domain. He ruled imperiously over the footmen who served at the table and was expected to present a sterling example to the male servants that he commanded. The best butler was known by the ease and elegance of service at milord's dinner table. Often a butler's commanding authority spilled over into other areas of household management, particularly where he ranked as the highest servant. He often performed the managerial duties of the house steward, groom of the chambers, and clerk of the kitchen.

In large households, the next in rank was the groom of the chambers. His duties included meeting visitors, taking charge of their visiting cards, and announcing them to the household or declaring that no one was "at home." In conjunction with these duties, he was to make sure all was kept immaculate for receiving guests. Lighting had to be maintained. Fires must be laid and fed. Writing desks must be stocked with ink, quill, and paper. He physically opened up the house and closed it down each day as he properly extinguished candles, lamps, and fires.

These four grades of upper male servants were set apart from the lower ranks by their status and prestige. They wore no livery unlike the lower servants. They also kept their meals in a room, separate from the servant's hall.

Footmen resplendent in dazzling livery were the backbone of the household. Inside the townhouse, they diligently waited at the table under the steely eye of the stern butler, served tea, relieved the groom of the chambers at the door, and generally made themselves useful whenever their assistance was needed. Often their master's friends borrowed footmen to assist at large entertainments. Outside, in the threatening streets of Regency London, footmen escorted their employers as they shopped, paid calls, and trotted from one amusement to another. Footmen gave one the proper cachet. A fashionable lady must have someone to scurry ahead and knock on doors!

Below the footmen in the servant hierarchy were ushers. They were the servants who waited on the servants! They tended the servant's hall and the upper servants quarters.

Lowest among the low within the servants group were the footboys, also known as provision boys. These eight- and nine-year-olds were used in every part of the household for odd jobs and were considered footmen in training. Pages were special footboys distinguished by their birth or a physical oddity. More than one fashionable lady kept an amusing little Negro boy as her page and dressed him in costly and luxurious livery.

On the distaff side of the domestic staff only two women enjoyed the distinction of being upper servants: milady's personal maid and the housekeeper. A lady's maid enjoyed the same benefits of the valet, the master's body servant. Her closeness to the mistress of the house made her very important in the servant's hall. Harriette Wilson kept a maid of fashionable French origin. If one couldn't have the real thing, at the very least, milady's maid should have a suitable repertoire of French phrases.

A housekeeper had direct control over all the other women servants. If the household boasted a steward, she served as his assistant. Her managerial authority increased greatly if she shared the house steward's responsibilities with the butler. She might be entrusted with household accounts, hiring servants through a registry office, and buying innumerable provisions to feed the large household. Typical everyday duties included supervising the repair of household linen and replenishing diminished food stuffs. Before the family returned to Town after a visit to their country estates or a sojourn in Brighton, she oversaw the cleaning and airing of the chambers. It was an important part of her job to make sure the house remained in a state of readiness to receive her employers.

The cook ranked next in importance to the housekeeper. Most prosperous households preferred a man cook or, at least, a woman cook who had trained beneath a male. Women cooks were given much lower wages though their duties and responsibilities were the same.

All cooks in fashionable households were expected to be familiar with French ways of preparing food, organizing a menu, and judging the quality and quantity of provisions. In a very social household, a variety of food preparation specialists assisted the cook or chef.

Chambermaids ranked highest among the lower female servants. Their sphere was properly in the bedrooms: dusting, straightening, cleaning, swatting insects in summer, laying fires and warming beds in winter, sweeping, closing windows, and turning down bedclothes the last thing at night.

Next came the hardworking housemaids and maids of all work. They toiled from dawn to dusk: scrubbing, dusting, polishing, and scouring every surface in the house. Then came the red-handed laundry-maid who labored among the dirty linens. The lowest among their number were the scullery maids. Assigned to the kitchen and pantry, they washed dishes and scoured pots from the servants' hall in addition to those from milord's table.

Domestic servants had many other benefits beyond their meager wages. The master granted them shelter, board, and clothing. The quality of these benefits varied with the enlightment of their masters. Lower servants usually lived in cramped, crowded quarters in either the attic, which was suffocating in the summer, or the basement which was dank, dreary, and cold in the winter. Rooms were often unheated and crawling with unwelcome pests. Food was generally plentiful and good, but upper servants had been known to severely ration lower servants and keep the majority of the food stuffs to sell for their benefit.

Food

An incredible array of food tempted the jaded palates of the Polite World. Multi-coursed, hours-long meals enhanced the never-ending round of pleasure in Town.

To achieve memorable culinary magnificence, rich *haut ton* hostesses employed all sorts of specialists to assist their fashionable French chefs. Bakers, confectioners, and male roasting cooks were only a few of the assistants necessary to aid the chef in creating masterpieces.

Good French chefs were highly prized and one of the most sought after was Antonin Carême who worked briefly for Prinny in the last years of the Regency. Though the Prince Regent offered him the enormous salary of £500 and should the Regent die a life pension of £250 to lure him back into his service, Carême refused.

Well-rewarded chefs were just one of the spare-no-expense extravagances of *beau monde* pleasure lovers. No ludicrously expensive appetite remained unfilled. One fashionable breakfast party featured strawberries that cost £150! Lord Alvanley's whim for an apricot tart every day drew the censure of his *maître de cuisine* because of the excessive expense. M'Lord promptly sent him to Gunther's to buy out the entire stock!

There was a widening gap between dinner and breakfast in the late eighteenth century. The new later dinner hour in Town also insured that breakfast would be larger and hardier than bread and chocolate. Large breakfasts including meat, egg, and fish dishes were *de rigueur* on fashionable sideboards.

The breakfast of 10 A.M. and the late 8 or 9 P.M. dinner left a long gap in the middle of the day. A substantial midday meal became common with the ritual of afternoon tea not emerging until Victoria's reign.

Dinner was the most social meal of the day. Keeping Town hours meant starting dinner at eight or nine. An elaborate, fashionable meal could take three or four hours. Dining out meant that guests were unable to go to the theater because they would have missed much of the evening's performance.

The servants served supper about four hours after dinner. Balls always included the supper dance. Partners minced and twirled around the dance floor, then retired to casually dine with each other from plates loaded with lobster patties and other delicacies. If one waltzed until dawn, weary dancers demanded a little extra sustenance!

Food was served in lavish helpings and there was a surprising variety of tempting dishes. All sorts of delicacies from around the world were available. Napoleon's stranglehold on the Continent had little effect on England's rule of the seven seas. Some of the notable treats that graced the English dinner table were:

Bolognese sausages
British West Indian limes
greenhouse peaches and pineapples
Indian curry
Italian and Turkish figs and dates
Jamaican bananas
Laplander reindeer tongues
Parmesan cheese
Russian caviare
Spanish olives
Westphalian and Portuguese hams

Visitors might complain about English cookery, but English meats were far superior to Continental cuts. Cattle, sheep, and poultry were herded from as far away as Wales and arrived in Town rather stringy compared to their fat succulent country cousins.

Gronow recalled the happy experience of dining in Regency England.

Even in the best houses, when I was a young man, the dinners were wonderfully solid, hot, and stimulating. The *menu* of a grand dinner was thus composed: — Mulligatawny and turtle soups were the first dishes placed before you; a little lower, the eye met with the familiar salmon at one end of the table, and the turbot, surrounded by smelts, at the other. The first course was sure to be followed by a saddle of mutton or a piece of roast beef; and then you could take your oath that fowls, tongue, and ham would as assuredly succeed as darkness after day.

Whilst these never-ending *pièces de résistance* were occupying the table, what were called French dishes were, for custom's sake, added to the solid abundance. The French, or side dishes, consisted of very mild but very abortive attempts at Continental cooking; and I have always observed that they met with the neglect and contempt that they merited. The universally-adored and ever-popular boiled potato, produced at the very earliest period of the dinner, was eaten with everything, up to the moment when sweets appeared. Our vegetables, the best in the world, were never honoured by an accompanying sauce, and generally came to the table cold. A prime difficulty to overcome was the placing on your fork, and finally in your mouth, some half-dozen different eatables which occupied your plate at the same time. For example, your plate would contain, say, a slice of turkey, a piece of stuffing, a sausage, pickles, a slice of tongue, cauliflower, and potatoes. According to habit and custom, a judicious and careful selection from this little bazaar of good things was to be made, with an endeavour to place a portion of each in your mouth at the same moment. In fact, it appeared to me that we used to do all our compound cookery between our jaws.

The dessert, — generally ordered at Messrs. Grange's, or at Owen's, in Bond Street, — if for a dozen people, would cost at least as many pounds.[8]

Visitor Prince Pückler-Muskau was not in the least enchanted with the service at English dinner tables. He complained, after the soup was removed and all the covers were taken off, that every one helped himself to the dish in front of him and offered it to his neighbors. Delicacies residing elsewhere had to be specially requested. He was always relieved when he chanced on an elegant household that had taken to its bosom the much more convenient Continental custom of sending footmen around with the dishes.

Dining at fashionable English tables meant vast quantities of food. One cookbook contained a diagram of an English dinner table laid out for the second course which featured twenty-five dishes. Roasted hare sat at the bottom of the table and roast pheasant was at the top. In the table's middle sat a pudding covered with a silver web. The side dishes consisted of a bewildering quantity of flavors and aromas. They were pistach cream, rocky island, fish mottoes, pea chick with asparagus, floating island, burnt cream, roast woodcock, snipes in savoury jelly, collared pig, macaroni, stewed mushrooms, and potted lamprey to name a few of the treats offered. And this was only one course! To accommodate these massive meals, Town houses usually had large dining tables which had sections that could be removed or increased as necessary to accommodate dinner guests.

The parade of wines that accompanied this multitude of food was astounding. Captain Gronow remarked:

A perpetual thirst seemed to come over people, both men and women, as soon as they had tasted their soup; as from that moment everybody was taking wine with everybody else till the close of the dinner; and such wine as produced that class of cordiality which eloquently wanders into stupefaction.

Gronow also stated that "wines were chiefly port, sherry, and hock; claret, and even Burgundy, being then designated poor, thin, washy stuff.[9]

Ratafia was popular with the ladies. The drink was based on the essence of bitter almonds (ratafia) and flavored with kernels of various fruits such as apricots, plums, or peaches.

Guests appreciated punches of various sorts. Negus and arrack or "rack" punch were frequently seen at Regency parties. Negus, named after English Colonel Francis Negus, was a concoction of wine, hot water, sugar, lemon juice, and nutmeg. Arrack was an alcoholic beverage of the East distilled from the juice of the coconut palm and was the chief ingredient in "rack" punch.

One special punch that titillated Regency palates was named especially for Prinny — Regent's Punch. The punch's alcoholic content came from numerous bottles of spirits: two bottles of Madeira, three of champagne, one of Curacao and hock, one pint of rum, and one quart of brandy. Four pounds of oranges, lemons, and raisins sweetened with sugar candy flavored two bottles of seltzer water which was added to the mix. The "receipt" recommended green tea to dilute the concoction rather than brandy.

All this gluttony and excessive drinking led to a high incidence of gout, "and the necessity of every one making the pillbox their constant bedroom companion."[10] Another direct result were the plentitude of stout aging dandies that paraded through Regency London. The corpulent Prince Regent was a prime example of too much of a good thing. Lord Folkestone commented in 1818 that the Prince's belly all but touched his knees since he had let it loose!

After the typical lengthy multi-course meal, ladies departed the dining room and left the gentlemen to an hour or two of heavy drinking. The gentlemen, now rather well to live from imbibing alcoholic beverages, rejoined the ladies who had been conversing among themselves in the drawing room. To entertain each other, they might share the latest *on-dit* with the company, play cards, or listen to one of their number perform musically.

Sometimes the gentlemen never appeared! It was not unknown for fashionable beaus to drink each other under the table after dinner. One special piece of furniture created to aid these multi-bottle fellows was the drinking table. They were designed specifically to hold bottles in concealed cavities and had spaces hollowed out in which a fellow's glass was set. The dining room sideboard served double duty. Designed for storing and serving, they were usually wide chests of drawers with cupboard space beneath for convenience. This cupboard space had been known to conceal chamber pots that were passed around with the bottles of port!

One hopes, after dinner, drinking, and conversation in the drawing room, that the reasonably sober guests made their way home, but before they left Captain Gronow related an essential practice:

> There was another custom in my young days which has luckily fallen into disuse. If one dined at any of the great houses in London, it was considered absolutely necessary to give a guinea to the butler on leaving the house. One hundred and thirty years ago this very bad habit (as I always considered it) prevailed to an even greater extent; for Pope the poet, whenever he dined with the Dukes of Montagu, finding that he had to give five guineas to the numerous servants at Montagu House, told the Duke that he could not dine with him in future unless his grace sent him five guineas to distribute among his myrmidons. The Duke, an easy, good-natured man, used ever after, on sending an invitation to the great poet, to enclose at the same time an

order for the tribute-money: he preferred doing this to breaking through a custom which had grown to be looked upon by servants as a right, and the abolition of which they would have considered as a heavy grievance.[11]

Cookbooks

To assist the Regency chef or cook there were several popular cookbooks. They included:

The Art of Cookery Made Plain and Easy which far exceeds anything yet published, by a Lady.
This cookbook published in 1747 remained a bestseller for over one hundred years. The author, Hannah Glasse, made the claim that the tome exceeded anything published to date; and generations of cooks seemed to agree with her.

She deplored the extravagant French sauces that used excessive amounts of butter and eggs and considered such extremes much too expensive. In her view a cook who used six pounds of butter to fry twelve eggs when half a pound per egg was sufficient was clearly a wastrel.

A typical Mrs. Glasse recipe for Chicken Pye included the following ingredients: anchovy with the liquor, sewet, veal, egg, lemon rind, bread, water, thyme, pepper, salt, and of course the chicken!

There was some controversy that there was no "Mrs. Glasse," but a polite invention of the cookbook's publisher and real author, Mr. John Hill.

The London Art of Cookery, and Housekeeper's Complete Assistant.
Published in 1783, John Farley, of the London Tavern, authored this cookbook. His recipe for Portugal Cakes reflected a characteristic "receipt" of the period—lavish ingredients with little attention to quantity of them. His assemblage of foodstuffs called for currants, rosewater, butter, flour, eggs, sugar, bread, and sack.

The Experienced English Housekeeper, for the Use and Ease of Ladies, Housekeepers, Cooks, etc., Written Purely from Practice.

First published in 1769, this explicit, practical cookbook had been through thirteen editions by 1806. The remarkable authoress, Mrs. Elizabeth Raffald, had been a housekeeper for fifteen years in country houses. In Manchester she opened her own confectioner's shop on Fennel Street, which also contained her registry office, one of the first employment agencies. She eventually established a full service catering business that featured all sorts of food and raised, according to one authority, sixteen daughters!

Her cookbook contained over 800 of her very own recipes. It was considered an excellent source of the best English cookery.

A New System of Domestic Cookery ... "by a Lady"

This bestselling cookbook was published in 1808 and its author was Maria Rundell, the widow of one of the partners of the famous jewelers. Notable among her "receipts" is the increasing use of unusual ingredients, which reflected the growing scope of British empire and influence.

Aspicius Redivivus, or *The Cook's Oracle*

This eccentric, amusing "receipt" book by William Kitchiner was published in 1817. It was the first cookbook to employ the use of quantity measurements of ingredients. Its author was an egocentric epicure with a variety of interests. *The Cook's Oracle* had the distinction of including only recipes of dishes the author had eaten. He felt quantity measurement was essential. He abhorred slapdash directions.

Livelihoods

The lavish lifestyles of the *beau monde* demanded

deep pockets. The sheer effort of manning and maintaining a London house was a tremendous financial drain. Expensive amusements also took a fearful toll on a gentleman's purse. In legal terms a gentleman was a man who had no occupation. A Regency gentleman of the *haut ton* needed about £10,000 a year to set himself up properly in Town and the country. His income properly came from his family's landholdings. Money smelling of the shop contaminated his good name, unless he had improved his fortunes by marrying a wealthy merchant's daughter.

But ten thousand a year would not cover ruinously expensive pursuits that struck many a gentleman's fancy and humbled his fortune. No amount of the ready could satisfy hardened Regency gamesters. Huge gambling losses combined with years of unpaid tradesmen's bills devastated many great fortunes on the day of reckoning.

Combined with this profligacy, a gentleman of the first consequence proved his mettle by the height of his indifference to filthy lucre. This devil-may-care attitude compounded the problems of reckless expenditure. Fashionable fellows who never counted the cost of anything lived on the edge of disaster.

Battling with this heedless pursuit of pleasure and cultivated indifference to money matters was his inbred paternalistic interest for those who tenanted his lands and entered his service. Proper stewardship meant a well-fed, prosperous countryside and fatter profit for his lordship's pocket. Some men of title and property did seek worthy occupations. They turned their backs on a life filled only with frivolous pursuits. Land magnates like Coke of Norfolk actively implemented and introduced new agricultural improvements.

Even wealthy spoiled gentlemen recognized that the land was the life's blood of their lifestyle. Reckless fellows forgot this fact at their peril!

The ranks of government and political life at every level abounded with landed gentlemen. The men of the *ton* actively sought to increase their prestige with new honors.

Government appointments were often extremely lucrative!
Heads of families and their eldest sons were the chief
recipients of glittering, profitable government appointments.
The eleven highly paid commissioners for the affairs of
India in 1820 were all titled heads of families or their
heirs.

Families with Irish titles vied for the chance to
advance into Great Britain's peerage. Irish titles were not
at all the thing! The Marchioness of Londonderry was in
transports when her husband, an Irish peer, was created
Earl Vane and Viscount Seaham of Wynyard and Seaham in
County Durham in 1823.

A life cushioned by a substantial yearly income also
allowed many the luxury of pursuing highly specialized
interests. Many gentleman actively patronized the arts and
became gifted amateurs themselves. Others collected
fabulous pieces of art that later became the basis of Great
Britain's art museums. Leisure time allowed those
gentlemen with an intellectual bent to dabble in literary or
scientific research.

Others pursued a life dedicated to sport. Their world
centered on the hunt, the ring, the racetrack, the shooting
range, the fencing parlor, cricket fields, and any other
playing field that suited their fancy. Some turned
exclusively to fashionable folly and followed the *ton* to
Town, to Brighton, and back to Town again finding
pleasure in the cut of their coat or devilish wit.

Most of all, the course they chose needed to respond
quickly to their greatest asset—their families influence and
patronage. Three institutions responded beautifully to
patronage: the army, the navy, and the church.

The lot of younger boy children who, unlike their
eldest brother, would not inherit their father's titles and
estates, could be exceedingly tiresome. Rarely did a
younger son have more than limited resources at his
command. It was imperative that they pursue careers to
supplement their meager incomes. This career should be
neither too arduous or demanding. They also wanted to
keep some access to the sporting life and better society.

Eminent families ruthlessly pulled strings to insure their sons bought into fashionable army regiments. To help preserve young men's exquisite sensibilities, families also exerted their influence to help them avoid service in dreaded India. Fellows with pockets to let and minimal connections served in line regiments and saw service with the working army during long stretches of hardship duty. Officers who anticipated promotion on merit grew grey waiting for a vacancy.

Brummell belonged to the dandified 10th Hussars. Known as the fashionable "Blues," the regiment teemed with the sons of dukes and earls during the 1790s — Charles Ker, son of the Duke of Roxburgh, sons of the Duke of Rutland, and the sons of Earls Darnley and Scarborough. Their Colonel-in-Chief was Prinny himself. They travelled with their thoroughbreds and curricles as they followed the Prince from Brighton to London and back again. The daily regime of the Hussars was none too arduous. They paraded at one o'clock, ceased imbibing about five, dined, and then adjourned to the theater. An independent income was essential to support the life style of a fashionable regiment.

Though influence could be wielded to keep officers at home in prime style, ambitious younger sons like Arthur Wellesley seized the opportunity and pursued his military career with all the ardor and vigor he possessed. The Napoleonic wars would offer young men a proving ground far superior to the hunting field.

Naval careers demanded more competence and experience. Officers often came from the families of gentlemen of modest means. Nelson was a poor parson's son.

Young boys were sent to sea at a young age to master seamanship and learn conduct befitting an officer. Noble connection and a private income could be very helpful.

The church reeked with patronage. Over 7,000 livings out of 11,342 in England and Wales were gifts to be distributed by aristocrats and gentry. Individuals with address and the right connections milked the system unmercifully. They amassed several livings, and as absentee vicars employed sniveling curates at a very small wage. The vicar pocketed the bulk of the living which could equal a hundred pounds or more.

Some unfortunate families did not have the means or influence to help their younger sons. Careers in the civil service, the law, or medicine would not be above these young men's touch.

The easiest way for a penniless, patronageless gentlemen to make his way in the world was to cast his eye over the marriage mart. Wealthy cits clamored for titled young fellows to wed their daughters, and many beaus answered the siren call of lucrative marriage settlements.

Health, Medicine, Disease, and Death

Regency Medical Care

Good health and a stolid constitution were attributes to cherish in Regency England. Dangers lurked around every corner! The dwellings of rich and poor bred every sort of vile germ. Inadequate drainage in even the grandest house resulted in many strange and noxious fevers, among them was dreaded, deadly typhoid. Treatments for wounds meant administering doctors who did not understand the simplest hygiene. Wounds often became infected, festered, and discharged loathsome pus.

Anesthesia awaited discovery. Gruelling, painful operations were performed on patients dosed with laudanum or spirits. If God were merciful, the patient lost consciousness. The uncleanliness of rusty knives and dirty hands plus poor methods of controlling bleeding led to numerous fatalities.

Prescribed treatments for every type of disorder often consisted of violent attacks on the patient's already weakened body. Doctors purged, blistered, and induced vomiting with pious impunity. Bloodletting or "leeching" was particularly popular. Every proper medical man knew letting out blood also let out the disease. Physicians smugly performed "cupping" with silver bleeding bowls and carefully chosen lancets produced from specially designed pocket carrying cases. They preferred cutting open a vein in the arm or hand made prominent by a skillfully applied tourniquet. Plump, sleek leeches applied to various portions of the patient's body were also used in the procedure.

Deliberate blistering with caustic agents applied directly to affected areas was appropriate therapy for drawing out infection. Clysters or enemas enhanced this blistering technique to achieve maximum benefit for the suffering patient. The Duchess of Devonshire had typical ophthalmic surgery. The inflamed left eye had developed a large swelling on her face. First, blood was drawn off the swelling. Then, leeches were applied to her left eyeball. The resulting corneal ulcer burst and destroyed her eyesight. A truly horrible operation followed. Post-operative treatment included neck blistering. Needless to say, the Duchess was never quite the same again.

The Duke of Wellington nicely summed up nineteenth-century attitudes to the medical profession.

> All doctors are more or less *Quacks*! ... and what they talk is neither more nor less than *nonsense & stuff*....[12]

Medical treatment advanced in some respects. Middlesex Hospital led the way about 1808 with a great many improvements: new large windows to admit light and increase ventilation, one patient per bed, clean attendants, and more privacy.

Edward Jenner's miraculous new treatment called vaccination offered new hope for people who lived in an age where smallpox scarring was an accepted facial feature. This fearsome disease had a mortality rate of one in four. Survivors were often horribly disfigured.

Inoculation had been known and used prior to Jenner, but the process had a high mortality rate using a smallpox vaccine. Jenner used controlled experiments to prove the validity of the widespread country wisdom that cowpox victims did not get smallpox; cowpox was a much milder disease. The first vital test of his theory was made in 1796. His successful results of this safer inoculation was first published in 1798.

After a brief period of ridicule by the medical community, the public and medical profession embraced "vaccination" wholeheartedly. In 1806, the unheard of happened! London went one whole summer without a single reported smallpox case.

Another researcher William Withering investigated the properties of foxglove, an old folk remedy. His experiments revealed digitalis, a foxglove derivative, as an effective treatment for heart disease.

Practicing along side Jenner and his more respectable colleagues were a plethora of quacks. Foremost among Europe's brotherhood of dubious healers was Luigi Galvani who discovered the results of an electrical charge on humans. Experiments on the legs of frogs in which a electrical current caused muscles to contract was the foundation of the idea of "animal electricity." The electrical charge applied to human patients was hailed as a cure-all. *The Times* reported it as a restorative in cases of suffocation and drowning.

For suffering souls who chose to doctor their own ailments, there were a multitude of powders, pills, and tinctures. Advertisements guaranteed cures for every symptom, ache, and pain known to man or woman.

One of these remedies, Burridge's Specific for the Rheumatic Gout and Rheumatism, sold for eleven shillings per bottle. Another, advertised for married ladies in particular, was Turner's Imperial Lotion for the cure of "inflamed Breasts of Lying-in Women, Sore or Ulcerated Nipples ... the Piles, Chilblains, Scalds...." etc., etc.[13] This wonder lotion could be had for only 4s. 6d. at Allan's, No. 76, Oxford Street opposite the Pantheon.

Folk medicine had a place in the Regency, too. A frog tied to one's neck was reported to cure nosebleeds. Pills made of cobwebs were used to treat asthma and consumption. Hog's dung was applied to bleeding wounds. The bleeding did stop, but the unfortunate sufferer contracted tetanus as a rule. Voluminous tomes on home remedies detailed even more horrifying treatments!

Dental Health

One of the most common and troublesome complaints was the toothache. A host of trades engaged in the business of extracting teeth and treating various tooth-related ailments. Apothecaries boasted immense lines of products to preserve teeth, eliminate bad breath, and cosmetically enhance the "ivories" appearance.

Toothdrawers, though dreaded and despised, were unconcerned with their unpopularity. The profession generated lucrative fees. The Prince Regent's dentist Charles Dumergue earned 100 guineas annually just from his royal customer.

Treatment sometimes involved cutting away the decay and filling the tooth with mercury-silver compound, though fillings were still rare. Most often, patients had the offending tooth extracted.

One replacement treatment involved plugging the cavity left in the gum with a healthy tooth. Poor, penniless souls often sold all their healthy teeth as replacements. Their extracted teeth then filled the holes in wealthier mouths.

Grave robbers also supplied teeth. They received £30 for a full set. Dealers made hefty sums selling "Waterloo teeth," which were shipped from the continent after the Napoleonic Wars.

Sets of false teeth fitted poorly and served only cosmetic purposes. Unwieldy dentures impaired speech and prohibited mastication. Mrs. Fitzherbert was universally hailed as a fine looking woman except for her ugly mouth

which housed a set of ill-made dentures.   Sound   teeth
were a blessing no Englishman or woman took for granted!

Death and Mourning

Mourning etiquette embraced a wide circle of family
and all the household servants in Regency England. The
greater the rank or importance of the deceased the more
elaborate the display. Important personages went to their
eternal rest with a lengthy funeral cortège which included
an elaborate procession of hearse, mourners, and hired
mutes. The length of the somber procession was propor-
tional to the importance and wealth of the mourned one's
friends, family, and associates.
     Deep mourning required clothes in dark or black
colors.   There should be a total absence of shine in the
material or on the accessories.   Ladies chose crape and
bombazine, a blend of wool and silk, because of their
supreme dullness. Clothes were refurbished by both sexes
and kept in readiness. Gentleman mourners removed shiny
gilt buttons and buckles from their clothing. They also
might outfit themselves in special mourning cloaks of black
to match the somberness of the occasion.
     American envoy Richard Rush attended the 1820
funeral of Mr. Benjamin West, artist and president of the
Royal Academy. He described it in his diary:

> Between forty and fifty mourning-coaches, the
> horses of each having covers of black velvet
> over them, made part of the train. There were
> the usual ceremonies in other respects of a
> funeral of this description in London; such as
> marshal-men, cloak-men on horseback, mutes,
> and pages. The hearse was drawn by six horses
> covered with black velvet; and the mourning
> coaches being also entirely black as well as the
> horses, the harness, and all the feathers and
> plumes, gave a solemn air to this pomp for the

dead. The effect of the whole was heightened as the corpse was slowly borne into the immense Cathedral of St. Paul's, pronounced the most imposing edifice for size and grandeur reared in Europe by Protestant hands.

Mr. West being a native of my country, I was invited by the Council and officers of the Royal Academy to the funeral as a pall-bearer, and attended in that capacity. The other pall-bearers were, the Earl of Aberdeen, Sir William Scott, Sir George Beaumont, General Phipps, the Honourable Augustus Phipps, Sir Thomas Baring, and Sir Robert Wilson. When the body reached the choir, the bier was set down and an anthem sung. It was then conveyed to the vault door, attended by the pall-bearers and mourners, and interred next to that of Sir Joshua Reynolds, the funeral church service being performed at the perforated brass-plate under the centre of the dome. The chief officiating clergyman was the Reverend Gerald Wellesley, brother of the Duke of Wellington. Altogether the scene was of much solemnity, and attested the honors paid by this distinguished Society to departed genius. Large and distinguished portions of the Society of London responded to the feeling which dictated them as was manifested by the private carriages belonging to the nobility and others seen in the procession, which exceeded the mourning-coaches in number.

Two of the mourning-coaches were appropriated to the pall-bearers. The one in which I was, conveyed also the Earl of Aberdeen, Sir William Scott, and General Phipps. The first, besides his eminence as a statesman, is distinguished by attainments in the arts; a testimonial of which is, his classical Treatise on Architecture, prefixed to an edition of Vitruvius, written during or after his travels in Greece.

> The slow pace of the procession until we arrived
> at the Cathedral was favorable to quiet
> conversation. The crowd along the Strand, and
> on passing Temple Bar, was very great.[14]

Three years previously the whole nation had plunged
into mourning. Princess Charlotte's death in childbed in
November 1817, devastated England. The court wallowed in
an orgy of mourning which foretold the excesses to come
in Queen Victoria's reign. Letter writers even sealed their
epistles with somber black wax.

The Lord Chamberlain, ordering court mourning for
Her Royal Highness Princess Charlotte, decreed that ladies
were to wear black bombazines and muslins accompanied by
crape accessories. Gentlemen were instructed to appear in
plain cravats, black cloth, and black accouterments down to
shoe buckles. Several fashion plate magazines featured
special mourning styles in the current mode. Ackermann's
Repository of Arts published a plethora of fashion plates to
cover every event in a mourning lady's day. Somber black
walking, evening, and carriage dresses of dull fabrics
graced its pages. Ladies in court circles needed a complete
wardrobe of suitable mourning gear made up!

After deepest mourning was over, only the most placid
of socializing was acceptable. The court did not indulge in
elaborate entertainments for many weeks. Two months
after Charlotte's death deepest mourning was declared at
an end, and court circles went into half-mourning. Ladies
put on black silk with white accessories such as gloves,
necklaces, and earrings. Grey for dresses and gentlemen's
coats became an acceptable color for "undress" or informal
wear.

The next stage of mourning signaled the return of
velvet as acceptable dress stuff. Colored ribbons, fans,
and tippets reappeared. White, gold, and silver materials
trimmed with black ribbons were also acceptable wear.
Men donned silver and gold brocaded waistcoats to relieve
the somber black of their clothes.

The first Drawing-room after the end of official

mourning found the ladies of the court arrayed in all the hues of the rainbow. As one observer described the scene, it was like spring had bursted out!

NOTES TO CHAPTER VI

1. Rees Howell Gronow, *The Reminiscences and Recollections of Captain Gronow*, 2:255-256.

2. Gronow, *Reminiscences and Recollections*, 1:301.

3. Princess Marie Von Liechtenstein, *Holland House*, 2:74-75.

4. Ibid., 1:158.

5. Gronow, *Reminiscences and Recollections*, 1:54-55.

6. *The Times*, July 1, 1813.

7. Mary Russell Mitford, *Our Village*, 1:261.

8. Gronow, *Reminiscences and Recollections*, 1:37-38.

9. Ibid., 1:38.

10. Ibid.

11. Ibid., 1:274-275.

12. Elizabeth Longford, *Wellington: Pillar of State*, p. 101.

13. *Le Beau Monde*, October 1807.

14. Richard Rush, *A Residence at the Court of London*, 1:277-279.

Chapter VII

THE REST OF THE YEAR

As the pleasures of Town life dissipated in late June or early July and the glittering social season ended, fashionable personages looked to other places and pursuits to relieve their tiresome *ennui.* Much of the landed aristocracy, core of the Polite World, spent most of the year settled on country estates. The Season, sometimes agreeable, always expensive, existed to make matches for offspring and provide amusement after dull winter months. Real life was the country way. To enliven their bucolic abodes, country dwellers hosted elaborate house parties, hunted game of every description fast and furiously, managed and mismanaged their agricultural enterprises, and celebrated life's major events with resplendent plentitude.

Brighton and its royal patron Prinny tempted many jaded senses to frolic at the seaside in the summer. Bath, though no longer as fashionable an inland spa as in Beau Nash's time, offered genteel entertainments and healthful waters. Travel abroad, though severely disrupted during Napoleon's reign, lured many to the continent after the Restoration, and even more after Waterloo.

Whatever pursuits put tonnish ladies and gentlemen in transports, London was sadly bereft of good company after the Season ended. The *beau monde* pursued their pleasures elsewhere.

Life in the Country

Landed noblemen and gentlemen whiled away their sojourn in the provinces by attending to multitudinous responsibilities and indulging in assorted pastimes.

Large landholders of lofty lineage fulfilled duties in country and local affairs. They were expected to be ready to offer advice and assistance in all aspects of local life in addition to administering their own estates and keeping watchful eyes on supervisory personnel.

Lady Caroline Stuart Wortley was thoroughly exasperated with her busy mate. She complained that her husband never stayed at home, but was off every day to one place or another. She lamented that his convictions kept him endlessly engaged at dinners and meetings all over the countryside. In short, he was naught but a foot ball tugged to and fro by his conscience and good nature. Their neighbors certainly never did their share, and her poor husband did their part plus his too. It greatly provoked the good lady to see her husband always so weary.

Women, too, were kept busy tending to family and household affairs. They oversaw the children (large families were common), the household servants, and spread out their maternal interest over the estate to encompass the tenantry.

A prosperous country estate typically included a residence of sufficient size to suit a gentleman with attendant parkland, gardens, stables, and paddocks. Radiating out of this center was a large agrarian business that consisted of a home farm and numerous tenanted farms and cottages. Revenues from agricultural enterprises and rents formed the backbone of a gentleman's financial well-being.

Land magnates possessed many country estates often in several different counties. They removed themselves from one household to the next like a medieval royal progression. Their stately march might signify the need for more and better game to improve sport. A smaller country house with its simpler life could also act as an escape from a stilted formal household. Ladies were known to breathe a sign of relief if their husbands didn't inherit another house.

To keep establishments running smoothly, a veritable troop of servants populated the house and countryside. Lord Fitzwilliam had 70 indoor servants at Wentworth Woodhouse. Blenheim employed 180 indoor and outside servants. Many of the indoor servants travelled with the master and the family as they removed from house to house. Milord had no intention of leaving thirty or forty servants idle and eating their heads off! The servants who waited on nature rather than their masters remained on their respective estates.

The land steward and/or the baliff stayed firmly fixed. They managed the agricultural enterprise at the home farm and in park land. They also supervised the tenantry, leased land, collected rents, and kept accounts of expenses. Landlords depended on worthy educated men to exercise a stewardship that showed a profit each year.

Supervised by the land steward were the parkkeeper, gamekeeper, gardener, and their subordinates. Gamekeepers protected the wildlife on the estate from poachers. They required knowledge of game laws and the strength to enforce them. Fields and woods were patrolled vigilantly. The parkkeeper cared for the deer. Keeping careful count, he protected the deer from poachers and repaired walls and fences. The gardener nurtured the landscape. He and his minions worked in flower beds, kitchen gardens, hotbeds, orangeries, and greenhouses. The mania for landscaping assured him much occupation in laying out walkways, placing urns and benches in propitious places, and constructing waterworks.

The stables, too, kept some staff though the head coachman and many of his underlings journeyed with the family. The dairymaids also continued to ply their trade. Cows must be milked, butter and cream made, and the excess sold at market.

Life continued on the estate with or without its owner, but practical business measures demanded that responsible landowners keep a close eye on their supervisory personnel. Unwise, self-absorbed Town beaus caught up in fashionable extravagance were poor stewards. They were not only cheated but, by their neglect, victimized their tenants. The whole countryside suffered! The best gentlemen landowners with an eye to increase profits sought out advanced methods of agricultural science to improve production. Coke of Holkham and the 5th Duke of Bedford were among many forward-thinking fellows who experimented successfully.

A variety of new methods improved farming. Four-course rotation increased fodder production. More fodder meant larger livestock herds. Coke of Holkham produced rich manure from stall-fed cattle, which, in turn, increased the crop yield. Improvements like these could double one's income. The community was also well served as the small farmer learned from Milord's success and, in turn, increased his production.

As diligent landlords went about their concerns, country households had access to good society. Provincial towns had balls, assemblies, and race meetings. The country houses around York always filled up with visitors as numerous parties arrived to view the races. Travellers of acceptable birth and connections were always welcome to break their journey at country houses on their route. Even if visitors were unknown to the residents, they were allowed to view notable houses. Housekeepers and butlers pocketed tidy sums from vails obligingly proffered by well-heeled sightseers.

Neither abundant duties on one's estate in the country, nor occasional visitors could satisfactorily fill one's time. Provincial assemblies attended by the neighborhood could be decidedly tiresome. Landowners of the first consequence looked to their fashionable friends to relieve humdrum days in the country. Why not enliven bucolic boredom with a house party?

The Country House Party

House parties could last a few days, a fortnight, or

many weeks. The host and hostess invited, they hoped, agreeable guests, though social obligations often resulted in odd mixtures of folk. The size of the party varied according to the size of the house and the event it could be planned around. A ducal heir's christening might boast hundreds of attendees as opposed to a handful of guests gracing family gatherings.

A typical house party revolved around a leisurely schedule that deferred to a loose timetable of meals. The day started with an immense breakfast. Informally served in the breakfast room, guests helped themselves to chocolate, hot bread, honey, cold bread, and a variety of meats, fowl, fish and egg dishes. Guests came at their own pace beginning about 10 A.M. Larger house parties clattered with the constant noisy comings and goings of hungry guests. Ladies, however, often kept to their bed chambers or dressing rooms and breakfasted there. Yesterday's *Morning Post* and *Gazette* usually arrived with the post. Guests often perused the papers and letters as they munched their way through a hardy repast.

The largest and most formal meal of the day was dinner. Served as early as 4 P.M., if the household kept country hours, the entire company retired to their rooms to change into more formal attire. Often a gong sounded thirty minutes before dinner to alert the guests, with another sounding when dinner was served. Everyone assembled dressed in evening clothes in the drawing room. Paired by importance, the ladies and gentlemen advanced to the dining room. The highest ranking male guest squired his hostess. The host did his duty with the highest ranking female. Others followed by precedence. Poor relations and guests of small consequence trailed at the end of the procession.

Country living also meant excellent food such as fresh butter, luscious cream, and all sorts of bounty from gardens on the estate. The wealthiest hosts impressed their guests with pineapples, specially nurtured in their greenhouses.

Elegant households used all the family's grandiose

plate. The grandest houses had dutiful footmen positioned behind each diner. As in Town, ladies withdrew to the drawing room and left the gentlemen to their port after dinner. The evening descended into genteel entertainments after the male and female contingents rejoined. Before retiring, a late supper was served between ten and twelve with times varying from household to household.

If dinner was served at later Town hours of six, seven, or even later, servants laid on nuncheon or luncheon to fill in the long gap between the morning and evening meal. The midday meal boasted informality and mostly female patrons. The gentlemen in the party often availed themselves of outdoor entertainments during fine days.

Men and women pursued many amusements together and apart. During the day gentlemen tested their mettle as crack shots as they hunted hare and fowl or practiced on shooting ranges. An exceptional stream might also lure men to its banks to fish. Ladies spent their time gossiping among themselves or drove around the neighborhood with their hostess to pay calls.

All sorts of outings were planned to take advantage of pleasant weather, from informal morning rides to elaborate *al fresco* meals at the local ruins. Visitors tramped diligently through gardens and parkland. Young ladies formed sketching expeditions and lugged along their pads and watercolors to immortalize the countryside. They hoped to commandeer the gentlemen to tote their supplies and abandon their game of battledore or shuttlecock. Practical young ladies intent on admiring nature's beauties discarded flimsy, fashionable sandals for sturdy half boots to avoid unhappy consequences.

The rage for amateur theatrics kept guests amused, too. Many large estates kept private theaters or rigged up a special stage for productions. Lord Barrymore built a most elegant little theatre at Wargrave in 1788 for just that purpose. Truly considerate hosts imported professional talent to bolster the sometimes meager skills of their guests.

On rainy days, guests retired to the library to read and converse. Gentlemen tried their luck at billiard tables, often making wagers to pique their interest. Visitors seeking pleasures in even the simplest things might play at crossquestions or jackstraws, popular children's games.

Inclement weather also signaled a chance to retire from the company and communicate by letter with acquaintances and family still in Town, at fashionable resorts, or at other country estates. The feathers of geese, turkeys, peacocks, and other fowl supplied the quills that made up writing instruments. A pen knife sharpened quill points after each use. If the host or one of the guests was a Member of Parliament, he could frank the letter, otherwise the recipient paid dearly to read the epistle. In 1812, there was a fourpenny charge for the typical letter consisting of one large sheet of paper folded several times and sealed with wax. This charge transported the epistle to a correspondent only 15 miles distant or less. Greater distances coupled with weight increased the price. Cheeseparing correspondents "crossed" their letters, i.e., lines were written top to bottom, then the page was turned sideways and lines were written top to bottom, perpendicular to the already inscribed lines. Verbose writers even crossed the page once more, diagonally! Reading crossed and recrossed prose presented a puzzling challenge to confused letter recipients.

Topping any guest's list of worthy things-to-do was touring the noble establishment itself. Visitors dutifully filed past generations of portraits chronicling family history. A young miss, specifically invited as matchmaking fodder, merited intense extra instruction on the family heritage.

Magnificent libraries graced many country houses. Thousands of tomes crammed on shelves represented the collection of generations of bibliophiles. These comfortable relaxed rooms proved suitable retreats on rainy days. The library often housed game tables, billiard tables, and musical instruments. They were a natural place for house guests to congregate.

The neighborhood hosted many entertainments to amuse visitors, as well as providing ample numbers of bodies to fill out the guest list for dinner parties and balls at the host's country house. Local hostesses vied with each other to entertain the lord of the manor and his friends with "Venetian" breakfasts, dancing parties, and card parties. Cards in the countryside were dull work though—chicken-whist featuring low-stakes and poor play.

Public days with invitations in the hundreds were expected by the neighborhood. One of the outstanding public days in Yorkshire was at Lord Fitzwilliam's Wentworth Woodhouse. They were usually held once a week. If one's name appeared on the list compiled by Lord Fitzwilliam, one could dine and bring friends to share the feast in the overflowing dining room at Wentworth on those public days.

Besides relieving *ennui* and promoting suitable matches among the young folk, country house parties celebrated the important milestones in life; birth, christenings, coming of age, and marriage.

The birth of an heir caused much rejoicing at the great house and surrounding countryside. Castle dwellers fired off cannons to mark the event. Landlords hosted great dinners for the tenantry. Church bells rang out to celebrate the news. Bells sounded in the whole county for very important families. The aftermath of a birth signaled the gathering of the far-flung family to celebrate baptism, and then, several months later the christening of the infant. Often relatives in the church, perhaps the younger sons of a previous generation, performed the religious ceremony before a gathering of house guests.

The Duke of Rutland spared nothing to celebrate his heir's christening in 1814. The baby Marquis of Granby had no less than Prinny and the Duke of York as his god-fathers. The Archbishop of Canterbury presided over the ceremony. The baby's grandmother, Dowager Duchess of Rutland, stood in as the Queen's representative as god-mother.

The Duke's spectacle began with a 21-gun salute to

both Prinny and the Duke on their arrival. After the solemn ceremony, the numerous guests settled down to stuff themselves and toast their host, their prince, and the heir far into the night. Prinny, overcome by the lavish displays of respect and admiration, showed his gracious best. He thoughtfully dressed in the Belvoir uniform of scarlet and buff to honor his host.

The tenants and respectable people of lower stations also shared in the lavish hospitality. Mr. Douglas, the Duke's butler, presided over an oval cistern that contained over 50 gallons of strong punch. The gracious Duchess flung open the grand rooms for inspection and similarly put the young Marquis on display.

The 200-plus guests at Belvoir celebrated for days. The party broke up January 7 as the replete Prince Regent left to visit the Earl of Winchilsea.

The tenantry always shared in their noble landlord's good fortune and celebrations. At Lady Buckingham's birthday dance in 1804 her guests laughingly danced with all the tenants, though there were complaints that the smell was beyond anything!

Belvoir Castle was also the site of one of the grandest coming of age celebrations that foreshadowed the lavish christening celebration in 1814. The 5th Duke of Rutland came of age in 1799 and hosted a series of splendid, costly festivities to celebrate his birthday. Months of preparation went into three days of continuous celebration. Over 18,000 bricks were laid by scores of specially hired workmen who built temporary buildings to house the entertainments. Domestic servants spent 11 days making up additional beds to accommodate the guests.

The quantity of food consumed put local suppliers in transports. Among the delicacies wolfed down by His Grace's guests were 112 sheep, 6 oxen, 23 turkeys, and 21 pigs. Libations imbibed included 46¼ gallons of brandy, 4 hogsheads of Lisbon wine, 23 gallons of rum, and several thousand gallons of beer. A baker worked 18 days to produce the required loaves. The cartloads of food and spectacular entertainment cost over £5,000. The young

Duke also spent another £4,500 to treat himself to a suitable assortment of presents.

Christmas, too, meant that it was time for enticing houseparties. Oatlands, reigned over by the jovial Duchess of York, offered many delights. The jolly Duchess gave presents! The German princess introduced the custom of gift giving among *haut ton* circles. It would be many years before the lower ranks of society would emulate her.

At Yuletide, the Duchess converted Oatlands's great dining room into a German fair. Booths stocked with the most delightful commodities lined the walls. In the center of the room stood a tree whose branches were lavishly loaded with cakes, gingerbread, oranges, and other confections. Presents which Town visitors had given the Duchess were displayed on one table and her presents to guests on another. She always insisted that her guests bring inexpensive token gifts rather than costly treats.

Servants dressed in their Sunday best also shared in the display and the Duchess's generosity. Even charity children dependant on her largess reaped the season's blessings. On the given signal, they raced to the loaded tree and stripped it of its delicacies in the blink of an eye.

Sport also drew the *ton* to the country houses. Beginning in November, the *battues* (hunts where beaters went before the hunter to flush game) started at Thomas Coke's Norfolk seat, Holkham Hall. Large parties took advantage of the excellent sport to be had here and elsewhere. Winter also signaled the start of foxhunting. Some sportsmen stayed with their local packs. Others toured the various hunting fields and rode with many different packs. Fashionable fribbles made for Melton country in Leicestershire and cadged hospitality from friends who owned snug little hunting boxes.

Other celebrations rejoiced in the fruitfulness of the countryside. The annual sheep shearing was the centerpiece of festivities designed to show off one's successful agricultural ventures. The 5th Duke of Bedford invited scores of guests to witness the Woburn Sheep

Shearing each year. He lavishly entertained visitors at breakfast, which was served at 9 A.M., then sent them on a farm tour and admonished them to admire the shearer's skills. Visitors then served as an appreciative audience for award giving and the adjourned to another hearty meal at 3 P.M.

American Richard Rush was invited to "Coke's Clipping" in 1819 and was mightily impressed with Holkham and its master.

> The occasion on which we were assembled, was called "The Sheep-shearing." It was the forty-third anniversary of this attractive festival; attractive even to Englishmen, accustomed as they are to agricultural beauty, and to fine old country homesteads, established and maintained throughout ages, in so many different parts of England. The term "Sheep-shearing," conveys, by itself, but a limited idea of what is witnessed at Holkham. The operations embrace every thing connected with agriculture in the broadest sense; such as, an inspection of all farms which make up the Holkham estate, with the modes of tillage practised on each for all varieties of crops; an exhibition of cattle, with the modes of feeding and keeping them; ploughing matches; haymaking; a display of agricultural implements, and modes of using them; the visiting of various out-buildings, stables, and so on, best adapted to good farming, and the rearing and care of horses and stock; with much more that I am unable to specify. Sheep-shearing there was, indeed, but it was only one item in this full round of practical agriculture. The whole lasted three days, occupying the morning of each, until dinner-time at about five o'clock. The shearing of sheep was the closing operation of the third day.
>   Such is the general scene, as far as agricul-

ture is concerned, which is its primary object. Mr. Coke explains to his guest and friends, all his processes and results. This is done without form, in conversation on his grounds, or at the dinner-table; and, even more impressively, on horseback.[1]

Rush stayed for a week and marveled at the hospitality.

The number of Mr. Coke's guests, meaning those lodged at his mansion, was, I believe, about fifty, comprehending those I have named and others, as I could scarcely know all in a visit of a week. But his friends and neighbours of the country of Norfolk, and other country gentlemen and visitors from parts of England farther off, arriving every morning after breakfast in carriages or on horseback during the continuance of the scene under invitations from Mr. Coke to be present at it and stay to dinner, amounted to about six hundred each day. On the second day I was informed that, including the home guests, covers were laid down for six hundred and fifty. All were comfortably accommodated, and fared sumptuously.[2]

Not all the guests were quite so enthralled with Mr. Coke's agricultural wonders. Mr. Rush noted:

The library, of many thousand volumes, is a treasure; and (shall I tell it?) *there*, on one of the days when I entered it during a short interval between the morning excursions and the dinner hour, did I catch stragglers of the home guests, *country* gentlemen too, who had not been out to the fields or farms at all, though they had come all the way to Holkham to attend the sheep-shearing.[3]

All house parties, whatever their *raison d'être*, must end. Some closed with the departure of the most important guest or because the visit had been scheduled as a set number of days, much like Rutland's coming of age celebration. Loosely arranged houseparties required ingenuity to prod guests who had overstayed their welcome. Clever hosts hinted vaguely about an outbreak of fever sweeping through the village or a case of smallpox among the servants. Cow-hearted visitors could be counted on to skulk to their rooms and oversee the rapid packing of bandboxes, portmanteaus, and trunks. Before the sun set, they clambered aboard their travelling carriages and headed down the post road at a fast clip.

Country Houses of Note

Belvoir Castle, Leicestershire

In 1801 the enormously wealthy 5th Duke of Rutland presided over numerous additions to the castle soon after he came of age. Architect James Wyatt turned the medieval pile into a gothic fantasy. When fire destroyed much of the interior in 1816, Wyatt's sons rushed to restore the original rooms.

The huge castle boasted a variety of styles. The saloon created by the 5th Duchess was in the rich, lush French style of Louis XIV. Even the gilded paneling on the wall had come from a chateau that once belonged to Madame de Maintenon. The entrance or guardroom was pure gothic and boasted a large collection of arms, armor, and other military accouterments. The Regent's Gallery dedicated to the Prince Regent exhibited a gilded classical flavor that was pure Regency.

Belvoir often hosted the Prince who visited during the christening celebration for the Duke's heir and to celebrate completion of the gallery that bore his name. Brummell was a great favorite of the Duchess. They often went sketching together on his visits. The Beau did heads, while the Duchess concentrated on landscapes.

Blenheim, Oxfordshire

The glorious Baroque palace built for the 1st Duke and Duchess of Marlbourough housed the reclusive unhospitable 4th Duke during most of the Regency. Chronicler Gronow recalled the Duke's oddities well.

> The Duke had been for some time a confirmed hypochondriac, and dreaded anything that could in any way ruffle the tranquil monotony of his existence. It is said that he remained for three years without pronouncing a single word, and was entering the fourth year of his silence when he was told one morning that Madame la Baronne de Staël, the authoress of *Corinne*, was on the point of arriving to pay him a visit. The Duke immediately recovered his speech and roared out, "Take me away — take me away!" to the utter astonishment of the circle around him, who all declared that nothing but the terror of this literary visitation could have put an end to this long and obstinate monomania.[4]

Not even Nelson was spared the odd turn of his grace's temper. On a visit in 1802 with his lady love, Emma, and her husband Sir William Hamilton, he was informed that the Duke would not receive them. The admiral toured the grounds with his party, but decidedly refused the proferred refreshments. The landscape they sulkily strolled through had been laid out by "Capability" Brown and featured a serpentine lake. Achille du Chêne had designed the majestic formal gardens.

Chatsworth, Derbyshire

Regency guests to Chatsworth saw the massive house that the 1st Duke of Devonshire had remodeled and restructured in the late seventeenth century. He transformed Bess of Hardwick's Elizabethan house into a splendid palace worthy of a ducal dynasty. Talman was his architect and the dithering Duke spent over twenty years on this house whose inspiration was Versailles.

The grounds owed their magnificence to the 4th Duke. "Capability" Brown designed the park, and Grillet, the French water engineer, planned the unique water delights in the style of Versailles. Among other lavish follies was a Thomas Archer designed Cascade House.

Visitors to this Baroque palace were treated to leisurely examinations of the excellent collection of drawings and paintings amassed by the 2nd Duke. Among these admiring guests were all the brightest stars of Whig society during the 5th Duke's reign. Beau Brummell was a favored guest of the Duchess. They wrote poetry together. Georgiana often gave the Beau special poems to put in his album of collected verse.

The "Bachelor" Duke or 6th Duke succeeded in 1811. By 1817, he began making plans to rebuild and expand the house to its present magnificence after deciding it much too small. The reconstruction lasted for twenty years. Sir Jeffry Wyatville designed the improvements. Especially notable was the magnificent new library created to house the bibliophile Duke's tremendous collection. Also included in the massive project was a huge conservatory and a new wing.

Holkham Hall, Norfolk

This severe Palladian mansion was the Norfolk seat of the extraordinary Mr. Thomas Coke. American Richard Rush visited Holkham Hall in 1819 and wrote:

> Holkham House covers an acre of ground. Looking at it on one of the mornings with the Duke of Bedford and others, and viewing its imposing centre, from which proceed four wings connected by corridors, the general conjecture

seemed to be that such an edifice could scarcely be built at the present day for less than half a million of pounds sterling. It was built, I understood, in the middle or early part of last century, by Lord Leicester, who was many years in Italy, where he studied the models upon which, after his return to England, it was erected.

Of the furniture in such a mansion, the paintings, tapestry, mirrors, rural ornaments, and all else, it need but be said that it is adapted to the mansion.[5]

The Marble Hall with its coffered ceiling and variegated, alabaster Ionic columns over fifty feet high ravaged the eyes with its magnificence. Twin Sicilian pink and white marble fireplaces, walls hung with crimson velvet, and furniture upholstered in green velvet distinguish the equally splendid saloon.

The long library housed the rare collection of manuscripts gathered by the family over several generations. Among these treasured tomes were many rare Greek manuscripts and a notebook of Leonardo da Vinci. Art treasures abounded too. Medieval tapestries, Roman and Greek statues, and paintings by Rubens, Kneller, and Gainesborough combined to kindle admiration in every eye.

Coke entertained innumerable guests. The hunting season and the annual sheep shearing strained accommodations. The Duke of Sussex, however, was always assured a room. The north state bedroom, featuring a plaque of Caesar Augustus that bore a striking resemblance to Napoleon, was reserved for this favorite guest.

Mr. Coke was just as remarkable as his house. He excelled with firearms, and was renowned as a hunter far into his old age. He refused a peerage for 30 years to retain his seat in the House of Commons. A feisty Whig, Coke used his Norfolk seat to promote his political principles.

Oatlands Park, Surrey

From the time of her marriage to the Duke of York to her death a few months after the mad old king's in 1820, the eccentric Duchess of York remained happily fixed at Oatlands. The jovial warmhearted Duchess left the tonnish whirl of London to others. Her royal husband had purchased Oatlands Park from the Duke of Newcastle in 1791 shortly before his marriage. The house had been a royal palace that both Henry VIII and later Charles I had used. Soon after the Duke's purchase, the original structure burnt to the ground. The Duke and his Duchess resided in a square undistinguished building built on the site of the former house. Left intact on the estate however was a magnificent grotto of stalactite rock and shells. The childless Duchess set up housekeeping here quite happily. The German princess was well loved by the royal family (except Prinny) and by the surrounding community, which greatly benefitted by her good works. Her kind heart, merry nature, and live-and-let-live attitude proved her a good match for the profligate Duke. They settled down to marital bliss of a sort.

The Duke trysted with his Duchess only on weekends, always with a party of his rakish, rowdy friends in tow. They gambled at whist for £5 a point, told vulgar jokes, and stayed up until the wee hours of the morning. The Duchess played cards for more genteel stakes with more agreeable guests or took her innumerable dogs (some authorities put the number as high as 100) on midnight strolls.

Among the Duchess' particular friends were "Monk" Lewis, "Kang-Cook" Major General Henry Cooke, and Beau Brummell. She adored Brummell's good manners and befriended him even in his Continental exile.

The informal Duchess was always a good-hearted hostess, but visitors had best beware! The dogs always got the warmest place by the fire.

Brighton

The bracing sea breezes of the Sussex coast worked like a tonic on the young Prince of Wales during his first visit to Brighthelmstone in 1783. Prinny was the guest of his wicked debauched uncle, the Duke of Cumberland, during this first sojourn in 1783. He would spend many years here basking in the town's approval, building an elaborate seaside palace, and luring the *ton* to his doorstep!

The young prince revelled in the free informal lifestyle and by 1786 had found a suitable residence on the west side of the Steyne. This respectable austere farmhouse won loud acclaim among his critics who had deplored his spendthrift ways.

Fashionable London followed Prinny in high gig to sample this new summer season at the seashore. All the *ton* agreed! Brighton was a devilish fine place to recuperate from the rigors of the London season. Even Yuletide visits became popular.

All his disreputable Carlton House set followed the pleasure loving prince to the salubrious seaside. Frequent guests included Colonel Hanger, Sheridan, Sir John Lade, and his hard-riding wife, Laetitia. Most notorious of all were the Barry siblings—Richard, the 7th Earl of Barrymore, was remembered for a vicious uncontrollable temper that earned him the nickname "Hellgate", Henry, the 8th Earl, was known as "Cripplegate" in honor of his clubfoot, the Reverend Augustus habitually dubbed "Newgate" to signify the only gaol which he had not graced, and their sister Caroline whose foul mouth and stable manners accounted for her sobriquet "Lady Billingsgate" (a quarter of London noted for the foul-mouthed porters in its fish markets). In the 1790s Brummell who held a cornetcy in the 10th Hussars was stationed nearby.

Until the 1802 remodeling and additions the Pavilion hosted only small groups of friends. The rowdy dissipation sported by Prinny's set perfectly suited Brighton. Twice-widowed, Mrs. Fitzherbert presided over the Prince's domestic life in these early Brighton years. Secretly and illegally married in late 1785, the royal couple maintained separate households for propriety's sake.

Brighton remained stylish through all the absurdities of the Prince's domestic arrangements and the numerous remodelings, expansions, and renovations of his Pavilion over the next thirty years. Fitzherbert would go out of favor, and in again, before finally dismissed by her royal husband.

The height of the resort's consequence among the *ton* was around 1810. Typically visitors to the seaside resort travelled on the New Road from London—the shortest route and in the best condition. A fashionable traveller had his prime cattle posted along the road and (with four changes) could make the journey in less than five hours. A very important visitor was greeted with pealing bells from the Assembly rooms. Public coaches were beneath the touch of the *haut ton*. For others, 28 coaches ran daily between London and Brighton in 1811. Public coaches made the journey in six hours.

Guests were usually asked to the Pavilion for only a few days and no more than a week's stay. The Prince did however constantly entertain visitors who had rented a fashionable address on the Steyne for the Season or took lodging at the two chief hotels, Old Ship and Castle Inn.

Brighton entertained her visitors with balls at Castle Inn and Old Ship on Wednesday and Fridays. There was a theater on the New Road with a large gallery, pit, and two tiers of boxes. The town boasted many other amusements. Brighton had a popular racecourse at which Prinny's horse Orville won the Brighton Cup in 1804. Cricket matches included Pavilion regulars Colonel Hanger and Lord Darnley. Gentlemen also indulged in bloodsports at the White Hart which featured a cockpit or in Hove where bullbaitings were staged as late as 1810.

Seabathing as a curative exercise had been prescribed and popularized by Dr. Richard Russell as early as 1750. At Brighton the rejuvenation promised by sea bathing was accomplished with the help of "dippers" and "bathers."

Martha Gunn and other sturdy women guided and dipped the ladies. Male "bathers" aided gentlemen. Famous among the bathers was "Old Smoaker," Prinny's support during his aquatic excursions as a young man. For a price, anyone who desired sea immersion entered a bathing machine, a wooden box on wheels pulled by a horse, by ascending several steps. Safely hidden from prying eyes, they made themselves ready to bathe. Ladies donned caps and long-sleeved shifts. The bathing machine was then backed from the beach into the ocean. Dippers waited halfway up the steps to assist descending bathers. After a dip, clients once more entered the machine to change clothes as the box was drawn back on to the beach by a reliable man who carefully guided the horse.

Bored young blades found titillation through the judicious use of telescopes trained on likely bathing machines. Patience was rewarded when their lecherous eye fixed on a diamond of the first water descending the ladder into the sea. Every curve was revealed through the wet clinging muslin shift as the damsel bobbed in the ocean under the watchful eye of an attendant!

The Assembly rooms in Brighton had a master of ceremonies named Captain Wade until 1808 when Mr. Forth replaced him. Strict rules governed the deportment and dress in the rooms. Much social life was also centered around the circulating library of Fisher's or Donaldson's. Here the *ton* gathered to gossip, read current periodicals, and select books.

The Polite World promenaded on the Steyne during the hour of nine o'clock. The fashionable parade served much the same purpose as similar traffic on both horseback and in carriages during the late afternoon in London's Hyde Park.

The Prince's fascination with the resort and his continuing presence ensured Brighton's popularity with the *beau monde*. Among the notable visitors were Lord Mansfield, Canning, the Creeveys, and Sir Philip Francis. Royalty also deigned to be entertained in Brighton. The illustrious Tsar Alexander and the King of Prussia came in

1814. Prinny's mother made two visits, the second attended by his daughter. Even ghastly Caroline of Brunswick had visited Brighton!

To accommodate the influx of gentlemen in the upper ten thousand, that redoubtable businessman, Raggett of White's, opened a clubhouse on the Steyne. And come they did! Even Byron succumbed to the resort's lure. He lodged with Scrope Davies and another friend on the Marine Parade in 1808.

Oddest of Brighton's residents was Henry Cope, the Green Man, who never failed to attract attention as he went about town. As reported in 1806, he was clad in green. Pantaloons, gloves, frock coat, waistcoat, and cravat were all green. He only ate green fruits and vegetables and lived among green chairs, tables, sofas, curtains, and bed. His gig, livery, portmanteau, and whip were green, too. Mr. Cope promenaded down the Steyne and in the libraries every day, singing and grinning to himself—ever happy with all the world.

To enliven his days at the Pavilion, Prinny indulged his fondness for music. Excellent German musicians made up his wind instrument band. Each afternoon they entertained Brighton from the Pavilion grounds. They performed works by Prinny's favorite composers—Beethoven, Bach, and Haydn. Music continued during evening meals and afterwards. The Prince often played his cello during musical evenings and raised his bass voice in song. As Creevey recorded in 1811:

> We were again at the Pavilion last night ... The Regent sat in the Musick Room almost all the time between Viotti, the famous violin player, and Lady Jane Houston, and he went on for hours beating his thighs the proper time for the band, and singing out aloud, and looking about for accompaniment from Viotti and Lady Jane. It was a curious sight to see a Regent thus employed, but he seemed in high good humour.[6]

Dinner at the Pavilion was served at 6 o'clock (much earlier than Town hours). The guest list numbered between thirty and forty and was made up of close companions staying at the Pavilion and those fashionable visitors staying elsewhere in the seaside resort. Dinner varied in length from one and a half hours to four hours. Food was served in sumptuous profusion. Antonin Carême's reign in the Pavilion's kitchen (several months in 1816-1817) was particularly notable for the culinary delights he set before the Prince and his guests. Ladies in the approved fashion sought the drawing room and were eventually joined by the gentlemen. Card playing, conversation, and music whiled away their evening hours.

Visitors appreciated their considerate prince. John Wilson Croker thought Prinny a splendidly considerate host who always spoke with everyone and shook hands with newcomers and particular friends alike. He always bade the ladies to be seated promptly. He led the highest-ranking lady on his arm to dinner. If there were two ladies of equal rank, he led both of them at the same time.

Guests, stuffed on the superb cuisine, sometimes needed a little exercise. Lady Ilchester preferred a walk up and down the gallery. At eleven a select few of Prinny's inner circle retired with him to a drawing room for a cold supper. Evening parties often lasted until three in the morning. Only excessively uncomfortable heating sometimes marred the entertainments. The eternal flames of hell could hold no surprises for any guest in Prinny's stifling rooms.

The annual celebration of Prinny's birthday on August 12 highlighted the Brighton season. A mock naval battle staged with soldiers in full uniform on Race Hill usually commemorated the holiday. The 1810 celebration featured about 10,000 troops. An infinite variety of fireworks illuminated the night sky as celebrants danced at Castle Inn's ball. Often, a few days after the event, the Pavilion hosted a birthday ball such as the one Byron attended in 1808.

The center of Brighton's fashionable whirl was

Prinny's fantasy palace — the everchanging Marine Pavilion. He first enlarged his Brighton residence with the aid of architect Henry Holland. Leaving his work at Althorp, Holland completed the Pavilion restructuring in 1787. The new Marine Pavilion obliterated the royal farmhouse. In its place emerged a long Palladian villa in prime style. Furnishings and decor reflected Prinny's love of French elegance. Few signs of the Sinomania that afflicted the Prince in later years graced this early Pavilion.

Between 1794 and 1801, the Prince's domestic life suffered a series of upheavals that affected his habitual sojourns in Brighton. His fickle favors were withdrawn from Mrs. Fitzherbert and bestowed on nasty, conniving Lady Jersey, who helped engineer the oh, so disastrous match with Caroline of Brunswick. Though fond of their Prince, Brighton could not countenance the downfall of beloved Fitzherbert. Crowds publicly hissed Lady Jersey as she passed along Brighton's thoroughfares. Affronted by this venomous display, Prinny stayed at Bognor during the 1796 season and rarely frequented the resort again until 1800, the year of his reconciliation with Maria Fitzherbert.

Buoyed by the renewed domestic tranquility, the Prince of Wales's building frenzy returned. Henry Holland in 1801 started the new construction that reflected Prinny's Sinomania, a passion for all things Chinese. Prinny single-handedly revived the vogue for Chinese, a fad of the 1750s. Stories circulated that the Prince of Wales had been much struck by the design and color of some Chinese wallpaper, and this had triggered his mania for the exotic. Whatever motivated the prince, the new interior of his seaside palace exclaimed his devotion to both oriental themes and motifs.

But the mercurial prince never stayed satisfied for long with either his surroundings or his paramours. In late 1806, he became estranged from Mrs. Fitzherbert. They never reconciled. Soon afterwards, he began to contemplate another extensive enlargement, remodeling, and redecoration of his Pavilion. John Nash was chosen to execute his exotic design for a fantasy palace.

Begun in 1815, the new Pavilion featured a "Hindustan Style" wedded with oriental motifs and designs. The seaside palace was more exotic than ever! Turrets and domes, derived from seventeenth century Mughal buildings, decorated the dramatic exterior. A host of artisans and craftsmen that included gilders, carvers, paperhangers and upholsterers contributed to the decor and furnishings.

Unfinished in its entirety until 1823, the reconstruction and redecoration of the Pavilion resulted in the most magnificent royal folly ever conceived. Particularly impressive was the banqueting room. The theatrical dragon chandelier hanging from the domed ceiling overpowered the room. Massive plantain leaves decorated the ceiling at whose center a carved silver Chinese dragon hung. From the winged dragon's claws draped an eye-arresting chandelier. By 1821 it was gas lit, and the lotus petal bowls burst with fiery light from the mouths of the six silver dragons perched around the brilliant body of the light fixture. It was only one of the many amazing sights. Exotic designs and a myriad of treasures filled each superbly original room.

Prinny exulted in the transformed Royal Pavilion for only a brief time. During the last five years of his life, Brighton's royal patron paid only one short visit in 1827. Lady Conyngham, his grasping, stupid, and final mistress, took mortal offense at supposed slights and urged her paramour to desert his seaside palace. Now king, aging and ailing, his magnificent royal folly completed, George IV readily complied. Other projects attracted his energy, money and attention. His seemingly insatiable appetite for change at the Royal Pavilion was fulfilled. Now he looked towards refurbishing Windsor Castle. Buckingham House awaited his touch, too! A king, after all, needed palaces worthy of him.

Bath

Stately Georgian Bath, nestled between the gentle

hills of Somerset and the Cotswolds, owed its fashionable glory to the natural hot springs that flowed beneath its streets. Regency England believed wholeheartedly in the water's curative powers. Legendary cures had been recorded for centuries. Celtic myths told of Bladud's leprosy and the skin disease suffered by the pigs he tended being miraculously cured. The site of the hot springs took his name, Bad-Lud, or Bath Waters. Romans turned the springs into a health resort that was renowned throughout the Empire. Medieval pilgrims travelled to worship at the Abbey as well as benefit from the healing waters. Even royalty sought its healthful restorative powers. Queen Anne, James I's consort, came to seek a remedy for dropsy.

This invigorating water so greatly desired by sufferers contained over thirty minerals and elements. Unpalatable flavors of sulphur and bismuth unfortunately dominated the healthful libation. Ailing souls immersed themselves in hot bathing pools and drank no less than three glasses of the smelly stuff per day in the Pump Room. They declared the Bath beverage decidedly nasty!

As a genteel watering place of the first stare, Bath's greatest glory existed in the eighteenth century. The arrogant leadership of Richard Nash, Bath's social arbiter, bullied vulgar, coarse nobility into pattern cards of perfection. Nash engineered a new type of society for Bath. The closed circles of the *haut ton* functioned ill in this resort town that also attracted baconfaced squires and their mates. Forceful Beau Nash orchestrated the intermingling of diverse classes by the enforcement of stringent codes of behavior. The sway of his personality kept even the peers of the realm beneath his thumb. It was not at all the thing to ignore the Beau's edicts!

Beau Nash's Assembly Room Rules

1. That a visit of ceremony at first coming, and another at going away, are all that are expected or desired by ladies of quality and fashion — except impertinents.

2. That ladies coming to the ball appoint a time for their footmen coming to wait on them home, to prevent disturbance and inconvenience to themselves and others.

3. That gentlemen of fashion never appearing in a morning before the ladies in gowns and caps show breeding and respect.

4. That no person take it ill that anyone goes to another's play or breakfast and not theirs—except captious by nature.

5. That no gentleman give his ticket for the balls to any but gentlewomen.—N.B. Unless he has none of his acquaintance.

6. That gentlemen crowding before the ladies at the ball show ill-manners, and that none do so for the future—except such as respect nobody but themselves.

7. That no gentleman or lady takes it ill that another dances before them—except such as have no pretence to dance at all.

8. That the elder ladies and children be content with a second bench at a ball, as being past, or not come to perfection.

9. That the younger ladies take notice how many eyes observe them.—N.B. This does not extend to the Have-at-alls.

10. That all whisperers of lies or scandal be taken for their authors.

11. That all repeaters of such lies and scandal be shunned by the company—except such as have been guilty of the same crime—N.B. Several men of no character, old women and young ones of questioned reputation, are great authors of lies in these places, being of the sect of levellers.[7]

The King of Bath ordered about recalcitrant duchesses and ousted coarse country squires with equal abandon. Among his greatest achievements were banishing swords from a gentleman's attire in the city, prohibiting duelling (which he considered unseemly), and refusing to let the hoydenish Princess Amelia (daughter of George III) dance after eleven. Odd Lord Peterborough was Nash's greatest failure. Under no circumstance would the eccentric peer be seen in anything but his riding boots!

Visiting Bath became the height of fashion by the mid-eighteenth century. Demand for housing brought about tremendous change as the medieval town became a Georgian jewel. Regency visitors to Bath resided and played in majestic Palladian and Georgian buildings erected during this period of furious growth.

Architect John Wood the Elder and Ralph Allen, wealthy postmaster and limestone quarry owner, together began Bath's transformation. Among Wood's projects were Queen Square, the Mineral Water Hospital, and Lindsey's Rooms. His grandest scheme, King's Circus, saw completion after his death under the direction of his son, John Wood the Younger. Wood's classically inspired architectural legacy dominated the style of the builders that followed him.

Considered the grandest Georgian building was the splendid Royal Crescent (Wood the Younger's design). The immense five hundred feet curve of thirty identical houses fifty feet high featured a ground-floor story and 114 columns twenty feet high that joined the first and second stories.

Extensive building and the layout of many new streets testified to the widening boundaries and increasing size of the city. Many areas familiar to Regency visitors such as Sydney Gardens, Laura Place, and Great Pulteney Street were built after 1770.

Bath's magnificent Georgian buildings did not, however, house the most fashionable members of Regency society. The *haut ton* flocked to Brighton's seashore in Prinny's wake. Lesser nobility, gentry, retired military men, parsons, and hypochondriac dowagers populated Bath, which in 1800 boasted 34,000 citizens.

The Polite World considered it a tiresome place at best, but the tedious town had its uses. Mourning demanded a suitable period of quiet social life. If London was out of bounds for the bereaved, surely not even the most censorious could find fault with a visit to tame Bath! Young chits mired in distressing scandal-bound situations in Town often sought refuge in respectable Bath until the social furor died down.

Vexatious rules governed Regency Bath much as they did Nash's Bath. Essential for every visitor was to enter one's name in the subscription books at both the Upper and Lower Assembly Rooms though the Masters of Ceremonies were but poor shadows of lordly Beau Nash. Ceremonial calls were paid on the most important new residents.

Those desiring to derive the most benefit from Bath's native advantage screwed up their courage and repaired to the baths. Usually a sedan chair conveyed the brave bather clad in a dressing gown to King's Bath, Queen's Bath, Cross Bath, or Hot Bath in the early morning hours. All, except the female only Queen's Bath, were patronized by both men and women.

The immersion process began in the "slips." Attendants dressed prospective bathers—women in voluminous gowns with wide sleeves and men in canvas waistcoats and drawers. The bathing attendant also gave each bather a floating dish or tray. Ladies put nosegays, handkerchiefs, oil essences, perfumes, confections, and whatever else they might need as they bathed. Guides maneuvered bathers into the 120 degree mineral waters for an hour's soak. Elderly women awaited to strip, dry, and redress the limp bathers who then retired by sedan chair to their lodgings.

Social life during the morning centered around the Pump Room. Gouty gentlemen and vaporish ladies gathered each day to take the waters (served by the glass) at the counter in the Pump Room. A portly statue of Beau Nash gazed sternly down on the assembly as the long-case Tompion clock made especially for the room ticked away the minutes. Tea was served to healthier souls who disdained the unpleasant waters. An orchestra housed in the musician's gallery supplied background music. More important than taking the waters was exchanging *on-dits* about other residents and speculating on new arrivals. Bath quizzes gained renown for the malicious enjoyment that they derived from their daily gossip fests.

After the obligatory visit to the Pump Room, various other amusements of a genteel sort entertained residents. Sydney Gardens, which opened in 1795, drew prominent visitors who strolled through its environs. Described as a miniature Vauxhall, the Gardens boasted delightful grottoes, an amusing labyrinth, and charming waterfalls. Entertainments included public breakfasts, concerts, and galas with dazzling illuminations and fireworks.

Shopping on Milsom Street also whiled away daylight hours. Circulating libraries often proved congenial gathering places. Bath notables were supplied with current periodicals, literary reviews, and newspapers from London as well as all the latest books and pamphlets.

Glittering nightlife, such as it was in sedate Regency Bath, centered in the New Assembly or Upper Rooms. The Lower Rooms were not as grand nor did they attract the better sort.

Wood the Younger designed the splendid new Upper Rooms, which cost £20,000 and were completed in 1771. Every detail had been planned to increase convenience and pleasure. A large paved section was provided to give plenty of room for sedan chairs at the main entrance to the west. There were two carriage entrances—one on Alfred Street and the other on Bennett Street.

The oblong ballroom to the left of the octagonal anteroom was one hundred feet long and lit by five glorious chandeliers. A semicircular recess provided musicians a place to ply their art. Balls were held on Monday and Thursday nights.

Balls always began about six and ended precisely at eleven. No exception was ever made! Even if dancers were in the middle of intricate figures, the music abruptly came to a halt. Generally only country dances and the minuet were permitted. No outlandish waltzes for this sedate company!

From the anteroom, subscribers to the Upper Rooms turned right to enter the tea-room. A two-story colonnade in the west end of the room housed musicians in its upper section. The card-room with its musician's gallery doubled as the concert-room on Wednesday nights. Another card room, smaller and octagonal in shape, had been added to the New Rooms several years after the original building was finished.

Visitors of some length to the inland spa let houses at fashionable addresses such as Laura Place, Pulteney Street, or the very elegant Camden Place. Fashionable suites of rooms were also available to rent. The White Hart on Stall Street was an excellent hostelry situated directly opposite the Pump Room. Other inns and hotels included York House and the Christopher.

A few notable souls did live in Bath. Dr. Johnson's friend, bluestocking Mrs. Thrale, resided in Bath after her husband's death in 1809. Her neighbors on Gay Street knew her as seventyish Madame Piozzi. Her second marriage had been made to a young Italian music tutor and had scandalized the prudish. Jane Austen resided in Sydney Place with her father for several years in the early part of the nineteenth century. Fellow novelist Fanny Burney, Madame d'Arblay, settled here with her French *émigré* husband in 1815 and became one of the sights of Bath.

All in all, the *haut ton* agreed. It was a devilish flat place populated with social climbers, boorish snobs, and boring respectable souls, but it had its uses!

Touring Abroad

Travel in Napoleonic Europe

The lure of European pleasures beckoned Englishmen

for generations. Young cubs and their bearleaders traditionally embarked at Dover to begin a "grand tour" of the Continent. These young fellows "finished" their education by sampling the decadent French court and eyeing the architectural wonders of Italy. The standard journey was overland from the disembarcation point at Calais. The journeyer advanced to Paris, then went on to Dijon, Geneva, Avigon, Rome and Naples. The Grand Tour could take six months or six years depending on the fortune and inclination of the traveller. The elegant society of France and the wondrous art and artifacts of Italy highlighted most tours, though all Europe became the playground for the touring English.

Revolution halted English travel in the late eighteenth century and reversed channel traffic as France's aristocracy scurried across the narrow channel for refuge. Social intercourse between the two nations ground to a halt until the brief Peace of Amiens (1802-1803). The francophile *ton* rushed back to beloved Paris, hungry for the latest French fashions and palate-pleasing food. Elated English tourists once again strolled Paris's wide boulevards. Outside cafes overflowed with good fellowship as cheerful French and English alike enjoyed wine, beer, cider, and lemonade as all the world and his wife promenaded by.

Lady Elizabeth Foster, a member of the Devonshire House *ménage à trois*, basked in the pleasures of Paris during the peace. She thought it would be impossible to find more amusement than all the excitement of visits by such fascinating fellows as the esteemed Baron Denon, Camille Jordan, and Monsieur de Narbonne. The international mix of society provided her endless entertainment and titillation. Lady Elizabeth was particularly impressed with a fine dinner that the inimitable Talleyrand hosted in a gallery lighted by almost five hundred candles and lamps. His guest list included a host of celebrities of all kinds. Could any place be more congenial to the *ton* than Paris?

Important visitors during the brief peace went to meet the great man himself. Napoleon entertained lavishly at Tuileries. English guests were charmed by his polished

hospitality and compelling personality.
Modest Englishwomen gasped at bare French fashions.
Miss Catherine Wilmot, member of Earl Mount Cashell's
party, was flabbergasted by women from fifteen to seventy
dressed in such revealing styles. In direct contrast, they
rouged their cheeks so heavily that they looked like
ancient statues that had suddenly been animated.
Paris delighted Miss Wilmot that spring of 1802. She
went vagabonding and poked her nose into every enchanted
corner of the blossoming city before her party continued
on through Europe. Arriving in Italy, they made
themselves known to the influential people there. They
thoroughly enjoyed being entertained in the best fashion at
balls, routs, and teas. Suitable pursuits in Florence
included visiting innumerable churches and museums.
Pushing southwards the travellers made their obligatory
trip to Naples. Naples meant Vesuvius and Miss Wilmot
dutifully ascended the historic volcano. She rested but did
not make the descent with the energetic gentlemen in her
party. Her fascinating sojourn on the Continent was cut
short when news arrived that Britain and France had
resumed hostilities. She found her way home overland to
Schleswig-Holstein and then crossed over to England.
Others were not so fortunate. Over a thousand
unhappy English souls were trapped in France. A majority
of these unlucky travellers spent the duration of the
Napoleonic Wars in Verdun and were not freed until 1814.
Touring grandly through Europe was now out of the
question for Englishmen. That Impious Monster, Napoleon,
kept the *ton* at bay as his power and sphere of influence
spread across Europe. English travellers ventured to the
Continent in safety only by passing themselves off as
American citizens. America remained neutral during the
conflict and was for a time even at war with Great Britain.
Although much of the Continent was unsafe, travel
around the theater of war was possible. Britain ruled the
sea. Byron travelled extensively during the Napoleonic
Wars in the Levant and Greece. Another touring
Englishman was Henry Holland, M.D. who wrote *Travels in*

the Ionian Isles, Albania, Thessaly, Macedonia, &c. During the Years 1812 and 1813. He left England in 1812 in order to visit a series of Mediterranean countries. Before this, however, he visited the Peninsula and observed the military hospitals. After the doctor had studied these establishments to his heart's content he began his tour. His resulting travelogue contained everything that made an impression on him in his far ranging journeys—Ali Pasha, antiquities, bazaars, ruins, the exotic Middle Eastern women, and all manner of natural wonders.

But Mediterranean tours did not satisfy fashionable tastes. All the Polite World dreamed of journeying to Paris again. Napoleon's defeat, abdication, then exile to Elba in May 1814, galvanized the upper ten thousand. Exultant, victorious occupation armies of England, Prussia, Russia, and Austria strolled Paris boulevards and dined in her cafes again. The occupying armies annoyed, frustrated, and enraged Parisians. Prussian and Russian soldiers were openly hated. Vindictive vandalism consumed Prussian general Blücher, and more than one Prussian soldier met an inglorious end in the dark Parisian streets.

Proud French officers challenged victorious enemy officers on the flimsiest of pretexts. Gronow remembered:

> Amongst the French themselves there were two parties always ready to distribute to each other "*des coups d'épée*"—the officers of Napoleon's army and the Bourbonist officers of the *Garde du Corps*. Then, again, there was the irritating presence of the English, Russian, Prussian, and Austrian officers in the French capital. In the duels between these soldiers and the French, the latter were always the aggressors.
>
> At Tortoni's, on the Boulevards, there was a room set apart for such quarrelsome gentlemen, where, after these meetings, they indulged in riotous champagne breakfasts. At this café might be seen all the most notorious duellists,

amongst whom I can call to mind an Irishman in
the *Garde du Corps*, W * * *, who was a most
formidable fire-eater. The number of duels in
which he had been engaged would seem incredible in the present day: he is said to have
killed nine of his opponents in one year![8]

With the restoration of the Bourbon monarchy in May
1814, London's fashionable fribbles joined the soldiers.
They dashed across to France to sample the city's elegant,
long-denied pleasures. Captain Gronow witnessed thousands
of oddly-dressed English flocking to Paris. He remembered

that the burden of one of the popular songs of
the day was, "All the world's in Paris;" and our
countrymen and women having so long been
excluded from French modes, had adopted
fashions of their own quite as remarkable and
eccentric as those of the Parisians, and much
less graceful.[9]

This state of affairs didn't last long. Englishwomen
put aside their small hats and donned large high-crowned
hats profusely adorned with plumes made of ostrich and
cock feathers. Dress sleeves lengthened to include mitten
cuffs falling over the hand. Elegant collarettes reminiscent
of sixteenth-century ruffs began adorning English necks.

In addition to the latest French fashions, the *haut
ton* had been starved for French flair, society, and food.
Napoleon's brief return in February 1815, to play out his
destiny in the one hundred days was a momentary break in
the amusing round of pleasures.

Captain Gronow wryly admitted that the "flower of
English society—men of fashion and distinction, beautiful
matrons and their still lovelier daughters" invaded Paris in
1815 and afterwards.[10] They built for themselves a tight
little enclosed world to which only the right people were
admitted.

Sir Charles Stuart was the popular English ambassador. Amiable and intelligent, he "paid as much attention to individual interests as to the more weighty duties of State." Gronow delighted in the ambassador's hospitality and largess.

> The British Embassy, in those days, was a centre where you were sure to find all the English gentlemen in Paris collected, from time to time. Dinners, balls, and receptions were given with profusion throughout the season: in fact, Sir Charles spent the whole of his private income in these noble hospitalities.[11]

Another center of tonnish entertainments were the charming *soireés* given by beautiful, accomplished Lady Oxford in her hotel in the Rue de Clichy. Among the *élite* of Paris society who gathered there, Gronow in particular noted "Edward Montague, Charles Standish, Hervey Aston, Arthur Upton, "Kangaroo" Cook, Benjamin Constant, Dupin, Casimir Perier, as well as the chief Orleanists."[12]

"Here, there, and everywhere" was the brightest star in Paris's filament in the autumn of 1815 — Lord Castlereagh.

> Indeed, the mass of business he had to transact was so immense, and the fatigue he had to undergo so great, that he was compelled to spend several hours each day in a bath; his nights being generally passed without sleep. His bath was always taken at the Bains Chinois, at the corner of the Rue de la Michodièere. He was there shampooed by the celebrated Fleury, and recruited his exhausted faculties by dozing for an hour or two. His favourite promenade was the gallery of the Palais Royal. In his walks he was almost always alone, and used to dress very simply, never wearing any orders or decorations.[13]

The simplicity of his dress was in direct contrast to
Lady Castlereagh's lavish adornment. According to
Gronow, she

> astonished the French by the magnificence of
> her diamonds. At the balls and parties she used
> to be followed about by envious women, affect-
> ing to admire, but looking daggers all the
> while.[14]

In addition to hobnobbing with the better sort at
Embassy entertainments and private amusements, English
visitors rushed to sample French cuisine. Gronow
reminisced that:

> The most celebrated restaurant was that of
> Beauvilliers, in the Rue de Richelieu; mirrors and
> a little gilding were the decorative character-
> istics of this house, the *cuisine* was far superior
> to that of any restaurateur of our day, and the
> wines were first-rate. Beauvilliers was also
> celebrated for his *suprême de volaille*, and for
> his *côtelettes à la Soubise*. The company
> consisted of the most distinguished men of Paris;
> here were to be seen Chateaubriand, Bailly de
> Ferrette, the Dukes of Fitzjames, Rochefoucauld,
> and Grammont, and many other remarkable
> personages.[15]

One of Napoleon's cooks, Borel, kept an excellent
dining-house called Rocher de Cancale in the Rue Mandar.
Dedicated English gourmets came over from England
expressly for the purpose of enjoying it. French officers
were often in Trois Frères Provençaux drinking fine wines
and indulging in tempting dishes of Provence.

English visitors also eyed the plundered art treasures
in the Louvre, Bonaparte's private apartments at St. Cloud,
victory monuments, and the best French actors. Roomfuls
of precious manuscripts awaited curious visitors to the

Bibliothèque Royale. Well-connected visitors managed to meet the noted Egyptologist Baron Denon and peruse his collection of curiosities. Notable among them was a mummy's foot from a once beautiful Egyptian princess.

The playground in Paris for gentlemen was Palais Royal, "the centre of European fashion and gaiety" and "the very heart of French dissipation."[16] Officers and gentlemen of fashion gathered here to indulge their passions. The notorious "oblong-square block of buildings" had originally been Cardinal Richelieu's personal residence (built in 1629).[17] It came into the possession of Phillippe d'Orléans, who held scandalous orgies within its walls. His descendant, Philippe Égalité, to collect funds to repair fire destruction, surrounded the gardens with galleries of shops on the ground and apartments to let above them. Housed in the notorious structure were all manner of cafes, gambling houses, and obliging ladies.

Seven P.M. was the busiest time of day. Immense crowds of officers of all the allied armies congregated in the corridors, gardens, and saloons. It was said European royalty indulged themselves *incognito* here too. Every vice and pleasure awaited gentleman visitors—from dining in renowned restaurants to flirting with painted females. Odd stories were told concerning the gambling-houses of the Palais Royal.

> An officer of the Grenadier Guards came to Paris on leave of absence, took apartments here, and never left it until his time of absence had expired. On his arrival in London, one of his friends inquired whether this was true, to which he replied, "Of course it is; for I found everything I wanted there, both for body and mind.[18]

The massive amusement center with its arcaded pavements hosted every indulgence and depravity. Gronow said:

A description of one of the houses of the
Palais Royal will serve to portray the whole of
this French pandemonium. On the ground-floor
is a jeweller's shop, where may be purchased
diamonds, pearls, emeralds, and every description
of female ornament, such as only can be
possessed by those who have very large sums of
money at their command. It was here that the
successful gambler often deposited a portion of
his winnings, and took away some costly article
of jewellery, which he presented to some female
friend who had never appeared with him at the
altar of marriage. Beside this shop was a
staircase, generally very dirty, which communicated with the floors above. Immediately over
the shop was a café, at the counter of which
presided a lady, generally of more than ordinary
female attractions, who was very much *décol-
letée*, and wore an amount of jewellery which
would have made the eye of an Israelite twinkle
with delight. And there *la crème de la crème* of
male society used to meet, sip their ice and
drink their cup of mocha, whilst holding long
conversations almost exclusively about gambling
and women.[19]

The gambling houses were "the very fountains of
immorality." They had tables for every class, so that
working men played with 20 sous, and gentlemen played
with 10,000 francs.

The floor over the gambling-house was
occupied by unmarried women. I will not
attempt to picture some of the saddest evils of
the society of large cities; but I may add that
these Phrynes lived in a style of splendour which
can only be accounted for by the fact of their
participating in the easily-earned gains of the
gambling-house régime.[20]

All these attractions, combined with the fact that "the Palais Royal was externally the only well-lighted place in Paris," made it a...

> rendezvous of all idlers, and especially of that particular class of ladies who lay out their attractions for the public at large. These were to be seen at all hours in full dress, their bare necks ornamented with mock diamonds and pearls; and thus decked out in all their finery, they paraded up and down, casting their eyes significantly on every side.[21]

Confirmed gamblers sought out the gorgeously furnished Salon des Étrangers conducted by the courteous Marquis de Livry. Visitors were provided with superb cuisine from the excellent kitchen as they lost huge sums in exceedingly reckless play. On Sundays the Marquis hosted amusements at his charming villa Romainville close to Paris.

> He invited not only those gentlemen who were the most prodigal patrons of his *salon*, but a number of ladies, who were dancers and singers conspicuous at the opera; forming a society of the strangest character, the male portion of which were bent on losing their money, whilst the ladies were determined to get rid of whatever virtue they might still have left. The dinners on these occasions were supplied by the *chef* of the Salon des Étrangers, and were such as few *renommés* of the kitchens of France could place upon the table.[22]

While the Polite World rediscovered Parisian delights, the great powers and petty princelings of Europe gathered in Vienna in the fall of 1814. The heads of five reigning dynasties and over 200 princely families descended on the Austrian city for six months. They came to participate in an international congress which was to settle European boundaries in the aftermath of Napoleon's defeat.

Entertainments were never ending. Among them were Metternich's Peace Ball on October 18 and costume ball on November 8. Metternich's hospitality also extended to inviting 250 guests for dinner each Monday night. November 23, 1814, was the Carrousel, an extravagant medieval tournament. Talleyrand's beautiful niece hostessed his excellent dinners prepared by Chef Antonin Carême at Kaunitz Palace. Invitation to Castlereagh's was much sought after because few were invited to their grand 22-room apartment in the Minoritzenplatz. Military parades, beautiful fêtes, and even a grand January sleigh ride amused the Congress, too.

The whirlwind of gossip that accompanied every gesture and word that passed the lips of the representatives of great powers kept the participants constantly amused. At the time of the Congress's Final Act on June 19, 1815, Napoleon had been finally defeated at Waterloo on June 18 and abdicated four days later. Europe was once more safe for the intrepid British tourist.

Touring—Post-Napoleon

After Napoleon's incarceration on Elba, then St. Helena following the Hundred Days, the English eagerly set forth to dally once again in Europe. Only remnants of the Grand Tour of the eighteenth century remained. Family parties of enthusiastic tourists replaced the young cubs of the eighteenth century who finished their gentlemanly education abroad.

These tourists dealt with travelling money much as it had always been done. They clutched their letters of credit to their bosoms and sailed forth to meet the unknown. Letters of credit were presented to the foreign correspondent of one's English bank, which gave authorization to the bank to meet the financial needs of the letter bearer. The amount was then recovered from London by the foreign bank.

After travellers settled the business of money, necessary accouterments had to be chosen. Opinion varied. In the 1790s Mariana Starke advised taking all of the medicines and spices one might need. She also recommended a whole range of eating utensils and one's own bedclothes. Mary Wollstonecraft thought touring was best served with one's own personal carriage with native servants acting as driver and interpreter. Other travellers insisted that a pocket bolt for lockless doors at Continental inns was essential. Eccentric Colonel Thornton embarked with ten horses, over one hundred dogs, numerous servants, and three carriages packed to bursting to sample Europe's pleasures.

Travellers without the means to journey abroad in luxury toured with a *vetturino* or *voiturin*. One fee assured tour members lodging, meals, and transportation to agreed-upon destinations. Package tours eliminated the fear of bothersome bandits. One traveller in Italy in 1818 reported to her mother in England that the horrifying rumors of bandits was greatly exaggerated. Only those parties in carriages travelling alone, at night, and with no escort need have any fear of vicious ruffians attacking them.

Travellers also encountered the wearisome chore of obtaining proper permits from local governments. Officious foreign bureaucrats could make this paperwork confusing, time-consuming, and costly. British tourists also had to be issued passports from their embassy to return to England or leave some foreign cities.

Travel inconveniences also included insolent and unhelpful inn servants, lodgings of dubious cleanliness, ghastly stomach complaints, and days of bone-shaking carriage travel. Intrepid English travellers were not daunted! The Polite World fervently plunged into European touring after Napoleon's downfall.

Waterloo's battle site lured many visitors to the fields outside Brussels. Brighton teemed with eager Englishmen ready to dash across the sea soon after victory to claim souvenirs. Tourists diligently searched the landscape for

bullets and buttons for many years. Stallholders at La
Belle Alliance and Hougoumont made tidy profits from the
sale of boots and badges. Byron tramped across the
battlefield and obligingly sent trophies back to friends in
England. Even George IV, guided by Wellington himself,
poked and prodded the battlescared ground for momentoes.
Sylvester Douglas (Lord Glenbervie) included the
Belgium battlefield on his tour. In his journal of August 6,
1817, he recorded the scene:

> We came yesterday over the field of battle of
> the eighteenth, having first passed through the
> village of Waterloo, between one and two miles,
> I should suppose, from the place where Colonel
> Alexander Gordon and General Picton were
> killed, and near which the battle seems to have
> commenced, the English army extending on a
> ridge to the right and left of the road, and I
> imagine in the road, which is in a considerable
> hollow just under and close to the high spot on
> the right where Gordon fell, and where a
> monument is now erecting to his memory, with
> a long inscription on the pedestal on one side in
> English and on the other in French, at the joint
> expense of his five brothers and his sister....
> About half a mile farther on the road, and
> also close to it on the left, is the little public
> house called "la Belle Alliance,".... On the spot
> where the monument ... of Colonel Gordon is
> erecting, one sees distinctly all the principal
> parts of this great scene where the greatest
> event perhaps recorded in history took place; on
> the left near the road, the place where Picton
> fell. About a mile more to the left and a little
> farther onward, the woods from whence about
> six in the afternoon Blucher's army was seen
> advancing.[23]

On most long Continental tours the elegant wickedness of Paris was the first major stop. The small, enclosed world of the best society greeted *haut ton* travellers who revelled in Parisian chic and divine food, as they did their best to ignore the filthy streets and stinking gutters. But one did not want to dawdle here. After all, Italy awaited! The captivating appeal of Italian sojourns had not diminished in post-Napoleonic Europe. English travellers enthusiastically wore Roman carnival masks and threw plaster sugar plums at friends. They stayed in melancholy Venetian palazzos and dutifully complained about the damp discomfort. They acquired suitably small antiquities from Herculaneum and carted them off to England.

Highlight of the southern dip in the Italian tour to Naples was menacing Vesuvius. Picnicking tourists trudged up the volcano, briefly rested, and ate their lunch. Gentlemen in the expedition and especially hardy ladies descended into the crater itself! One lady visitor claimed she pelted down the side in eight minutes.

English tourists admired the wondrous architecture of ancient and modern Rome, Renaissance Florence, and palatial Venice. Second only to these great monuments were the amusing people everywhere. Rome, which in 1818 was only the capital of the tiny Papal states, hosted international society. Her salons rang with chatter in French and English. Conversable residents of the ancient city included the ageing Countess of Albany, the Young Pretender's widow, and numerous members of the Bonaparte family. Lord Glenbervie particularly delighted in his invitation to Lucien Bonaparte's grand Roman seat, Ruffinella. The illustrious company that he encountered there on his 1816 visit included Madame Mère, Princess Borghese (Napoleon's tempestuous sister), and the former ruler of Holland, Napoleon's brother Louis. To join in this amusing company, English travellers had to submit to intense scrutiny by Papal customs. All luggage was sternly eyed in order to find and confiscate banned books!

Byron, disgraced in society and living in exile in various places throughout Italy, also became one of the sights. English wayfarers often sought him out or at least sought out the latest *on-dit* about the notorious poet. Equaling Byron in scandal was the ghastly Princess of Wales, who when not cavorting through Europe, set up housekeeping with her entourage at the Villa d'Este on Lake Como. Caroline had not improved with age and became more eccentric every year. Rumor reported numerous indiscretions and erratic behaviors performed by the Princess with her startling dyed black hair.

The lengthy trip which Lady Caroline Stuart Wortley, her husband and children took in 1817 typified the Grand Tour after Napoleon. They stayed in magnificence at the Hotel Breteuil in Paris and delighted in their view of the Tuileries Garden. When they sampled French theater, Lady Caroline reported to her mother that the celebrated French actor Talma had pleased them far beyond their limited expectations, but Mlle. Mars had been seen in much too small a part to make a judgement.

Mingling with good society had proved as satisfying as Talma's performance. They attended numerous dinners of fashionable addresses. Among their hosts were Sir Charles Stuart and the Duc de Rohan.

Their planned departure from Paris was postponed because a fit of gout afflicted milady's husband. Their journey on to Rome was delayed as he took muriatic acid foot baths on the advice of his doctor. They managed to amuse themselves quite nicely with a visit to the Tuileries to witness a spectacle given for the French royal family and attendance at the opening of the Chambers.

The attack of gout abated and the family continued on their way. They reached Lyons on November 23, travelling three hundred miles in a week. By December 1, 1817, the party arrived in Turin. Lady Caroline was enraptured with the scenery, especially on their ascent of Mount Cenis.

They journeyed onward to Bologna where she was gratified to see St. Jerome by Coreggio restored to Parma after spending three years among the other looted treasures in the Louvre. Equally interesting were Bonaparte artifacts! The magnificient cradle that had held little Nap and Marie Louisa's toilette were both on display. Florence disappointed Lady Caroline who thought it dingy, sad, and dark. They finally reached Rome by Christmas, thoroughly delighted to be in the "Eternal City," the trip from Florence had been fraught with unpleasantness. Not only did the terrible quality of the horses impede one's progress, but the tremendous poverty sadly dampened one's spirits! Also, a blight on the landscape were the ghastly blackened remnants of captured bandits hanging from the tops of poles. But all the unpleasantness was worth it for Rome was glorious. The children and their parents saw ancient Rome in the mornings and in the afternoons read in Eustace about what they had seen. She was particularly taken with the Coliseum and St. Peter's.

By February 1818, they were in Naples. They of course, made the obligatory trip to nearby Pompeii. The highlight of their visit was actually dining in one of the ancient houses. After a brief sojourn in Naples, they spent three days travelling to Rome for a lengthier visit to enjoy the delightful springlike weather in February. The children took drawing, Italian, dancing, and French lessons during their stay.

They eventually departed for Venice and arrived there in April, journeyed through the Tyrol in May, and reached Munich on May 13. By June 6, 1818, they were once again in Paris and made ready to return home. At journey's end, any English family would have no doubt agreed with other intrepid English tourists if queried upon the advisability of travelling abroad. No matter what discomforts and hardships they faced, nothing was quite so exciting as adventuring in foreign places.

NOTES TO CHAPTER VII

1. Richard Rush, *A Residence at the Court of London,* 1:120-121.

2. Ibid., 1:122.

3. Ibid., 1:123.

4. Rees Howell Gronow, *The Reminiscences and Recollections of Captain Gronow,* 2:51-52.

5. Rush, *Residence,* 1:122-123.

6. John Gore, ed., *The Creevey Papers,* p. 89.

7. Alfred Barbeau, *Life & Letters at Bath in the XVIIJth Century,* pp. 33-34.

8. Gronow, *Reminiscences and Recollections,* 1:104-105.

9. Ibid., 1:90.

10. Ibid., 1:299.

11. Ibid., 1:99.

12. Ibid., 1:91.

13. Ibid., 1:299.

14. Ibid.

15. Ibid., 1:96.

16. Ibid., 1:86.

17. Ibid.

18. Ibid., 1:89-90.

19. Ibid., 1:87.

20. Ibid., 1:89.

21. Ibid.

22. Ibid., 1:121.

23. Francis Bickley, ed., *The Diaries of Sylvester Douglas (Lord Glenbervie),* pp. 238-39.

Prince Riding in Hyde Park   *Stubbs*

New York Public Library
Picture Collection

Chapter VIII

THE HORSE

At the center of life in Town and country stood the noblest of beasts — the horse! Horses were of course the major component of the overland transportation system. A huge network of inns, stables, coaching lines, and horse servants catered to travellers and travelling coaches, both public and private. But beyond this utilitarian purpose, horses reigned as the plaything and passion of the Polite World.

The *beau monde* donned elegant riding clothes to parade down Rotten Row atop a bang-up piece of flesh and blood during society's fashionable afternoon hours. Ladies decked out in stylish carriage dresses and the latest mode in bonnets ordered out their barouches, and then had their coachman tool them around the park at a sedate pace. Eccentric Lord Petersham took endless trouble matching his horses, carriage, and harness to a particular shade of brown of which he was fond.

Driving-mad gentlemen joined fashionable coaching clubs like the Whip Club. Wearing outrageous uniforms, they drove four-in-hand coaches for amusement. The most passionate and noble Jehus learned to handle the ribbons aboard a commercial coach beside skillful Knights of the Whip, long distance coachmen.

Horses stood at the center of two great addictive sports: foxhunting and horse racing. Chasing the illusive, crafty fox had entered its Golden Age during the Regency. Gentlemen showed their mettle by riding neck or nothing over tortuous hedges and fences as they rode straight to the hounds. Equal excitement was also found on the racecourse. The painstaking breeding and training of a blood horse, the thrill of the actual race, and the stimulation of gambling on the outcome made racing the perfect pastime for Englishmen of wealth and position.

Whatever function horses were put to on the King's highway in Town and in the countryside, every gentleman ached to develop prowess as a rider and driver. And every lady whispered a prayer before she settled down into her death trap of a sidesaddle!

An Essential Guide to the Language
of the Road, the Turf, and the Hunting Field;
or Horse Talk Explained

Astronomer — a horse with a high-held head.
Bit of blood — thoroughbred horse.
Bit of cavalry — a horse.
Black Bess — highwayman Dick Turpin's mare.
Black work — night driving.
Blood-horse — thoroughbred horse.
Bo-kickers — a hard-to-control horse.
Box figures — coachmen.
Cattle — horses. Prime cattle — the best horses.
Chopping — hitting horse with a whip.
Copenhagen — Wellington's ill-tempered horse.
Coper — a dishonest horse dealer.
Crack-whip — good driver.
Crimp match — a fixed race.
Eclipse — the unbeaten racehorse of legendary prowess. Raced in 1769-70 and defeated all comers.
Fanning — whipping.
Fast trotters — good horses.
Handling the ribbons — driving a coach.
Highpad — highwayman.
Horse of good bottom — horse of endless pluck.
Jarvey, or Jarvis — hackney coach driver.
Jehu — a fast driving coachman. From II Kings 9:20: "... and the driving is like the driving of Jehu the son of Nimshi; for he driveth furiously."
Knight of the crooked whip — Tom Hennesy, a well known artist of the road.
Knight of the road — highwayman.

Knight of the whip—long-stage coachman.
Knowing ones—turf sportsmen wise in the ways of both
  jockeys and horses.
Leader—horse which led the team.
Leg or blackleg—bookmaker.
Marengo—Napoleon rode this white stallion at Waterloo.
McAdamites—foxhunters who bring up the rear.
Neck or nothing—all-out effort, from horse racing.
Ostler—one who tended traveller's horses at an inn,
  jokingly known as an oatstealer.
Pad—the highway.
Penciller—bookmaker.
Peter—portmanteau.
Peter-hunters—robbers who stole parcels from
  coaches.
Piper—a horse who is broken and winded.
Prads—horses.
Queer lot—horses with an infirmity of temper.
Rattler—a hackney coach.
Rattler and prads—a coach and horses.
Rattling cove—a coachman.
Riding à la Chifney—standing up in the stirrups.
Rig—horse and carriage.
Stones—the cobbles of London streets and other paved
  streets of the provinces.
Thrusters—Foxhunters who thrust themselves in front of
  the pack.
Tigers—grooms of small stature who wore striped waistcoats.
  Also tyger.
Tipping the double—slipping away without tipping the
  coachman.
Tits—horses.
Tooling—driving a carriage.
Towelling—flogging.
Wheeler—horse that worked next to the wheel.
The Turf—the race course or profession of horseracing.
Yard of tin—the coach guard's horn, usually a good yard
  long, it was used as a signaling device.

The Horse in Town

When the Polite World journeyed to Town each spring in their travelling carriages, they came to see and be seen. Just as fashionable society judged the drape of a gown or the cut of a coat, so did they take note of the mounts that their peers rode and the horse flesh that they tooled through London streets. Prime goers meant a gentleman was of the first stare.

Adding to the fashionable necessity of maintaining a decent stable, Regency England was horse mad. The sheer enthusiasm for driving and riding was at its height. Smart rigs with high-stepping horses were all the crack.

Horses destined to pull these elegant equipages were matched with precision and groomed to a high gloss. The elegant Georgian townhouses had a plethora of stables in the mews behind them. A troop of specialists catered to the animals' every need; coachmen, grooms, ostlers, and stable boys. All coddled these prime bits of blood. And London's thoroughfares teemed with wagons bearing straw, hay, and fodder from the surrounding countryside to feed this army of animals.

Hyde Park at the fashionable hour of 5 P.M. was the backdrop for the grandest show in London. Footmen, elegantly powdered in remembrance of a bygone age and attired in lavish livery, handed highborn ladies into beautifully appointed carriages. Gentlemen ordered their phaetons with precisely matched bays or greys to be made ready or had a high spirited tit saddled. And thus the show commenced. As Captain Rees Howell Gronow recalled the fashionable parade:

> The company which then congregated daily
> about five was composed of dandies and women
> in the best society; the men mounted on such
> horses as England alone could then produce.
> The dandy's dress consisted of a blue coat with
> brass buttons, leather breeches, and top boots;
> and it was the fashion to wear a deep, stiff

white cravat, which prevented you from seeing your boots while standing.... Many of the ladies used to drive into the park in a carriage called a *vis-à-vis*, which held only two persons. The hammer-cloth, rich in heraldic designs, the powdered footmen in smart liveries, and a coachman who assumed all the gaiety and appearance of a wigged archbishop, were indispensable. The equipages were generally much more gorgeous than at a later period.... The carriage company consisted of the most celebrated beauties, amongst whom were remarked the Duchesses of Rutland, Argyle, Gordon, and Bedford, Ladies Cowper, Foley, Heathcote, Louisa Lambton, Hertford, and Mountjoy. The most conspicuous horsemen were the Prince Regent (accompanied by Sir Benjamin Bloomfield); the Duke of York and his old friend, Warwick Lake; the Duke of Dorset, on his white horse; the Marquis of Anglesea, with his lovely daughters; Lord Harrowby and the Ladies Ryder; the Earl of Sefton and the Ladies Molyneaux; and the eccentric Earl of Morton, on his long-tailed grey.[1]

Young ladies on horseback preened in their finest feathers to impress the *ton* as it dallied through the park. Typical riding habits had very full skirts with plenty of leg room so legs could be positioned properly on the side-saddle. The skirt was topped with a jacket to the waist with or without small tails and plain tight-fitting sleeves. Accesories included short gloves of fine tan leather, half-boots, and an elegant hat decorated with plumes. Ornamentation often drew inspiration from the military. The shape of a button, the cut of a collar, and the trim and embroidery on the jacket reflected this influence.

Gentlemen, too, dressed to impress their tonnish audience. Top boots or tops were fashionable for riding. They were close fitting to foot and leg. Buff or white tops turned below the knee contrasted with the black body of the boot. Riding breeches were high-waisted and fit very snugly. After 1809 they were most often made of leather. Breeches were topped with tailcoats, either cut or sloping, which were constructed of kerseymere or shag. Fashionable gentlemen also wore trousers with Wellingtons or pantaloons with half boots. Elegantly tied cravats and a striped waistcoat were *de rigueur.*

But not only the *ton* graced the park. Sumptuously bedecked Cyprians displayed their womanly charms in spanking turnouts, always ever hopeful of luring a wealthy protector. They were much bolder than gently reared misses who demurely caught the eye of an eligible *parti.* Procuresses with a tonnish clientele also put on display their newly caught ladybirds to whet the appetites of aging debauchees of rank and fortune.

There was a great variety of carriages driven by gentlemen and coaches driven by carriage servants or postilions. Among the most general types to be seen were:

Barouche

This stylish vehicle had a fold-back top that when unfolded, covered only the back half of the carriage. It could be driven by a coachman or ridden postilion with two, four, or six horses. Some amateur aristocratic coachmen preferred this carriage over the private drag.

Cabriolet

Similar to the curricle in appearance, the cabriolet crossed the Channel from France. It was a light two-wheeled carriage for only one horse. It featured a folding leather hood, curving shafts, and a large apron. There was only a small platform at the back and it was recommended that a tiger rather than a full-size groom stand there.

Curricle

This two-wheeled carriage was pulled by two horses. Prinny helped popularize this low-wheeled vehicle. A steel bar connected to the horses' back pad balanced the weight of the pole. The curricle had a seat at the back for groom or tiger.

Drags

These were four-wheeled gentlemen's coaches built to enhance the fashionable interest in four-in-hand driving. They resembled mail coaches but had extra seats on the back to carry two grooms. Captain Gronow remembered these drags as one of the glories of the Regency.

> ...There was a perfection in the minutest detail that made a well-appointed four-in-hand appear like a choice work of art. The symmetry of the horses, the arrangement of the harness, the plain but well appointed carriage, the good taste of the liveries, the healthy, sturdy appearance of the coachmen and grooms, formed altogether one of those remarkable spectacles that make a lasting impression on the memory.[2]

Drags distinguished themselves by the noble crest painted on the boot door and on each side door.

Gigs

This two-wheeled one-horse carriage enjoyed much popularity in all its forms. One style was the Dennett Gig built by Mr. Bennett from Finsbury. Also popular among the *beau monde* was the Stanhope gig built by Tilbury. His inspiration came from the Fitzroy Stanhope's design. It boasted a very comfortable ride because of the four springs it hung upon.

> ...Lord Barrymore sported a very pretty "Stanhope" in which he used to drive about town accompanied by a little boy, whom the world denominated as his tiger.[3]

Another gig was the tilbury. Its heavy body was well supported by excellent springs. Even the roughest roads did not daunt the two passengers aboard this gig.

Landau
     This versatile four-wheeled coach had a roof which
opened in the center and folded back flat. It could carry
four people. A pair of horses pulled it through London's
streets. The *ton* favored it for less formal occasions such
as drives in the parks and excursions into the countryside.

Phaeton
     These light four-wheeled carriages were drawn by
two, four, or six horses. Over the front wheels hung a
very high seat. The hind wheels were one or two feet
higher than the four to five feet front wheels. The
precarious height turned them into a challenge that no
game buck refused. Prinny's love of tooling his phaeton to
Brighton helped usher in driving as a fashionable pastime.
Various types of phaetons included perch, crane-neck,
high-perch, and highflyers.

Town coach
     This large, impressive four-wheeled vehicle carried
four tonnish passengers and was pulled by two, four, or six
horses. The family's heraldric arms were carefully painted
on the doors of its enclosed body. It was used for official
business, social calls in Town, and all formal occasions.

Vis-à-Vis
     The lean lines of this vehicle were a miniature
version of a coach. Only two people, face to face could
ride in this carriage. It was often used for stately
occasions.

     The coachmen who drove families of rank and fashion
in Town wore liveries that were precise in every detail.
The basic uniform included top boots, white leather
breeches, vertically striped waistcoats, dark tailored coats,
white cravats, white shirts, hogskin gloves, and top hats.

The single-breasted coats were a different color than the collars or the collars were trimmed with special lace to signify each family. The color scheme for livery and coaches was chosen from the colors on the family arms. The family crest adorned each button. The groom wore identical livery except the coat was shorter. Six buttons trimmed his coat back instead of the coachman's four. The most elegant turnouts also had carriage servants who matched each other in size, conformation, and hair color, much like a prime set of cattle.

Lady Salisbury, known as Old Sarum, was a *grande dame* of the old school who demanded transport in the first style of elegance. As Raikes recalled:

> Lady Salisbury scrupulously adhered to the state of former days; she always went to court in a sedan-chair with splendid liveries, she drove out in a low phaeton with four black ponies in the Park, and at night her carriage was known by the flambeaux of the footmen.[4]

Even Prinny at his most reclusive never forsook the pleasure of a jaunt through Town with his carriage and horses.

> For years even before he came to the throne, he very seldom appeared in public, or went anywhere, but to Manchester House, where his visits were as regular as clockwork. At four o'clock the gates of Carlton House were opened daily, and the plain *vis-à-vis* with the gray liveries, and the purple blinds down, was to be seen wending its way through the crowd to its usual destination, unremarked by any but the experienced eye, which knew the royal incognito, and the superb bay horses unequaled in London.[5]

Driving a coach was not always left to menial horse servants. The excitement of skillful driving challenged many tonnish fellows. Horse-mad gentlemen who had a passion for the ribbons formed driving clubs to practice their four-in-hand skills. The Benson Driving Club included Lord Sefton, Mr. John Warde, and Sir Bellingham Graham among its members. The Whip Club or, as it was known after 1809, the Four-in-Hand Club was one of the most prestigious of the clubs where one dressed like a gentleman and drove like a coachman.

Members of the Four-in-Hand Club met four times a year in London. Atop their private drags or barouches, they drove their high-bred cattle (none cost less than three hundred guineas) in single file from their usual meeting place at George Street, Hanover Square, to Salt Hill, a distance of 20 miles. A bountiful dinner awaited them at the Windmill served up by Botham, the innkeeper.

These gentlemen coachmen wore white drab driving coats which featured no less than fifteen capes and two tiers of pockets. They also sported large bouquets of yellow geraniums, myrtle, and pinks in their buttonholes. The finery underneath this massive driving coat consisted of a single-breasted blue coat which was rather long at the waist and sported brass buttons engraved with "Four-in-Hand Club." Their distinctive kerseymere waistcoat had yellow and blue stripes. The prescribed muslin cravat was white with black spots. White corduroy breeches came down rather long at the knee and buttoned in front just over the shin. They were worn with short top boots with long, turned down tops. A hat with an Allen brim and conelike crown perched on their heads.

The trip to Salt Hill and back was steady going at a trot. No coach was allowed to pass another. Usually the only problem occurred when one of the gentlemen coachmen imbibed too abundantly of the inn's celebrated port wine and tooled back to London while a trifle foxed.

Among the original members of the club were Mr. Lewis, Colonel Berkeley, Lord Barrymore, Mr. Clutterbuck, Tom Richards, and Sir John Lade. One of the club's leaders was the Earl of Sefton who "drove splendid bay horses, and was acknowledged to be a man of considerable taste."[6] Lord Barrymore was equally dazzling among all the "turnouts." He "drove four splendid greys, each matched in symmetry, action and power."[7] At variance with the elegance of milord's equipage was his profound proficiency in vulgar phraseology and slang. "It would have been safe to back his lordship as the winner against the most foul-mouthed costermongers."[8]

Lord "Tommy" Onslow, though the acclaimed master of four fine black cattle and possessing coaching skills second to none, was considered a little too eccentric to be admitted into the club. The combination of his black horses with his somber black carriage gave his whole turn-out the morbid appearance of an undertaker! Not good *ton*!

All the most prestigious members of the Four-in-Hand Club spent time either driving public coaches or sitting alongside coachmen talking about "life upon the road" and a variety of horse related matters. Ardor for the ribbons and the road drove one gentleman to have his teeth filed so a space was made to expel "his spittle in the true fashion of some of the more knowing stage-coach drivers."[9]

Any gentlemen fascinated by coach driving were advised to seek tuition from professional coachmen busily plying their trade on the Holyhead Road, Oxford Road, and the rest. As Captain Gronow remembered:

> In the days of which I speak there were amateur coachmen, who drove with unflinching regularity, and in all weathers, the public stage-coaches, and delighted in the opportunity of assimilating themselves with professional Jehus. Some young men, heirs of large landed proprietors, mounted the box, handled the ribbons, and bowled along the highroad; they touched their hats to their passengers, and some among them did not disdain even the tip of a shilling or half-crown, with which it was the custom to remunerate the coachmen. Many persons liked travelling to Brighton in "The Age," which was

tooled along by Sir Vincent Cotton, whilst others preferred Charley Tyrrwhit.[10]

Coaching was enormously expensive. Not everyone could afford to set up stables in Town, much less drive as a hobby. For impecunious young beaus on the Town, Mr. Tilbury kept a livery stable in Mount Street that was much frequented by the *ton*. He hired out not only elegant rigs, but could also mount a gentleman on a decent hack.

Those poor souls devoid of coach, carriages, and a stable in Town also took public conveyances—the hackney coaches. These vehicles usually resembled gigs or coaches and were previously used carriages of different sorts. Sedan chairs, litter-like boxes powered by husky men, were also still used, especially on state occasions.

Tattersall's stood at the center of the horse world not only in Town, but in all England. Richard Tattersall established this auctioneering yard expressly for the sale of horses at Hyde Park Corner in 1766. His reputation for high standards gained as the Duke of Kingston's Master of the Horse combined with his encyclopedic knowledge of equine lineages assured the yard's success.

Sales were held twice a week. Not only were prime bits of blood sold to the highest bidder, but so were carriages and hounds. The dispersal sale of the Duke of Kingston's stud in 1773 helped bring the business into prominence.

The opening of the Subscription Room in 1780 also increased its prestige. Members paid annual dues for use of the room graced with a painting of Eclipse over the fireplace. The core of the membership was the aristocratic members of the Jockey Club who dominated horse racing. Monday had prime importance to gentlemen who paid their dues here. It was settling up day and head-to-head wagers were paid. The aegis of the Jockey Club members helped prevent sharp practices and defaulting on bets. Those who failed to pay were banned from the race course, which, in turn, insured that they would not recoup their fortune through future bets.

The auctioneering yard consisted of many stables, loose boxes, and a round enclosure for watching the paces of thoroughbreds and other cattle being put up for sale. In the middle of this enclosure stood a cupola atop which a bust of Prinny resided.

Prime horseflesh brought enormous sums. The sporting aristocracy thought nothing of paying 1000 guineas for an elegant bit of blood. At Tatts gentlemen could expect to receive the highest prices for their cattle when they were auctioned off. Buyers knew they would have the opportunity of choosing superior animals. Even royalty sold up at Tattersall's. In 1819 the old Queen's stables were sold at one of Tattersall's famous dispersal sales. Her 55 horses brought £4,544 and her 18 carriages fetched £1,077.

Besides the yard's function as horse seller, it was Mecca to every sporting man forced to take up residence in Town. How else could these poor fellows exist in London without the conviviality to be found at Tatts? Here one could always find a receptive audience for a hoary old hunting tale or discover the latest *on-dit* circulating through the sporting fraternity. A grand cross section of the horse-mad Regency world frequented the yard—tulip of the goers, military types, sprigs of nobility, canny horse dealers, fox-mad clericals, racing touts, gamblers, blacklegs, and owners of fabulous blood-horses.

Travelling in Regency England

Approximately 16,000 miles of travel-ready road awaited journeying Englishmen in 1816. Many were newly macadamized for smoother, quicker paced rides. Others had been widened in the French style to thirteen yards across for a faster, safer trip. Regency England readied itself for the beginning of the golden age of coaching! Travellers made overland journeys faster than they ever had before. In 1700 the Norwich to London run took 50 hours. In 1800 it took only 19 hours. Even more dramatic was the decrease in time for the Edinburgh-London route, which went from 256 hours to a mere 60 hours of travelling time by 1800! This lengthy trip featured the average 3 stops for meals of 25 minutes duration.

Going at a fast clip down these roads were private travelling chariots, post-chaises, mail coaches, and stage coaches. Each served different needs and different segments of society.

Private Travel

The gentry and aristocracy preferred to travel in the comfort and privacy of their own vehicles. The grandest travellers had coachmen, footmen, and postilions dressed in lavish livery. They horsed their coaches with post horses, which were hired at each stage of the journey. The wealthiest travellers kept their own horses stabled at the first two or three stops on regularly travelled routes. As the horses were changed on the carriage, so, too, at regular intervals were the postboys or postilions.

Aristocratic carriages proclaimed their lineage by crests on the side doors and the boot. All the ornamental parts of the carriage such as the joints and mountings, were in brass or silver. Travellers without their own travelling chariot or barouche could still go privately by hiring a post-chaise. All important inns throughout the country had coaches and teams for hire. Usually a pair of horses pulled a post-chaise, though two pair were hired as needed. Post-chaises always used the services of a post-boy, who rode one horse while leading the other. In 1815, a typical fee of one shilling, six pence per mile included carriage, post-boys, and horses. A four horse team doubled the fee. Post-chaises generally came from the ranks of old and cast-off travelling chariots. Their usual galloping pace and bright yellow color earned them the sobriquet "Yellow Bounder."

Travellers who broke their journey into several stages stayed overnight at inns. When they entered, a porter rang a bell for the hostler and waiter. The innkeeper or an upper servant rushed out into the hall to see what was required and assigned the visitor rooms for the night. Wealthy travellers hired private rooms to dine in and use as sitting rooms to avoid the scruffy assortment of humanity in the public rooms. Waiting on the inn visitor and his equipage were ostlers, stable-boys, waiters, chambermaids, and boots. Typical fare included potatoes, kidneys, beef, cold hams, pigeon or game pies, bread, and cheeses.

Only the most ill-advised travellers put up at inns whose bedrooms were placed above the stables. Vermin and pests kept one awake so in the night!

Paterson's British Itinerary by Daniel Paterson kept travellers on their route. Between 1785 and 1832, 17 editions enlightened and edified the public. He detailed all the roads used by stage and mail coaches. Toll-gates, bridges, the body of water crossed, and every country house and family of importance near the routes were just some of the innumerable travel tidbits listed.

Public Transport

The black-and-maroon mail coaches with their scarlet wheels and undercarriage plus the Royal cipher and "Royal Mail" on the door were a familiar sight to Regency journeyers. John Palmer of Bath introduced this mail delivery system as a replacement for postboys on horseback in 1784.

The first responsibility of the mail coaches was to keep to the timetable and protect the mail. Passengers on these coaches always came second to the mail. Parliament allowed no more than four passengers on the inside who each were allotted 16 inches of seat space. Cheaper seating for four atop the coaches roof was also available.

The Royal Mail was by far the fastest of the public transport systems because the coaches did not have to stop to pay tolls. When Harriette Wilson fled Lord Craven's protection, her black footman secured her a place on the furiously fast mail. In no time at all, it dashed from Brighton to Hull where the young and handsome Fredrick Lamb waited to ravish the willing Harriette.

The emphasis on speed coupled with tightly-adhered-to schedules forced innkeepers to speed up horse care. A good time to unharness a team and put on a fresh one was three minutes. Excellent inns could change teams in one minute flat! Mail coaches had a mandate to insure fast, safe delivery of the mail. Parliament allowed passengers aboard the mail in order to defray expenses. The Post Office owned none of the horses or coaches. Contractors supplied both. Even the coachman was supplied by a contractor. Only the guard, the custodian of the mail, was directly employed by the government. Clothed in royal scarlet, the guard, in order to insure that his timetable was kept, wielded a three-foot tin horn. With his "yard of tin" he signaled innkeepers that the mail approached and needed a speedy change of horses. He summoned weary passengers back to their seats, warned other traffic to yield the right of way, and blew at toll gatekeepers who ran to fling open their gates. The guard rode at the rear of the coach with the precious mail tucked away safely in the boot beneath his feet.

Stage coach lines competed with the mail for passengers. These privately-owned stages ran their routes by day. The busiest time at any inn was the 5 A.M. to 8 A.M. stretch. Courtyards rang with the noisy arrival of mail coaches and the departure of brightly painted stage coaches with their destination printed on the coach body.

Owners of stage coaches worked hard to cram as many passengers as possible aboard the vehicles. Only four passengers sat on the inside, but the roof offered enormous potential. At least eight or more passengers crowded atop the coach in these cheap seats which were often dangerous and unhealthy. Some unlucky souls toppled off, breaking a limb or their necks. Others suffered terribly in bad weather. For passengers who could stay firmly fixed upon the roof of the coach, other dangers lurked. Unwary travellers could be struck by a wild whip wielded by a clumsy coachman. Gusts of wind blew off hats, and rain poured down to drench the poor soul huddled atop the coach. And the other passengers sharing this precarious rooftop perch? The outside seats were cheaper, and one's travelling companions were not always what they should be. The guard at the rear could also add his share of irritation if he were musical and blew his horn at every opportunity.

Various perils lurked on the road to endanger unwary passengers. The quest for more and more speed, overloading, bad loading, and careless maintenance by any of the large troop of horse and coach laborers caused numerous problems. Drunken coachmen and high-spirited young gentlemen racing down the turnpike presented difficulties, too.

One of the greatest hazards of the road for passengers was trying to get sustenance. The quest for speed by coachmen and their coaching lines sent travellers scurrying to grab any tiny morsel at the inn before the coach sped on its way. Too often the cry of "all ready" sounded just as food came to the table. Nip-cheese innkeepers watched passengers carefully to make sure no food was carried out. No one was allowed to eat aboard the coach. Hungry passengers dashed to wait on themselves desperately trying to eat their money's worth before the coach was off again. Unscrupulous innkeepers had been known to serve the same fare to each coach that stopped in a day—always insuring that no passenger from any coach load tasted more than a morsel.

The threat of highwaymen had all but been eliminated by 1815. The heavy traffic and greater speed made "stand and deliver" obsolete. Now robbers concentrated on the parcels that journeyed on the mail coaches. Finchley Common on the Great North Road no longer hosted the likes of Dick Turpin mounted on Black Bess and Sixteen-string Jack, who was said to be Lady Lade's paramour.

The coaching lines kept great terminal coach yards in London. Massive stables housed innumerable horses and coaches that were maintained by an army of workers.

There was a coach office that handled booking passengers and accepting parcels for transport. For the young men of the *ton*, the White Horse Cellar in Piccadilly was one of the prime sights in Town. They thrilled to the arrival of admired coachmen cracking their whips in the approved fashion.

Coaching-mad gentlemen eagerly sought the seat beside accomplished coachmen driving four-in-hand, and just as eagerly laid out their blunt to drive the coach themselves. Sir St. Vincent Cotton could often be seen aboard the Age.

The coachman, his coat sporting many capes, was considered at the peak of his profession when he arrived at his destination exactly to his timetable with horses in good condition and the trip accident free. Of particular admiration was the coachman's way with the whip — an important tool in controlling an eager team. Whipsters of note had been known to wield the whip so well they caught game with it as they tooled along. Adroit coachmen could boast a tasty duck or two fetched in this fashion.

A coachman in prime style was called an artist. What they did best was a jolly good job of "hitting 'em and holding 'em." But some were not so skilled! Some particularly inept coachmen made disastrous tries at controlling fractious teams. Cringing passengers were sure the end was near as the careening coach pitched back and forth across the road. Often accidents were only avoided because the horses stopped of their own accord and in spite of the driver's nonexistent skills.

Foxhunting

The slapping pace set by a crack pack of foxhounds demanded bold, fearless riders in Regency England. Foxhunting had undergone enormous changes in the Georgian era, and during the Regency it entered its Golden Age. Hounds had been bred to be faster. This new speed and the gradual enclosure of the countryside with fences and hedges demanded fast, bold horses who could jump. The speed and new danger made it a thrilling and hazardous sport. Good horses bred for the hunt were known as "flying leapers" because they jumped obstacles from a gallop. Now quick, crafty foxes were treed by a fast pack rather than dug out from their holes with a pick ax as in earlier and slower-paced times.

The love of the sport bred devoted gentlemen foxhunters who rode straight to the hounds six days a week. They threw their hearts over the most treacherous bullfinches knowing their horses would follow. According to Charles James Apperley, the much-admired correspondent for *Sporting Magazine* known as Nimrod, a good rider to hounds needed a firm seat and a light hand. Added to these talents he should also be cool no matter what difficulty presented itself, self-controlled, and sharply perceptive.

All knew that a man showed his mettle on the hunting field. The highest accolades were to be called "game to the back bone" or lauded as "in nerve, no superior" while pursuing the hapless fox over bullfinches and wicked ox-fences. To be a bruising rider of rare pluck was to be all the crack! And nothing could keep a man who was game to the backbone down. A passionate sporting Yorkshireman named Shaw, though severely crippled by gout, rode six seasons with Lord Derby's hounds. He had to be lifted onto his splendid horse Comet, but he rode as hard as anyone in the field, even though chalkstones were slowly and painfully coming out of his hands.

Even disabled veterans answered the siren song of the hunting horn. Nimrod noted Captain Harvey's splendid pluck. A slight man with only one arm (the other had been left at Waterloo), he rode well up to the hounds. Nothing stopped this valiant Irishman. He rode over fences that some whole men would have declined. His ingenuity in using his one arm and teeth to open gates and move other obstacles combined with his splendid good humor filled Nimrod with the utmost admiration.

The popularity of the sport and large number of participants demanded organization. Though there were still private packs owned by the likes of Thomas Assheton Smith and the Duke of Rutland, the enormous expense of maintaining packs made them out of reach for most. Many areas were hunted with subscription packs, which took the name of their locality. Private packs were only hunted with permission of the master or a personal invitation. Subscription packs charged a fee to hunt.

Sporting men came from every walk of life. No class distinctions marred the winter months on the hunting field. Hunting-mad clergymen came to the pulpit clad in hunting boots and ready to ride to the hounds. Lowly Mr. Gunter, the confectioner on Berkeley Square, was a faithful follower of the hounds. He was even treated to Lord Alvanley's tonnish wit.

> Everybody knows the story of Gunter the pastry-cook. He was mounted on a runaway horse with the King's hounds, and excused himself for riding against Alvanley by saying, "O my lord, I can't hold him, he's so hot!" "Ice him, Gunter—ice him!" was the consoling rejoinder.[11]

Subscription packs chose their own master who usually owned and kept the pack of fox hounds and managed the country they hunted. A large pack like the Quorn had nearly 200 subscribers. Typical smaller packs had 50-odd subscribers.

The best hunting packs were a credit to the neighborhood. Their meets were greeted with appreciative expectation. Packs depended on the good nature of the surrounding countryside. Popular masters who always compensated farmers for fox-related damages and took care to avoid crops had a plentitude of foxes for sport. Packs that alienated the local yeomen and raised hackles had poor hunting. Angry farmers nefariously destroyed the foxes themselves and all that lovely sport was lost!

Desperate packs imported French foxes to repopulate their hunting fields, though hunting a frog fox was considered damn dull work.

The pack met at 10:30 or 11 A.M. on regular hunting days. The hounds, horses, riders, and liveried hunt servants gathered at cross roads, inns, market places, or even the lawns of great country houses. Though fox-hunters could traditionally wear anything, a red or black coat was generally worn. White leather breeches, top boots, and a silk hat completed the outfit.

Though the subscription packs extended a welcome to milord's lawyer and pastry cook, his lordship's female relatives would probably not be out riding hard to the hounds! Newfangled galloping at fences and hedgerows that dotted the enclosed Regency landscape made their two-crutch sidesaddle deadly. Ladies' saddles were unsteady creatures for fast-paced hunting. The Regency sidesaddle firmly placed the right leg in position with two crutches. The top crutch on the saddle curved downward, and the second crutch, directly beneath the first, curved upwards. The left foot was placed in the stirrup. Over rough country the left leg with nothing to support it or anything to grip became useless for maintaining balance. The saddle's design would not be really safe nor would women hunt in great numbers until the 1830s with intro-duction of a third crutch or leaping-head which held the left thigh in place. The sidesaddle presented another difficulty. A lady always needed assistance to mount from a sturdy male or an inanimate mounting block.

Ladies perched atop a horse sat with their shoulders square, face forward, and keeping their weight centered over the horse's spine. The position of their legs man-dated a voluminous special skirt of uneven cut so that the hemline was horizontal when mounted. The flowing, full skirts tried these often drawerless ladies' ingenuity. To preserve their modesty, lady riders strapped their skirts down, a most uncomfortable ride, or pinned back and front skirt together.

Only the most exceptional, lion-hearted women really

hunted hard. Lady Laetitia Lade gained acclaim as a neck-or-nothing equestrienne. Most notable however was the audacious Lady Salisbury, who not only rode to the hounds, but was the Master of her family's pack at Hatfield hunt (1775-1819). As Thomas Raikes recalled:

> She was one of the beauties of her day and famed for her equestrian exploits. Till a late period in life she constantly hunted with the Hatfield hounds, in a sky-blue habit with black velvet collar, and a jockey cap, the uniform of the hunt; riding as hard and clearing the fences with as much ardor as any sportsman in the field. In earlier life she hunted with Mr. Meynell's hounds at Quorn, in Leicestershire, which was the scene of many curious anecdotes in those days.[12]

Men generally didn't care to hunt with the fairer sex—no matter how good they were! If the lady was a terrible rider or just not good enough to triumph over her bad equipment, they slowed the pace and got in the way. If she was a Lady Salisbury or Lady Lade, she was much, much too good and outshone most of the males in the field.

The slapping pace of an invigorating foxhunt ended successfully with the capture of the fox. Traditionally, three acts followed the catch; treeing, brushing, and capping. Treeing was the act of holding the fox aloft in a tree to be bayed at by the hounds beneath before throwing the fox to them. The first man up to the kill was rewarded the fox's brush—which was brushing. Capping meant gathering money from the field, usually half a crown per hunter for the huntsman making the kill.

For the *haut ton*, Melton, Leicestershire, was the Almack's of the hunting field. Titles and expensive horses abounded in the little town during prime hunting season. Other areas were equally good, considerably cheaper, and much less populated with fashionable fribbles, but none had the cachet of Melton. Located in the middle of Quorn country visitors also had easy access to other good packs such as Belvoir and Cottesmore. A gentleman could find sport here every day of the week except the Sabbath.

Though enthralled with the perfection of Leicestershire as England's premiere hunting field, Nimrod was not immune to its problems. He counted the immense crowds that descended on the area after Christmas as the greatest disadvantage to finding good sport. Melton's fashionableness often turned it into a dangerous squeeze much like a fashionable London party at the height of the Season. The great crowd also increased the dangers of foxhunting which was already quite perilous enough without added difficulties.

The most dazzling private pack in Leicestershire was the Duke of Rutland's noble pack of foxhounds at Belvoir. The Duke spent £1,200 annually maintaining his pack and untold thousands on hospitality and entertaining at the castle during hunting season. The estate boasted a considerable number of stables and housing for resident grooms and visitor's servants which stood outside the park. The castle would have been hard put to accommodate the huge numbers that descended upon it in hunting season.

The Master of the Hunt was an important as the country hunted and the pack of foxhounds put in the field. Tom Smith, Master of the Craven, had an eerie affinity with the fox. He held the phenomenal record of ninety foxes in ninety one days in the field. Also notable among Masters was coarse unflagging "Squire" Osbaldeston. Though he faithfully hunted six days a week, the "Squire" never faltered. Once Nimrod suggested that they might take the Stanhope gig to their destination after a hard day's hunting, but Osbaldeston insisted that nothing could replace the pigskin, and they rode instead.

Thomas Assheton Smith also earned accolades as a Master of the Quorn hounds and other packs. Nimrod praised Smith as a consistent, determined hunter who exhibited unparalleled nerve in the saddle. Not only was his determination unequaled, but his prowess in the field was remarkable.

The quality of the horseflesh was also very important. Most hunters showed a great deal of blood, that is, had a good dash of thoroughbred in their lineage. Dedicated sportsmen spent enormous sums on their mounts. Nimrod believed Lord Sefton to be the best mounted man in England for his weight. He paid dearly for this fine horseflesh. Horses in his stable such as Gooseberry, Plato, and Rowland cost almost a thousand pounds each. He also offered one Lorraine Smith eight hundred guineas for his renowned horse Hollyhock.

Equally important was the quality of the hounds. Speed was essential but it was also important that hounds be bred from the noses, that is, hounds with good noses should be consciously bred over all others. Nothing was so essential to excellent hunting as a pack that could turn quickly with a scent. The makeup of a pack and what made for the best hunting was examined at length in *Le Beau Monde*, April 1807.

> The most experienced sportsmen are of opinion, that the pack for Fox-Hunting should consist of twenty-five couple. The hour for the diversion is an early one, and he thinks that the hounds should be at the cover by sun-rising. The huntsman should then throw in his hounds as quietly as he can, and let the two whippers-in keep wide of him on either hand, so that a single hound may not escape them. It is particularly recommended to keep all the hounds steady, and to make them all draw. Much depends on the first finding of a fox, for a fox well found may be looked upon as half killed. There are but few instances where sportsmen are too noisy, and too fond of encouraging their hounds, which seldom do their business as well as when little is said to them. Most fox-hunters wish to see their hounds run in good style. This is extremely natural. It is disagreeable to see them run in a string, or creep slowly on when

they should exert their utmost vigour. A pack of harriers, if they have time, may kill a fox, but they cannot kill him in the style in which he ought to be killed; they must hunt him down. "If you intend," says Mr. Beckford, "to tire out the fox, you must also expect to be tired yourself." The duration of the chace should never be less than one hour, nor ought it to exceed two, which will, in most cases, be found sufficiently long if properly followed. Indeed, very few fox-chaces would ever exceed two hours, if there were not a fault somewhere, either in the day, the huntsman, or the hounds.

The best season for fox-hunting is in January, February, and March; and at these times the skin of the animal is in the highest perfection. Hounds hunt fox best in the coldest weather, because at such season he leaves the strongest scent behind him.[13]

Avid sportsmen even took their hounds to war. The Duke of Wellington was particularly fond of hunting. In the spring of 1813 he kept a stud of eight good horses and hunted almost every day in the Peninsula. He wore a light blue frock coat sent to him by the redoubtable Lady Salisbury. A young subaltern even chased a fox into the French lines!

Even the fastidious Beau Brummell took to the hunting field, though admittedly he never stayed the course. Foxhunters got caked with mud and returned absolutely filthy, don't you know! He couldn't bear the pristine white tops of his top boots to be sullied by dirt and almost always turned back at the first fence.

The Turf

Horse-mad Englishmen of good birth and full pockets found the breeding of blood-horses and racing them more

than fit occupation. Gentlemen of the *ton* eagerly
patronized the race courses dotting the English countryside
in 1800. Patronizing, though no longer actively participating
in the sport, was Prinny. Though the Prince of Wales had
eagerly embraced the Turf in his younger days (his stud
won 190 races between 1788 and 1791), the dreadful scandal
and rumors surrounding his horse Escape, ridden by
Chifney in 1791, forced him peevishly from the Turf.
Escape had lost a race the day before the race in question.
The odds were raised. Miraculously the horse won handily
the next day, and the Prince won a substantial sum at
greatly increased odds. Though for once the Prince seemed
blameless, rumors of race-fixing swirled around his head.
The Jockey Club ruled against the Prince's jockey Chifney.
They demanded that Prinny divest himself of Chifney's
services. In a great huff he did so and withdrew himself
from racing. The hard feelings between Prinny and the
aristocratic racing establishment eased in 1805 when he was
presented with a nicely worded apology, but he did not
race again until the last years of his life. He never gave
up however the fun and feverish excitement of watching
the races and gambling on their outcome.

> The Prince made Brighton and Lewes races the
> gayest scene of the year in England. The
> Pavilion was full of guests; the Steyne was
> crowded with all the rank and fashion from
> London during that week; the best horses were
> brought from Newmarket and the North, to run
> at these races, on which immense sums were
> depending; and the course was graced by the
> handsomest equipages.[14]

The shrine at which gentlemen of the Turf worshipped
was the interlocking network of courses at Newmarket. It
had a perfect situation for racing and boasted far more
racing than any other course in England. There were
seven race meetings a year (circa 1820). Over one-third of
the entire racing population of horses trained in the

numerous nearby stables. For the tonnish fellows who frequented racecourses, it offered perfection. Spectator attendance hardly ever exceeded 500, and nearly all that number were members of the upper class. There were no booths or crowds to block the view as they did on Derby Day at Epsom. Most gentlemen watched the spectacle on horseback (some even rode in with the winner) or clambered on top of coach roofs for a better view. No admission fee was levied against spectators at Newmarket or indeed at any racecourse in the Regency. Spectators did pay to sit in the grandstands at Epsom Downs and other courses but to watch was free to all of every class. Even women were welcome to view the racing contests, but the spartan discomfort of Newmarket daunted most members of the fairer sex.

Two of the premiere Newmarket races were established in the early part of the nineteenth century. In 1809 at the Second Spring Meeting, a sweepstakes for three-year-olds began to be run over the Rowley Mile, a straight, taxing course. At the first running there were 23 horses racing with entry fees of 100 guineas each. It was dubbed the 2000 Guineas. A three-year-old filly race was established in 1817. Fillies ran the less harsh Ditch Mile. The race became known as the 1000 Guineas because 10 fillies at 100 guineas each ran that first race. The July Stakes for two-year-olds was another notable race.

Races were run in a variety of ways. Heats had been common since the Restoration, but they had lost favor at most race meetings by the turn of the century. The winner of a heat event was the horse that could win two heats. Heats meant long gruelling contests for valuable horseflesh, because in early Georgian England, the length of a single heat could be four endless miles. This distance gradually shortened throughout the eighteenth century. Though heats had become unfashionable, matches were still a favorite event. Here individual owners pitted their horses directly against each other in head-to-head contests. They agreed on a wager and winner took all. Hambletonian vs. Diamond was one of the greatest matches of the

Georgian Age. The owners wagered 3000 guineas on the outcome. The enormous sidebets by tonnish spectators totaled almost 300,000 guineas! Plate and cup races in which horses raced for the prestige of winning an admirable trophy had long been run and were common also. Sweepstakes races however reigned supreme among the various events. A whole field of horses ran against each other. Each owner who subscribed to the race put up the same sum. The winner of the event took the total amount. It was by far the most agreeable way to win a lot of money without risking quite so much of one's own blunt!

Many racecourses drew fashionable racegoers. Ascot had outstanding race meetings that lured the gentry and nobility to its environs. Its proximity to London, consistent royal patronage, and a Gold Cup in 1807 assured its popularity with the *ton*. Racing enthusiasts ignored the grand field of horses only once. The presence of popular heroes Blücher, Tsar Alexander, the King of Prussia, and Hetman Platov in 1814 drew all eyes and interest. Prinny as George IV began the first Royal Procession in 1825, which forever assured that Ascot would remain all the go!

Epsom Downs, nurtured by the Earl of Derby, developed into a fashionable haunt. Eclipse's legendary racing career on the Downs (He retired unbeaten through two racing seasons, 1769-70) added to the course's fame. Derby Day which was highlighted by the one-and-one-half mile race for three-year-olds called the Derby drew the *ton* and hoi polloi in droves. Attendance often topped 100,000. Among them and sitting pampered in his own stand, the only permanent fixture on the racecourse, sat Prinny. His miniature castle had small battlements and a facade of three Gothic arches. The flat roof provided ample space to view the races for the Prince and his ever-present retinue of disreputable cronies.

York was the center of racing in the north. Goodwood under the patronage of the Duke of Richmond also had good *ton*. Other provincial racecourses dotted through the countryside included Newcastle, Chester, Warwick, Winchester, and Doncaster.

The Jockey Club whose membership exclusively boasted blue-blooded aristocrats governed the large, widespread fraternity of racing known as the Turf. In 1790 members included Prinny and the Dukes of Bedford, Devonshire, Grafton, York and Norfolk. These noble fellows and those that followed them by their power and prestige insured that the rulings of the organization were accepted, implemented, and final. The club did much to regularize the sport of kings by establishing consistent rules that were fairly applied and instituting detailed record keeping and documentation. An example of this was having owners register their colors and start to use those colors consistently at race meetings.

There were several publications essential to a sporting gentleman's enjoyment. The bible of the Turf was the Stud Book. *Introduction to a General Stud Book* by James Weatherby was first published in 1791. After several revisions and a supplement, an 1808 version declared itself the final one. The Stud Book firmly put all breeding on record and established the pedigree of all blood horses. Equally important to the horsey set was the *Calendar*. The Jockey Club first appointed James Weatherby in 1773 to keep the Match Book and publish a racing calendar. The Weatherby family continued the tradition throughout the Regency. Other publications consulted included *Baily's Racing Register, Pick's Racing Calendar, The Turf Register,* and *The Sporting Magazine.*

Great fortunes were made and lost on Regency racecourses. The alluring combination of blood horses and lady luck appealed directly to the heart of a Georgian gentleman. Huge sums were wagered on horseraces just as they were on the turn of a card upon green baize tables at gentlemen's clubs. Mr. Roger Brograve, a former captain in the 2nd Dragoons and brother of Sir George Brograve, had frittered away his competent fortune on the Turf. He lost £10,000 on one Derby. His debts eventually overwhelmed him and he committed suicide in June 1813. Brummell, too, was sadly addicted to gambling on horseracing. As Raikes recalled:

The spell was good (this was, I think, in 1813); during more than two years he was a constant winner at play on the turf, and I believe realized nearly 30,000*l*. The blind goddess then deserted him; but not till after he had formed some projects of domestic life in which Miss____, the late Lady____, was the object of his addresses, which were not accepted. The tide, however, turned, but I never could understand that his losses were very considerable, and I never was more surprised than when, in 1816, one morning he confided to me, that his situation had become so desperate, that he must fly the country that night and by stealth. The next day he was landed in Calais, and, as he said, without any resources. I had several letters from him at that time written with much cleverness, in which his natural high spirits struggled manfully against his overpowering reverses; but from the first he felt confident that he should never be able to return to his own country.[15]

Bookmakers were a recent innovation on Regency racecourses. The first known bookmaker, blacklegs, or "legs" surfaced just before the turn of the century and were common by 1804. Legs offered varying odds on different horses and accepted bets on any horse in any race. Dandy Scrope Davies supplemented his income by bookmaking at Newmarket. Working in tandem with legs were racing touts who spied on racehorses as they ran trials and wormed out stable secrets for nefarious purposes.
 The animals who provided this wealth of entertainment (or devastation if one's horse did not win) suffered innumerable indignites at the hands of their Regency trainers. Severe sweats, trials, and purges were the cornerstone of their existence. They were kept rugged in heated stables with never a whiff of fresh air to threaten them. They usually stayed in the region where they

trained and only raced there. Transport was very difficult, and even dangerous for the horse. Most often the horse was walked to the race course. With the type of training the poor animal endured and the walk on top of it, a horse with very far to go could barely lift his hoof, much less win a race.

NOTES TO CHAPTER VIII

1. Rees Howell Gronow, *The Reminiscences and Recollections of Captain Gronow*, 1:52-53.

2. Ibid., 2:109.

3. Ibid., 2:257-258.

4. Richard H. Stoddard, ed., *Personal Reminiscences by Cornelia Knight and Thomas Raikes*, p. 289.

5. Ibid., p. 307.

6. Gronow, *Reminiscences and Recollections*, 2:110.

7. Ibid., 2:257.

8. Ibid.

9. Ibid., 2:113.

10. Ibid., 2:112.

11. Ibid., 1:322.

12. Stoddard, *Raikes*, p. 288.

13. *Le Beau Monde*, April 1807, p. 355.

14. Stoddard, *Raikes,* pp. 298-99.

15. Ibid., p. 272.

Chapter IX

THE REAL WORLD AND THE REAL PEOPLE

The small enclosed world of the *haut ton* played only a slight part in the rich tapestry of life in early nineteenth century England. In the real world, the lower classes were grappling with the sometimes devastating effects of the Industrial Revolution. The middle class was growing by leaps and bounds, and their moralistic repulsion for raffish Regency decadence became the herald for a new age. And the talented minds, as in every age, were busily at work inventing, writing, painting, governing, experimenting, and reforming. To put these diverse elements in perspective a select chronology and biographical dictionary follow.

A Select Chronology of
Late Georgian England (1800-1821)
With Particular Emphasis on the Regency

1800

Summer and Fall	Food both scarce and costly generated a series of food riots in London.
Published:	*Castle Rackrent* by Maria Edgeworth

1801

January 1	Union between Great Britain and Ireland was enacted. The Union Jack was adopted as the official flag.

February 20   George III suffered a brief recurrence of his episodic madness.

March 14   Pitt resigned as Prime Minister.

March 21   French army defeated decisively at the Battle of Alexandria by the British.

May 15   John Hadfield took ill-aimed potshots at George III as the king attended a performance at Drury Lane.

October 16   *Morning Post* reported that over 20,000 French prisoners were being held in England.

November   A Bill was brought into Parliament to take the first modern census. The unscientific collection of data revealed 15,717,287 souls residing in England, Wales, Scotland and Ireland.

Published: *Moral Tales for Young People* by Maria Edgeworth.

1802

March   The Peace of Amiens was signed by France, England, Spain, and the Batavian Republic.

November   Colonel Edward M. Despard and three dozen followers plot to kill the king. He was arrested and executed.

Observed: The flight of Garnerin made ballooning a topic of conversation.

The West India Docks were completed and opened.

Published: *Peerage of England, Scotland, and Ireland* by John Debrett
Edinburgh Review and Cobbett's *Weekly Political Register* began publication.

1803

May 18   The brief interlude of peace between Britain and France came to an end.

Observed: Master Betty or "The Infant Roscius" amazed and delighted audiences for the first time.

Published: *The Minstrelsy of the Scottish Border* by Sir Walter Scott. (His first published work)

1804

May   Napoleon became the French Emperor.

July   Great Britain, Austria, Sweden, and Russia created the Third Coalition to ally themselves against France.

December   Napoleon was crowned at a grand ceremony with the Pope in attendance.

Observed: British and Foreign Bible Society began.

1805

October 21   Nelson was mortally wounded at Trafalgar. This naval victory broke Napoleon's navy; Great Britain ruled the seas.

December 2   Napoleon, though outnumbered, defeated the allied Russian and Austrian armies at Austerlitz. Austria hurriedly sued for peace, and the Third Coalition was broken.

Published: *Madoc* by Robert Southey

1806

January 23   William Pitt the Younger, the Prime Minister, died.

September 13 The Whig leader Charles James Fox died.

October   The renowned opera singer, Madame Catalani, debuted on the London stage.

November 21   Napoleon's Berlin Decree declared the entire British Isles under blockade and closed Continental ports to British shipping.

Observed: The first of the Elgin marbles arrived in Great Britain.

Published: First of the thirty-six volumes of *The Parliamentary History of England* by William Cobbett.

1807

March 25   Parliament abolished the slave trade. The institution of slavery was not outlawed until the 1830s.

September 2   The English attacked Copenhagen and captured the Danish fleet.

Observed: Ascot had its first Gold Cup.

Published: *Tales from Shakespeare* by Charles and Mary Lamb

1808

August   The first British forces landed in Portugal.

September 20   Covent Garden burned to the ground.

Demonstrated: Richard Trevithick's "Catch-Me-Who-Can", a steam railway locomotive, chugged around a track near Euston Road in London.

Published: *Marmion* by Sir Walter Scott
               Introduction to a General Stud Book (the final version) by James Weatherby
               Baronetage of England by John Debrett

1809

February   The Duke of York resigned as Commander-in-Chief of the Army due to the   scandal surrounding Mary Anne Clarke, his mistress, who sold commissions using her influence.

February 24   Drury Lane burned to the ground.

May 12   Wellington defeated Soult at Oporto.

June 27-28   British and Spanish forces defeat French at Talavera.

July 2   Byron set sail for an inspiring tour of the Mediterranean.

October 25   Britain celebrated "The Jubilee," the beginning of the fiftieth year of George III's reign.

Observed: The first 2000 Guineas at Newmarket was run.

1810

May 31   Rumors began to circulate that the vile Duke of Cumberland had murdered his valet.

October 15   *Morning Post* reported 12,000 English prisoners are held by the French.

December   George III suffered complete mental incapacity and was confined.

Observed: The intrepid, eccentric Lady Hester Stanhope sailed to the Middle East and never returned to Britain.

Published: *Lady of the Lake* by Sir Walter Scott

1811

February 6   The Regency Bill had passed and es-
                    tablished the Prince of Wales as Regent
                    for his mad father. Prinny's oaths were
                    witnessed by the Privy Council on this
                    day.

Spring   Severe labor unrest resulted in widespread
                    machine wreckage and rioting. Workers
                    who feared replacement by machinery were
                    dubbed Luddites. Rioting began in
                    Nottingham and spread throughout the
                    country.

March 5   General Graham's English troops beat a far
                    superior French force at Barrosa.

May 16   The British claimed a Pyrrhic and con-
                    troversial victory over the French at
                    Albuera.

May 25   The Regent reappointed the Duke of York
                    to his former position as Commander-in-
                    Chief.

June 19   Prinny hosted a grand fête to celebrate
                    his regency for 2,000 of his closest friends
                    for the paltry sum of £15,000.

August   The old king's apartments at Windsor were
                    padded. No hope was held out for his
                    recovery.

Observed: "The Great Schism" a large group of
                    disenchanted Protestants left the Anglican
                    church.

| Published: | *Sense and Sensibility* by Jane Austen |

1812

January - May	Labor troubles continued. Rioting came to Leeds, Macclesfield, Bolton, and many other towns.
May 11	Perceval, the prime minister, was shot and killed by John Bellingham in the lobby of the House of Commons. The Tory government of the Liverpool ministry came into power and remained so until 1827.
June	United States declared war on Britain.
	Napoleon invaded Russia.
July 22	Wellington and his troops defeated the French army at Salamanca and captured two French eagles!
September 30	The two captured French eagles from Salamanca joined two taken at Madrid and one captured near Ciudad Rodrigo in Whitehall Chapel during an elaborate military ceremony.
October	Napoleon and his troops abandoned Moscow and began the almost three month retreat from Russia.
Observed:	Gas lit lamps began to replace the oil lamps in London streets.

Exhibited:	*Snowstorm: Hannibal and His Army Crossing the Alps* by J.M.W. Turner at the Royal Academy.
Published:	*Vivian* by Maria Edgeworth *Childe Harold's Pilgrimage* (first two cantos) by Lord Byron

1813

June 21	Wellington led his allied troops to a brilliant victory at Vittoria.
July	After Prinny gave Brummell the cut direct, the impudent dandy inquired, "Alvanley, who's your fat friend?" They never spoke again.
July 20	Vauxhall staged a grand public *fête* to celebrate the victory at Vittoria.
Summer	The visiting bluestocking Madame de Staël became the darling of the *ton*.
October 16-19	The Allies defeated Napoleon at the Battle of Leipzig. The fall of his empire became inevitable.
Published:	*Pride and Prejudice* by Jane Austen *Life of Nelson* by Robert Southey "Queen Mab" by Percy Bysshe Shelley *The Giaour* by Lord Byron *New View of Society* by Robert Owen

1814

Winter	One of the coldest winters ever settled over London. The Thames was frozen

over between London Bridge and Black-
fiars.

February 1   A great Frost Fair featuring all sorts of
amusements and booths opened on the
stretch of frozen Thames River. It closed
on February 5 when the ice began to
crack.

March   The Duchess of Oldenburg, the Tsar's
sister, arrived in London in advance of her
brother's state visit. She and Prinny
detested each other on sight.

April 6   Napoleon abdicated.

May 3   Wellington was created a duke.

Louis XVIII entered Paris and reclaimed
the Bourbon throne.

May 4   Napoleon arrived at Elba.

May 30   The First Treaty of Paris was signed. It
returned France's borders to those of
1792.

June   Tsar Alexander, King Frederick of Prussia,
and Blücher visited England. Blücher
became the center of fanatical adoration.

July 21   An elaborate *fête* at Carlton House was
given for the recently returned Duke of
Wellington.

August 1   The great victory celebrations ordered by
Prinny took place in London's Hyde Park,
Green Park, and St. James's Park.

August   Prinny's consort Princess Caroline left for Europe. She led a scandalous life abroad for the next six years.

September   The Congress of Vienna began. The English were first represented by Lord Castlereagh, later by Wellington.

December   Britain and United States signed the Treaty of Ghent which ended hostilities.

Observed: Edmund Kean debuted at Drury Lane as Shylock.

Published: *The Corsair* by Lord Byron
Waverley by Sir Walter Scott

1815

January 15   Nelson's Lady Hamilton died.

February   Rumors abounded that a pig-faced lady of great fortune known as "her sowship" had taken up residence in London.

March   Anti-Corn Bill riots swept across London to protest the sharp increase in food prices due to the passage of the bill.

March 20   Napoleon, having escaped from Elba, landed in France and the Hundred Days began.

June 15   The Duchess of Richmond gave a ball in Brussels. It was here Wellington learned that Napoleon was on the march and began to mobilize. Many of her guests would die

	or be wounded in the days to follow.
June 18	Napoleon defeated at Waterloo.
June 19	The Congress of Vienna ended.
June 22	Napoleon abdicated for the second time.
	The Tower guns and the guns of St. James's Park roared in jubilation after news of Waterloo victory reached London.
August	Napoleon embarked for St. Helena aboard the *Northumberland*.
Observed:	Journals of Parliament reported Prinny £339,000 in debt. Other sources believed his indebtedness to be over £1,000,000.
	Sir Humphrey Davy introduced his safety lamp for miners.
	John Nash began rebuilding the Brighton Pavilion.
Published:	*Guy Mannering* by Sir Walter Scott *The Present State of Roadmaking* by John McAdam *Emma* by Jane Austen

1816

May 2	Princess Charlotte, heir presumptive, married her prince charming, Prince Leopold of Saxe-Coburg-Saalfeld.

May 17	Beau Brummell, fleeing his debts, departed for the Continent. He would never return to England.
December 2	Spa Field Riots occurred. It was just one of the many incidents of rising social and political unrest which happened throughout the year.
Observed:	The House of Commons apportioned £35,000 for the British Museum to acquire the Elgin Marbles.
Published:	*The Prisoner of Chillon* by Byron "Kubla Kahn" by Samuel Coleridge

1817

January 28	Angry crowds hoot, hiss, and scream at the wildly unpopular Prince Regent as he makes his way to open Parliament.
July 18	Jane Austen died.
November 6	Princess Charlotte died after giving birth to a stillborn son. The whole nation plunged into prodigious mourning.
Observed:	Waterloo Bridge was completed after six years of construction.
	The new Custom House was completed.
	John Kemble retired from the stage.
Published:	*Ormond* by Maria Edgeworth "Ozymandias" by Percy Bysshe Shelley

1818

May 14   Matthew "Monk" Lewis, dramatist and
            novelist, died.

Fall   Congress of Aix-la-Chapelle

Observed: The death of Prinny's heir galvanized his
            siblings. Eighteen hundred and eighteen
            became the year of the royal marriages.
            They included:
            Duke of Kent to Mary Victoria, Dowager
                Princess of Saxe-Meiningen
            Duke of Clarence to Princess Adelaide of
                Saxe-Meiningen
            Duke of Cambridge to Princess Augusta
                of Hesse-Cassel

Published: *Nightmare Abbey* by T. L. Peacock
            Frankenstein by Mary Shelley
            "Endymion" by John Keats
            Northanger Abbey and *Persuasion* (post-
                humously) by Jane Austen
            Thomas Bowdler's sanitized version of
                Shakespeare.
            "Bowdlerism" entered the language.

1819

March 20   Burlington Arcade, Piccadilly, London,
            opened.

May 24   The future Queen Victoria was born to the
            recently married Duke of Kent.

August 16   "Peterloo," A meeting of reformers in
            Manchester addressed by "Orator" Hunt

was dispersed by cavalry. The resulting death and injury toll was outrageous.

December
: The Six Acts, which were aimed at curbing freedom of the press and other rights, were passed to insure the maintenance of public order.

Observed:
: Hobby horses are ridden on London streets.

The first ship powered by steam to cross the Atlantic took 26 days.

Published:
: *Don Juan*, Cantos I and II, by Lord Byron
: "Ode to a Nightingale" by John Keats
: *Ivanhoe* by Sir Walter Scott

1820

January 1
: The Cato Street Conspiracy, a plot instigated by Arthur Thistlewood to assassinate government ministers, was uncovered.

January 29
: The old mad king died.

June 6
: Queen Caroline returned to England after her six year romp through Europe. The populace acclaimed her!

Summer-Fall
: George IV plotted to rid himself of his queen. Queen Caroline endured a farcical trial that ended unsuccessfully for the new king.

Published:
: "Prometheus Unbound" by Percy Bysshe Shelley
: *Melmoth the Wanderer* by Charles Maturin

1821

July 19   George IV was crowned at a lavish, spectacular coronation ceremony. His wife Caroline unsuccessfully attempted to gain admittance.

August 7   Queen Caroline died.

Observed: William Cobbett began his famous "rides" through rural England.

Exhibited: *Hay Wain* by John Constable

Published: *Life in London* by Pierce Egan, illustrated by George and Isaac Robert Cruikshank

A Select Biographical Dictionary

Adam, Robert (1728-1792)

After several years on the Grand Tour on which he diligently studied ancient domestic Roman architecture, Adam returned to Britain in 1757. He was destined to be in the forefront of neo-classical architects in Georgian England. Shelburne House in Berkeley Square was one of many triumphs. The innovative genius of his interiors usually surpassed the exterior designs of such establishments as Home House, Wynn House, and Derby House. Diversity, simplicity, delicate colors, close attention to every detail, and the belief that every object in the interior must complement each other characterized his best work.

Alexander I, Tsar of Russia (1777-1825)

Regency England flattered, adored, and flocked around the heroic Tsar during his state visit to Britain in June, 1814. The Tsar of Russia (1801-1825) was a vacillating, devious leader. On the homefront he wavered between reform and suppression. In foreign affairs he opposed Napoleon (1805-07), then sued for peace in 1807 and joined the Continental System until 1810. Mutual distrust between the two emperors led to a breakdown of relations, and Napoleon marched upon Russia in 1812. The Tsar became instrumental in Napoleon's downfall and helped to redesign European borders. In the last uneventful years of his reign, he followed a moderate course.

Austen, Jane (1775-1817)

This English novelist brilliantly chronicled the follies and foibles of the English gentry during the Napoleonic Wars. Her first published novel was *Sense and Sensibility* (1811), followed by *Pride and Prejudice* (1813), *Mansfield Park* (1814), *Emma* (1815) and *Persuasion* and *Northanger Abbey* (post. 1818). *Emma* was dedicated to the Prince Regent with his permission. Austen gently turned down the suggestion that she write a history of the illustrious Prince's family, stating that her meager talents could not do justice to the subject.

Blake, William (1757-1827)

This unconventional poet and artist earned his living as an engraver. He published and imaginatively illustrated his own poetic works which were considered much ahead of their time; among them were, *Songs of Experience* and *Songs of Innocence*.

Blücher, Gebhard Leberecht von (1742-1819)

Regency England fell in love with this crusty, coarse Prussian general during his visit to England during Victory Summer, 1814. He was pursued with frantic devotion wherever he went. He had enjoyed a long, hard fighting military career, and by the end of the Napoleonic wars was the premiere Prussian military hero. His presence was crucial to victory at Waterloo in 1815.

Brougham, Henry Peter (1778-1868)

This Scot, who helped establish the *Edinburgh Review* (1802), went into the House of Commons as an outspoken Whig in 1810. During the Regency he voraciously defended Caroline of Brunswick, especially during the farcical Queen's Trial in 1820. His bravura performance as he discredited one crown witness after another made him a much sought after lawyer.

Brummell, George Bryan "Beau" (1778-1840)

This Regency fashionplate graced the 10th Hussars with his presence from 1794 to 1798. His indifferent career as a soldier came to an abrupt end when he inherited a fortune and found out that the Hussars were being posted to Manchester. "Beau" caught the fancy of the Prince of Wales as early as 1794, and he quickly became a favorite. His own attributes and the friendship of Prinny insured his prompt social success in London at his new residence at No. 4 Chesterfield Street, Mayfair.

Brummell's adroit wit, innate fashion sense, and elegant social graces soon catapulted him into the ultimate Regency dandy and supreme social arbiter. His comments on the terrible cut of Prinny's coat had even reduced his royal friend to tears. Brummell's approval could lend cachet to any aspirant to fashionable circles; his disapproval could ruin the unlucky souls who had gained his contempt.

Brummell and Prinny eventually parted ways. The impudent "Beau" had slighted Mrs. Fitzherbert, acted nastily over some snuff, and then uttered those infamous words, "Alvanley, who's your fat friend?" in 1813. The break was final and complete. Brummell's social consequence was such that he remained the darling of the *haut ton* after the break. What drove him to utter ruin was the crippling fault that ruined many others — incredible extravagance and suicidal gambling. By May 1816, he had completely dissipated his respectable fortune and fled Britain to escape his creditors. The former king of the *ton* lived in obscurity on the Continent for the rest of his life.

Byron, George Gordon Noel, became 6th Baron Byron in 1798 (1788-1824)

This handsome, clubfooted young lord enraptured the *ton* with his brilliant poetry and titilating romantic exploits. The publication of Cantos I and II of *Childe Harold's Pilgrimage* in 1812 propelled him into instant celebrity. His many liaisons with social hostesses, most notably with the unbalanced Caroline Lamb, provided ample fodder for gossips. During his years as a social lion, he also wrote *The Giaour* and *The Corsair*. Separation from his wife of a year, Anne Isabella Milbanke, in 1816 and the accompanying nasty rumors of incest between Byron and Augusta Leigh, his half-sister, turned him into a social outcast among the *haut ton*. He left England in 1816 and spent the rest of his life abroad. *Don Juan* and the third canto of *Childe Harold* were produced during his exile.

Canning, George (1770-1827)

Sharp-witted Tory MP, George Canning enjoyed a long illustrious career in government. During a stint as Foreign

Secretary (1807-1809) he vigorously pursued war against
Napoleon. Differences with Castlereagh, his party's
Secretary of War, led not only to his resignation, but a
duel between the two men. He reentered the Foreign
Office after Castlereagh's suicide in 1822. At his death in
1827, he was serving as Prime Minister. He died at
Chiswick, the Devonshire villa, in the same room where
Fox had expired.

Carlton House Set

The Prince of Wales acted like a magnet to all the
worst rakes and rogues in the kingdom. His particular
cronies who were most intimately involved in the decadent
dissipations of the Prince were known as members of the
Carlton House set. They included:

Colonel George Hanger — a wild amusing rogue noted
for the oddity of his wagers.

Henry Barry, 8th Earl of Barrymore, "Cripplegate" — a
dissipated, foulmouthed noble of extravagance tastes
and woeful morals.

11th Duke of Norfolk — a multi-bottle man given to
extremely low behavior.

Sir John Lade — a famous whip whose wife Letty was
noted for her coarse language and horsemanship.

3rd Marquis of Hertford (known as Lord Yarmouth
until his succession in 1822) — a rake addicted to
gaming of every sort.

Other members of Prinny's rakehelly inner circle at
various times included Lord Cholmondeley, Prince Boothby,
the fabulously wealthy Ball Hughes, and Lord Alvanley.

Caroline of Brunswick, Princess of Wales (1768-1821)

Prinny's consort, a stolid German princess, wed her first cousin, later George IV, on April 8, 1795. It proved a disastrous mismatch of monumental proportions. After a few months of marriage and the birth of their only child, Princess Charlotte, they lived separate lives. The promiscuous unstable Princess of Wales became a rallying point for Whig opposition during the Regency. She left England in 1814 and wallowed in Continental exile until 1820. Prinny's attempt to divorce her in 1820 was unsuccessful, but he did insure that she remained uncrowned at her death.

Castlereagh, Lord (Robert Stewart) (1769-1822)

Lord Castlereagh was the architect of Britain's foreign policy through much of the first quarter of the nineteenth century. He served in various positions in the Tory government including War Minister (July 1805 to January 1806; April 1807 to September 1809). Foreign Secretary (February 1812 until his death). He also represented Britain at the Congress of Vienna (1814-1815) and Congress of Aix-la-Chapelle (1818). Exhaustion and depression overcame him in 1822, and the austere unpopular statesman committed suicide.

Cobbett, William (1763-1835)

Cobbett denounced and exposed corruption, glorified the English countryside, deplored industrialism, and opposed Napoleon in over thirty years of scribblings. Much of his work appeared in his own publication the *Weekly Political Register* (1803 to 1835). *Rural Rides* (1830) recounted a series of journeys to the English countryside in the 1820s and was filled with astute observations.

Coleridge, Samuel Taylor (1772-1834)

The intellect of this English poet and critic illuminated the Romantic movement. Notable among his poetry was "Kubla Kahn" and "The Rime of the Ancient Mariner." Between 1808 and 1819 he gave a series of seven lectures on various literary subjects, one of which was Shakespeare. Some of his best literary criticism was in *Biographia Literaria* (1817).

Constable, John (1776-1837)

This superb English landscape painter enjoyed little success during the Regency. Admiration and acclaim eluded him until 1824 with the exhibition of *Hay Wain* at the Paris Salon.

Cruikshank, George (1792-1878) and Isaac Robert (1789-1856)

The sons of Isaac Cruikshank were popular satirical caricaturists, artists, and book illustrators whose long careers began in the early nineteenth century. Both gained fame by turning their prolific and wicked pens on the fashionable follies and scandals (particularly Prinny and Caroline's marriage) of the Regency. Though George's greater popularity overshadowed his brother's career, Isaac Robert was noted for his humorous depiction of the dandy in all his ridiculous glory. The quintessential guide for young bucks on the town, Pierce Egan's *Life in London* (1821) benefitted from illustrations by both brothers.

Edgeworth, Maria (1767-1849)

This Irish novelist wed sympathetically drawn regional settings, spritely dialogue, and realistic characters to gain her reputation as a literary lion in Regency London. Her first important works included *Castle Rackrent* (1800), a novel depicting cruel Irish landlords, and *Belinda* (1801). By 1806 her novels of manners had propelled her into a full, rich life at the center of literary London. During the Regency she continued to be productive, writing: *Tales of Fashionable Life*, in six volumes, (1809-1812); *Vivian* (1812); *Patronage* (1814); *Harrington* (1817); and *Ormond* (1817). She returned to Ireland in 1820 following a bout of depression and ill health. She revelled in rural pursuits and continued to write here until the end of her life.

Fitzherbert, Maria Anne (1756-1837)

Prinny fell madly in love with twice-widowed, Catholic Mrs. Fitzherbert in 1785. Despite the legal impossibility of their union, the determined, lovesick Prince secretly married the older, Junoesque woman of his dreams on December 21, 1785. They struggled off and on for eighteen years to achieve domestic bliss. They parted forever in 1803. Prinny, with customary childlike sentimentality, cherished momentoes of their union. He died with her portrait hung around his neck. A settlement of £6,000 a year kept Mrs. Fitzherbert in the style to which she was accustomed until her death.

Fox, Charles James (1749-1806)

Whig leader Fox delighted in hard drinking and extravagant gaming as much as he enjoyed opposing the policies of George III and William Pitt the Younger. Throughout his tempestuous political career, Fox championed the cause of liberty in Parliament with ample debating skills. He condemned Britain's actions in her American colonies and welcomed the liberating force of the early part of the French Revolution. He was a particular favorite of Prinny's (George III considered Fox a terrible influence on the young Prince of Wales) and was sorely missed at Carlton House after his death at Chiswick in 1806.

George III (1738-1820)

While Prinny celebrated the beginning of his Regency with a glorious *fête,* his father was beginning ten long years locked up in Windsor Castle as a madman. George III had succeeded to the throne in 1760 on the death of George II, his grandfather. He dutifully married Charlotte of Mecklenburg-Strelitz, a fruitful German princess. They settled down to a thoroughly domestic existence and produced a quiverfull of children. He suffered his first brief bout of madness in 1765. A much longer recurrence in 1788-89 prompted the suggestion of establishing a regency. His recovery stopped all talk of a regent until the final devastating and complete descent into madness in 1810.

George IV, earlier Regent for George III (1762-1830)

The pleasure-loving Prince of Wales gaily entered into the decadent high society of raffish Georgian England even before he came of age in 1783. At his independent household at Carlton House, he surrounded himself with the dissolute and brilliant Foxite Whigs, in particular Fox and Sheridan. He eagerly pursued friendships with rakehells and rogues of every description. He indulged his love of finery and amusement with a zestful passion, always intent on sampling everything. Prizefighting, horseracing, gambling, and expensive women whiled away many a day and night. He enjoyed the life of a beau on the town, and spent enormous sums maintaining his exciting life. Though he had enjoyed popularity as a young, handsome prince with the world at his feet, his wild unchecked spending, which demanded frequent appeals for money from an increasingly unsympathetic Parliament, badly tarnished his public image.

Troubled domestic arrangements reinforced the growing contempt heaped upon him by the populace. His marriage to Caroline of Brunswick in 1795 (a ploy to get his massive debts settled) was a public and private disaster. Their many marital troubles provided ample fodder for the ravenous pens of caricaturists. They lived together until their first and only child, Princess Charlotte, was born. Prinny, as the Prince of Wales was known to his intimates and enemies, always had a profusion of female company. His paramours from "Perdita" to Lady Conyngham reflected his decided taste for full-bodied ladies after their youthful bloom had faded. The greatest love of his life was Catholic Mrs. Fitzherbert whom he secretly and illegally married in 1785. Their liaison lasted off and on until 1803. After the final break, he occasionally shed a few sentimental tears over his lost love between conquests.

His public and private life generated more and more contempt, ridicule, and antagonism as he grew older. He excelled in planning great ceremonial occasions which cost unforgivably huge sums. After Fox's death in 1806, he gradually drifted away from his old Whig friends and supporters. They never forgave him for happily accepting Perceval's Tory ministry when he became Regent. His debts never seemed to be paid no matter how often he pleaded for additional funds.

George IV was a curious mixture of charm, childish willfulness, sentimentality, and utter selfishness. He earned every ounce of contempt heaped upon him and yet he could be the most charming of hosts and a loyal friend. Wellington described him as "the most extraordinary compound of talent, wit, buffoonery, obstinacy, and good feeling—in short, a medley of the most opposite qualities, with a great preponderance of good—that I ever saw in any character in my life."[1]

This affable buffoon of a prince became Regent in 1811. He had been known as the "First Gentleman of Europe" in his early dashing years on the town as a beau of the first water, but he was fat, florid, and nearly fifty by the commencement of his regency. There was little of the handsome "Florizel" left.

He succeeded to the throne in 1820, and soon after treated his countrymen to a ludicrous trial of Queen Caroline, as he tried unsuccessfully to divest himself of his queen. It could safely be said that the monarchy had reached its lowest popularity by his death in 1830. Ironically his greatest legacy was the massive building projects he instigated and the marvelous furnishings and art on which he had squandered so much money.

Gillray, James (1757-1815)

This savage caricaturist who alternately amused and outraged Georgian England became famous with a particularly wicked cartoon concerning Prinny and Mrs. Fitzherbert entitled "Farmer George and His Wife." He produced over 1500 vulgar, boisterous engravings until mental illness ended his career in 1811.

Hazlitt, William (1778-1830)

This important critic and essayist had a long prolific career as a journalist and author. He contributed to a variety of periodicals and newspapers during the period: *Morning Chronicle* (as theater critic), The *Examiner, Champion,* the *Edinburgh Review* and *The Times.* His books included the *Characters of Shakespeare's Plays* (1817), *A View of the English Stage* (1818), and *Lectures on the English Poets* (1818). His criticism was noted for being discerning, readable, and learned.

Holland House Circle

Wealthy Whig society gathered at the Kensington mansion known as Holland House as guests of the 3rd

Baron Holland and Lady Holland. The imperious Lady Holland reigned over dinner guests that included the most brilliant luminaries of the Whig opposition, as well as the most interesting, talented men in society. Included in this circle were Sheridan, Sir Philip Francis, cousin Charles James Fox, "Monk" Lewis, Byron, Payne Knight, Brougham, Tom Moore, Henry Luttrell, and Sydney Smith.

Jackson, John (1769-1845)

Gentleman Jackson reigned as the boxing champion of England from 1795 until his retirement in 1803. Admired by the Fancy for his prowess and grit, he parlayed his fame into a successful pugilistic school for the bucks and beaus of the *ton*. Byron was just one of his many admirers of the prizefighter who patronized the school.

Kean, Edmund (1789-1833)

This small man with his compelling voice and magnetic stage presence became a star at Drury Lane in 1814 in the role of Shylock. His unstudied acting style galvanized the London theater audience and critics alike. In time he played all the great tragic Shakespearean heroes. Though immensely successful, his reckless uninhibited lifestyle, drunkenness, and profligate generosity kept him penniless and he died deeply in debt.

Kemble, John Philip (1757-1823)

In direct contrast to the natural, magnetic Kean, actor and theater manager John Kemble performed in a stiff, studied manner. Not even opposite his glowing sister Sarah Siddons (They first performed together in 1785) did his cold oratorical manner catch fire. As a theater manager he reigned over Drury Lane from 1788 to 1803.

He began managing Covent Garden in 1803. He unhappily suffered through the theater's fiery destruction in 1808, the costly rebuilding, and the months of rioting by unhappy patrons protesting price increases after reopening in 1809. His health broke under the strain, and he was not seen on a London stage for two years. He, as all actors of his generation, suffered badly in comparison to the formidable Kean. Kemble's last performance was in June 1817 as Coriolanus.

Lawrence, Sir Thomas (1769-1830)

Lawrence relished his position as the fashionable portrait painter of the *ton* and Court. In 1786 he had a growing reputation as an artist when he left Bath to seek his fortune in London. By 1789 he had been called to Windsor to paint Queen Charlotte. Within three years he became the Painter to the King. Notable among his work were the series of portraits of current leaders commissioned by the Prince Regent in 1814. His style, though firmly based in eighteenth-century, had a theatrical drama in keeping with the romantic ideal.

Lewis, Matthew (1775-1818)

"Monk" Lewis, an admirable fellow of many talents, enjoyed his first great success as an author with the publication of the melodramatic "gothic" *The Monk* in 1795. He wallowed in its gratifying success and the acclaim and affection of the fashionable world. He delightedly numbered royalty among his friends, in particular the amiable Duchess of York. During his varied life, he served as an MP, supplied numerous tonnish gatherings with amusing chatter, wrote innumerable plays, scribbled much verse, and humanely ran the vast Jamaican estate which he inherited from his father in 1812. He succumbed to yellow fever during a return trip from Jamaica in 1818 and was sorely missed by his large circle of fashionable friends.

Louis XVIII (1755-1824)

After many years of exile, both on the Continent and in Britain, the oldest living brother of Louis XVI triumphantly returned to France in 1814. His ten year reign was briefly interrupted when Napoleon returned from Elba, but after Waterloo, the gout-ridden obese old king returned to Paris to follow a moderate policy during his rule.

McAdam, John (1756-1836)

The Scottish engineer provided the best possible means for fashionable beaus and their ladies to reach the site of their Regency frolics—a new method to build roads of outstanding smoothness and durability! Roads were to be "macadamized," that is, a carefully constructed convex, well-drained road was layered with broken stones of the same size (preferably granite and greenstone), and then traffic compacted the stones into a smooth, solid surface. McAdam put his road building ideas into action after he was appointed Surveyor General of Bristol Roads in 1815.

Metternich, Clement von (1773-1859)

This brilliant statesman served as Austria's Foreign Minister from 1809 to 1848. Metternich wanted to ally Austria with Napoleon from 1809 to 1813. He helped achieve this end by actively championing the match between Marie Louise and Napoleon. When he realized that Napoleon's empire was doomed, Metternich gradually pulled Austria away from France and allied with Russia and Prussia in 1813. When European boundaries were redrawn at the Congress of Vienna, the substantial territorial gains of the Austrian Empire owed much to the machinations of this wily negotiator.

Napoleon (1769-1821)

This brilliant Corsican shrewdly parlayed the French populace's disillusionment with the Directoire and his own successful French military career into an emperor's crown for himself and an empire for his people. The French paid a high price for their Empire as they plunged into a continual series of military campaigns throughout Europe. Britain's press called him such things as "Odious Tyrant" and the "Monster" though the Holland House circle admired him greatly. After a series of serious defeats, he abdicated in 1814 and was exiled to Elba. Victory generated a frenzy of excitement in Britain and the summer of 1814 was known as "Victory Summer" for good reason. People at every level of society attended all manner and fashion of celebratory entertainments. Napoleon's last brief moment of glory, the "Hundred Days," when he fled Elba and attempted to regain his throne, ended in defeat at Waterloo. He spent the last years of his life incarcerated on St. Helena.

Nash, John (1752-1835)

John Nash enjoyed the distinction of being the Prince Regent's favorite architect. This was no small honor considering the magnitude and scope of Prinny's building fever. Among the monumental jobs which Nash tackled for the Prince were: the rebuilding and transformation of Brighton Pavilion into a fantasy palace (1815-1823); the structures erected in London's various parks to celebrate victory on August 1, 1814 as decreed by Prinny, which included a Chinese bridge in St. James's Park; and the ill-fated attempt to transform Buckingham House into a grand palace. The design of Regent's Park and Regent Street, the "Royal Mile," mark Nash's greatest achievement. The grandeur and scope of his vision along the street which Prinny commanded be built to connect Carlton House to Regent's Park stands as a suitable monument to the age.

Nelson, Horatio (1758-1805)

As Admiral Nelson lay wounded aboard his ship *Victory* at Trafalgar, his officers and men helplessly watched as the finest of British Naval commanders died at the moment of his greatest victory. The defeat of the French under Villeneuve gave Britain total command of the sea during the Napoleonic wars. Nelson's long, brilliant career at sea turned him into a revered figure. Not even his adulterous and public affair with Lady Hamilton could diminish the stature of the one-eyed, one-armed naval hero.

Rowlandson, Thomas (1756-1827)

This gifted painter and illustrator achieved his greatest fame as a caricaturist of particularly wicked bent. His critical, satirical eye fell on every level of society. His most notable series were the *Tours of Dr. Syntax,* begun in 1812, which he produced with William Combe. Also memorable was his series *The Comforts of Bath.*

Royal Dukes

Never in the history of Great Britain has the populace been inflicted with so expensive a batch of Royal Dukes. The sons of George III were an immense and unpopular drain on English pocket-books. Though Prinny was by far the most expensive of the royal brood, his brothers were rightly called great millstones around the neck of the government. The six younger brothers of George IV who survived childhood included:

1. Frederick, Duke of York (1763-1827)
The Duke of York spent most of his adult life in the military. He was uninspired, though painstaking, in the field, but shone as Commander-in-Chief. His organizational skills did much to insure victory over Napoleon. His military career was briefly marred by the scandal involving his mistress Mary Anne Clarke and the nefarious sale of army commissions. He resigned as Commander in 1809, but was reinstated in 1811. He stayed deep in debt throughout his life, recklessly overspending year after year. He married his affable Duchess in 1791, and their weekend marriage at Oatlands suited him very well.

2. William, Duke of Clarence, later William IV (1765-1837)
Prinny's bluff, hearty brother had a short naval career as a young man and never lost his quarter deck manner and sometimes startling informality. His active naval career was virtually over in 1788 when he was created Duke of Clarence. Soon after this he began a lengthy liaison with Mrs. Jordan. They produced an ever-increasing and expensive brood of Fitzclarences (10 in all) over their 21-year relationship (1790-1811). When Princess Charlotte, George IV's heir presumptive died in 1817, the Duke of Clarence joined the royal race to the altar. His union to Princess Adelaide of Saxe-Meiningen proved unfruitful, but the death of his elder brother, the Duke of York, in 1827 insured that he would reign as king, if he could outlive the ailing Prinny. The brief reign of the jovial, informal William helped restore some of the popularity of the monarchy that Prinny lacked through years of debts and dissipation.

3. Edward, Duke of Kent (1767-1820)
This son of George III's chief acknowledgment was fathering the future Queen Victoria. Like most of his brothers, he was wildly extravagant and remained in debt

throughout his adult life. His military career was marred by harsh discipline, bestial behavior, and mutiny by men under his command. He heartily despised Prinny and eagerly took any position in opposition to him.

4. Ernest, Duke of Cumberland, later King of Hanover (1771-1851)
The reviled Duke of Cumberland embraced the most rabid reactionary Tory positions. His forceful personality dominated Prinny's political philosophy during his Regency and his reign as king. The Duke felt it was his duty to stiffen Prinny's backbone in dealing with any reform. His battle-scarred face (he had lost an eye) combined with his coarse, crude company manners and stringent political philosophy made him universally disliked. Public animosity followed him throughout his rather sinister life. Dark rumors of murder and incest were readily believed.

5. Augustus, Duke of Sussex (1773-1843)
The Duke of Sussex gained great popularity among the people in his career as an ardent Whig. His championship of Catholic Emancipation and other reforms often put him at odds with his reactionary brothers. His unapproved and later-dissolved marriage to a commoner in the 1790s produced two children. He had a pronounced passion for books and collected them until the end of his life.

6. Adolphus, Duke of Cambridge (1774-1850)
Adored by his parents, this charming Royal Duke lived a blameless, virtuous life unsullied by scandal and well within his income. This changeling in the House of Hanover spent much of his life in Hanover—as an officer in the army, Governor General (1814-1830), and Viceroy (1831-1837). He married Princess Augusta of Hesse-Cassel, and their union was blessed by three children.

Scott, Sir Walter (1771-1832)

"The Wizard of the North" obtained much of his inspiration for his novels and poems from the history and legends of his native Scotland. His narrative poems which earned him great popularity included *Marmion* (1808), *The Lady of the Lake* (1810), and *The Lord of the Isles* (1815). His ability to portray historical periods with brilliant vigorous detail made his novels immensely popular. His novels, which he wrote anonymously in the beginning, include *Waverley* (1814), *The Heart of Midlothian* (1818), and *Ivanhoe* (1819). Unfortunately losses in his publishing business bankrupted the genial Scott in 1826, and he spent the last years of his life busily scribbling away to pay off his enormous debts.

Shelley, Percy Bysshe (1792-1822)

The flower of English romanticism wrote his first important poem, "Queen Mab," in 1813. Shelley embraced a whole range of enlightment ideas that shocked his more staid contemporaries. Like Byron, his domestic life was riddled with strife. He separated from his first wife in 1814, and then he ran off with William Godwin's sixteen-year-old daughter Mary a few months later. Shelley was free to marry in 1816 after Harriet committed suicide. The runaway lovers eloped that same year. The couple spent the last years of Shelley's life on the Continent. Shelley had a prodigious output which included: "Alastor, or the Spirit of Solitude" (1816), "Ozymandias" (1817); *Prometheus Unbound* (1819); and *The Defense of Poetry* (1821). Mary, too, began to write and produced *Frankenstein, or The Modern Prometheus* (1818). Shelley drowned in 1822 at the age of thirty.

Siddons, Sarah (1755-1831)

Georgian England's best Lady Macbeth was a dignified woman of high moral character and a tragic actress of electrifying stage presence. Her first major triumph on the London stage was playing Isabella in *The Fatal Marriage* in 1782 at Drury Lane. She spent much of the rest of her professional life playing London during the winter seasons and touring in the provinces in the summer. Her first resounding success as Lady Macbeth in 1785 remains a legend in theater history. She enjoyed a long, successful career on the stage until her retirement in 1812.

Skeffington, Sir Lumley (1771-1850)

This amiable Regency dandy typified the reckless rowdy fellows who hovered around Prinny and were known as the Carlton House set. Sir Lumley spent much time on his dress. (Prinny often consulted him about clothing.) He made the most of his appearance and even resorted to the paint pot on occasion. Sir Lumley, though just as wild as any of his friends in this expenditure of the ready, loved the theater. His passion for attending and actively writing plays consumed him. He often visited as many as four theaters in one night. His own rather unsuccessful plays were usually comedies or melodramas. Among his ventures were *Word of Honour* (1802) and *The Sleeping Beauty* (1805). Despite inheriting his father's considerable estate and baronetcy in 1815, he lived the last years of his life in straitened circumstances.

Smith, Sydney (1771-1845)

A honest, uncompromising clergyman and brilliant wit, Smith came to London in 1803 flushed with literary successes in Edinburgh. At his own dinner table and in the dining room at Holland House, he shared his splendid wit and his liberal beliefs. He wrote *Letters to Peter*

Plymley (1807-8) in support of Catholic Emancipation. With the passage of the Clergy Residence Act in 1809, Smith had to assume his rightful place at his living in Yorkshire. He dived into his new life with admirable enthusiasm. He always remained a man of high principle, a champion of social reform, and a lively, quotable wit.

Soane, Sir John (1753-1837)

The renowned architect who dutifully studied his craft in Itly during his youth (1777-80) rose to the top of thearchitectural profession with his outstanding original design of the Bank of England (1788). Many important appointments followed. They included: Clerk of the Works at St. James's Palace and the Houses of Parliament (1791); Superintendent of Works to the Fraternity of Freemasons (1813); and Joint Architect to the Board of Works (1815) with Smirke and Nash. His extensive personal collection of books, art, and antiquities became the basis for the Soane Museum.

Stanhope, Lady Hester (1776-1839)

Lady Hester Stanhope was a formidable, independent woman who became known as one of the nineteenth century's most outstanding eccentrics. She served briefly (1803-6) as housekeeper and hostess to her uncle William Pitt the Younger. After his death in 1806, she drifted for several years before beginning her travels. In 1810 with a tiny entourage, she set sail for the Middle East. She never returned to Britain. Instead, she wholeheartedly adopted Arab customs. The Druses, an Arab tribe on Mount Lebanon, adopted her in 1814, and she eventually became their prophetess. The tales of her eccentricities endlessly titillated the *ton,* and her political meddling kept the Foreign Office on its toes for the rest of her life.

Turner, Joseph Mallord William (1775-1851)

Turner gained early acclaim as an artist and became a Royal Academician at the precocious age of 27 in 1802. Even at this young age he was already considered Britain's premiere landscape artist. His endless fascination with rain, sunlight, and mist lasted throughout his artistic career. Among his early works are *The Fifth Plague of Egypt* (1801) and *Dido Building Carthage* (1815). In the 1820s he began developing a new, intense style as a direct result of a visit to sun-drenched Italy. Before his death in 1851, he achieved legendary status that few artists ever received in their own lifetime.

Watt, James (1736-1819)

This Scottish engineer and inventor spent much of his professional life perfecting an effective steam engine. Using Newcomen's early engine design, he tinkered and toyed with improvements over many years. At the time of this revered inventor's death, the great burst of steam-powered transportation was just beginning.

Wellesley, Arthur, created 1st Duke of Wellington, 1814 (1769-1852)

The hero at Waterloo had a long illustrious career in the British Army. After a lengthy stint in India and other posts, he assumed command of British and Portuguese troops in the Peninsula (1809-1814). He played a brilliant strategic waiting game with the French while building a tough cohesive fighting force with strong lines of supply. Important victories against French forces, such as Salamanca (July 1812) and Vittoria (June 1813), eventually routed the French from Spain and Portugal. By October 1813 the allies were fighting the French on their own soil and Napoleon's downfall was assured. A grateful nation

created him Duke of Wellington in May 1814. On Napoleon's return to France, Wellington was recalled from the
Vienna Congress and placed in command of the Allied
troops. The Waterloo victory assured his status as a
legendary hero. He began a controversial political career
in 1818, eventually serving as Prime Minister. His resolute
conservatism, which made social and parliamentary reform
repellent, brought his popularity to low ebb. After
Wellington's retirement from the political arena, the legend
soon rehabilitated itself. Victorian England smothered the
"Iron Duke" with more adulation than he could stand.

Wilberforce, William (1759-1833)

This political activist and advocate for social reform
was instrumental in securing passage of the 1807 Bill which
abolished the slave trade. He continued for the rest of his
life to tirelessly champion the abolition of slavery and
other social reforms. His high Christian ideals and the
immense respect afforded him gave him a powerful moral
voice in British and international politics. Just before his
death in 1833, Britain formally abolished slavery.

NOTES TO CHAPTER IX

1. Richard Henry Stoddard, ed., *Personal Reminiscences by
   Cornelia Knight and Thomas Raikes*, p. 188.

Chapter X

A DICTIONARY OF RUDE AND VULGAR CANT AND SLANG

A

Addle pate — a silly unkind person.

Addle plot — a marplot.

Address — "having address," being socially adroit.

Agog, all-a-gog — eagerly astonished.

Apartments to let — an empty-headed person.

Apothecary — "to speak like an apothecary," to employ difficult words. Apothecaries were noted for hiding their lack of knowledge by the use of multisyllable words.

Awake — "He was awake upon every suit." He was very shrewd.

B

Bacon-faced — very full of face.

Banbury story of a cock and a bull — a foolish, digressive tale.

Barking irons — pistols.

Bartholomew baby — a garishly clothed person, dressed like the dolls on sale at the Bartholomew Fair.

Bean — a guinea.

Bear-garden jaw or discourse — crude or indelicate language, such as that heard at bear-gardens.

Beat — a watchman's round. The area where he has free license to beat peace-loving subjects at his pleasure.

Bedizened — frightfully over-dressed.

Beetle-headed — slow-witted.

Belcher — Large red neckerchief with yellow and black spots named for pugilist Jem Belcher.

Big ones — men of importance such as the Duke of Wellington and The Lord Chancellor.

Big wigs — judges; from the saying "the wisdom's in the wig."

Bird-witted — flighty and inconsiderate.

Black book — "He was in the black book," i.e., his character was blemished. A black book was kept in most regiments, and the names of all persons sentenced to punishment were recorded.

Blood money — the reward offered when highwaymen, footpads and other villians were convicted.

Blow a cloud — to smoke tobacco.

Blue devils — heavy-heartedness.

Blunderbuss — a foolish, incompetent person.

Blunt — money.

Bluster — to brag.

Boxing a charley — overturning a watchman in his shelter.

Brandy-faced — a reddened countenance from freely imbibing.

Bran-faced — branded by freckles.

Brass — money or brazenness.

Break-teeth words — difficult to say.

Breeze — "raising a breeze," to make a commotion.

Brown study — contemplative, preoccupied.

Buffle-head — perplexed, dullwitted.

Bully ruffians — unmannerly highwaymen who use abusive language when robbing passengers.

Bumble bath — a muddle.

Bunch of fives — a fist.

C

Cake or cakey — a silly, foolish person.

Came up to scratch — a boxing term. One who meets his obligations or lives up the expectation that surrounds him.

Canary — a sovereign.

Cant — the language of the rabble.

Canterbury story — a lengthy circuitous tale.

Caper merchant — a dancing teacher.

Carbuncle face — a scarlet face riddled with pimples.

Cat's paw — to be a cat's paw was to be the tool of another. From the story about the monkey who secured a chestnut from the fire by using the cat's paw.

Cat sticks — skinny legs.

Cent per cent — a usurer.

Chalk — to take advantage. Habitués of public houses use chalk marks to keep score in gaming. Advantage is taken when a chalk mark is rubbed out.

Chalk up — public-house credit marked on a slate behind the door.

Chawbacons — rustic fellow from the country.

Cheeseparing — niggardly.

Chitty-faced — one who has a babyish countenance.

Chuckle-headed — dull witted, slow.

Chum — a companion, friend.

Cit — a citizen of London.

Clanker — a terrible untruth.

Cloth market — "he came from the clothmarket," he arose from the bed.

Clunch — a clumsy lout.

Clutch-fisted — stingy.

Cock of the game — a sporting man.

Cock-sure — overconfident.

Cock-a-whoop — overjoyed.

Cold — to catch cold; to get in a sorry plight.

Coming — too coming, to be too forward.

Complete to a shade — dressed in the height of fashion.

Cork-brained — stupid.

Court holy water or court promises — insincere flattery and ingratiating promises with no substance.

Cow-handed — clumsy.

Cow's thumb — done in just the right way is done to a cow's thumb.

Crack or all the crack — to be in prime style, ultrafashionable.

Cracksman — a burglar.

Crook shanks — a man with crooked, imperfect legs.

Crow — to bluster or brag.

Crusty fellow—a gruff, sullen fellow.
Cully—a fopish ninny.
Cut direct—to go out of one's way to avoid an approaching loathsome fellow.
Cut indirect—to look another way and unconcernedly go by the loathed person without seeming to see him.
Cut sublime—to admire the scenery and sites and sublimely avoid seeing the loathed person.

D

Dab—a skilled practitioner.
Dash—"cutting a dash," making oneself a place in the fashionable world.
Deep-one—a cunning rascal.
Devilish—very.
Devilish queer—strange.
Diamond squad—persons of quality.
Dished up—"he was dished up," he was ruined.
Done the thing right—managed matters properly. Taken care of one's self and one's friend.
Dry boots—an amusing scamp.
Dudgeon—ire. "high dudgeon," very angry.
Dun—an insistent creditor.
Dun territory—to be in deep debt.

F

Face—"boldly facing things out," to unblushingly assert a falsehood.
Facer—a hard blow to the face.
Fallalls—women's ornaments.
Fine as a fivepence—well turned out.
First consequence—"to be of the first consequence," to be of the highest social level.
Flea bite—a slight injury of no account.

Floor—to floor, to knock down.
Flummery—insincere compliments.
Flush in the pocket—loaded with riches.
Fob—fob off: to put off with a trick. The fob is also a
small breeches pocket for holding a watch.
Foundling—an abandoned child, found and reared by the
parish.
French leave—to leave unannounced.
Friday-faced—sad-faced.
Fudge—humbug.
Fuss—much to-do about unimportant matters.
Fustian—bombastic speech.

G

Gabster—a chatterbox.
Gingerbread—"he had the gingerbread;" he was wealthy.
Ginger-pated or Ginger-hackled—red headed.
Glimflashy—wrathful.
Go, the.—in the best style. "He was all the go, he was in
the mode."
Go-by, the.—to pass someone or something without stopping.
Gooseberry-eyed—lackluster grey eyes.
Great Unwashed—the lower classes.
Green—inexperienced, immature.
Gudgeon—a gullible soul.

H

Hanger on—a depenent.
Hatchet face—a sharp phisiogomy.
Havycavy—vacilating.
Hen-hearted—uncourageous.
High ropes—"to be on the high ropes," to be fervent.
High water—"It was high water with him," he was rich.
Hoaxing—mocking. "Hoaxing a quiz," ridiculing a peculiar
man.

Hop merchant—a dancing teacher.
Hubble-bubble—a muddle.

I

Inexpressibles—breeches.
Ivories—teeth.

J

Jackanapes—an impertinent fellow.
Jaw—to jaw: to talk.
Johnny raw—a country bumpkin.

K

Kick—"all the kick," in style.
Kick over the traces—out of control.

L

Leg—"to execute a leg," to bow.
Line—"to keep the line," to be correct.
Loaf—"to be in bad loaf," to be in a undesireable circumstances.
Loggerhead—slow witted.
Lombard Fever—"sick with the lombard fever," bored and idle.
Long shanks—a tall person.
Loon or lout—a clod.
Low water mark—penniless.

M

Maggotty — whimsical, capricious.
Marplot — a spoilsport.
Megrims — low spirits.
Merry-begotten — a love child.
Mill — a boxing match.
Monkey — £500.
Moped — dull, morose for lack of company.
More than Seven — to have an adult understanding of a situation.
Mushroom — a person or family suddenly gains wealth and importance, an allusion to a rapidly, growing fungus.
Mutton-headed — a dullwitted fellow.

N

Nick — Old Nick, the devil.
Nick ninny — a stupid fellow.
Nip cheese — a miserly person.
Noddle — the head.
Noddy — a half-wit.
None-such — one who has no equal.

O

Oar — "putting in his oar," meddling or giving an unsolicited opinion.
Old dog at it — expert.
Out at heels or out at elbows — in a bad financial situation.
Out of blackgloves — no longer in mourning.
Outrun the constable — "to outrun the constable," to live beyond one's means.

P

Paper scull—a fool.
Pate—the head.
Peepers—eyes.
Peg—"at home to a peg," at ease.
Pell-mell—with great haste.
Pet—"in a pet," in a huff.
Platter-faced—wide-faced.
Playing a deep game—having ulterior motives.
Plum—a hundred thousand pounds.
Plump—"plump" in the pocket, well supplied with money.
Polite World—high society.
Pony—£25.
Prittle prattle—trifling talk of no significance.
Pucker—"in a pucker," disorder or scared.
Pudding-headed—dull-witted.
Purse proud—one who is overwhelmingly proud of his
   wealth.

Q

Queer—to perplex.
Quiz—an odd or unusual looking fellow.

R

Rattle—to rattle: to chatter aimlessly.
Rattle-pate—a thoughtless, haphazard person.
Ready, the—money.
Rich as a nabob—as wealthy as one of the merchants who
   made his fortune in India.
Rig—trick, scheme, or game. "up to every rig," awake to
   every trick.
Rig out—clothing.
Rum—excellent, good. "Rum one," knowledgable fellow.

S

Sapscull — a lack-wit.

Scandal broth — tea.

Scrape — "to get into a scrape," get into a troublesome situation.

Scapegallows — one who has merited the gallows but has evaded that fate.

Shallow pate — a ninny.

Sharp set — ravenous.

Sixes and sevens — "at sixes and sevens," jumbled, chaotic.

Skin — "in bad skin," irate.

Sly boots — a shrewd fellow behind an innocent countenance.

Smokey — strange, curious.

Snuff — "to take snuff," to take offense. "Up to snuff," versed in the ways of the world.

Spanish coin — flattery.

Spindle shanks — thin legs.

Sport — to display.

Spout — to speak theatrically.

Spree — a bit of fun, a romp.

Stiff-rumped — arrogant, proud.

Stubble it — Be quiet!

Suds — "in the suds," in a troublesome situation.

T

Take-in — a hoax.

Tame — "to run tame in a household," to treat another's home as one's own.

Ten in the hundred — a usurious money lender, more than five percent interest was considered excessive.

Thatch-gallows — a rascal.

Thumping — large.

Tittle-tattle — chitchat, gossip or idle chatter.

Touch — "above one's touch," on a higher social level. "Beneath one's touch," on a lower social level.

Trim — clothing, state; "in a fine trim," in excellent condition.

Twig—to see.
Twig, in—in fashion.
Twit—to admonish or chid someone, particularly about
    obligations owed.
Twitter—"in a twitter," frightened.

U

Upper ten thousand—the aristocracy.
Uppish—irritable, oversensitive.
Upstarts—persons raised above their stations.

V

Vagaries—romps, frolics.

W

Wag—a mischievous, playful fellow.
Waggish—mischievous.
Warm—wealthy.
Waspish—petulant, querulous.
Weasel-faced—sharp featured.
Whisker—a falsehood.
Windmills in the head—foolish, whimiscal.

Z

Zany—a clown.
Zounds—ejaculation, from God's wounds.

SELECTIVE BIBLIOGRAPHY

Adburgham, Alison. *Shopping in Style: London from the Restoration to Edwardian Elegance.* London: Thames and Hudson, 1979.

————. *Silver Fork Society: Fashionable Life and Literature from 1814-1840.* London: Constable, 1983. Good overview of the *ton* and fashionable authors of the period.

Adolphus, J.H. *The Royal Exile: Or Memoirs of the Public and Private Life of Her Majesty, Caroline, Queen Consort of Great Britain: Embracing Every Circumstance Connected with the Memorable Scenes of Her Eventful Life from the Earliest Period to Her Late Arrival in England. A Full and Impartial History of the Charges against Her and Proceedings in Parliament and of All Important Events That Have Transpired since Her Return.* 18th ed. 2 vols. London: Jones, 1821.

Alsop, Susan. *The Congress Dances: Vienna 1814-1815.* New York: Harper & Row, 1984. Good narrative of the personalities of post-Napoleonic Europe who shaped the future of Europe at the "waltzing" Congress.

Angelo, Henry. *Reminiscences of Henry Angelo with Memoirs of His Late Father and Friends: Including Numerous Original Ancedotes and Curious Traits of the Most Celebrated Characters That Have Flourished during the Past Eighty Years.* 2 vols. London: H. Colburn and R. Bentley, 1830. Anecdotes abound on fashionable life and pursuits.

Angelo, Mr. *The School of Fencing With a General Explanation of the Principal Attitudes and Positions Peculiar to the Art.* 1787. Reprint. New York: Land's End Press, 1971.

Anglesey, Marquess of. *One Leg: The Life and Letters of Henry William Paget, First Marquess of Anglesey K. G. 1768-1854.* New York: William Morrow, 1961. Good biography of the heroic and scandalous Marquess.

Aprà, Nietta, trans. *The Louis Styles: Louis XIV, Louis XV, Louis XVI.* London: Orbis Publishing, 1972. Well-illustrated introduction to French furniture styles re-popularized during the Regency.

Arch, Nigel, and Marschner, Joanna. *Splendour at Court: Dressing for Royal Occasions since 1700.* London: Unwin Hyman, 1987. Superb illustrations and lively text.

Ashton, John. *The Dawn of the XIXth Century in England: A Social Sketch of the Times.* London: T.F. Unwin, 1886. Reprint. Detroit: Singing Tree Press, 1968. All Ashton's books are filled with multitudinous gleanings from primary sources loosely woven together with a satisfactory narrative.

————. *English Caricature and Satire on Napoleon I.* London: Chatto & Windus, 1888. Reprint. Singing Tree Press, 1968.

————. *The History of Gambling in England.* London: Duckworth, 1899.

————. *Old Times: A Picture of Social Life at the End of the Eighteenth Century....* London: J.C. Nimmo, 1885.

————. *Social England under the Regency.* London: Chatto & Windus, 1899. Reprint. Detroit: Singing Tree Press, 1968.

Austen, Jane. *Jane Austen's Letters to Her Sister Cassandra and Others.* Ed. R.W. Chapman. 2d ed. New York: Oxford University Press, 1952. Her letters abound with delicious details of every aspect of everyday life.

Austen-Leigh, James E. *A Memoir of Jane Austen.* London: R. Bentley, 1882. Reprint. Folcroft, Pa.: Folcroft Library Editions, 1979.

Ayling, Stanley. *George the Third.* New York: Alfred P. Knopf, 1972.

Baker, H. Barton. *History of the London Stage and Its Famous Players 1576-1903.* 1904. Reprint. New York: Benjamin Blom, 1969. Good overview.

Barbeau, A. *Life & Letters at Bath in the XVIIJth Century.* London: W. Heinemann, 1904.

Beard, Geoffrey W. *Craftsmen and Interior Decoration in England 1660-1820.* New York: Holmes & Meier, 1981.

Birkenhead, Sheila S. *Peace in Piccadilly: The Story of Albany.* New York: Reynal, 1958.

Blew, William C.A. *Brighton and Its Coaches: A History of the London and Brighton Road with Some Account of the Provincial Coaches That Have Run from Brighton.* London: J.C. Nimmo, 1894. Lots of detail and many colorful anecdotes.

Bloodgood, Lida F. *The Saddle of Queens: The Story of the Side-Saddle.* London: J.A. Allen, 1959.

Blum, Stella, ed. *Ackermann's Costume Plates: Women's Fashions in England 1818-1828.* New York: Dover, 1978. Wonderful illustrations from *The Repository of Arts.*

Blyth, Henry. *Caro the Fatal Passion: The Life of Lady*

Caroline Lamb. New York: Coward, McCann & Geoghegan, 1972. Fine biography of Byron's paramour, society's darling, and social outcast.

Borer, Mary I. *The Story of Covent Garden.* London: R. Hale, 1984.

Borowitz, Albert I. *The Thurtell-Hunt Murder Case: Dark Mirror to Regency England.* Baton Rouge: Louisiana State University Press, 1987.

Boulton, William B. *The Amusements of Old London: Being a Survey of the Sports and Pastimes, Tea Gardens and Parks, Playhouses and Other Diversions of the People of London from the 17th to the Present 19th Century.* 2 vols. 1901. Reprint. New York: Benjamin Blom, 1969.

Bovill, E.W. *The England of Nimrod and Surtees 1815-1854.* London: Oxford University Press, 1959. Excellent look at sporting England and golden age of coaching.

————. *English Country Life 1780-1830.* London: Oxford University Press, 1962.

Bradfield, Nancy. *Costume in Detail: Women's Dress 1730-1930.* Boston: Plays, Inc., 1968. Superb drawings which illuminate function and form. Lucid text.

Brander, Michael. *The Georgian Gentleman.* Farnborough: Saxon House, 1973. Lively, anecdotal survey of the pleasures and pastimes of a gentleman.

————. *The Life and the Sport of the Inn.* New York: St. Martin's Press, 1973.

Braun-Ronsdorf, Margarete. *Mirror of Fashion: A History of European Costume 1789-1929.* Trans. Oliver Coburn. New York: McGraw-Hill, 1964.

Briggs, Asa. *The Age of Improvement 1783-1865.* London: Longmans, Green, 1959. Excellent.

————, comp. *How They Lived.* Vol. 3, *An Anthology of Original Documents Written between 1700 and 1815.* New York: Barnes & Noble, 1969.

Brooke, Iris. *Dress and Undress: The Restoration and Eighteenth Century.* London: Methuen, 1958. Reprint. Westport, Conn: Greenwood Press, 1973.

————. *English Costume of the Nineteenth Century.* 1929. Reprint. London: A.&C. Black, 1977. Well-organized history of fashion's evolution.

Brown, Lucy M., and Ian R. Christie, eds. *Bibliography of British History 1789-1851.* Oxford: Clarendon, 1977. Superb bibliography for every approach to subject. Heavy slant toward primary sources.

Brownlow, Emma Sophia, Countess. *The Eve of Victorianism: Reminiscences of the Years 1802-1834.* London: John Murray, 1940.

Bryant, Sir Arthur. *The Age of Elegance 1812-1822.* New York: Harper & Row, 1950. All of Bryant's books are vividly written with superb bibliographies, full of primary sources. Good historical narrative.

————. *The Great Duke: Or The Invincible General.* New York: William Morrow, 1971.

————. *Years of Endurance 1793-1802.* London: Collins, 1942.

————. *Years of Victory 1802-1812.* London: Collins, 1944.

Buck, Anne. *Dress in Eighteenth-Century England.* New York: Holmes & Meier Publishers, 1979.

Buckingham, 2nd Duke of. *Memoirs of the Court and Cabinets of George the Third: From Original Family Documents.* 2d ed. 2 vols. London: Hurst and Blackett, 1853.

Burgess, Anthony. *Coaching Days of England: Containing an Account of Whatever Was Most Remarkable for Grandeur, Elegance and Curiosity in the Time of the Coaches of England: Comprehending the Year 1750 until 1850.* London: Elek, 1966.

Burke, Thomas. *English Night Life From Norman Curfew to Present Black Out.* London: B.T. Batsford, 1941. Amusing anecdotal history.

Burnett, T.A.J. *The Rise and Fall of a Regency Dandy: The Life and Times of Scrope Berdmore Davies.* Boston: Little, Brown, 1981. Detailed biography based on recently discovered papers.

Burney, Fanny. *The Famous Miss Burney: The Diaries and Letters of Fanny Burney.* Eds. Schrank, Barbara G., and David J. Supino. New York: John Day, 1976. Pertinent selections from her copious pen.

Burton, Elizabeth. *The Pageant of Georgian England.* New York: Charles Scribners' Sons, 1968. Superb study of all the little things of everyday life. Everything from gardening to medicine to washing clothes. Excellent bibliography. Published also as *The Georgians at Home 1714-1830.*

Bury, Lady Charlotte. *Diary Illustrative of the Times of George the Fourth Interspersed with Original Letters from the Late Queen Caroline and from Various Other*

Distinguished Persons. 2 vols. Philadelphia: Carey, Lea and Blanchard, 1838. Gossipy narrative.

Calder-Marshall, Arthur. *The Grand Century of the Lady.* London: Gordon and Cremonesi, 1976. Wonderful social history of the Georgian lady. Filled with astute observation and fine use of diaries and letters.

Cassin-Scott, Jack, and Haythornthwaite, Philip. *Uniforms of the Napoleonic Wars 1796-1814.* Poole, Dorset: Blanford Press, 1973. Illustrations in color.

Cate, Curtis. *The War of the Two Emperors: The Duel between Napoleon and Alexander—Russia, 1812.* New York: Random House, 1985.

Chambers, Jonathan D., and Mingay, G.E. *The Agricultural Revolution 1750-1880.* New York: Schocken Books, 1966.

Chancellor, E. Beresford. *Life in Regency and Early Victorian Times: An Account of the Days of Brummell and D'Orsay 1800-1850.* London: B.T. Batsford, 1926. Lively account with much detail.

————. *The Lives of the Rakes.* Vol. 5, *Old Q and Barrymore.* Vol. 6, *The Regency Rakes.* London: P. Allan, 1925-26. Full of gossipy details about thoroughly reprehensible fellows.

Chandler, David G. *The Campaigns of Napoleon.* New York: Macmillan, 1966.

————. *Waterloo: The Hundred Days.* New York: Macmillan, 1980.

Cheeson, Wilfrid H. *George Cruikshank.* New York: E.P. Dutton, 1908.

Churchill, Randolph S. *Fifteen Famous English Homes.* London: Verschoyle, 1954.

Clarke, Michael, and Nicholas Penny, eds. *The Arrogant Connoisseur: Richard Payne Knight 1751-1824.* Manchester: Manchester University Press, 1982. Beautifully illustrated plus art catalogue listings.

Clark, Kenneth. *The Gothic Revival: An Essay in the History of Taste.* London: Constable, 1928.

Cobbett, William. *Advice to Young Men, and (Incidentally) to Young Women, in the Middle and Higher Ranks of Life in a Series of Letters Addressed to a Youth, a Bachelor, a Lover, a Husband, a Citizen or a Subject.* New York: J. Doyle, 1833.

————. *History of the Regency and Reign of King George the Fourth.* 2 vols. London: William Cobbett, 1830-34.

————. *Rural Rides in the Counties of Surrey, Kent, Sussex, Hants, Berks, Oxford, Bucks, Wilts, Somerset, Gloucester, Hereford, Salop, Worcester, Stafford, Leicester, Hertford, Essex, Suffolk, Norfolk, Cambridge, Huntingdon, Nottingham, Lincoln, York, Lancaster, Durham, and Northumberland in the Years 1821, 1822, 1823, 1825, 1826, 1829, 1830, and 1832: With Economical and Political Observations Relative to Matters Applicable to, and Illus. by the State of Those Counties Respectively.* 2d ed. London: A. Cobbett, 1853.

Collard, Frances. *Regency Furniture.* Woodbridge: Antique Collectors' Club, 1985.

Colson, Percy. *White's 1693-1950.* London: Heinemann, 1951.

Connely, Willard. *The Reign of Beau Brummell.* New York: Greystone Press, 1940.

Cook, Sir Theodore. *Eclipse & O'Kelly: Being a Complete History So Far as Is Known of That Celebrated English Thoroughbred Eclipse (1764-1789) of His Breeder the Duke of Cumberland & of His Subsequent Owners William Wildman, Dennis O'Kelly & Andrew O'Kelly....* New York: Dutton, 1907.

————. *History of the English Turf.* 3 vols. New York: Charles Scribner's Sons, 1901-1904.

Cooper, Charles. *The English Table in History and Literature.* London: Sampson, Low, Marston, 1929.

Corson, Richard. *Fashions in Hair: The First Five Thousand Years.* New York: Hastings House, 1965.

Creevey, Thomas. *The Creevey Papers.* Ed. John Gore. London: Folio Society, 1970. Interesting accounts given by a frequent guest of the Prince Regent.

————. *The Creevey Papers: A Selection from the Correspondence & Diaries of the Late Thomas Creevey, MP, Born 1768—Died 1838.* Ed. Sir Herbert Maxwell. 2 vols. London: John Murray, 1903.

————. *Creevey's Life and Times: A Further Selection from the Correspondence of Thomas Creevey, Born 1768—Died 1838.* Ed. John Gore. London: John Murray, 1934.

Croly, George. *Life and Times of His Late Majesty George the Fourth: With Ancedotes of Distinguished Persons of the Last 50 Years.* 2d ed. New York: Harper, 1840.

Cruickshank, Dan, and Wyld, Peter. *London: The Art of Georgian Building.* New York: Architectural Book Publishing, 1975.

Cruse, Amy. *The Englishman and His Books in the Early Nineteenth Century.* 1930. Reprint. New York:

Benjamin Blom, 1968.

Cumming, Valerie. *Gloves.* London: B.T. Batsford, 1982.

Cunliffe, Barry. *The City of Bath.* New Haven: Yale University Press, 1986.

Cunnington, C. Willett, and Phillis E. *Handbook of English Costume in the Nineteenth Century.* Boston: Plays, 1970. Standard source book.

Cunnington, Phillis E., and Lucas, Catherine. *Costume of Births, Marriages & Deaths.* New York: Barnes Noble, 1972. Excellent reference.

Cunnington, Phillis E., and Mansfield, Alan. *English Costume for Sports and Outdoor Recreation from the Sixteenth to the Nineteenth Centuries.* London: Black, 1969. Outstanding.

Curtis, Mattom M. *The Story of Snuff and Snuff Boxes.* New York: Liveright, 1935. Well-illustrated with numerous photographs.

Darvall, Frank O. *Popular Disturbances and Public Order in Regency England: Being an Account of the Luddite and Other Disorders in England during the Years 1811-1817, and of the Attitude and Activity of the Authorities.* London: Oxford University Press, 1934.

Davies, Andrew. *The Map of London from 1746 to the Present Day.* London: B.T. Batsford, 1987.

de Courtais, Georgine. *Women's Headdress and Hairstyles in England from AD 600 to Present Day.* London: Anchor Press, 1973. Excellent illustrations and text.

Dinkel, John. *The Royal Pavilion Brighton.* New York: Vendome Press, 1983. Fabulous illustrations, excellent social and architectural history. Good detailed descriptions of each remodeling.

Drummond, Jack, and Wilbraham, Anne. *The Englishman's Food: A History of Five Centuries of English Diet.* 2d ed. London: Jonathan Cape, 1958.

Drury, Elizabeth. *The Butler's Pantry Book.* New York: St. Martin's Press, 1981. Contains several of Adams's *The Complete Servant* household hints and other household helps of the period.

Durant, Will, and Ariel. *The Story of Civilization.* Vol. 11, *The Age of Napoleon.* New York: Simon and Schuster, 1975. Adequate general overview of period.

Edgeworth, Maria. *Letters from England 1813-1844.* Ed. Christina Colvin. Oxford: Clarendon Press, 1971.

Edwards, R., and L.G.G. Ramsey, eds. *The Connoisseur Period Guides to the Houses, Decoration, Furnishing, and Chattels of the Classic Periods.* Vol. 5, *The Regency 1810-1830.* New York: Reynal, 1957. Excellent introduction to the period which covers a variety of subjects from fashion to architecture and music.

Emsley, Clive. *British Society and the French Wars 1793-1815.* Totowa, N.J.: Rowman and Littlefield, 1979. Analyses effect of lengthy wars on British homefront.

Endelman, Todd M. *The Jews of Georgian England 1714-1830: Tradition and Change in a Liberal Society.* Philadelphia: The Jewish Publication Society of America, 1979. Interesting, contains everything from Mendoza the Jew to moneylenders. Cruikshank and Rowlandson caricatures illustrate.

Erickson, Carolly. *Our Tempestuous Day: A History of Regency England.* New York: William Morrow, 1986.

Recent and wonderfully written social history.

Ewing, Elizabeth. *Dress and Undress: A History of Women's Underwear.* New York: Drama Book Specialists, 1978. An amusing look at the contraptions and improving underpinings on the feminine form.

Farington, Joseph. *The Farington Diary.* Ed. James Greig. 8 vols. New York: G.H. Doran, 1923-28. Excellent look of fashionable life. Many everyday details.

Farnol, Jeffrey. *Famous Prize Fights: Or Epics of The Fancy.* Boston: Little, Brown, 1928. Stories of the greatest matches.

Farrell, Jeremy. *Umbrellas & Parasols.* London: B.T. Batsford, 1985.

Ford, John. *Prizefighting: The Age of Regency Boxiana.* London: David and Charles, 1971.

Foster, Vanda. *Bags and Purses.* London: B.T. Batsford, 1982.

Foster, Vere, ed. *The Two Duchesses: Georgiana, Duchess of Devonshire, Elizabeth, Duchess of Devonshire. Family Correspondence ... 1777-1859.* 2d ed. London: Blackie & Son, 1898. Two members of the Devonshire House *menage á trois.*

Franks, A.H. *Social Dance: A Short History.* London: Routledge and Kegan Paul, 1963.

Franzero, Charles M. *Beau Brummell: His Life and Times.* New York: John Day, 1958.

Fraser, Flora. *Emma, Lady Hamilton.* New York: Alfred P. Knopf, 1986. Sympathetic and excellent study of Nelson's great love.

Fussell, G.E., and K.R. *The English Countryman: His Life and Work from Tudor Times to the Victorian Age.* London: Andrew Melrose, 1955. Reprint. London: Bloomsbury Books, 1985. Excellent discourse on changing country life.

George IV. *The Correspondence of George, Prince of Wales 1770-1812.* Ed. A. Aspinall. 8 vols. New York: Oxford University Press, 1963-71.

———. *The Letters of King George IV 1812-1830.* Ed. A. Aspinall. 3 vols. Cambridge, Eng.: The University Press, 1938.

George, M. Dorothy. *Hogarth to Cruikshank: Social Change in Graphic Satire.* London: Allen Lane, Penguin P., 1967. Glorious illustrations, outstanding text that matches the superb reproductions of Britain's greatest caricaturists.

———. *London Life in the Eighteenth Century.* London: Kegan, Paul, Trench, Trubner, 1925. Reprint. New York: Harper & Row, 1965. Wonderful detail in this authoritative study.

Gilbert, Edmund W. *Brighton: Old Ocean's Bauble.* London: Methuen, 1954.

Gillis, John R. *For Better, For Worse: British Marriages 1600 to the Present.* New York: Oxford University Press, 1985. Outstanding study of the changing relationships between men and women. The analysis of various societal and familiar pressures on the marriage contract are perceptive and thoughtful.

Ginsburg, Madeleine. *Wedding Dress 1740-1970.* London: Her Majesty's Stationery Office, 1981.

Girouard, Mark. *A Country House Companion.* New Haven: Yale University Press, 1987.

———. *Life in the English Country House: A Social and Architectural History.* New Haven: Yale University Press, 1978. Excellent story of the development of the country house lifestyle.

Glenbervie, Lord. *The Diaries of Sylvester Douglas (Lord Glenbervie).* Ed. Francis Bickley. 2 vols. London: Constable, 1928. Lots of fashionable doings, includes a European tour.

Glover, Michael. *The Napoleonic Wars: An Illustrated History 1792-1815.* New York: Hippocrene Books, 1978. Good introduction to a confusing series of alliances, coalitions, and campaigns.

———. *The Peninsular War 1807-1814: A Concise Military History.* Hamden, Conn: Archon Books, 1974. Well-told account of British presence in Spain and Portugal.

———. *A Very Slippery Fellow: The Life of Sir Robert Wilson 1777-1849.* London: Oxford University Press, 1977-78. Biography of an erratic, charming rogue at the center of history.

Glover, Richard G. *Britain at Bay: Defense against Bonaparte 1803-14.* New York: Barnes and Noble, 1973.

Goldring, Douglas. *Regency Portrait Painter: The Life of Sir Thomas Lawrence P.R.A.* London: MacDonald, 1951.

Gomme, George L., ed. *The Gentleman's Magazine Library: Being a Classified Collection of the Chief Contents of the Gentleman's Magazine from 1731-1868.* 11 vols. London: E. Stock, 1883-94. Reprint. Detroit: Singing Tree Press, 1968.

Gould, William, and Patrick Hanks, eds. *Lives of the Georgian Age.* New York: Barnes & Noble Books, 1978. Excellent concise biographies of major figures, includes bibliography with each biography.

Graham, Helen. *Parties and Pleasures: The Diaries of Helen Graham 1823-1826.* Ed. James Irvine. Edinburgh: Paterson, 1957. The typical social whirl in upper class society from the viewpoint of a young woman.

Greaves, Margaret. *Regency Patron: Sir George Beaumont.* London: Metheun, 1966.

Grego, J. *Rowlandson the Caricaturist.* London: Chatto & Windus, 1880.

Greville, Charles. *The Greville Memoirs: A Journal of the Reigns of King George IV, King William IV and Queen Victoria.* Ed. Henry Reeve. 8 vols. London: Longmans, Green, 1896-99.

Grey, J. David, A. Walton Litz, and Brian Southam, eds. *The Jane Austen Companion.* New York: Macmillan, 1986. Wonderful reference to Austen and her period.

Gronow, Rees Howell. *The Reminiscences and Recollections of Captain Gronow: Being Ancedotes of the Camp, Court, Clubs, and Society 1810-1860.* 2 vols. London: J. C. Nimmo, 1889. Wonderful memoirs of war, club life, and fashionable pursuits in London and Paris. Filled with one quotable anecdote after another.

[Grose, Frances?] *1811 Dictionary of the Vulgar Tongue: A Dictionary of Buckish Slang, University Wit, and Pickpocket Eloquence.* Reprint. Northfield, Ill.: Digest Books, 1971.

Grosvenor, Caroline Stuart Wortley, and Charles Beilby, Lord Stuart of Wortley, eds. *The First Lady Wharncliffe and Her Family 1779-1856.* 2 vols. London: Heinemann, 1927. Brimming with upper-class domestic details. Includes Post-Napoleonic tour of Europe by herself, husband, and children.

Hamilton, Lady Anne. *Secret History of the Court of England from the Accession of George the Third to the Death of George the Fourth: Including among Other Important Matters Full Particulars of the Mysterious Death of Princess Charlotte.* 2 vols. 1832. Reprint. Boston: L.C. Page, 1901. Gossipy history.

Hamilton, Leo, ed. *Ladies on the Loose: Women Travellers of the 18th and 19th Centuries.* New York: Dodd, Mead, 1981.

Hanson, Harry. *The Coaching Life.* Manchester: Manchester University Press, 1983. Amusing, well-researched look at the golden age of coaching.

Harris, John. *Regency Furniture Designs from Contemporary Source Books 1803-1826.* Chicago: Quadrangle Books, 1960.

Harris, Stanley. *The Coaching Age.* London: R. Bentley and Son, 1885.

Hazlitt, William. *Table Talk: or Original Essays.* Everyman's library. Essays and belles lettres, no. 321. London: Dent, 1952.

Hecht, J. Jean. *The Domestic Servant Class in Eighteenth Century England.* London: Routledge and Kegan Paul, 1956. Comprehensive study.

Herold, J. Christopher. *The Horizon Book of the Age of Napoleon.* New York: Bonanza Books, 1983. Excellent introduction to period, well-illustrated.

————. *Mistress to an Age: A Life of Madame de Staël.* Indianapolis: Bobbs-Merrill, 1958.

Hibbert, Christopher. *The Court at Windsor: A Domestic History.* New York: Harper & Row, 1964.

————. *The English: A Social History 1066-1945.* New York: W.W. Norton, 1987.

————. *George IV: Prince of Wales 1762-1811.* New York, Harper & Row, 1972. These two volumes are the best life of Prinny.

————. *George IV: Regent and King 1811-1830.* New York: Harper & Row, 1973.

————. *The Grand Tour.* New York: Putnam, 1969. History of intrepid British tourists, liberally illustrated.

Hinde, Wendy. *Castlereagh.* London: Collins, 1981. Good political biography.

Hindley, Charles. *The True History of Tom and Jerry: Or The Day and Night Scenes of Life in London from the Start to the Finish: With a Key to the Persons and Places Together with a Vocabulary and Glossary of the Flash and Slang Terms Occuring in the Course of the Work.* London: C. Hindley, 1890. Excellent glossary.

Hoare, Sir Richard. *The Journeys of Sir Richard Colt Hoare through Wales and England 1793-1810.* Gloucester: A. Sutton, 1983.

Hodge, Jane Aiken. *The Private World of Georgette Heyer.* London: The Bodley Head, 1984. Good biography of the popularizer of Regency period novels.

Holcombe, Lee. *Wives and Property: Reform of the Married Women's Property Law in Nineteenth Century England.*

Toronto: University of Toronto Press, 1983. Excellent study of the evolution of laws affecting women and their property.

Holland, Henry. *Travels in the Ionian Isles, Albania, Thessaly, Macedonia, etc.* Physician Travelers, ed. Robert M. Goldwyn, no. 8. London: Longman, Hurst, Rees, Orme, and Brown, 1815. Reprint. New York: Arno Press, 1971.

Holland, Henry E. *The Journal of the Hon. Henry Edward Fox (afterwards fourth and last Lord Holland) 1818-1830.* Ed. the Earl of Ilchester. London: Butterworth, 1923.

Holland, Vyvyan. *Hand Coloured Fashion Plates 1770 to 1899.* London: B.T. Batsford, 1955. Excellent bibliography. Contains detailed account of the development of fashion illustrations and women's magazines.

Horstman, Allen. *Victorian Divorce.* New York: St. Martin's Press, 1985. Good discussion of divorce laws before the Victorian reforms.

Howe, P.P. *The Life of William Hazlitt.* 2d ed. Hamondsworth: Penguin, 1949.

Hudson, Derek. *Holland House in Kensington.* London: P. Davies, 1967.

Hunn, David. *Epsom Racecourse: Its Story and Its People.* London: Davis-Poynter, 1973.

Hussey, Christopher. *English Country Houses.* 3 vols. London: Country Life, Ltd., 1955-58.

Hyde, H. Montgomery. *Princes Lieven.* Boston: Little, Brown, 1938.

Jackson-Stops, Gervase, and Pipkin, James. *The English Country House: A Grand Tour.* Boston: Little, Brown, 1985. Wonderfully illustrated with numerous color photographs of country houses of many different periods.

Jaeger, Muriel. *Before Victoria.* London: Chatto & Windus, 1956.

Jerrold, Blanchard. *The Life of George Cruikshank. 1898.* Reprint. Chichely, Eng.: Minet, 1971.

Joint Publishing Committee Representing the London County Council and London Survey Committee. *Survey of London,* vols. 29-30. *The Parish of St. James Westminster: Part 1, South of Piccadilly.* London: Athlone Press, 1960. These oversize volumes detail every building and site of historical interest in this highly fashionable part of London. Copious illustrations include floor plans, interior and exterior views of Almack's, White's, Boodle's etc. Detailed maps illustrate St. James's Square in 1814 and Pall Mall in 1821.

Jones, Howard M. *The Harp That Once ...: A Chronicle of the Life of Thomas Moore.* New York: H. Holt, 1937.

Jones, Louis C. *The Clubs of the Georgian Rakes.* Columbia University Studies in English and Comparative Literature, no. 157. New York: Columbia University Press, 1942.

Jourdain, Margaret. *Regency Furniture 1795-1830.* 2d ed. London: Country Life, 1965. Well-researched text is surrounded by numerous photographs of many and varied furniture styles. Excellent.

Kennedy, Carol. *Mayfair: A Social History.* London: Hutchinson, 1986.

Knight, Cornelia. *The Autobiography of Miss Knight, Lady Companion to Princess Charlotte.* Ed. Roger Fulford. London: W. Kimber, 1960.

Laver, James. *The Age of Illusion: Manners and Morals 1750-1848.* New York: David McKay, 1972.

Leveson Gower, Granville. Earl of Granville. *Lord Granville Leveson Gower: Private Correspondence 1781 to 1821.* Ed. Castalia Granville. 2 vols. New York: E.P. Dutton, 1916.

Lewis, Wilmarth S. *Three Tours through London in the Years 1748, 1776, 1797.* The Colver Lectures, Brown University, vol. 21. New Haven: Yale University Press, 1941.

Liechtenstein, Princess Marie. *Holland House.* 2 vols. London: Macmillan, 1874. Anecdotes plus a room by room tour.

Lockwood, Allison. *Passionate Pilgrims: The American Traveler in Great Britain 1800-1914.* New York: Cornwall Books, 1981.

Longford, Elizabeth. *Wellington: Pillar of State.* New York: Harper & Row, 1972. Wonderful Wellington study. Well organized and immensely readable two-volume biography.

———. *Wellington: The Years of the Sword.* New York: Harper & Row, 1969.

Longrigg, Roger. *The English Squire and His Sport.* New York: St. Martin's Press, 1977. The evolution of sporting squires.

———. *The History of Foxhunting.* New York: C.N. Potter, 1975.

————. *The History of Horse Racing.* New York: Stein and Day, 1972.

Low, Donald A. *That Sunny Dome: A Portrait of Regency Britain.* London: Dent, 1977.

————. *Thieves' Kitchen: The Regency Underworld.* London: Dent, 1982. The darkside of Regency life.

Lowndes, William. *The Royal Crescent in Bath: A Fragment of English Life.* Bristol: Redcliffe Press, 1981.

MacCarthy, Bridget G. *The Female Pen.* Vol. 2. *The Later Women Novelists 1744-1818.* Cork: Cork University Press, 1946-47.

McClellan, Elisabeth. *Historic Dress in America 1607-1870.* 2 vols. 1904-1910. Reprint (2 vols. in 1). New York: Arno Press, 1977. Extensive use of primary sources of English origin.

Macdonald, John. *Memoirs of an Eighteenth-century Footman, John Macdonald: Travels 1745-1779.* 1790. Reprint. London: Routledge, 1927.

Mackay-Smith, Alexander; Druesedow, Jean R.; and Ryder, Thomas. *Man and the Horse: An Illustrated History of Equestrian Apparel.* New York: Metropolitan Museum of Art, 1984. Good overview of both equipment and apparel evolution featuring excellent period portraits, sporting scenes, and fashion plates.

McKendry, Maxine. *Seven Hundred Years of English Cooking.* Ed. Arabella Boyer. New York: Exeter Books, 1973. Good introduction to subject.

Mackey, Howard. *Wit and Whiggery: The Reverend Sydney Smith (1771-1845).* Washington: University Press of America, 1979.

Macquoid, Percy. *History of English Furniture.* Vol. 4, *The Age of Satinwood 1770-1820.* London: Lawrence & Bullen, 1908. Reprint. New York: Dover Publications, 1972.

Mahan, Captain A.T. *The Life of Nelson: The Embodiment of the Sea Power of Great Britain.* 1897. Reprint. New York: Haskell House, 1969.

Marchand, Leslie A. *Byron: A Biography.* 3 vols. New York: Alfred P. Knopf, 1957.

Margetson, Stella. *Regency London.* New York: Praeger, 1971. Superb social history of the city, includes architecture, amusements, and lifestyles.

Marples, Morris. *Six Royal Sisters: Daughters of George III.* London: Michael Joseph, 1969.

Masefield, Muriel A. *Women Novelists from Fanny Burney to George Eliot.* 1934. Reprint. Freeport, N.Y.: Books for Libraries Press, 1967.

Mayne, Ethel C. *A Regency Chapter: Lady Bessborough and Her Friendships.* London: Macmillan, 1939.

Melville, Lewis [Lewis S. Benjamin]. *Beau Brummell: His Life and Letters.* New York: George H. Doran, 1925. Contains many primary source materials including his album, a book of poems by assorted friends.

———. *The Life and Letters of William Cobbett in England & America: Based upon Hitherto Unpublished Family Papers.* 2 vols. London: John Lane, 1913.

Mennell, Stephen. *All Manners of Food: Eating and Taste in England and France from the Middle Ages to the Present.* Oxford: B. Blackwell, 1985. Well-written, intelligently organized narrative.

Mercer, General Cavalié. *Journal of the Waterloo Campaign: Kept Throughout the Campaign of 1815....* Reprint. New York: Praeger Publishers, 1969.

Metropolitan Museum of Art. *Early Firearms of Great Britain and Ireland from the Collection of Clay P. Bedford.* Greenwich, Conn.: The Metropolitan Museum of Art, 1971. Wonderfully illustrated with photographs.

Mingay, G.E. *English Landed Society in the Eighteenth Century.* London: Routledge and Paul, 1963.

————. *The Gentry: The Rise and Fall of a Ruling Class.* London: Longman, 1976. Good overview of the subject.

Mingay, Gordon. *Mrs. Hurst Dancing: And Other Scenes from Regency Life 1812-1823.* London: Victor Gollancz, 1981. Charming contemporary watercolors illustrate domestic matters and country affairs.

Mitford, Mary R. *Our Village: Sketches of Rural Characters and Scenery.* 2d ed. 2 vols. London: H.G. Bohn, 1852. Domestic and country detail galore.

Mitton, Geraldine E. *Jane Austen and Her Times.* New York: G.P. Putnam's, 1905. Good study of both the author and the period.

Monsarrat, Ann. *And the Bride Wore...: The Story of the White Wedding.* New York: Dodd, Mead, 1973. Delightful narrative on the evolution of the love match, wedding customs, and bridal clothes.

Montague-Smith, Patrick W., ed. *Debrett's Correct Form: An Inclusive Guide to Everything from Drafting Wedding Invitations to Addressing an Archbishop.* New York: Arco Publishing, 1977.

Moore, Thomas. *Memoirs, Journal, and Correspondence of Thomas Moore.* Ed. Lord John Russell. 8 vols. London: Longman, Brown, Green, and Longmans, 1853-56. London literary life.

Morris, Thomas. *The Napoleonic Wars.* Ed. John Selby. Hamden, Conn.: Archon Books, 1968.

Murstein, Bernard I. *Love, Sex, and Marriage through the Ages.* New York: Springer, 1974.

Musgrave, Clifford. *Regency Furniture 1800-1830.* New York: T. Yosaloff, 1961. Well-illustrated.

————. *Royal Pavilion: An Episode in the Romantic.* 2d ed. London: L. Hill, 1959. Wonderful history of Pavilion's heyday.

Neumann, Philipp von. *The Diary of Philipp von Neumann 1819 to 1850.* Trans. and ed. E. Beresford Chancellor. 2 vols. London: P. Allan, 1928.

Newark, Peter. *The Crimson Book of Highwaymen.* London: Jupiter Books, 1979. Good introduction to legendary rogues.

Nichols, John. *Reminiscences of Literary London from 1779 to 1853: The Rise and Progress of the Gentleman's Magazine.* New York: Harper, 1896. Reprint. New York: Garland Publishing, 1974.

Nicoll, Allardyce. *The Garrick Stage: Theatres and Audience in the Eighteenth Century.* Manchester: Manchester University Press, 1981.

Nicolson, Sir Harold. *The Congress of Vienna: A Study in Allied Unity 1812-1822.* New York: Harcourt, Brace, 1946. Excellent straightforward account.

Nightingale, Joseph. *Memoirs of the Public and Private Life of Queen Caroline.* Ed. Christopher Hibbert. London: Folio Society, 1978.

Nimrod [Charles James Apperley]. *Nimrod's Hunting Reminiscences: Comprising Memoirs of Masters of Hounds, Notices of the Crack Riders and Characteristics of the Hunting Countries of England.* 1843. Reprint. New York: Alfred P. Knopf, 1927.

Oman, Carola. *Nelson.* New York: Doubleday & Company. Reprint. Westport, Conn.: Greenwood Press, 1970.

Palmer, Alan. *An Encyclopaedia of Napoleon's Europe.* New York: St. Martin's Press, 1984. Excellent reference to the people, places, and events during the cataclysmic years of Napoleon's ascendancy.

Palmer, Alan W. *Alexander I: Tsar of War and Peace.* London: Weidenfeld & Nicholson, 1974.

Palmer, Iris I. *The Face Without a Frown: Georgiana, Duchess of Devonshire.* 2d ed. London: F. Muller, 1944.

Palmerston, Lady Emily. *The Letters of Lady Palmerston.* Ed. Tresham Lever. London: John Murray, 1957. Epistles by Lady Melbourne's daughter Emily, sister-in-law to Caroline Lamb and first married to Lord Cowper. She was one of Almack's Lady Patronesses during the Regency.

Parker, Derek. *Byron and His World.* London: Thames & Hudson, 1968. Copiously illustrated, puts Byron in perspective.

Partridge, Eric. *A Dictionary of Historical Slang.* 2d ed. New York: Penguin, 1972.

————. *A Dictionary of the Underworld: British &
American Being the Vocabularies of Crooks, Criminals,
Racketeers.* 2d ed. London: Routledge and Kegan Paul,
1961.

Pearson, John. *The Serpent and the Stag: The Saga of
England's Powerful and Glamourous Cavendish Family
from the Age of Henry the Eighth to the Present.* New
York: Holt, Rinehart and Winston, 1983.

Pemberton, W. Baring. *William Cobbett.* Harmondsworth:
Penguin, 1949.

Phillips, M., and Tomkinson, W.S. *English Women in Life
and Letters.* 1926. Reprint. New York: Benjamin Blom,
1971.

Pilcher, Donald. *The Regency Style 1800-1830.* London: B.
T. Batsford, 1947. Excellent study.

Pine, L.G. *The Story of Titles.* Rutland, Ver.: C.E.
Tuttle, 1969.

Plumb, J.H. *The First Four Georges.* London: Collins,
1966.

————. *Georgian Delights.* Boston: Little, Brown, 1980.

Plumb, J.H., and Wheldon, Huw. *Royal Heritage: The Story
of Britain's Royal Builders and Collectors.* 1977.
Reprint. New York: Crescent Books, 1985. Much
emphasis on Prinny's projects and purchases.

Priestley, J.B. *The Prince of Pleasure and His Regency
1811-20.* New York: Harper & Row, 1969. Sumptuous
reproductions of portraits, paintings, fashion plates, and
caricatures illustrate this lively year-by-year account.

Pückler-Muskau, Hermann. *Puckler's Progress: The Adventures of Prince Pückler-Muskau in England, Wales and Ireland as Told in Letters to His Former Wife 1826-9.* Trans. Flora Brennan. London: Collins, 1987. London high society observed by a fortune-hunting prince.

———. *A Regency Visitor: The English Tour of Prince Pückler-Muskau Described in His Letters 1826-1828.* Trans. Susan Austin; ed. E.M. Butler. London: Collins, 1957.

Pullar, Phillipa. *Gilded Butterflies: The Rise and Fall of the London Season.* London: Hamish Hamilton, 1978. Amusing history of English upper classes in Town.

Quennell, Marjorie, and C.H.B. *A History of Everyday Things in England.* Vol. 3, *The Rise of Industrialism 1733-1851.* 5th ed. London: B.T. Batsford, 1950. Excellent study of all manner of things that affect everyday life. Everything from farm equipment to light fixtures to house drains.

Quennell, Peter. *Byron in Italy.* New York: Viking, 1941.

———. *Byron: The Years of Fame.* New York: Viking, 1935.

———. *Romantic England: Writing and Painting 1717-1851.* New York Macmillan, 1970. Good overview and superbly illustrated.

Quinlan, Maurice J. *Victorian Prelude: A History of English Manners 1700-1830.* Columbia University Studies in English and Comparative Literature, No. 155. New York: Columbia University Press, 1941. Good study of changing etiquette and attitudes.

Raikes, Thomas. *A Portion of the Journal Kept by Thomas Raikes, Esq., from 1831 to 1847: Comprising Reminiscences of Social and Political Life in London and Paris during That Period.* 4 vols. London: Longman, Brown, Green, and Longmans, 1856-57. Vivid anecdotes of high society.

Ramsey, Stanley C. *Small Georgian Homes and Their Details 1750-1820.* 2 vols. New York: Crane, Russak, 1919-1923. Reprint. (2 vols. in 1). New York: Architectual Book Pub., 1974. Comprehensive.

Reid, Robert W. *Land of Lost Content: The Luddite Revolt 1812.* London: Heinemann, 1986.

Richardson, Joanna. *The Disastrous Marriage: A Study of George IV and Caroline of Brunswick.* London: Johnathan Cape, 1960. Reprint. Westport, Conn: Greenwood Press, 1970. Interesting dual biography.

————. *The Everlasting Spell: A Study of Keats and His Friends.* London: Johnathan Cape, 1963.

————. *George the Magnificient: A Portrait of King George IV.* New York: Harcourt, Brace & World, 1966.

Richardson, Philip J. *The Social Dances of the Nineteenth Century in England.* London: Jenkins, 1960.

Roberts, Henry D. *A History of the Royal Pavilion Brighton: With an Account of Its Original Furniture and Decoration.* London: Country Life, 1939.

Rogers, Samuel. *Recollections.* Ed. William Sharpe. Boston: Bartlett and Miles, 1859.

————. *Recollections of the Table-talk of Samuel Rogers: To Which Is Added Porsoniana.* Ed. Alexander Dyce. 2 vols. New Southgate: H.A. Rogers, 1887.

Rudé George F. *Hanoverian London 1714-1808.* Berkeley: University of California, 1971. Companion to Sheppard's *London 1808-1870.* Both excellent.

Rush, Richard. *A Residence in the Court of London: Comprising Incidents Official and Personal from 1819 to 1825: Amongst the Former Negotiations on the Oregon Territory and Other Unsettled Questions between the United States and Great Britain.* 2d ed. 2 vols. London: R. Bentley, 1845.

Rust, Frances. *Dance in Society: An Analysis of the Relationship between the Social Dance and Society in England from the Middle Ages to the Present Day.* London: Routledge & Kegan Paul, 1969.

Sanders, Lloyd C. *The Holland House Circle.* 1908. Reprint. New York: Benjamin Blom, 1969. Anecdotes throughout.

Schmidt, Margaret Fox. *Passion's Child: The Extraordinary Life of Jane Digby.* New York: Harper & Row, 1976. Childhood at Holkham Hall and a scandalous society divorce.

Shelley, Frances W. *The Diary of Frances Lady Shelley.* Ed. Richard Edgcumbe. 2 vols. London: John Murray, 1912-1913. Diary of a very fashionable member of the *ton.* Includes a lengthy visit to the continent after Napoleon's downfall.

Shelley, Henry C. *Inns and Taverns of Old London: Setting Forth the Historical and Literary Associations of Those Ancient Hostelries Together with an Account of the Most Notable Coffee-houses, Clubs, and Pleasure Gardens of the British Metropolis.* Boston: L.C. Page, 1909.

Shepherd, Thomas H., and Elmes, James. *London and Its Environs in the Nineteenth Century.* London: Jones &

Co., 1829. Reprint. New York: Benjamin Blom, 1968.

Sheppard, Francis H. *London 1808-1870: The Infernal Wen.*
Berkeley: University of California Press, 1971.
Companion to Rudé's *Hanoverian London 1714-1808.*

Sichel, Marion. *The Regency.* 1978. Reprint. Costume
Reference, No. 5. London: B.T. Batsford, 1987. Fine
study describes costumes and accessories in great detail.
Illustrated with accurate line drawings.

Simond, Louis. *An American in Regency England: The
Journal of a Tour in 1810-1811.* Travellers in History,
ed. Christopher Hibbert. London: R. Maxwell, 1968.

Sitwell, Dame Edith. *Bath.* London: Faber & Faber, 1932.
Reprint. Westport, Conn.: Greenwood Press, 1979.

Smith, John T. *A Book for a Rainy Day: Or Recollections
of the Events of the Years 1766-1833.* Ed. Wilfred
Whitten. London: Methuen, 1905.

Smith, Robert A. *Late Georgian and Regency England
1760-1832.* New York: Cambridge University Press, 1984.
A lengthy bibliography that comprehensively covers
period.

Smith, Sydney. *Wit and Wisdom of the Rev. Sydney Smith:
Being Selections from His Writings and Passages of His
Letters and Table-Talks.* 1856. Reprint. Freeport, N.Y.:
Books for Libraries Press, 1972.

Somerset, Anne. *The Life and Times of William IV.*
London: Weidenfeld and Nicholson, 1980. Liberally
illustrated, straightforward account.

Southworth, James G. *Vauxhall Gardens: A Chapter in the
Social History of England.* New York: Columbia

University Press, 1941. Excellent history of this pleasure garden. Includes maps.

Spiel, Hilde, ed. *The Congress of Vienna: An Eyewitness Account.* Trans. Richard H. Weber. Philadelphia: Chilton Book, 1968. Numerous diaries and letters of various participants organized into a vivid account of the Congress.

Stanhope, Lady Hester. *Travels of Lady Hester Stanhope.* 3 vols. London: Colburn, 1846. Reprint. Salzburg: Universität Salzburg, 1983. The ultimate eccentric.

Stirling, Anna M. *Coke of Norfolk and His Friends: The Life of Thomas William Coke, First Earl of Leicester of Holkham: Containing an Account of His Ancestry, Surroundings, Public Services & Private Friendships....* 2 vols. London: John Lane, 1908.

Stoddard, Richard H., ed. *Personal Reminiscences by Cornelia Knight and Thomas Raikes.* Bric-a-brac series, No. 7. New York: Charles Scribners' Sons, 1887.

Stone, Lawrence. *Dearest Bess: The Life and Times of Lady Elizabeth Foster afterwards Duchess of Devonshire: From Her Unpublished Journals and Correspondence.* London: Methuen, 1955.

———. *The Family, Sex, and Marriage in England 1500-1800.* New York: Harper & Row, 1977. Good study of evolution of family life.

Street, George S. *The Ghosts of Piccadilly.* New York: P. Smith, 1930.

Stuart, Dorothy M. *Daughter of England: A New Study of Princess Charlotte of Wales and Her Family.* London: Macmillan, 1951.

Summers, Montague. *The Gothic Quest: A Short History of the Gothic Novel.* New York: Russell & Russell, 1964.

Summerson, John N. *Georgian London.* 3d ed. Cambridge: MIT Press, 1978.

Summerson, Sir John. *John Nash: Architect to George IV.* 2d ed. London: George Allen & Unwin, 1949.

Swinton, Blanche A. *A Sketch of the Life of Georgiana, Lady de Ros: With Some Reminiscences of Her Family and Friends, Including the Duke of Wellington.* London: John Murray, 1893. Includes all names of the guests at the pre-Waterloo ball at the Duchess of Richmond's. Lady de Ros was the daughter of the house.

Sykes, Christopher. *Private Palaces: Life in the Great London Houses.* New York: Viking Penguin, 1986. Abundant illustrations and photographs. Interesting text.

Tannahill, Reay. *Food in History.* New York: Stein and Day, 1973.

Taylor, Lou. *Mourning Dress: A Costume and Social History.* London: George Allen and Unwin, 1983.

Tegg, William. *The Knot Tied: Marriage Ceremonies of All Nations.* 1877. Reprint. Detroit: Singing Tree Press, 1970.

Thompson, F.M.L. *English Landed Society in the Nineteenth Century.* London: Routledge and Kegan Paul, 1963. Excellent survey of the lifestyles and attitudes of this class. Highly recommended.

Thornton, James. *Your Most Obedient Servant: Cook to the Duke of Wellington.* Exeter: Webb & Boner, 1985.

Tolstoy, Nikolai. *The Half-Mad Lord: Thomas Pitt, 2nd*

Baron Camelford (1775-1804). New York: Holt, Rinehart and Winston, 1978. Interesting biography of a gentleman with high connections and a hot temper.

Trease, Geoffrey. *The Grand Tour.* New York: Holt, Rinehart and Winston, 1967. Amusing survey of intrepid British travellers through the centuries.

Trench, Charles C. *A History of Horsemanship.* New York: Doubleday, 1970. Good introduction to subject.

Trevelyan, George M. *Illustrated English Social History.* 2d ed. Vol. 3, *The Eighteenth Century.* Vol. 4, *The Nineteenth Century.* London: Longmans, Green, 1949-52.

Tristram, W. Outram. *Coaching Days and Coaching Ways.* London: Macmillan, 1888. Reprint. London: Bracken Books, 1985. History of various roads.

Turner, Ernest S. *A History of Courting.* New York: Dutton, 1954.

Vamplew, Wray. *The Turf: A Social and Economic History of Horse Racing.* London: Allen Lane, 1976.

Warwick, Christopher. *Two Centuries of Royal Weddings.* New York: Dodd, Mead, 1980.

Watkin, David. *The Royal Interiors of Regency England.* New York: Vendome Press, 1984. Well-researched text, magnificent watercolors by W.H. Pyne done in 1817-1820.

Watney, John B. *Travels in Araby of Lady Hester Stanhope.* London: Gordon and Cremonesi, 1975.

Watney, Marylian. *The Elegant Carriage.* London: J.A. Allen, 1961. Wonderful illustrations and an immensely readable text.

Waugh, Norah. *The Cut of Men's Clothes 1600-1900.* New York: Theatre Arts Books, 1964.

Weinreb, Ben, and Christopher Hibbert, eds. *The London Encyclopaedia.* London: Macmillan, 1983. Reprint. Bethesda, Md.: Adler & Adler, 1986. Indispensable reference book.

White, Cynthia L. *Women's Magazines 1693-1968.* London: Joseph, 1970. Good bibliography.

White, R. J. *The Age of George III.* London: Heinemann, 1968. Good introduction to period. Excellent background.

————. *Life in Regency England.* London: B.T. Batsford, 1963.

————. *Waterloo to Peterloo.* London: Heinemann, 1957. Reprint. New York: Russell & Russell, 1973.

Wilcox, R. Turner. *The Mode in Costume.* New York: Charles Scribner's Sons, 1948. One of several costume books by Wilcox. All well-illustrated with well-organized discussion of changing fashions.

————. *The Mode in Furs: The History of Furred Costume of the World from the Earliest Times to the Present.* New York: Charles Scribner's Sons, 1951.

————. *The Mode in Hats and Headdress Including Hair Styles, Cosmetics, and Jewelry.* New York: Charles Scribner's Sons, 1959.

Wilcox, William B. *The Age of Aristocracy 1688-1830.* 2d ed. Lexington, Mass.: D.C. Heath, 1971.

Wildeblood, Joan, and Brinson, Peter. *The Polite World: A Guide to English Manners and Deportment from the*

Thirteenth to the Nineteenth Century. London: Oxford University Press, 1965.

Wilkins, W. H. *Mrs. Fitzherbert and George IV.* 2 vols. London: Longmans, Green, 1905.

Williams, Guy. *The Age of Agony: The Art of Healing 1700-1800.* London: Constable, 1975. Well-written account of the horrors perpetrated by the medical profession. Contains many gruesome details.

Wilmot, Martha, and Catherine. *The Russian Journals of Martha and Catherine Wilmot 1803-1808.* Ed. Marchioness of Londonderry and H.M. Hyde. London: Macmillan, 1934.

Wilson, Harriette. *Harriette Wilson's Memoirs.* Ed. Lesley Blanch. London: The Folio Society, 1964. Regency England's most famous courtesan tells all. The promised second volume never appeared. Her former customers promptly paid hush money to still her pen.

Wilson, Michael I. *The English Country House and Its Furnishings.* New York: Architectural Book Publishing, 1977.

Wilton, Andrew. *J.M.W. Turner: His Art and Life.* New York: Rizzoli, 1979.

Woodforde, James. *The Diary of a Country Parson: The Reverend James Woodforde.* Ed. John Beresford. 5 vols. London: H. Milford, 1924-31. Copious details of everyday life.

Wright, Thomas. *Caricature History of the Georges: Or Annals of the House of Hanover, Compiled from the Squibs, Broadsides, Window Pictures, Lampoons and Pictorial Caricatures of the Time.* 2d ed. London:

Chatto & Windus, 1898. The best English caricaturists batter the Hanovers.

Wright, Thomas, and Evans, R.H. *Historical and Descriptive Account of the Caricatures of James Gillray: Comprising a Political and Humorous History of the Latter Part of the Reign of George the Third.* 1851. Reprint. New York, Benjamin Bloom, 1968.

Wriston, Barbara. *Rare Doings at Bath.* Chicago: Art Institute of Chicago, 1978.

Wroth, Warwick W. *The London Pleasure Gardens of the Eighteenth Century.* London: Macmillan, 1896. Reprint. Hamden, Conn.: Archon Books, 1979.

Wynne, Elizabeth and Eugenia. *The Wynne Diaries 1789-1820: The Adventures of Two Sisters in Napoleonic Europe.* Ed. Anne Fremantle. 1935. Reprint. London: Oxford University Press, 1982. Charming diaries of young ladies which are filled with a wealth of everyday detail.

INDEX